TURNCOAT'S DRUM

'*Turncoat's Drum* paints a vivid and accurate picture of seventeenth-century battle. I woke in the dew, wood-smoke and foul breath of the camp, stood shoulder to shoulder with that indomitable Cornish infantry at push of pike on Lansdown Hill and smelt the fear that coursed through the Parliamentarian cavalry as they lurched over the bone-cracking drop into "Bloody Ditch" at Roundway Down. Quite simply, I know of no other novel that takes me back, sure as a pike-thrust, to glimpse the realities of an England "by the sword divided".'

Richard Holmes (author of *Firing Line*)

Also by Nicholas Carter

STORMING PARTY
THE SHADOW ON THE CROWN BOOK 2

NICHOLAS CARTER

TURNCOAT'S DRUM

The English Civil War in the West, 1643

THE
SHADOW
ON THE
CROWN

Part One

PAN BOOKS

First published 1995 by Macmillan

This edition published 1996 by Pan Books
an imprint of Macmillan General Books
25 Eccleston Place, London SW1W 9NF
and Basingstoke

Associated companies throughout the world

ISBN 0 330 34478 1

1 3 5 7 9 8 6 4 2

A CIP catalogue record for this book is available from
the British Library

Typeset by CentraCet Limited, Cambridge
Printed and bound in Great Britain

DRAMATIS PERSONAE

MENTIONED IN HISTORY

King Charles I.
Prince Rupert of the Rhine, his nephew.
Prince Maurice, Rupert's younger brother.
Sir Ralph Hopton, Royalist general in the west, former comrade of Sir William Waller.
The Earl of Caernarvon, cavalry commander.
Richard Atkyns, Captain, Prince Maurice's horse.
Sir Nicholas Slanning, Cornish Colonel of foot.

Sir William Waller, Parliamentary general in the West.
Colonel Nathaniel Fiennes, Governor of Bristol for the Parliament.
John Pym, Oliver St John, Sir Henry Vane, principal Parliamentarian leaders.
Colonel Alexander Popham, west country Parliamentarian leader.

UNMENTIONED IN HISTORY

Parliamentarian:

William Sparrow, pamphleteer, afterwards officer of militia.
Master Percival Greesham, a printer, his employer.

Major Archibald McNabb, Scots officer of horse, attached to Bristol garrison.

Major Tobias Fulke, a gallant but rather elderly gentleman.

Master Ignatius Webster, Master Herbert Lyle, Commissioners of Parliament.

Sir Gilbert Morrison, MP, Colonel of militia, wool merchant and turncoat.

Captain Jamie Morrison, his son, officer of militia.

Bella Marguerite Morrison, his daughter.

Mary Keziah Pitt, her maid.

Master Algernon Starling, clerk to Sir Gilbert.

Gregory Pitt, driver, Zachary, Eli, Mordecai, his sons, serving in militia.

Colston Muffet, Sergeant, Merrick's regiment, serving with Waller.

Hereward Gillingfeather, as above, an agitator, William Butcher, as above, sharpshooter.

Matthew Culverhouse, Davey Buchanan, cavalry troopers, Waller's horse.

Royalist:

Captain Hugo Telling, officer of horse, Prince Maurice's regiment.

Jack Cady, Ned Jacobs, his troopers of horse.

Colonel Maurice Butler, officer of Cornish foot.

Captain Scipio Porthcurn, officer of Cornish foot.

Jethro Polruan, Denzil Petherton, Judd Downderry, Simon Shevick, Isaac Thrush, Gideon Wooly, Cornish foot soldiers.

Sir Marmaduke Ramsay, Royalist squire.

Margaret, Lady Ramsay, his aggressive wife.

Thomas Ramsay, his son, recuperating from wounds.
Anneliese Ramsay, his daughter, Thomas's twin sister.
Findlay, their gamekeeper and sharpshooter.
Matilda Dawkins, a Royalist camp follower.
Peggy Rake, a bawd.
Ambrosio di Meola St Corelli, an Italian surgeon serving with Hopton.

PROLOGUE

Let peace be sought through war

CROMWELL'S PERSONAL MOTTO

BY
THE PALACE OF
WESTMINSTER

LONDON, APRIL 1643

Sir Henry Vane – Young Harry to noisy jostling backbenchers and sober-minded Parliamentarian greybeards alike – paused at the massive studded door, stroked his large nose. He thought for a second, then rapped loudly and strode in. The room was large but barely lit, screens had been carried in and positioned to make the most of the meagre fire flickering in the grate, entice the warmth from the gloomy corners. He had hurried from one end of London to the other that day, busy about Parliament's (and therefore the Lord's) work, and hadn't seen a decent flame yet. The people, shivering and snapping at one another, had been even more ill mannered than usual. They had stared out of their sooty rooms and smoky alehouses with undisguised suspicion, whispered and muttered to their neighbours as he hurried along the filthy backstreets. It was as if he had hung a forked tail from his black breeches. Parliament needed a victory, a clear-cut, decisive, unquestionable triumph to dispel the mood of gloomy uncertainty which pervaded the capital from the most magnificent town house to the meanest hovel. A buff-coated Caesar to march down Tower Hill trailing a thousand shackled prisoners was what they needed now. A Hannibal who could humble these King's men, reduce their precious cavalry to a procession of peacocks dragging rusty chains. Then the people would find their voices once more. Harry was sure of it, indeed, he dared not be sure of anything else. He snorted under his breath, tried to imagine which of their current commanders could deliver the spectacular success they craved. The Earl of Essex? Manchester? They were ponderous windbags, skilful enough strategists with pen and ink but rather less forthcoming with guns and powder. They delivered fine speeches but precious little in the way of action. In the meantime London shivered, pondering its uncertain future. The capital without its King was like a road without an inn, a room without a fire. And there would be plenty more cold days and nights before this war was done, Vane reflected miserably. Especially if the King's powerful forces in the north tightened their stranglehold on the capital's coal supplies. His increasingly active armies in the south had already begun to paralyse the wool trade up the Thames Valley and the navy had its hands full sweeping sudden swarms of pirates from the seas.

Trade, commerce, enterprise at home and abroad. The lifeblood of Parliament's cause, the self-made men who had heckled King Charles to distraction every time he had dared call a Parliament, who had drawn up their Grand Remonstrance in an attempt to shape this monumental mercantile movement, to redefine their role in the running of the country. Strangle trade, ruin the mighty merchants, and Parliament would be nothing but a shouting house of frightened men, their armies naked and unpaid, rotting around frozen campfires.

Vane shivered involuntarily, straightened the collar of his plain but immaculately cut coat, and strode into the room with his usual jaunty confidence. Good Young Harry, here to cheer us this misty evening.

Three rigid armchairs had been pulled up close, the seats on either end occupied by a pair of black-suited men bent over an assortment of papers and reports. Vane glanced behind the screen, saw a large map of England weighted down over a table, wooden blocks supporting colourful painted flags, a tiny trace of gaiety in the grim chamber. He nodded to the elder of the two gentlemen, who had glanced up to see what was keeping him.

'Harry, thank you for coming,' he said, holding his stomach and climbing to his feet with a painful wince. John Pym, Leader of the House, was a portly but pale man of medium height, his grey hair brushed back in waves from his calm, intelligent face. Vane shook his hand, took the proffered chair and nodded to the second man who returned the briefest of acknowledgements. Oliver St John, brilliant lawyer and Solicitor-General, taciturn to the point of rudeness. Pym was the talker, the gifted diplomat who could stitch the most diverse political and clerical elements of the country into uneasy alliance against their King. The unlikely triumvirate had lashed themselves to the rudder of Parliament's fortunes, and if ever again Charles Stuart marched into London a free man, there would be few ahead of them in the queue for the scaffold. Pym made himself comfortable again, and handed the younger man a crumpled news-sheet.

'Another defeat?' Vane scanned the Royalist pamphlet with his quick, large eyes. They were no strangers here to bad news. Unwelcome reports of desperate routs, shattered hopes, scattered armies. They had all felt the icy fingers of miserable defeat, heard the whispers in the dim corridors of Westminster, black swarming crickets heralding another disaster, drowning out the heady, rollicking debates in the House. Vane remembered the dark days after Edgehill, the opening battle in their great crusade. Their great crusading host shot down in smoke and ruin. The wings, rank upon rank of russet cavalry, shredded and shorn, its bare belly charged and piked and charged again. Only the Earl of Essex's infantry had held firm, clinging to the slope like bloodied wrestlers, fighting their Royalist counterparts to a standstill until night had swept down over the hills to whisk the light of battle from their bleary, sooty eyes. Edgehill, where the war of words had grown teeth and claws, turned on the talkers and rounded on ranters alike. Please God, no more Edgehills.

'*Mercurius Aulicus,* one of their scurrilous news-sheets, printed at the King's court in Oxford and smuggled into the capital under the skirts of some trollop,' Pym recited. Vane looked up at the small man, the flames picking out the heavy shadows under his tired blue eyes, the sunken cheekbones and slack skin around the precise, measured mouth. He had never been a strong man, and he was clearly straining his constitution grafting twenty-five hours a day to keep Parliament's hold on the war as tight as possible. Just lately his grip had been slipping as the various Royalist successes around the country weakened the will of all but the most devoted and fanatical Parliamentarian.

'Reporting Waller's defeat at Ripple Field,' Vane observed. 'I've already heard about it. Waller was mortified, of course.'

'He always is. Just as Essex and Manchester are mortified when they get a drubbing. But it's not the content we are particularly concerned about.'

'What John is trying to point out is that the enemy is stealing a march on us in the war of words. Infecting their hearts and minds, undermining the people's will to fight for us. This trash is selling in Oxford for tuppence. In the capital people are paying eight pence and more for it. This material is the toast of every street corner!'

'And we are not talking about Royalist spies or sympathizers,' Pym went on. 'The people find this trash, as Oliver rightly calls it, far more entertaining than our own bulletins.'

Well, that was hardly surprising, Vane had read Parliamentarian reports which would have put an ox to sleep.

'Their lack of integrity and principle, and basic disregard for the gravity of this situation, is typical of their Cavalier attitude,' Vane commented dutifully. 'Precisely what we have taken up arms against.'

Even amongst themselves, Parliamentary hardliners were careful to spare the King as much direct criticism as possible. They said His Majesty was badly advised. That his evil counsellors kept vile pacts with the Devil, or worse, the Pope. His wife Henrietta Maria was French, a devout Catholic who had urged His Majesty into this terrible folly of war, promising aid from France, Spain and the Empire, if necessary. Unfortunately for the King his kindly, well-wishing brother monarchs were already up to their necks in blood as the German wars raged from one end of Europe to another. Charles, for the moment, would have to see to his own house, his own turbulent House of Commons.

Pym held up his hand as Vane coloured, drummed his knuckles on the arm of the chair in youthful agitation.

'We know all that, Harry, we know that very well. But it must be said our bulletins, principled, honest and well intentioned, are about as popular out there as the Black Death.' Even St John was moved to snicker a little.

'Are you suggesting we lie and distort as they do? Inflate

their casualties, slander their generals and flatter our own?'

'What I am saying, Harry,' Pym said carefully, 'is that one good pamphleteer is worth a thousand doubtful pikemen. We already have several people working on similar projects to this. We feel we must go out to the provinces, go to the cities and towns and win this war, this vital war of words, right there on the streets.' He straightened, a little breathless.

Vane frowned. 'Turn up a few liars, in other words,' he said.

Pym bristled. 'The people are weather-vanes, Harry. They'll blow about in the slightest breeze, carry Charles into London on their shoulders one day, execute him the next.'

Vane didn't imagine Parliament or the people would ever countenance *executing* their sovereign, but he took Pym's point.

'Needs must when the Devil drives, Harry, and he drives us now, to the very edge of the pit. We need to find our own hacks, who will match lie for lie, who will muddy the waters while we set our course. Call them what you will.'

Vane thought for a moment. 'Recruit some of our brave trained bandsmen, they seem free enough with their tongues,' he suggested.

'What you might call Militia's Gossips,' St John suggested, the faintest trace of a smile playing about his mouth.

'Militia's Gossips; very good, Oliver, very good,' Pym congratulated. 'Although I wonder whether our beloved countrymen, our dear readers, will be aware of the pun?'

Vane sat back in the rigid armchair, wondering also. As far as he could see, it was pikemen, not pamphleteers, Parliament needed now.

PART ONE

AMBUSH

*The Parliamentary Party in Somerset, with a
view to prevent the junction of Sir Ralph
Hopton with the Marquess of Hertford,
summoned the whole county to rise and keepe
their randevouze at Taunton Deane*

A PERFECT DIURNAL, MAY 1643

BITTERWELL WOOD

SOMERSET, JUNE 9, 1643

He had concealed himself as best he could, given his kingfisher coat of bright blues and sea greens did not exactly blend into the tangled undergrowth along the overgrown road. The captain tilted his curly brown head, impatiently anticipating the wool wagon which they had been informed would be on its way to market that afternoon. He listened for the wheel creak over the busy hum of the heavy insects, wallowing from sticky bud to trumpeting bloom on the warm summer breeze. Willow wands fell over his head, coiled and curled over his stooped shoulders, an unkempt Medusa working her choking roots about him, tangling the good leather bridle and tying elf-locks in his sweating charger's mane. A fearful farmer peering in at the captain might have imagined him to be a demonic centaur, a wild wood-imp in Satan's service, loosely lashed to his ruined willow by dozens of umbilical fronds and creepers. Lurking in the leafy shadows for passers-by busy about their rightful business on the old road over the hill. Had he stood his ground a moment more and peered through his crossed fingers the farmer would have recognized instead a slightly built youth leaning along the twitching shoulders of a chestnut horse, whispering reassurances. Thin, unremarkable features gathered up in concentration, listening intently for the wayward wheels. A long nose twitching above a fine russet moustache – perhaps a recent addition to his frowning, not overly ferocious face. His pale eyes, green grey and mottled with tiny brown motes, flickered in the dappled sunlight filtering through the fronds, the pesterfly clouds shifting and settling around the hot flanks of the horse. The spirited chestnut hadn't taken kindly to being backed into the spray of willows and it was all the rider could do to hold him steady as he swished his tail, swatting the hungry midges.

Too near the brook, he thought ruefully. He should have trusted to surprise, hidden beyond the next bend and come hurtling out on the overloaded wagon as the driver negotiated the narrow hump-backed bridge. His first ambush, his first command. The rest of the patrol awaiting his orders.

Wait! There it was. He could hear the timbers groaning and shrieking under a heavy load, bulging sacks of greasy ripe wool balanced precariously within the oak ribcage of the cart. Here was one back-road delivery which wouldn't see the scales up at Bristol market. One load which wouldn't fetch the booming prices demanded by the war-wearied merchants, help their mongrel Parliament dress up and arm the misguided traitors flocking to those hated colours. Hugo Telling eased the twin pistols from the leather buckets tucked against his thighs, risked one last whisper to his snorting horse. He heard the low whistle, Cady's signal that the wagon had cleared the bridge and was lumbering up the slope towards his hideaway. The captain had left Cady, his corporal, and one of the new Gloucester men on the far side of the merry stream, ready to run out with their carbines if the driver proved lively enough to risk running back to the slumbering village at the bottom of the hill. To call the militia boys out to help while Telling helped himself to his load. Parker and Jacobs, the rest of his patrol, were holding the horses further up the wooded hill and keeping watch to the north. At least, he hoped they were keeping watch. Just as likely to be squatting on a log at smoke, or keeping an eye on some damned goose-girl.

The captain eased the willow curtain apart with the sooty barrels of his pistols, peered out over the road as the creaking built to a teeth-grinding cacophony and the great wagon lumbered into view at last. Immense wooden wheels fully six feet across dug new creases in the corduroy track, jammed loose stones into the summer-baked mud. A fat owl of a man in a stained smock, reins wrapped around his generous belly, flicked a switch over the broad backs of his six-horse team, his gleaming red face freckled beneath a huge straw hat. He was whistling to himself as he straightened the glistening shires for the long pull up Bitterwell Hill. From there he would have an easier drive, the gentle ridges beyond folding away northwards, carrying the old Wells road up to and beneath Bristol's tall grey walls. Carrying Morrison's wool to market. Not that they'd get there now. The animals alone would be worth the morning's wait, two sweaty, nervous hours exposed as they were this far ahead of Prince Maurice's vanguard. Rustling a wool wagon not ten miles from the Redcliffe Gate, from under the hairy noses of Bristol's rebel garrison. Cocking a snook at Governor Nathaniel Fiennes' buff-coated troopers would be a prize to boast about, a feat to make his name back at camp. The talk of the toadstool tents and reeking horselines, envy of every anonymous officer queuing for the latrine pits on a cold morning, stamping shapes in slurry with their pinch-toe boots. So many young nobodies bent on history. Captain Telling, scourge of the west, the grey robber.

He smiled to himself as he watched the wagon creak closer. Eyed the sturdy shires, hoofs as big as a squire's best plate, flicking their tails at the hordes of gnats they had enticed from the bulrushes by the bridge. They would be pulling the Prince's culverins before the week was out, and he would be riding stirrup to stirrup with his chief, exchanging pleasantries with the King's own scowling young cousin. Telling leaned over the chestnut's twitching ears, scanned the road behind the leaning wagon. An enormous piebald cob had been tied to the backboard, but there was no sign of any rider. Not that Telling could imagine anybody would want to ride such a lumbering, wall-eyed beast. Perhaps the driver had secured the cob cross behind as a fail-safe brake, to stop the wagon in its tracks if it started rolling back down the hill. The blowing beast's black and white hide bore the clear impression of saddle and girth, but it had obviously been untacked for the trip. Not even a barefoot boy or a hungry hound to accompany it, who might raise the alarm.

Merchant Morrison would rue the day he'd trusted his wares on the high road over the Mendips. Up until that summer the strong Parliamentary party thereabouts had secured the hills, held every stone-flanked gorge and windblown combe. Now Prince Maurice and General Hopton had united at Chard, turned their men north to challenge the passes, push the Dorset, Devon and Somerset militias out of their road and clear a way to Bristol, the open sea. Telling wasn't exactly privy to his generals' candlelit deliberations, but surely the strategy was clear enough: by pushing north across the great upland highways the army would cut the greedy merchants off from their bases in the west, prevent their wretched goods from getting to market and so strangle the pulsing umbilicus which fed their embryonic rebellion. Waller? Ha! They would deal with Sir William Waller and his western rogues, push Essex and his crop-headed ranters aside and reclaim the capital for their King.

Telling smiled to himself, delighting in the simple beauty of the remarkable plan. And who rode point, who carried the King's sword furthest into Parliament's sprawling underbelly? Why, Hugo Telling the rector's boy. That's right, he thought energetically, remembering for a moment the beatings he had taken at the hands and feet of his elder brothers and the cheeky village boys. Re – Re – Re – Rector's boy no longer! Let them try and fight him now, he mused, with his horse and his sword and his paired pistols! He pictured the scene. The camp, no, Windsor Castle, bursting with crowds of wildly cheering people. Step aside there, make way for the King! The grateful Sovereign tipping his bowed shoulders with his sword. Arise, Sir Hugo, most faithful of the faithful! How that fat beetle, that turncoat moth Morrison would beat his velvet wings and bleat when he heard the news, a month's shearing whisked away to clothe the King's men. His moment had come at last. Drawing his sword in anger for the first but surely not the last time! He closed his eyes in an ecstasy of expectation, jammed his spurs into his horse and reared out of the willows, a demon of the wild wood.

'I told Father Gregory could drive me, and you'd be there too of course,' Bella lied to the tousled apprentice as he picked and pulled at the strings of her bodice. William

Sparrow, spreadeagled on the warm bales beside her, tugged at the ribbons in frustration. The hulking youth was nettled to think his sweetheart rated the doddering old driver of more use than him in case of trouble. He gazed at the merchant's feckless daughter for a moment, exasperated by her careless teasing.

'Your father trusts me more than he does that old pot walloper,' he snapped, making himself comfortable in the back of the creaking wagon.

'He wouldn't trust you to look after me,' the girl pointed out archly. 'And don't talk about him behind his back.'

'Whose back? Your father's?'

'No,' she hissed, elbowing him in the ribs. 'Greggy there.'

William glanced up at the top of the driver's straw hat, bobbing merrily over the rim of their oak bower.

'Well, I look after you, don't I?'

'Oh, is that what you call it? What d'you think Father would say if he could see us now, eh?'

William grinned and returned his attention to the girl's partially freed cleavage. What a day this was turning out to be! He had been more than delighted when Sir Gilbert's wayward daughter had decided to accompany her father's produce to market in Bristol. It wasn't every day the printer's apprentice got a chance to corner Bella Morrison on a bale of warm wool. Back at the yard, William had stowed his precious snapsack in the back of the wagon and had reached down to help the merchant's daughter clamber up, relishing the treasures of her tightly bound cleavage.

'Are you sure Sir Gilbert's given you permission to come with us?'

'Of course I'm sure. I wouldn't go running off halfway across Somerset without his say-so, would I?'

Five minutes down the road he had managed to persuade her to climb over on to the bales, to get a better view of the countryside, he'd explained with a wink. It wasn't the first time he'd rolled in the hay with Morrison's free-spirited young daughter. Bristol was a twenty-mile journey from Chipping Marleward though, and this time he would have her all to himself – unless of course she decided she wanted to get down and walk. She always seemed to find some reason for cutting short their momentary liaisons in the stables, their snatched moments of youthful passion.

She smacked his prying fingers away from her breasts as if she could read his suddenly smug expression. William sighed with disbelief as she ducked out of his hungry embrace and scrambled up excitedly on to the warm bales to gaze about her. She was as beautiful as a carving on the prow of a ship. He rolled over on to his back and gazed at the bewitching creature as she pirouetted on the bales, throwing her arms out to balance herself against the unsteady rhythm of the grinding wheels. He felt as if he had been lashed to a mast like those sailors of legend while this temptress sang siren songs to the rolling countryside. She grinned slyly, kicked off her shoes and trampolined around the rocking wagon as Gregory dozed on the running-board. Her dress billowed up around her shapely legs as she leapt higher and higher, throwing mad shadows over William as she eclipsed the bright noonday sun. Warm rays glinted and sparkled in the halo of her hair as she tossed her head, screaming in delight. She leapt higher, sending up great clouds of dust and tiny fibres that made them both cough.

The overloaded wagon lurched as Gregory woke himself up long enough to negotiate the narrow bridge at the foot of Bitterwell Hill, tipping the hysterical girl from the bales and sending her crashing down beside the leering youth. He threw his leg over hers, pinned her to the wool sacks as he pressed his hot mouth against her lips. She kissed him hungrily as he manoeuvred his hands between the loosened strings of her bodice, her skirts pulled up and open about her. William raised himself on one elbow, caught his breath as the girl smiled her wickedest chestnut-roasting smile.

The willow wands snapped loudly as the spirited stallion erupted out of the trees, startling the paired shires and bucking the dozing driver from the running-board. The bloated fellow lost his hat, sprawled over the traces with an agonized yelp, startling the whinnying team into attempting panicked flight. Telling spurred his horse past the frightened team, cut across their path as the heavy wagon pitched like a galleon in a gale, came to a halt in a hazy cloud of dust. The captain gripped the prancing charger, levelled his pistol at the driver, still entangled with his reins but pawing and keening over his smashed foot, ground into the hard-baked track by his own wheels.

'Stand in the name of the King!' Telling crowed, turning the chestnut close against the restless shires, pawing the dust and tossing their heads in apple-eyed agitation. The driver propped himself up, lifted his leg and gazed at the bleeding bones, the purple flesh bulging between the rents in his old boot.

'Stand? Stand, yer reckon?' he mouthed, tobacco teeth clenched, sweat beading on his horrified brow. His unattended wagon rocked on its heels, Cady and the Gloucester man hurrying up to drag the handbrake on before the whole enormous load rolled slap bang down the hill and into the stream. Cady leaned over the mortified driver, made a sooty face.

'Y'll need the bone setter and a bucket for that, my old matey,' the corporal commented with a smirk. The fat driver turned a fearful eye on him, gazed back at the blossoming rosebush, all the wagon had left of his dirty foot.

Telling frowned at the silly mundanity of it, felt slightly cheated it had been the wooden wheel which had drawn blood, not his brave sword. His carefully laid ambush looked more like a cruel prank, a practical joke on the village idiot. He had expected screaming, slashing and pleading, not resentful conversation. Damn it all, the Gloucester man was looking up at him as if he had deliberately picked on the old fellow! He swallowed, glanced up at the sudden movement from the top of the wagon. Ah, he knew it, they weren't finished yet. He brandished his pistol, opened and closed his dry mouth.

'Come down, in the name of the King,' he cried, hoarse.

'We're unarmed!' An equally dusty answer from among the fragrant sacks, all tipped to one side against the wagon's heavy beams. Some damned boy sunning himself on the bales instead of watching out behind as his master had bidden him.

'Stand up, steady about it,' Telling called as Cady climbed up the stalled wagon like a monkey, grinned at the frightened occupants clutched within.

'Oh, my chicks, you'll crack those eggs, carryin' on so! Let's have you out of it!' He waved them from their straw bower. He spied a curly head all stuck with straw and tufts of fatty yellow wool rise from the stacked bales. A broad forehead and a pair of startled green eyes fixed on the impish corporal as if he'd dropped from the very sky itself. Telling snorted, waved the barrel of the pistol.

'Come down.'

'Don't shoot, we're all civilians here!' the youth called, turning from captain to corporal and back again.

'Come down, all of you,' Telling repeated, mastering his prancing horse and his rasping voice. The youth threw a leg over the side of the wagon, climbed to the ground holding on to his breeches. Telling frowned, looked up as Cady clicked his tongue, helped the girl to her unsteady feet. Slim as a weasel, her warm brown breasts straining at the trellis of lace the grinning youth had obviously been busy picking open. Telling felt himself flush, watched her as she swung her loose hair from her eyes, peered down at his wavering pistol, fumbled with the helplessly knotted strings of her bodice.

'There's only the two of us, sir, don't shoot us down like dogs, sir,' the youth called, rearranging himself as he stepped from one foot to the other beside the stalled wagon. His heavy leather shoe trod the driver's out-stretched fingers into the stony road. The furious driver yelped, pulled his hand back and cracked his head against the running-board. He fell back in a faint, pulled about like a harpooned porpoise by the nervously stamping horses, still harnessed by the straining reins. Cady guffawed but Telling's Gloucester man, a farmer himself by the everyday breeches and hacking jacket he still wore under his blue sash, took pity on the driver. He lifted him out of the way and rolled him over the dandelion verge, bending over to unpick the crippled drayman from the tangled reins.

Cady grinned, helped the barefoot girl clamber between the wagon's ribs. Telling stared as she threw out a shapely tanned leg, found her footing on the massive studded wheel and eased herself to the ground. The corporal studied their abandoned love nest, his nose twitching, and fished the youth's forgotten snapsack up on the point of his carbine. He flicked it to the ground between the boy's buckled shoes, then swung himself down and prodded the smoky muzzle into the stranger's chubby arm.

Telling turned from the fearful farm boy to his captivating companion. He watched as she leaned forward to fasten her dress, her rich brown hair glinting silkily in the warm afternoon sun, apricot cheeks burning. Apparently satisfied, she folded her fringe from her high forehead, looked up at him unconcernedly. He stared as she curled a finger in the knotted strings of her bodice, bit her tongue between her full red lips. Christ's wounds! He rammed the pistol into the bucket holster along his thigh, blinked down at the mouthwatering apparition. Sweet-talked into the hay by this lecherous, what, clerk, if he was any judge of those pudgy white hands, fidgeting with the snapsack he'd picked from the dusty track. The leather bag was smeared in sticky blood from the unconscious driver's crushed foot.

'What do we do with 'em, bring 'em along?' Cady wanted to know.

'Eh? Oh, yes.' Telling turned his attention back to the heavy-set youth, gazing intently from the business end of the corporal's ready carbine.

'The bag?' Telling asked, nodding at the dirty sack its owner was pulling to pieces.

'The bag, sir? My lunch sir, if you please sir. A stale loaf and a bottle of ale, which you're welcome to try if you've a mind . . .'

Telling nodded impatiently. 'Keep your ale for now,' he hinted darkly. 'The wool is another matter. It's for the King.' He tipped his hat back, glanced at the girl again, her bold hazel eyes flickering from the nervy horse to equally nervy rider. He raised his eyebrows as menacingly as he was able, inclined his head. 'Not so?'

'Not so? Why no, sir, that is, yes, sir, whatever you say, sir. Of course it belongs to the King, God save him sir, with all his troubles and all.'

'God will save him sir, from all his troubles.' He rolled the word around his narrow mouth, enjoying himself as the girl fussed and preened, tugged some of the fluff from her shoulders, carelessly blew it away on her slim fingers. He opened his mouth, lurched in the saddle as if he'd been caught in the blast of a demi-cannon and finally managed to fix his gaze back on the clerk.

'And how comes such an enthusiastic and loyal servant of His Majesty to be travelling in a cart belonging to that treacherous rogue Morrison? What do you say to that, sir?'

The youth fiddled with the straps of his sack, looked awkward. 'We must all serve where we may.'

'Serve? But who do you serve, master?'

'Sparrow, sir. Starling. Billy Starling,' the youth spluttered, colouring up to the roots of his dark curly hair. He was no Roundhead then, at least.

'Sparrow? Starling?' Telling exclaimed. 'Are you one or the other? Are you Thrush or Rook or Jay or Jenny Wren, which?' the captain enquired, turning his horse in elaborate circles beside the patiently waiting shires. 'And what of your companion,' He leaned forward, gazed sideways at her. She gazed sideways at him, gave a tiny, electrifying smile that seemed to inflate his saddle up tight around his worn breeches, crush up his narrow chest so he could barely breathe in the stuffy gorge.

'Starling,' the youth lied. 'Billy Starling, apprenticed . . . that is, er, indentured to Mr Morrison sir, from an early age,' he added as an afterthought. Telling nodded.

'Apprentice, eh? And what of your companion?' he repeated. The girl went to open her mouth, seemed to stumble as the heavy youth took a step forward.

'Nellie Smith, sir, parlour-maid up at Pitt's farm, sir.'

Telling jerked at his reins at the sudden clatter of hoofs from up along the rutted track. Two riders bent low over fresh horses, tugging two more with empty saddles behind.

'Patrol!' The first, wrapped in a filthy brown coat despite the sultry heat, bellowed a warning. A patrol? Enemy patrol? Suddenly the prank had purpose, the silly game had soured all over again. Telling peered up the hill, the road hidden by a sudden turn. They would never move the wagon in time, from this God-damned alley. The riders pulled up, held the reins to their startled colleagues.

'How far?' Telling called, drawing his pistol once again.

''Alf-mile, mebbe more,' the scout panted.

'We'll burn it, fetch out your . . .' The heavy youth cowering behind the wheel suddenly swung the snapsack into the stallion's face, ducked under its lashing hoofs as it reared up in alarm. Telling lurched over the chestnut's mane, accidentally pulling the trigger. The pistol shot cracked around the narrow gorge, echoed gleefully from ledge to ledge down the stream. The captain grabbed the

23

reins as the sprightly youth recovered his wits, kicked the terrified horse in the fetlock and dived into the thick undergrowth beside the road. Cady raised his carbine, fired into the rattling branches and coiling vines.

'Captain, they are upon us,' the scout warned, pointing up the road. Telling mastered the snorting stallion, walked it in circles looking along the track. A dozen and more horsemen, breastplates glittering, a compact troop cantering stirrup to stirrup down the rutted track. Telling wrenched his prancing horse about, glared down at the girl cowering beside the wagon.

'Tell your master—' He held on with furious determination, gasped: 'I'll mark him for his insolence, I'll have him flogged at the tumbler when the King's men come!' he cried, twisting his head to gaze at her for a moment longer. He shouted something, spurred his horse away down the road and over the bridge, his tiny patrol closing up behind him.

The girl peered after them as they disappeared around the bend and into the quiet trees. The rumble of their hoofs diminishing, drowned by the Roundhead troop cantering after them with no evident determination to actually catch up with the fugitives. The girl stepped behind the wagon as they shouted and clattered away over the grey stone bridge. Their leader reined in expertly, swung himself out of the saddle before the horse had stopped moving. A beefy, bow-legged cavalryman in lobster pot, back and breast, an enormous orange sash knotted around his middle proclaiming his allegiance. There seemed to be somewhat more of the stocky officer than his uniform would credit. He straightened himself, looked over the unconscious driver, groaning on the verge with his arms closed over his red face. The newcomer finished his reconnaissance, stepped around the wagon and gave the girl a stiff bow, rolling the heavy helmet from his rusty cropped head in one practised movement.

'M'name's McNabb. Archibald McNabb, at your service, Miss . . . ?'

'Morrison,' the girl beamed, modestly straightening her dress. 'Bella Morrison.' He held out his rough paw, but jumped back in surprise before he could take possession of her hand. He grabbed for his sword as the willow wands parted and her companion stepped out, brushing the worst of the bruised bark from his torn shirt and ripped breeches.

'Archie. Was I ever glad to see your smiling face!' William exclaimed breathlessly.

McNabb scowled, ran his hand over his creased brow. The girl noticed the newcomer's eyes were pale blue, watering from the exhilarating ride down the hill.

'Och, away wi' ye now, and that's Major McNabb to you, my laddie,' he growled, tugging a neckerchief from his sweat-stained buff coat and running it over his livid face. 'Saved you from yoursen agin, no doubt?' he asked.

'That kill-calf candle waster would have shot me dead like a dog,' the youth moaned, opening his snapsack to check the contents, wad after wad of badly smudged pamphlets, tied with string. The Scotsman watched him with unconcealed contempt.

'Are you still peddlin' that drivel aroun' the town?' he asked, regaining his breath. 'Will ye not see sense and leave it by? A wretched wee trade in times like these, do you not think so, Miss Morrison?'

Bella was gazing wistfully over the bridge, the rumble of hoofs heralding the return of McNabb's troop and not, as she had secretly hoped, that dashing young man in blue.

'I beg your pardon, sir?'

'I was telling your friend here, put his pen aside and pick up a sword, would you not agree?'

Bella shook her head, absent-mindedly. Let them prick themselves on pens or swords, but please God bring the handsome King's man back. He looked devilish sweet, colouring up so easy. Bella shaded her eyes, peered toward the bridge as McNabb's troop trotted back the way they had gone. Their commander bit his lip, nodded at his cornet, a fleshy youth with an oily, forked beard.

'Clean away, sir. Prob'ly more of them and all, hidden up, like,' the youth called in a thick Devon accent.

McNabb sighed, settled the helmet over his bristly red thatch as he digested the breathless report. 'Two on the hill there and three by the bridge,' he replied shortly. 'You had the better of them five to one!'

The cornet flushed. 'They 'ad the better harses, mind you, sir.'

The major shook his head, nodded at the forgotten driver being helped up by the pamphleteer.

'Ah, steady Will, steady.' The crippled wagoner hopped on his good foot, balancing himself on the youth's broad shoulders.

'Lend a hand with your man there,' McNabb snapped. 'We'll escort Mr Sparrow on to Bristol with his precious pamphlets. Even a set of sad scoundrels like yourselves should reckon to get the best of a few bags of wool,' he observed contemptuously.

Sparrow straightened slowly under his groaning burden, grinned at him.

'And ye can steek ye gob as well, laddie,' he warned.

TEMPLE BACK

BRISTOL, JUNE 1643

The excitement of the ambush had worn off by the time they had followed the high road in off the hills, leaving Will feeling unusually glum. Perhaps it had something to do with the fact Bella hadn't stopped gabbling about their miraculous encounter, had seemed more energetic with every turn of the creaking wheel. We could have been killed, carried off to slavery, she'd wondered, her lively hazel eyes busier than the goldfinch flock tumbling along the hedge beside the rescued wagon.

'No, I could have been killed, you could have been carried off into slavery,' he'd corrected, prickly and hot as they perched on the running-board, poor old Gregory Pitt groaning in their abandoned bower. It was no use fretting, he told himself. He'd lost his chance and he knew it. He could have been rolling in the wool with his own true love if it hadn't been for that damned captain. Praying for time to stand still while they cuddled and cavorted. Grinning broadly with his tongue between his teeth as his clumsy fingers pulled and picked at the pretty portcullis of strings that held her bodice together. William pulled at his suddenly cramped breeches, made himself as comfortable as he could. God's wounds, he wouldn't have minded moving at ten yards an hour, wasting an entire afternoon if he had been buried in the back with Bella all to himself.

He would have delayed the journey, slowed their progress in every way he could think of. Applied the handbrake when Greggy wasn't looking, taken short cuts over flooded fords, insisted on frequent stops to let the tired shires get their breath while he panted and gasped up on the warm bales with the feckless maiden. Instead, he found himself wishing the miserable miles away, and snapped the switch over the shires' broad backs to hurry them along.

'What have you been feedin' those horses on, lead? I've never seen such a set of broken-winded old nosebags,' he said waspishly.

Gregory Pitt looked up from the bales, stung by the youth's criticism. 'These yeres' the best beasts in the county,' he objected. 'You'll not find better.'

Even so, the twelve-mile journey seemed a relentless drag, the unkempt road confined by narrow belts of tangled hedges offering limited glimpses of the commons and enclosures, sudden gullies and dales giving out into boggy hollows studded with arthritic rowans. Travellers were few and far between, those who had made up their minds to go north to escape the King's vengeful western army had already made themselves scarce, left the high road to the lonesome crows and grey-beaked ravens. Major McNabb's endless anecdotes about his various adventures seemed to weigh the heavy wagon down even more. He'd been in Balfour's brigade at Edgehill, and seemed to have memorized a dozen diverse events for every moment of that miserable October day. William whittled a stick to nothing and tossed it over the side as the cheerful Scot rode alongside providing a running commentary on the diverse twists and turns of his damned war. Confusing his big mare as he nodded and pointed and gesticulated, taking sly glances at Bella as she sat on the running-board flushing and sighing and heaving herself half out of her dress.

'It makes you shiver, when you think of it, the King's men so close,' she had chimed in when the well of his recent experience had run dry at last. 'I wonder if they are all like him? The captain I mean,' she chattered on. 'So dashing and handsome it makes you wonder how these dirty draymen and tapsters Father's recruiting will ever be able to stand up to them.'

Sir Gilbert had been commissioned by Parliament to raise a regiment from the farms thereabouts, but for all his energetic campaigning on Mr Pym's behalf he had only managed to enlist a few dozen vagabonds so far.

'I think it's important for a captain to look the part, don't you?' she asked as McNabb rode on in rugged silence.

Will fiddled with the rents in his breeches, pulled at his baggy stockings.

'But there I go ... blathering on. He is our enemy, after all, and he would certainly hang poor Father, if he had the chance.'

He wouldn't be the only one ready to knot a length of hemp around Morrison's chubby chins, Will reflected sourly.

'Such a pity he's a Loyalist.'

'Royalist,' Will and McNabb corrected in unison, with feeling.

The Scots officer had practically fallen off his horse fussing over Bella, bowing in his saddle as the convoy eventually parted company under Bristol's Redcliffe Gate. They watched him trot off, his suddenly formidable troop closing in behind him, clattering down the narrow cobbled streets shadowed by the handsome spire of St Mary Redcliffe. The great town houses bulged above the streets like over-baked cakes. Riotous inns served garrison and civilian alike while spies moved in the back bars, listening for traitor talk. The goodwives of Bristol bustled down the streets with baskets of greens, stopping to stare as the troops rode by, heralds of an uncertain future. The town was not exactly a hotbed of Puritanical fanaticism, most of the town elders would have preferred to stay on the fence as long as possible, keep an open city as their colleagues across the North Sea had preserved the Hansa-town trading partnerships even in the midst of their terrible long wars. Could this struggle last nigh on thirty years and all? A doctor would have had good cause for concern, taking the erratic pulse of the port. The occasional encouraging psalm drowned out by the ribald choruses bawled from the treacherous taverns: 'Merchants do quake, their loyalty fake, their soldiers' mothers heads do shake.' With Bristol the second most important seaport in the land, though, it would have been foolish in the extreme to imagine it would be left to its own devices long. At the end of February Parliament had installed Colonel Nathaniel Fiennes, rosy-featured son of Lord Saye and Sele, in a bid to inspire the defences, beef up the city's crumbling walls. He was a plucky if pedestrian commander, but many of his troops, like his townsfolk, would have preferred to leave the war to others, them that wanted it. Let sleeping dogs lie could have been the motto on their brave banners. He and his brother John had shouted themselves hoarse, emptied their coffers of coin, but their strenuous recruiting had only managed to attract a few hundred men to the colours. The Popham brothers had brought in more from Wiltshire, and they had also picked up a few stragglers from Edward Hungerford's rapidly disintegrating regiment along with refugees from Devon and the far west. Bristol, however, had not proved to be as enthusiastic for the cause as London and the south-east. Looking out over the narrow hovels, the brothers in the keep could almost imagine the tumbledown houses turning their backs on them and Parliament. Not that they would have kept much of a welcome for the King, for that matter.

Will had taken the reins, steered the heavy wagon to Sir Gilbert's warehouse in the heart of the busy city. A warren of tiny alleys and tall houses with gaping windows, noisy ragged children running behind the cart in place of their steel-helmeted escort. Will turned the heavy load into the busy yard behind Morrison's warehouse, trotted around the sweating team to help Bella down. The damned girl had already hoicked up her skirts and clambered over the wheel, attracting a crowd of carters and carriers who tipped hats, tugged forelocks and good-dayed Miss Bella until the overseer scuttled out of his ramshackle office to shoo them back to work. Will stood glowering as Bella tugged her shoes from beneath the running-board, slipped them on her brown feet before the clerk could catch her going barefoot like a gypsy and carry more tales to her father. It had taken all her charm and well-practised wiles to convince Sir Gilbert to let her ride to town in the first place. So she told Will, anyway. In actual fact she hadn't asked her father's permission at all. She had been bored rigid at home with her dull old books and her badly tuned piano. The whole world in a spin of smoke and excitement, and there she was cut off from her friends with a few gossiping servant girls for company. Even her dullard brother Jamie had been packed off to Shepton Mallet with the militia. She wanted to see some action, even if he didn't! She had convinced herself she deserved better, and had jumped at the chance of a change of scenery, a trip to Bristol. Surely her father wouldn't have made too much of a fuss, even if she had asked him. He had indulged her hopelessly, ever since her mother had died, and would generally go along with her every whim and fancy. Sir Gilbert had, however, drawn the line at Kilmersden Hall, the Ramsays' sumptuous manor house on the hill above their quiet hamlet. There was a war on and Sir Marmaduke and his son were for the King. Enemies. Old Henpeck and his Crybaby Boy? She had protested, miserably. 'Enemies all the same, my dear,' Sir Gilbert had assured her, giving his daughter his most serious frown. She had been con- fined to the house, prevented from running up the hill to see her friend Anneliese, Crybaby Tom's spirited twin. Bella and Annie had grown up together, two of a kind. High-spirited romantics who had run rings around their insufferably stuffy brothers. She wondered whether the war would wake them up a little, make men of them. As long as it didn't make corpses of them, she thought guiltily. Then again, she hadn't started the war, had she? If they wanted to go and make fools of themselves, they would only have themselves to blame if they were injured, she decided primly.

'Miss Morrison, charmed.' Algernon Starling, Sir Gil- bert's charmless but trusted deputy, closed his hands in front of his chest, gave the object of Will's breath-taking, stomach-aching, brain-burning lust a short, stiff bow. Will glared at the clerk's slick black hair, worn long over his knobbly white head, and clambered up the wheel to help poor Gregory to the floor. They had tied his foot as best they could, but it wouldn't have needed a surgeon's mate to tell him he needs must lose it.

'Ah, God's bud, but it hurts so,' Gregory gasped, leaning precariously on the youth's arm as he hopped awkwardly to the back of the wagon, sat down heavily on a greasy bale.

William helped him down, supported him as Starling stepped around to count the bales.

'Miss Bella tells me your journey was not without incident,' he remarked. Will nodded, regarding the clerk's narrow brow, crow's feet features frowning as he scribbled in a ledger. Starling was clothed head to toe in black broadcloth, as cold as a fish while the men sweated and worked about, stacking crates, rolling barrels. Morrison's warehouse was a regular hive at the best of times. With Waller's army near by, six thousand troops to supply, he had been forced to take on extra men, working shifts day and night. As far as Will knew, Algernon Starling had no roost. He stayed in his office, taking occasional catnaps on his neat little bunk, presently stacked with newly forged swords. Gregory tugged off his hat and held it in front of him as he balanced himself as best he could.

'Gregory's been run over, Master Starling, hurt his foot summat awful,' Will reported.

Starling flicked his eye from his inky columns for a moment, studied the ragged bundle, already blossoming with blood. 'The wagon goes back tomorrow, whether he drives or no. Collect your wages from Master Hollingsworth,' he retorted, climbing up like a giant insect to beetle about in his master's wares.

By the time Will had helped Gregory into the warehouse and had one of the coopers take a look at the driver's smashed foot, Bella had disappeared. She had flitted up the narrow staircase to the cramped and damp apartment behind the warehouse which Morrison kept when he was in town. William sighed, ordered his old piebald stabled for the night, threw his satchel over his shoulder and left the hive of uncaring activity, made his way to the quieter quarters of his other business associate, Master Percival Greesham, printer by appointment to the Parliament.

'I was banging to wake the dead, could you not hear me?' Sparrow snapped as the gruff printer opened the door to his grubby, ink-splattered premises, peered out into the narrow street of darkened hovels.

'Oh, it's you.'

'Who did you think, Prince Rupert?' William shouldered by the printer, lifting his heavy satchel from his shoulders and dropping it on to a table buried under a mountain of lead type. Spilled, sorted and serrated as if it had been gushed out by some iron basilisk and not a rolypoly bad-tempered old misery wrapped in a blanket and clutching a candle in his stained, calloused hands. He patted his pockets for his eye glasses, put the candle on the table and opened the bag.

'Did he like them?'

'Morrison? Oh yes, he liked them all right.'

Master Greesham picked the familiar pamphlets from the sack, stacked them on a leaning shelf with dozens of others. Bruised, yellowing paper advertising their age as well as the tone of the arguments and opinions expressed within. As the war had gone on so the pamphlets had plummeted new depths of expression, turned fiction into fact, fact into fiction. Lied and manipulated and exaggerated the way the war was being run and why. To save the King from his evil councillors. As the deadly struggle went on the gloves came off. Master Greesham's clients wanted more blood and bile, less complicated political procrastination, more blatant prejudice. Lay it on thick, boy! William, his lively and imaginative apprentice, was particularly gifted when it came to inventing scenes of horror and rapine. He could turn a chaplain's tea party into the sack of Magdeburg in three paragraphs, and even the grudging Greesham had been forced to admit he had helped turn a tottering print shop into a booming business.

The guns might well have fallen silent but pens were scratching furiously from Cornwall to the remote wild isles of Scotland. Presses were clanking to feed the ravenous hunger of Royalist and Roundhead alike. As well as their lying fantasies, the country needed facts and figures to help tear itself apart, precise instructions on pulling one of its limbs from the other. Soldiers needed drill books, gunners instructions on elevation and effect, pikemen hints on balancing eighteen feet of steel-tipped ash, musketeers diagrams on charging and discharging their unreliable weapons. Even the poor surgeon's mate needed a hand, sawing bleeding limbs from broken bodies, packing muslin bags of maggots to the infected stumps. A maggot wouldn't touch clean meat. Master Greesham had tried to bar the door as they crowded in with their ridiculous orders for outrageous print runs to ludicrous deadlines. Paper didn't grow on trees, ink didn't fall from the sky and good help was hard to come by. Still, business was business and the Parliament had money if the King didn't.

Master Greesham listened as Sparrow improvised a description of the day's events, sketched out the latest episode in a bitter civil war. A humble wagoner going about his lawful business for his kindly old master, hideously tortured by a gang of cut-purses lurking in an evil ambuscade. Satan's own imps masquerading as merry Cavaliers, hatched of the cockatrice's eggs and suckled by pox-diddled harlots. How the old man cried piteously for them to stop as the King's men rolled his enormous wagon over his poor old foot, again and again as his poor shrieks shivered the lying rooks! A typical greeting from the Royalist army even now on its way north, burning and looting as it came like a crazed and bloated dragon of legend. See to your weapons, ye citizens of Bristol, see to your walls!

'Legend? You wouldn't recognize legend from God's holy books,' Greesham scolded, settling his glasses on his nose to read one of the newly printed tracts. 'You're letting your imagination run riot, young man. The people, you know,' he said piously, looking over the thin frames of his spectacles, 'will only believe so much. Add one too many sticks to the fire and you'll burn down the chimneys of their belief, mark my words.'

Chimneys of belief? William shook his own chimney of disbelief, nosed about the shop among trays of print, galleys and presses and frames and pots, picked a crust from an abandoned pewter plate.

'You can ask Miss Bella, if you don't trust me,' he said through a mouthful of chewed dough. 'Old Greggy'll lose his foot or I'm a Dutchman.' He swallowed, wiped his generous lips. 'I'm surprised you didn't hear the commotion back here, shots, galloping horses and all.'

'Hear a few shots? I've had the lad printing off two thousand *Mercuries*, it's been hell here, I can tell you.'

William recognized their conversation was set to follow a familiar path, a series of interchangeable and vaguely attributed opinions, casually exchanged disinformation which never bore more than a passing resemblance to true fact. He yawned mightily.

'And if all this nonsense is true, why the long face?' Master Greesham pointed out, craftily as ever.

'I'll tell you what,' William replied earnestly, 'I stand there protecting Sir Gilbert's own flesh and blood from the good Lord knows what, from being sold as slave to the very Turks themselves, I shouldn't wonder,' he improvised, 'and what does the little ingrate say?'

Master Greesham tugged the blanket around him, nodding him to continue.

'"He was ever so brave,"' he mimicked in a shrill falsetto. 'I stood there, puffing me chest out right enough, and realized she was on about this bloody noodle!'

The amply proportioned printer chuckled, making his greasy chins wobble. 'I tell you, that girl's got Royalist tendencies, believe you me.'

'Bella Morrison? She couldn't give a fig for any Royalists, dashing young men on big chargers, that's all that one's interested in. She's little more than a strumpet, the way she walks in here bold as brass.' William frowned, shut the thought out of his mind. She was no strumpet. She was generous with her affections, was all. All the time. To everybody.

Greesham retrieved the candle, studied the morose youth for a moment, the light dancing about the gloomy shop, the dull racks of cold type that fired imaginations around the country.

'Well up to bed with you anyway, we've an early start

tomorrow, up to the castle to see Fiennes himself. Seems he's not convinced the town is ready to fight to the death to keep the King out.'

William shrugged. 'And there's you saying he wasn't worth his job. Sounds like our Nathaniel's more of a realist than we thought,' he smirked, following the master up the suicidal stairway to the gloomy garret above.

BY

CHIPPING MARLEWARD

SOMERSET, JUNE 1643

True to Algernon Starling's word, Sir Gilbert's empty wool wagon rolled into the cramped yard behind the merchant's bustling house at a quarter to two the following afternoon. The clerk had in a fit of uncharacteristic generosity allowed poor Gregory to slump in the back with the ticks and the tufts, while a new driver hired from the city stews saw to the tired team. Bella had stared morosely at the countryside throughout the tiresome journey home, gazing sourly at the heather and bracken slopes she had admired the day before, her high spirits sapped in turn by Starling's eunuch stare and the ever increasing proximity of her gaudily appointed prison, her shrinking doll's house room with the view of the yard. Every creak of the great studded wheel, every lazy crack of the driver's whip dragged her back there, thrust the hazy horizons further away than ever. She had cupped her face in her hands and moped, frowned at the hedgerows, holding their birdsong breath as if the empty ark lumbering by was some vast oak-ribbed sparrowhawk. Mile after mediocre mile of quietly expectant countryside.

The canny farmers, smelling the change in the wind, had herded their stocks down from the hills, from their neat, lush pastures. Gathered what crops they might before the ravaging armies descended on their tilled slopes. Each broken-winded cart horse or crumple-horned cow had been sent to market along with the last pickings from the kitchen garden, a final cracked dish of warm white double yolkers. Gold now, there was something worth having. Gold could be hoarded, a hoard could be hidden. Bella eyed each tumbledown haystack, every lone elm or guardian oak. That's where she would plant her fortune, under the biggest tree she could find. She wondered for a moment if they meant to fight their silly war just there, over the hedge and down the creeping soiled slopes. Perhaps she would climb that sentinel elm, see if she couldn't spy the enemy, a colourful horde of handsome gypsies, the captain in the kingfisher coat out ahead, an enormous plume in his hat as if he served the Sultan, the Grand Turk himself.

Her friend Anneliese could see the towers and spires of Bristol, if she cared to clamber out on to the flat roof of the Manor, high on the hill. The fortified roof from which her father's gamekeepers were drawing beads on their lowly neighbours. The squire had sent his best men and only son to join the King early in the war, and the rumour-mongers had it the house was actually occupied by less than two dozen loyal retainers. Luckily for the squire the barely trained town band – hardly more numerous than their concealed counterparts on the hill – had proved reluctant to come to blows and the two sides had settled instead on an uneasy truce. The tiny hamlet, thirteen miles south of Bath, sat astride the Fosseway, an uncertain sword blade thrust between the warring counties. The numerous but inexperienced forces of Parliament to the north, the smaller but battle-hardened Cornish Royalists approaching from the south.

It was a tricky fellow, war, Sir Gilbert reflected, pacing

the study of his large but rather ill-fitting house in the middle of Chipping Marleward's muddy High Street. He had found it every bit as worrying as wool, twice the bother of dairy cattle, thrice that of sheep. It could quite throw you over, if you didn't take care to stay one jump ahead. Just like a handsome gelding at a horse fair, it could carry you to your fortune or throw you down into the nettles. You couldn't buy its loyalty, you couldn't shake its hand and spit on a deal. You got on and off you went, where you may. The merchant stomped up and down the Persian rug in his best black boots, heard the wagon rumble into the yard. He peered out of the leaded windows, wondered why Bella had bothered running out to meet them. Stuck to her room these days, couldn't bear the talk of pigs and prices, war and wealth. Young Jamie wasn't cut out for commerce either. Not cut out for anything else, as far as his father could see. He frowned, focused his watery blue eyes on the heavy wagon. Was that a new man down there with Starling? And why was old Gregory taking his ease in the back like the lady of the manor? He rapped his knuckles on the glass, tugged at the window in irritation.

'Starling! Not you! Get Greggy to his feet there! I don't pay drivers to pick their noses in the back of my wagons!' he called, his fleshy face flushing easily. 'What's that? He's been hurt? Wool gathering again, I dare say!'

Starling peered up at the window, shook his narrow reptilian head, and walked up the short flight of steps to the back door of his master's mansion. Bella stood by awkwardly as Gwen Pitt was called from the wash house to collect her crippled husband. Gregory had fashioned a crutch from a broken broomstick, hobbled on out of the yard to meet her. Gwen, an enormous bag of a woman with wild red hair and cheeks to match, hurried across the

41

narrow street, her great pendulous breasts straining her bodice, to see the damage for herself. Greggy lifted the crutch in greeting, almost impaled himself on his master's railings.

'In the wars, is it? We've fools enough in our house without ye playing the poltroon up yonder!' Gwen cried, holding her face in her red-raw washerwoman's hands.

'It'll mend, it'll mend,' Greggy muttered as the neighbours gathered to see what the fuss was about. 'Away indoors, woman.' He limped on down the street, Bella hurrying alongside.

'He was hurt in the ambuscade, the wagon went over his foot,' she reported, as dourly as she could.

'Ambuscade? Over 'is foot an' all?'

'I'm sure Mr Starling will mention it to Father, see about some compensation for you.'

Gwen rounded on the girl, the full extent of her old man's injuries beginning to dawn on her.

'What, he'll work again, though?'

'I'll work, course I'll work.'

'He will work, miss, won't 'e?'

'I'm sure we can find him some lighter tasks about the yard, Mrs Pitt.'

'Lighter tasks, he'll not drive, then?'

'I'm sure he'll be able to turn his hand to most anything,' Bella said, colouring.

Gwen eyed her. 'Mayhap he'll be able to turn his hands, miss, 'sis bliddy foot's worryin' me.' Bella watched the elder Pitt boys race down the road to help their hobbling father. He shooed them off with his stick, limped on down the muddy street between his great ragged boys. They opened a path for their cursing father, turned to nod and hallo to Bella, biting her lip as pretty as a picture beside their worrying mother. Gwen tugged at her bonnet, which had slipped from the back of her frizzy red hair, pulled at the knotted strings. 'We'll not keep those boys another week, that's the thing, see, miss,' she said flatly, tears misting her bright eyes. 'We've bare enough to feed 'em now, great lumps that they are. They'll be off, see, miss, off to join the army like as not.'

Bella held a hand to her brawny red forearm. She felt acutely useless, brought up short by the bitter reality of this horrid, back-door war. It was all very well for these handsome Cavaliers and dour Roundheads to go tearing about the country attacking one another to no apparent reason. It was the women, left at home, who did all the worrying, held families together, darned their wounded husbands when they eventually staggered back along the high road. The big woman gazed miserably at Bella's fine fingers, nodded distractedly and hurried on after her man. The boys scratched and laughed, fell about each other like baited badgers as Bella bowed her head and hurried back inside the yard. Zachary, the eldest, thumped his brothers away, stalked off after his parents, leaving the rest brawling in the dusty street. She had eased her way through the steamy kitchen and was halfway across the scullery when her red-faced parent appeared in the doorway like a heavy sack barrel bobbing in the chop, his round belly straining the bands of his breeches. Mr Starling had evidently given him a full report on the previous day's adventures. Bella gave him her sweetest smile as he blustered.

'We thought you'd run away to Bristol! We thought you'd been taken by these damned brigands!' he cried, as if Bella's long-dead mother had still been at home, peering over his shoulder to scold her. Elspeth Morrison had been eaten up by the fevers shortly after delivering the almost identical eight-pound three-ounce twins. Sir Gilbert and his country relations had brought the two of them up in place of the broken, bloodless woman. He remembered her clutching his chubby hand in her red-eyed delirium, imploring him to send the babes to her sister's in Bristol. Sir Gilbert had promised to do just so, his fingers crossed behind his back. He ranted on about ungrateful wenches and saucy girls, hinted darkly at the dire punishments which awaited them in the back streets of the city.

'That apartment's nothing more than a garret,' he roared.

'Jinks was there,' she pouted, refusing to name Mr Starling, her accuser. 'It was perfectly safe.'

'I only pay that feeble old pot walloper to keep the rats down, not look after me only daughter,' Sir Gilbert went on, his beetroot face draining a few shades, country accent reasserting itself strongly. 'I don't want the place runnin'' with vermin when I'm about me business.' He didn't say which business.

Bella bowed her head, nodded as wretchedly as she was able. 'I know you were worried, Father, beside yourself,' she whispered.

Sir Gilbert spluttered, smoothed his lively, tight grey curls back into oil-assisted order on his hot head. She knew full well he hadn't realized she had gone. He would have assumed she'd taken to her bed by the time he had finally finished with his heavy ledgers the evening before. 'The next time, young lady, you'll kindly take the trouble to inform me when you go gallivanting about the country. Let this robbing bandit of a Royalist remind you, the roads are too dangerous for ladies. Now away and change while I have words with Mr Starling.'

The gaunt jackdaw of a clerk coughed quietly in the

hallway as if to advertise his fetid presence. Bella hurried on along the corridor, tugging her dress up about her knees. Starling stepped back against the wall as she shot him a look, licked his thin lips as she strode past. Sir Gilbert frowned at her slim, shapely back. Just like her mother at that age, he thought ruefully, opened the door to his plain, barely furnished counting room. A deal table worn smooth by countless piles of notes and coins, polished by shirtsleeves trapping heaps of cash, wads of inky receipts. Algernon Starling eased his scrawny rear on to a straight-backed chair, ran his crooked finger over the heavy volume to find his place. Sir Gilbert paced beneath the barred window, amber with dust and forgotten webs.

'Well? Did it make the weight?'

Starling extracted a bottle and quills, shaking his long, narrow head. 'You said seven shillings, they'll not pay that while the roads are open.'

'Good enough, good enough.' Starling continued to shake his head. The merchant frowned. 'Well?'

'You shouldn't have extended yourself so. The wool cost us—'

'Cost me,' Sir Gilbert interjected.

'Cost you, three hundred and eighty-five pounds, all told. If we let it go at the current prices, we could realize a few pounds besides. A tidy profit.'

Sir Gilbert closed an eye, poked a sausage finger at the ledger. 'Speculate to accumulate, Starling, speculate to accumulate,' he advised. 'Seven shillings? They'll pay twelve and think themselves lucky, if the King's men get across the Marlborough road. I didn't grow this house from seed, you know,' he declared.

Starling closed his heavy lidded eyes at this opening shot in the merchant's frequently expanded life history.

Was it a barrow of eggs he'd started with, or a sixpenny seat on the London coach? Either way, he'd end up taking Ludgate, if he wasn't careful. Starling ran the quill into the ink, drew small circles on his blotter while Sir Gilbert reminisced. He didn't need the merchant's books to tell him where they stood. They were out. Out by several thousands pounds, a pretty penny, sir. They should have been counting coin while they could, not throwing money around like seed corn.

Of course, he knew all about Sir Gilbert's little stratagems. The winter just gone, the merchant had tucked himself into his most martial outfit, a breastplate he claimed had been worn by one of his ancestors at the time of the Armada, and ridden up to Bristol. He had managed to secure a brief interview with the city's previous governor, Thomas Essex, and had extracted a commission, a *commission* mind you, to raise a regiment of troops for the Parliament. A regiment from Chipping Marleward? If you had pressed every last man jack, wives, children, dogs and all, you would have struggled to find a company. Starling had made himself scarce the day Morrison had been called back over the water to the great keep, half expecting to hear the wily merchant had been arrested on the spot for his fearful insolence. When he spied the pair of cavalry troopers escorting Sir Gilbert back to his warehouse he thought the game had been up before it had begun, and had been on the verge of making a run for it down the leaning alleys and grubby cobbled backstreets. Then he had spotted the small bound chest the troops were carrying, and realized with a start the idiots in Whitehall had authorized the merchant's merry game.

Sir Gilbert had spent the next six months recruiting his motley band, attracting a few shepherds in off the hills, a dozen vagabonds from their wanderings up and down the Fosseway and a sprinkling of Chipping Marleward's upright yeomen. He had used less than twenty pounds of his gold mobilizing his militia, and had borrowed the rest to buy up every ounce of wool, every last cow, sheep, pig and fowl from the farms as far south as Yeovil. The fearful farmers had been only too pleased to sell their stock, the King's ravenous Cornishmen with their wild hair and funny talk on their way and all. He had pulled off a dozen good deals, financing his purchases with Parliament's gold, and shipped the produce up to Bristol, his fortified warehouse by Temple Back. Starling pulled at his beaked nose, not daring to imagine what would happen if his master's enterprises came to light.

Sir Gilbert wound up his improvised history, rubbed his knuckles into his constantly watering eyes.

'How much are we out, if we take it we paid full prices, full prices, mind, for the upkeep of the regiment?'

'Pay and provision for six hundred men for six months, let's see, two thousand eight hundred and seventeen pounds, eighteen shillings and thruppence.'

Sir Gilbert waved his pudgy paw. 'You don't grow six hundred men from seed, man!' He snorted. 'Take it we've recruited three hundred.'

'Well, then, one thousand four hundred and—'

'Yes, yes, there's no need to spell it out,' Sir Gilbert muttered, pacing the narrow room from one whitewashed wall to another. He had heard tell of regiments in the King's army with fewer men. Battle, desertion, disease would surely take its toll, he reasoned. It wasn't as if he had deliberately set out to swindle Parliament, not at all. He was a man given to sudden inspirations and quicker decisions. It was how he had got on, after all. Snap it up, open your palm to see what you'd caught later. It had been an obvious step, siding with Parliament in the first place. Men like him needed a say in government, a say in who got taxed, how much and what for. The King couldn't expect to go on living from hand to mouth year after year, calling up parliaments and dissolving them on a whim. Interfering with religion, trying to impose his Book of Common Prayer on decent, sober folk who remembered the bad old days of Elizabeth and Mary, the continual papist plotting. Look how Charles had got his fingers burnt up in Scotland trying to appoint his blasted bishops. The English army he'd sent to enforce his appointments sent scurrying home, routed like the ragged peasants they were. Armies didn't grow from seed, you know. They needed officers, they needed pay. Who paid? Merchants like him paid, sure enough. Trade you see, trade was driving things now.

Sir Gilbert's secondary consideration had been his politely hostile relationship with the local squire, Sir Marmaduke Ramsay. The hook-nosed devil up on the hill. Ramsay was old blood, aye, and old hat. He squeezed his tenants hard but hardly earned a bean from his open fields. Morrison would have enclosed the pastures, and got a good hard manager in there to sort the stock. Cut down half that standing timber, drained the boggy slopes which weren't fit for three-legged goats. Good hunting country maybe, but Sir Gilbert hadn't made his pile trying to stay in a saddle. It had been no surprise to anyone when Ramsay had declared for the King, sent his only decent tenants off with his worthless son to hunt Roundheads on Edgehill, assuming in his overbearing arrogance the village would continue to bow and scrape, tug their forelocks as usual. Tug their forelocks no longer, not to Squire Ramsay anyway.

Sir Gilbert threw out his chest. 'All we've done—'

'All you've done,' Algernon Starling simpered.

'All I've done, is round up the numbers in each company a little.'

'Claiming pay and provision for six hundred men. Why all you have, 'tis nothing but a shilling's worth of shadows, sir,' the clerk added gloomily.

The merchant squinted, kept his brimming eyes on the little man in black. 'Well, I wouldn't be too cocksure if I was you, Master Starling. If I go down I'll make damn sure I take you with me,' he threatened.

The clerk looked unimpressed. 'I am merely an ignorant scribe, you've said so many a time. I have merely recorded the figures you've given me,' he said curtly.

'Oh, it's like that, is it?'

Further unpleasantries were interrupted by the soft knock on the door. Sir Gilbert strode over, tugged it open. 'Bella, my dear. Come to apologize for yesterday's little escapade?'

Escapade indeed, she thought, smiling. 'I've been thinking, Father.'

'I'm a little busy with Master Starling now, dear.'

'I want to see Anneliese, Father.'

Sir Gilbert frowned. Old Ramsay's daughter. He had once hoped he could have married young Jamie off to her, sealed the breach and shared their old country blood. She was a hothead, though, same as her mother, and Jamie, well Jamie wasn't the man to ride on up there and throw her over his saddlebags, was he now?

'It's no surprise I went off with Will, I'm bored stiff

sitting up in my room. The piano tuner's serving in the King's Life Guards, so they say in the village, and I can't play a one-fingered jig without . . .'

Sir Gilbert soothed her, nodded his fleshy red head. 'You know the situation, my dear . . .'

'But I've been speaking to Mary Keziah and she says the squire's had enough of the war now, what with his boy hurt and all . . .'

'Hurt? Thomas?'

'Hurt in the big battle near Banbury. Sideways, Edgewise . . .'

'Edgehill,' Sir Gilbert corrected. 'Hurt, you say? Hurt bad?'

'Mary doesn't know. She was sworn to secrecy,' Bella replied.

The maid had relations in just about every house in the hamlet, and most of the larger isolated properties round-about. Sir Gilbert tugged at his coat in irritation. Why was he always the last to learn of Chipping Marleward's affairs? Last in line for the pump-house gossip. Had enough? Old Ramsay? He'll never have had enough, not with that harridan of a wife egging him on, anyway, he thought. Interesting.

CHEWTON MENDIP

JUNE 10, 1643

The silent night had laid a cold dew over the lush grass, jewelled their ready carbine barrels as the dismounted riders waited at the edge of a dripping oak plantation. The star-studded night had cooled everything but Hugo Telling's vile temper. Emptying an ounce of lead into some Roundhead's belly might well. He pictured that curly headed youth running over an open field, imagined himself spurring alongside, cutting him down with a glorious stroke of his untried sword. He felt the dewy ground vibrate as if in sympathy beneath his aching boots, heard a heavy horse wheeze and pant as it cantered up the sparsely wooded slope. The rider urged the beast on, steering blindly between swarms of fireflies buzzing over the coiled brambles. It was Jacobs.

'Captain?' he hissed into the darkness.

'Here.'

The scout tugged his grey nag around, walked him to a steaming halt under the hanging boughs.

'They're ours all right, singing to wake the dead,' Jacobs reported, slipping from his saddle and tugging his shapeless felt hat from his unruly black hair. ''Undreds of 'em, campfires from one end of the valley to the other.' Telling nodded as the patrol tugged their horses from the shelter of the trees, tightening the girths and easing the reins over their tossing heads. Telling's charger was still limping. They had outrun that cautious Roundhead troop after a mile or so, cleared the gorge and headed south across the rolling downs before the stallion had begun favouring its left foreleg. Jacobs had tried several of his own remedies including urinating over a handful of dock leaves and holding the compress to the swelling but the vicious kick and sudden gallop had obviously damaged the chestnut's fetlock. Damn that fellow, kicking a man's horse. What kind of a trick was that? Telling had been forced to walk the beast back to the camp, fuming the feathers from his hat as he stamped along in his ungainly riding boots. By God, that Starling would have blisters enough before he'd finished with him! He'd know him again, by the scoundrel's mammoth cob, for one thing, by the insolent curl of his generous lips. His patrol had plodded along behind, sniggering and whispering to each other. Telling had rounded on them, demanded to know what they were laughing at.

'Nothing, Captain,' Cady had grinned cheekily. 'Just sayin' as 'ow we wouldn't have minded swapping places with that curly 'eaded feller who kicked your horse. Good God and all his angels, did you ever see such a beauty, lads?'

Telling smouldered to think of that hulking farm boy pawing at the girl, glowered as Jacobs thrust his lean crotch backward and forward in his high worn saddle.

'I'd 'ave fought off the very 'ounds of 'ell, keep her to meself,' the Gloucester man observed with a gap-toothed leer.

Telling had pulled his horse on, swearing under his breath as the patrol exchanged winks.

'Did you see the flirt-gill's teats?' Cady crowed. 'I'd 'ave given a year's wage from this damn army to get a shavin' of that . . .'

'Shut that racket, you'd think you had never seen a woman before,' Telling had bawled, the hair on his head bristling uncomfortably under his hat.

A moment later and the riders were ready to depart. They swung up into their saddles and settled themselves. Cady offered to let the captain ride his horse, but the youth waved his hand distractedly, marched on leading the stallion by the reins. He led his grinning patrol down the hill, tendrils of mist curling around their legs. They were forced to change course, follow a brimming duck-weed ditch along the edge of a water meadow, and paused by a large gate hanging drunkenly beside a narrow, overgrown lane. They could see and smell the fires burning brightly through the tall hedges, shadows passing this way and that as sleepy sentries made their rounds about the camp.

'Halt or we shoot 'n!' The shout rang out from the gloomy, dew-laden hedge as Telling rested his hand on the gate's splintered crossbar, stared at the musket barrel which had been unceremoniously shoved under his nose. He jumped, looked up in bewilderment as a ragged red musketeer stepped from the foliage, eyed him suspiciously.

'Shoot 'n anyways, Jethro,' another called from the shadows to the left.

'Hold hard or I will,' Jethro said from the side of his mouth, his tangled blond hair and wild beard illuminated in the firefly glow from his match cord. He blew gently on the glowing red point, held in the musket's iron-mouthed mechanism. A squeeze on the trigger and the matchlock would snap shut on the primed pan, ignite the powder charge and send a glob of hot lead burning through

Telling's trembling skull. The captain had barely understood the musketeer's warbling accent, and wondered for
a moment if the giant was some German mercenary,
fighting for English gold.

'Captain Telling, Prince Maurice's Horse,' he stammered, looking down the sooty black eye of the gun.

''Ear that now, Matthy, comes from that Princy fellow
now,' he said.

Half a dozen figures climbed through the hedge like
wood demons, closed in on the patrol. Jacobs spurred his
nag forward, his short carbine held like a club.

'Have you lost yer wits, comin' this far, you Cornish
baboon?' he rasped. 'Cassn't ye tell an officer when ye see
one?' he demanded. Jacobs was a Dorset man, and he'd
had dealings with his belligerent neighbours before.

'Shoot 'n anyways, Jethro,' one of the smoky devils
urged.

Jethro eased the match from the pan, glowered at his
prisoner. 'What's the field sign?'

'Henrietta Maria,' Telling replied promptly. At the
mention of the King's Catholic spitfire of a wife – she took
fierce pride styling herself the She-Generalissima – the
Cornish troopers seemed to shimmer, shrink back into the
dripping foliage as if the Queen herself had walked in
over the dewy meadow.

'Well, why dissn't thee say so first goin' off,' Jethro
snorted, lowering the musket.

Telling, recovering his nerve, pushed the gate back on
the giant's meaty paw. 'Get out of my way, you damned
ape.'

The giant musketeer inspected his grazed knuckles
while his colleagues muttered in their barely comprehensible dialect.

'I said, open the damned gate,' Telling snarled.

The blond man in the worn red suit regarded him down his broken nose, a school bully with a big gun.

'We be King's men all right but we bain't your bliddy slaves, my little house dove,' he hissed.

'Downderry ... Polruan ... you sacks, you kill-calf bloats! What the devil are you playing at now?' An officer in an expensive full-length coat barged his way through the muttering gang, beat them away with his enormous black hat. 'I've warned you about this, get back there, I've ... out of my way ... Polruan, now then.' He eyed the chief musketeer, who looked as if he would shoot the newcomer for sixpence.

'Sez they'm out from the Princy,' Polruan growled sulkily. 'Crept up quiet like, no shout, no sign, no nothing. I tell 'ee 'ere now, the next bleater tries spiderin' up on us, we'll 'ave 'n.'

The officer heaved the gate open, nodded reassuringly at Telling. 'Maurice Butler. Colonel.' He shook the younger man's hand, tugged him closer. 'Don't pay any mind to my lot. Worst set of rascals you could find for obeying orders, but I'd rather have them at my back than to my front, eh?' he whispered confidentially. Telling nodded. 'Brave enough boys for all that though,' the colonel called to a ragged chorus of approval and one loud, reverberating fart.

'I'm to report to the commander,' Telling told him.

'Commander? Which one? There were more generals than musketeers, last time I looked,' Butler said cheerfully, leading the way into the lane past his unrepentant sentinels. 'Let's see if we can find the one giving the orders tonight.'

Telling handed his reins to Jacobs, hurried after the

brisk figure as he strode along the lane, turned and vaulted over a stile into the busy field. It was by far the largest military encampment Telling had ever seen. A great mushroom city of soggy white tents, illuminated by a thousand idle embers. Men in dozens of different-coloured coats huddled, squatted and stamped around the miserable flames, their faces lit like the wild natives from the Americas. Stark black shadows and fierce red stripes. Telling could smell horse dung, sweat and human excrement. Frying bacon made his hungry nose twitch.

'Six and a half thousand and more,' Butler said, noticing the youth had stopped still by the gate. 'Our General Hopton and your Prince Maurice, what's the other old duffer's name? Marquess of somewhere or other. More than enough to deal with Waller, I'll wager. Talking of a wager, would you care for a drink and a smoke at my tent? We get quite a good crowd around usually, you know.' Quite a good crowd? Telling had barely slept a wink the last few nights, listening to their wild carousing, their early morning pistol practice beyond the latrine pits. He wondered for a moment what his father, the Reverend Edmund Telling, pious Rector of St Clement's, Wainbridge, would make of him keeping such company at such an early hour, and delightedly accepted the colonel's unexpected invitation.

Butler poured Telling a generous measure, tilted the flask to his mouth and drained it noisily. 'Ahh, that's better. One of my boys relieved a gouty Roundhead gentleman of it this morning. Madeira, if I'm not mistaken,' he said, wiping his lips on his sleeve. 'Look here, old man, don't take any notice of my lot. You have to treat them like a strumpet, beat 'em one moment, flatter 'em the next. They're not keen on orders, and they've no time for the popinjays that shout orders from the back. The front, Telling, get to their front and lead 'em on,' Butler enthused. 'They'll follow you into the pits of hell.'

Telling sipped at the fiery liquor, felt his cheeks flush as the unfamiliar alcohol seared his throat. Eighteen years at the rectory, his experience with strong spirits had been rather limited. He'd get a taste now though, now he'd gotten away from his narrow-minded, impossibly precise father and his three like-minded elder brothers. Hugo had never shared their taste for clerical argument, pointless chitchat as far as he could see. In his younger days back at the rectory he would sit for hours in his tiny room, secretly devouring pamphlets on the great German wars of religion. Relishing the lurid woodcuts depicting scenes of rape and torture, massed pikemen advancing like great hedgehogs toward city walls sprouting cannon, that reminded him of the outstretched necks of hungry iron chicks. Hugo would ride his pony around the neatly laid out rectory garden, putting whole rows of beans to flight, hacking and harrying the hoary old apple trees around the orchard until the air was full of great fragrant clouds of blossom. He would ride the panting pony in ever decreasing circles in the pink storm, crying and laughing with juvenile delight, until his mother hurried into the depleted orchard to shoo him back to his books. On his eighteenth birthday his despairing parents had given in and allowed him to go up to Oxford to read the classics. Eighteen years and three months, and poor Hugo had been bored rigid over his dusty tomes, idly scraping his name in the smoky oak panelling of the common room, when he had heard the commotion out in the quad. He had tumbled outside with the rest, wild-eyed students and venerable old masters alike shouting themselves hoarse as they welcomed the King's army, fresh from the ridge of Edgehill. Sweating, laughing men had pegged tents and parked their artillery in Magdalen Grove. They paraded through the narrow streets and waved to the girls hanging out of the windows. Telling had looked up at those beautiful flushed young faces, felt himself inflate near to bursting with fanatical pride and righteous zeal. He had run through the camp and been first in the queue to join the prancing pack of peacocks who rode behind the King. Hugo smiled at the pleasant memory, gulped the heavy wine and disguised his cough behind his glove. Butler belched and tugged his coat open, made himself comfortable on an empty cheese barrel. He knocked the lantern as he sat down, sending it swinging from the crossbeam of the grubby marquee. A gaggle of officers careered by the tent, pulling one of the camp doxies between them as if she was an angry calf going to the slaughter pens. Arguing at the tops of their shrill voices, they tripped and cursed as they got themselves entangled in the guy ropes.

'Damn these snares!' one of them bawled, measuring his length in the narrow gutter between Butler's quarters and those of his neighbours.

'Were we expecting Hannibal and his elephants? Staking out the camp like a damned tennis court,' another called drunkenly.

Telling peered at the puppet shapes silhouetted by the dirty canvas flank of the tent, watched the shadowy shapes pick themselves up and dust themselves down with the careless enthusiasm of the seriously inebriated. The woman shape lolled like a doll, pulled between two bawling beasts in baggy breeches.

'Get out of it, you drunken monks,' Butler yelled, hurling his empty flask at the darkest staggering shadow. The officer yelped and fell to his knees. He crawled over the guy ropes and into the tent, clambered to his feet hitting his head on the swinging lantern.

'Who threw that grenade? What, Butler, you again?' the cavalryman slurred. The intoxicated officer took another step, collapsed at the colonel's feet, reclining gratefully against his mud-splattered boot. Cornet Montgomery Gabriel, a clean-shaven pudgy young Cavalier, his generous mouth, usually gathered into a superior sneer, slack and red with drink. His quick dark eyes had been dulled and mired by the heady wine. One of the dandy young gentlemen who had formed the King's élite show troop back at Oxford, he had volunteered for service as one of Prince Maurice's dashing young aides-de-camp, and inherited a life expectancy he could reckon in days. He peered up at the colonel's companion, standing awkwardly by the tent pole.

'Is that you, Tyler?'

'Telling.'

'Telling. Ha! Managed to miss another one?'

'Another what?' Telling demanded, indignantly. After the indignities he had suffered in the last twelve hours, any stray spark was likely to ignite his frayed temper. Gabriel, too drunk to notice the colour draining rapidly from his colleague's set features, looked up distractedly as the other two officers dragged the protesting woman into the tent. Telling swallowed, watching the wild-haired creature struggle to tie her gaping bodice.

'Ah! Hands off, Till!' A tall officer, expensive shirt tugged open to his sweating chest, knocked the girl's grubby fingers from her strings, eased his hand beneath her bodice. The girl swung round into his arms, her bushy brown mane devouring his head. The second officer steadied himself, closed in behind her, hands busy tugging her skirts up her brown legs. Gabriel stretched his leg, kicked Telling in the shin.

'Fight. You missed another good fight, boy. There's more to this than riding around with a stick up your arse!'

'I've been out on patrol since yesterday noon,' Telling stammered, tearing his eyes off the groaning girl and her laughing companions. 'Have I missed something?' he grated, fixing his pale eyes on the recumbent cornet.

'You've missed a good scrap, my lad! How long is it you've been with us? Since Oxford? And you haven't drawn sword yet.' Butler nudged his friend in the back.

'Are you implying I deliberately avoided a battle?'

'Don't be so touchy, Telling, you'll get your chance,' the colonel reassured him. 'We caught up with some of their rearguards. Seems they're shadowing us just over the next ridge.' The tall officer reached up, tore the girl's bodice open. Telling stared at the girl's pointed brown-tipped breasts before she could cover herself.

'Careful now, sir,' she scolded, arms pinned by the shorter man behind her. 'You'll have me in rags yet!'

'Rags? Pah! A shilling will get you the finest gown in Somerset, once we've kicked Waller's arse out of our way! I'll take you round all the fine houses in Bristol, clothe you like a queen,' the taller officer boasted, leaning forward to nuzzle her bare breasts.

'The Queen of Whores!'

'I'm no whore!' the girl pouted, half-heartedly pushing the tall man away.

Butler frowned at their antics, Gabriel turned his bleary eyes on Telling.

'Even our little rector's boy'll get his chance, if the Prince lets that fool Caernarvon take point!' The Earl, an impossibly handsome youth with a mass of blond curls, had forged a reputation as a hothead, even among the dashing Cavaliers of the Prince's army. A reputation he was about to underline, in red.

THE GREAT KEEP OF BRISTOL CASTLE

JUNE 10, 1643

William Sparrow pushed the writing stand aside, stretched extravagantly, and leaned over to blow the smuts from his latest tract. He had been up since dawn finishing it, assembling an ink-smeared proof from half a dozen scrawled jottings, abandoned drafts. He held the paper up to the dim candlelight, chuckled as he read his version of the previous day's ambush. Lay it on thick, lad, they'd said. So he had. Percy Greesham bustled around the gloomy workshop in a stained night gown, picking over a tray of type as if it was a plate of titbits, peering over the youth's shoulder to read his latest effort. He shook his grizzled grey head.

'Have you been at the metal polish again, my lad? You expect anybody to believe this trash?'

'I'm just giving them what they want. Since when have you objected to us making a few shillings?' Sparrow tucked the even more outrageous final draft into his sack, glared at his tormentor. He had been apprenticed to Mr Greesham at eleven years of age, his mother being a distant cousin of the sourly complexioned printer, and had spent the next six years learning every aspect of sweeping shops, delivering papers and running errands as far as the neighbouring villages. Greesham though, true to his grudging word, had also taught the clumsy, hulking boy his letters. The printer was nosy, irritable and highly opinionated, a familiar figure among the huge number of small traders who scratched a living in Bristol's smoky stews. A magician with molten metal, he could set a six-page double-sided leaflet before the author had finished dictating it. Greesham was not above altering an opinion here or there either, or dropping whole sentences which did not fit with his view of the world. If he was challenged, he would shrug his shoulders and blame Will. He had kept his head above water for a number of years, watching Sparrow metamorphose from a useless overgrown child into a rather useful overgrown youth, riding about the town on his great wall-eyed piebald Jasper, delivering leaflets and catalogues, picking up orders from the other struggling tradesmen and suggesting themes for the local aldermen's addresses.

Greesham had been struck practically dumb by the sudden eruption of work the war had created, and he had at first relished the extra income. As the war had dragged on and the Royal armies marched from one success to another, however, he had sunk back into his old ways, becoming more despondent by the day. Sparrow had taken on more and more of the workload, and Greesham had realized with a shudder that the youth was now practically indispensable. Worse still, his young apprentice had hinted he could manage perfectly well without his old master. Now, instead of standing meekly by, nodding his head as Greesham ranted, Sparrow would thrust his chin out, remind him who was bringing in the lion's share of their income. Giving him advice into the bargain, the saucy devil. Don't look gift horses in the mouth?

'Cheer up? Cheer up? I'll dance a jig all the way to the scaffold, when the King's men come and settle this lot,' he had scolded the hulking youth, throwing a handful of pamphlets outlining the principal elements of the Solemn League and Covenant on to the dirty floor. 'Do you think your Prince Maurice is going to drop in and have a good laugh, all these jokes you've put round about him? Saying he can't ride his horse and talk at the same time, that he took a cannon ball in the head, missed his brain by three feet? It's all very well standing there grinning my lad, you wait till he drops in for a word with you, that's what I say,' he had raved.

'He's got to get here first. Through Waller's army and Bristol's walls.'

Bristol's walls. Five miles of fortifications and two rivers. The Avon, broad but slow, and the Frome, swift but narrow. Bristol had grown up in the boggy bowl where the rivers met, surrounded by ranges of green hills. The newly appointed governor, Nathaniel Fiennes, had ridden from one end of the perimeter to the other, improving the defences, thickening the walls, moving cannon into the strongpoint forts that studded the long line. But stout walls needed stout men, and Fiennes' motley garrison of four thousand soldiers and townsfolk were not exactly itching for a fight. The stocky colonel had already arrested the previous governor and had two Royalist plotters, Messrs Bourchier and Yeomans. They had been hanged in the market place in front of a sullen crowd of dispirited grey faces, looking to the energetic Fiennes as if they had been beaten already. A good hanging usually cheered everybody up, but the sorry Bristolians watched as if he had strung up their own sons.

'I don't know why you're on your high horse,' Will complained. 'What do you think I brought back from

Morrison's, eh? A bag of washers? You know he practically offered me a commission into the bargain?'

'Into his make-believe militia? Oh, that's rich,' Greesham sneered, gathering his dirty gown about his fleshy shoulders. 'And never you mind about Morrison's money. That's my business,' he scowled, crabbing up at the mention of hard cash.

Sparrow jumped to his feet, towered over the dishevelled old printer. 'No, it's our business. I write it, you sell it, got it?'

Greesham huffed and hahed, rattled the tray of type in agitation. Sparrow picked his coat from the hook by the door, threw the bulging sack over his shoulder and stalked out into the bright morning sunlight without a backward glance at the miserable old screw in the shop. Greesham rubbed a hole in the filthy leaded window-pane, watched his protégé march off down the bustling alley.

Will's spirits rose as he made his way along Temple Street, nodding and waving to the familiar faces in the morning rush. He picked his massive cob cross from the livery stable to speed his mission to the great grey keep towering over the middle of the city like some enormous chimney. The youth directed the heavy piebald over the High Street bridge, turned right along the river. Mud-smeared work parties trudged along the streets, off to repair some section of the walls. Ragged pikemen drilled in the open land overlooking the Avon, a bawling sergeant holding his grey-flecked head as the recruits dropped their weapons, marched into one another and about-faced the wrong way. Sparrow watched them for a moment, wondering how long they would stand against Prince Rupert's young scoundrels, and kicked the piebald along the closely built-up bluff and approached the castle. The massive keep had been built by the Normans in eleven something or other, and Fiennes had naturally chosen the monstrous pile as his headquarters. Sparrow passed long files of better dressed troops, three troops of russet-coated cavalry in back and breast, brand new buff coats and newly issued sidearms. The troopers grinned as they watched the youth urging his enormous black and white gelding under the gates.

'Get off and milk it,' one wag shouted.

'Well, we won't go 'ungry, at least,' a veteran commented.

'Our horses will, if he's put in among 'em!'

Their fresh-faced captain suppressed a smile, urged them on as Sparrow trotted into the swarming courtyard. He paused to study the gleaming new cannon which had been rolled into wickerwork emplacements around the walls, wondered apprehensively at the carnage the guns would wreak on the mass of shabby huts, the mushrooming hovels stretching beyond the extended walls. The crowded, stinking suburbs built out into the marshy meadows. All those people – his sort of people too – seeped out of the city like unwanted waste. Sparrow watched as teams of gunners stockpiled balls, rolled barrels along rocky leges, hauled the great sakers and culverins around so their black mouths gaped over the ranked houses, the broad river below.

Every gate had been fortified, covered by carts creaking under the weight of murderer guns, simple but effective multi-barrelled weapons. Beyond the walls thickets of brambles and sedge smothered the greasy, muddy banks of the Avon. Barges and boats glided silently, sailors sculled between the bigger ships lying at anchor in the inner harbour, a forest of masts and rigging. Above all the frenzied activity a forlorn hope of screaming gulls wheeled and dipped as if waiting to snap up the souls of the men who would die beneath the grim cannon-weary walls.

'Have a care! That's finest priming powder, not smoked fish!'

Sparrow swung around in the saddle and recognized Archibald McNabb striding through the busy crowd directing the careless labourers. He slipped out of the saddle as the Scot shook his head at the wall-eyed piebald.

'Is that beast or basilisk you've found yoursen?' he asked, his pocked features stretched in a broad grin.

'Don't you start. I'm a pamphleteer, not one of your fancy princes.'

McNabb raised his colourless eyebrows, nodded over his armoured shoulder. 'Pamphleteer, eh? A wee bit grand, do ye not think? Besides, you're late, as usual.'

'I got stuck behind some wagons in Redcliffe Street. More food for your greedy garrison.' Sparrow tied the horse up at the crowded rail, followed the bow-legged cavalryman into the dark heart of the keep. The Scot's scabbard scraped and tapped against the wall as he trotted up a short flight of stone steps, squeezed past a small drake which had been set up on the landing.

'I've never seen so many guns,' Sparrow commented.

McNabb snorted. 'You should have seen Magdeburg, my laddie. That was guns.'

'Magdeburg fell,' Sparrow pointed out.

The Scot paused at a formidable studded door, nodded ruefully. 'Aye. It fell.'

The Protestant capital in eastern Germany had been taken after a ferocious bloodbath siege, plundered and burnt to the ground by the frenzied, starving Imperialist troops under Count Tilly almost ten years before, but the news-sheets weren't about to let the good citizens of England forget it. The tremendous massacre, lurid high spot of the never ending carnage they called – for the sake of simplicity – the German wars, was a favourite topic for the Parliamentarian propagandists, along with the more recent outrages in Ireland. Just across the narrow Irish sea whole families of God-fearing Protestants and Scots colonists had been put to the sword by the rampant papist heathens. The very same papist heathens Charles Stuart was negotiating to bring over to fight his dirty war for him! Would you ever believe it? The *Mercuries* were full of horror stories, eyewitness reports of villages wiped out and maidens ravished. See to your walls, stand by your colours, protect your innocents!

'I saw Tilly mysen, riding through the bluddy streets, a swaddling babe cradled to his armoured breast. The wee bairn was trying to suckle the very rivets of his armour, aye.'

Sparrow gave him a wearied grin. 'Tilly's Life Guard wouldn't have let a damned Calvinist like you within a mile of the old man,' he snorted.

McNabb narrowed his pale blue eyes. 'You go callin' folk this and that, mind you have the facts right, my laddie,' the Scot advised, tapping his breastplate. 'Tilly's Life Guard were all deed, and though I'm of Presbyterian stock mysen, I'm not one to ram my opinions down other folks' throats,' he added, looked up as a couple of long shadows detached themselves from the crumbling grey walls, stepped into the weak sunshine filtering through the gunport.

'A most excellent and respected creed, my good captain,' the shorter one said, his great stovepipe hat clutched to his shrunken chest. Both staring strangers were dressed head to toe in black broadcloth suits, yellowing stocks tied around their impossibly long necks. Sparrow wondered if they were the bloody traitors Fiennes had ordered hanged a few months before, with their chaffed red necks and bulbous, fanatically glinting eyes. Whether they had returned to haunt the lair of the officer who had sealed their doom.

McNabb looked them up and down, smiled thinly. 'Master Webster, Master Lyle,' he bowed stiffly. 'I didn't see you there.'

'People very often overlook our person,' the shorter one, Webster, said without moving his lips. 'Master Lyle and I can often be found where folk would never expect us. You would be surprised at some of the conversations we have been privy to, standing by, quiet like,' he said silkily.

'I was recalling the sack of Magdeburg, sir.'

'They say the River Elbe runs red to this day, on the very day the city fell,' Lyle commented. 'And that no crops will grow, the fields being so sick with death.'

McNabb nodded. 'I'd not be surprised.' He turned, rapped on the great oak door, stood by as the black-suited duo ducked under the low doorway. Sparrow rolled his eyes at the Scot, who nodded him in after them. William found himself in a low stone chamber, sparsely furnished with table and chairs, a neatly made bunk. A great column of sunlight illuminated a short, stocky officer, leaning over a large creased map, a pair of compasses clutched in his hand. The gunport overlooked a slow bend of the river, the banks overgrown with ranks of sedge and sagging bulrushes. A gaggle of ragged children called and laughed as they played hide and seek among the rushes, up to their dirty knees in rich brown mud.

The governor gave McNabb and Sparrow the briefest of acknowledgements, and jabbed the compass point into a heap of fly-blown papers.

'Will you look at this nonsense?' the agitated officer invited, turning his wandering attention back to the trying correspondence he had been wrestling with all that morning. He read aloud from a savagely torn letter he had speared on the compass point, as if the hated note might be carrying some pestilential contagion. 'Your honour is most respectfully and earnestly pressed to make a sortie west and secure the south Wales seaports! Hah! What with, my footman? Wife? Daughters? My brother tried to intercept Prince Maurice at Frome, what could he do with a few dozen doubting dragoons, eh? What do these fools expect me to . . .' Fiennes looked up, his friendly smile freezing on his rugged face as he caught sight of the two black-suited crows. He cleared his throat, nodded.

'Master Webster, Master Lyle. I wasn't aware you would be attending our trivial meeting,' he spluttered, recovering himself. The commissioners dragged up a pair of rigid chairs, held their coat-tails out and made themselves comfortable, folding their identical hats in their laps. McNabb came to attention behind them, chin out. Sparrow stepped awkwardly from one foot to the other.

'I am afraid we could not agree with your assessment of the situation, Colonel,' Webster said stonily. Fiennes reddened again. 'We wouldn't call our pamphlet campaign trivial, would we, Master Lyle?'

'Indeed not, Master Webster.'

Fiennes opened his mouth, glanced from one to the

other, then to Sparrow. 'I wonder if you have met our principal pamphleteer in these parts, William Sparrow of Greesham's?'

'Greesham's foot?'

'Greesham's the printer, sir,' Fiennes corrected.

Webster turned his black eyes on the youth, inclined his head a fraction. 'I must congratulate you sir. It is seldom indeed one meets such an artful and accomplished, what should we say, distortionist?'

'Distortionist, that's a . . .'

Fiennes flashed McNabb a warning look, walked over to the big printer as he struggled to pull the sack over his head. Sparrow opened the bag and extracted a wad of leaflets and his hastily scrawled draft, which Fiennes glanced at, passed to the silent commissioners for approval.

They digested the document carefully, Sparrow felt the cold rock-locking frozen fingers around his bones as their eyes followed the closely printed argument. Webster frowned, studied Sparrow through his deadly dark eyes.

'Another pack of lies, sir.'

'A transparent tissue of patent untruths,' Lyle, a slower reader, added.

'Two score Cavaliers seen off by a one-legged driver and a clerk? A milkmaid with a pail?'

'And divers eggs and refuse?' Lyle recited from the grubby pamphlet.

'What have you to say for yourself, sir? Well?'

Sparrow swallowed, his mouth dryer than the crumbling mortar oozing between the stones. 'Well, sir . . . I was told, sir . . . I had been given the impression—'

'It is passable effort, sir,' Webster interrupted. 'Master Lyle and I do not personally agree with Mr Vane's instructions on these matters, nevertheless, we recognize the importance of securing an efficient dissemination of Parliament's case.'

Fiennes sighed with relief, Sparrow blinked quickly. 'Thank you sir. Most kind.'

'I believe in Master Sparrow we have struck upon a man with the gift of communicating directly with the masses,' Fiennes blustered enthusiastically. 'I fear the townsfolk are not soundly behind our great cause. Why, in London, we recruit several hundred men a day, here I am lucky if I replace the scoundrels who deserted the night before! This lot here don't know whether to piss or kick over the pot, if you'll pardon my soldier's talk,' the officer muttered.

'You must watch your men, Colonel,' Webster advised.

'And your language, sir. Battle is no excuse for a foul mouth,' Lyle scolded.

'You must punish all such desertions, emphatically, sir,' Webster proposed.

'And ungodly language,' Lyle seconded.

'Emphatically, yes, sir.' Fiennes grinned weakly at them, blinking like a pair of magpies before him. How dare Whitehall send these pale creepers to hang about his headquarters as if he was about to sell the city off to the highest bidder. Did they not trust him? He had been in arms since the beginning, after all. It had been his cavalry Prince Rupert had scattered at Powick Bridge, the very first fight of the war. Spurring back over the bridge, riderless horses galloping alongside and his men screaming the black devil himself was after them, Fiennes had wondered where he had gone wrong. Asked God's mercy, begged him to point out his mistakes. He had set up his squadrons, exactly as the manuals described. They had been well equipped, well armed and on good horses. The fine russet troops had trotted forward in perfect order, like knights across a chessboard. And what had happened? They had been bowled aside by a flashing, deafening tornado of blues and crimsons and yellows. A rainbow of screaming, colliding colours. His men had drawn up, emptied their pistols at the terrifying mass of enemy horsemen, struggled to hold their prancing horses, holster their smoking pistols and draw their swords in the same senseless second. Fiennes had hacked about him for all he was worth, but his support troops had melted like fat on a grate, disintegrated into a mass of panic-stricken fugitives, bolting for the bridge. Why? Where had he gone wrong? He'd led his men as Rupert had his, from the front, not cowering like a ninny in the rear. Why then had Prince Rupert thrown him out of the way as if his armoured cavalry had been so many turnips impaled on beanpoles? He had lain awake, night after night, worrying himself sick. How would they ever, ever beat him?

At least it had been somebody else's turn to catch it, those few weeks later at Edgehill. Fiennes' troops had been brigaded into Sir William Balfour's cavalry reserve that day, waiting just behind the great psalm-singing blocks of Essex's foot. Rupert's flashing silk and steel tornado had rolled down the slope like a ball of fire, just as before, demolished the squadrons of horse quaking in their stirrups at the bottom of the hill. The flank regiments had dissolved as his troop had dissolved at Powick Bridge, and Rupert had swept after them, unbeatable and unstoppable. Fiennes had thought he had misheard, when the dour Balfour had ordered the cavalry reserve regiments to charge the King's exposed foot, grappling at push of pike with Essex's men. Charge? Those years of service with the

Dutch had softened his brains! Shouldn't they fall back by squadrons, cover the retreat? Balfour had waved his sword above his helmeted head, pointed the gleaming blade at the thickest outcrop of enemy colours. Fiennes had found himself cantering forward, the terrified infantry of both sides leaping out of the way or being bowled over like milk bottles. The Parliamentarian reserve had sliced clean through, helped Essex's tired, bloodied foot hold the King's men to an honourable draw. By the time Rupert's blown squadrons had returned, night had fallen and Charles Stuart's fantastic opportunity to settle the wars there and then had been lost. It wouldn't be the last time Rupert's horse charged victoriously and in vain, but Fiennes, shuddering in the brisk breeze which had blown up from the river, wasn't to know that. As far as he was concerned, Rupert was a demon, a prince of air and darkness. He could change his shape, was a master of disguise. No pistol nor sword could harm him for he bore the devil's shield. God help Nathaniel Fiennes, if Rupert came before these wretched walls. He glanced up, realized he had missed Webster's impassioned speech about the importance of leafleting the cities.

'Well, Master Sparrow? Will you go to London and join our busy writers, help the *Mercuries* tell our side of the story?' Sparrow opened his wide mouth, dumbstruck. 'I am sure we have no need to entice you with offers of salary, times such as they are, but I have been directed to inform you that you can expect board and lodging, and five shillings a week for your troubles,' Webster offered.

Sparrow said nothing. Five shillings? He was making ten and more on the side, working for Greesham. Move to London, all those hundreds of miles away, for five shillings a week? Sir Gilbert had already promised him a commission in his village militia. That would give him a far more useful income and a uniform into the bargain! Maybe it was time to bite the bullet, join the fight instead of hovering on the fringes like a greedy mosquito. Yes. He could just picture Bella's adoring face as he paraded in his finery!

'There is no need to give us an answer immediately, Master Sparrow,' Webster allowed. 'We hear you spend a deal of time working for Colonel Morrison down in, let me see, Chipping something?'

'Who? Oh, Sir Gilbert, yes.'

'Yes, indeed. We are about to pay a visit to Sir Gilbert, to see for ourselves how his fine regiment is shaping up.'

'His regiment? Oh yes, that regiment,' Sparrow stammered.

'Has the colonel raised more than one? Would the cause had more Sir Gilberts,' Lyle joked, mirthlessly.

Sparrow smiled glumly. Depended on how many men they reckoned on making up a regiment, he supposed. But if Sir Gilbert's shadow battalion made a regiment, three sixpences made a fortune.

CHEWTON MENDIP

JUNE 10, 1643

The big borrowed bay was prancing and bucking, entirely unused to the distant rattle of musketry and the occasional sharp cough of a pistol nearer at hand. Telling gripped the reins, turning them over and over his hands, weaving the greasy leather through his fingers. The strange and unfamiliar horse tossed its head again and Telling wrenched the reins back in response, cursed the beast for the hundreth time. His own charger would have stood his ground, hardly troubled by the distant explosions and drifting clouds of acrid smoke tumbling and tangling with the mist rising sullenly from the valley below. He coughed, looked up and down the double-ranked troop. His chestnut was still lame, and he had been forced to send Cady and Jacobs out to requisition a new mount.

'It was the fattest farm I've seen,' Cady had reported, leading the fine hunter they had 'requisitioned' on a stolen rope. 'And our boys had already carried off everything the farmer 'adn't bolted down. Didn't he rave, when we 'ad 'is 'orse, an' all?' The wiry trooper had glanced at Jacobs, who had nodded his stubbled head in agreement. 'Fat as a moth, he were. Showed us all the letters of credit he had already. "When's this lot goin' to be paid, then? Who'll honour these chits?" The King'll 'onour 'em when 'e's won, it's that simple, I told 'im, didn't I, Ned?'

Telling had nodded glumly, felt an unwelcome twinge of conscience. He hadn't expected to be looting fearful farmers when he'd joined up in Oxford. He thought guiltily about his own home, the comfortable rectory at Wainbridge, imagined a gang of cut-throat Roundheads knocking his parents aside as they tugged poor old Ben, his father's saddle horse, from the stable. Well, the sooner they gave up and allowed the King to take his rightful place in London, the sooner they could all go back to a decent living.

Telling's troop had joined the rest of Prince Maurice's fine regiment on a humpbacked hill above Wells. The grassy knoll rose like a pale whale from the shifting Sargasso of fog and mist which seemed to have sought out every corner of the boggy levels, entangled itself on the ranks of sedge, patient files of rushes. They had expected a grandstand view of the enemy rearguard as it made an orderly fighting retreat across the neat checkerboard farmlands towards Chewton, hidden in another fold of the lush green hills. Instead all they could see were the flat tops of the hills, so many toads' eyes in the rippled grey pond. They were drawn up in two long, stamping lines on the forward slopes while the sullen Cornish foot shuffled and grumbled through the thinning mist along the road below. Hugo watched them, shook his head. You couldn't describe it as a march, more like a procession of drunks thrown out of an alehouse. Then again, this ragged band had already come well over two hundred miles. They had taken Taunton without a fight and thrown garrisons into Dunster Castle and Bridgwater. The enemy had melted away north, their brown columns swollen with Parliamentary sympathizers, merchants, shop keepers and well-to-do farmers who had read lurid reports about the Cornish host. Infidels and cannibals to a man.

The hardy few who hadn't loaded their belongings on to carts and joined the throng were now bitterly regretting their stupidity. The sober-minded townsfolk of Taunton had attempted to buy off the Royalist army with eight thousand pounds, but even this hefty gift hadn't stopped the wild horsemen from ransacking shops and drinking themselves silly in the abandoned alehouses. Telling and some of the other officers had beaten men out of the inns with the flat of their swords, attempted to restore discipline where they could. The rumour-mongers told a different story. That some poor haberdasher had been dragged before the strutting peacocks, ordered to pay his share toward the cannibals' keep. He had pleaded to be excused on the grounds he had eighteen children. The evil earls and princes had told him to go and drown them, come back with the money. A young maiden, whose widowed mother scraped to keep a roof over their heads sewing clothing for the ladies thereabouts, had begged them not to take their small savings, offered herself up to the drooling German himself, Prince Maurice. The next morning the grinning prince had rolled the ruined virgin out of his bed, snatched up their pitiful sack of coins, and ridden off on his charger, laughing at the dawn. Cady and Jacobs, grinning and nattering behind Telling's back, had heard all the stories. The vicious tales seemed to spread like a pestilential plague through the gossipy camps of both armies, gathering extra embellishments along the way. The conniving rascals spent most of their spare time hanging around with harlots and whores down by the horsclines, and were as well informed as the average Parliamentary hack busy scribbling lies in Bristol.

'Maurice? That booby? He wouldn't know where to stick it,' Cady commented.

'He'd know where to stick it all right, but it wouldn't be up front.'

'They say he has a little sambo to pull off his boots,' the corporal theorized.

'Pull a few other . . .'

'Will you two idiot jackdaws stow that chatter?' Telling snarled, twisting around in his saddle. 'The next man who repeats any lie about the Prince will be flogged at the tumbler for his troubles. Is that clear?'

'Yes, sir. Meaning no offence, sir. Only we heard from Matilda Dawkins how the Prince don't like—'

'I don't want to know about Matilda Dawkins,' Telling lied. In actual fact, he hadn't been able to think straight about anyone else since he had seen her being groped and mauled in turns by those halfwits the night before. Well, it had looked like a mauling to him, staring curiously over the rim of his tankard. Their brutal lovemaking reminded him of his childhood, the way his bullying brothers would pinch his arms to the floor, gleefully ignoring his feeble kicks and punches. What had bothered him the most was how the wretched girl had seemed to enjoy it, cooing and screaming and arching her back like a little cat. He blinked, held his hand over his eyes as the mist blew away, revealed the brief green fields and narrow lanes to the front. A sudden shadowy movement like a flock of blackbirds over to the right. Not another ambush, surely?

The Royalist advance party had already been given

several bloody noses by the Roundhead rearguard, which would run and then turn like a hunted wolf. The old fox Waller himself had hurried his own regiment of horse south to support the retreat and attack any over-enthusiastic advance guards. The impatient Royalists, snapping at the enemy's heels, had pursued the Roundhead cavalry through Somerton and straight into a carefully laid ambush. The enemy commander had filled a ditch with his dragoons, the cunning snipers who rode around the battlefield on their ragged nags, dismounting to fire off a few shots and then cantering off out of trouble. The foolhardiest Royalists had been knocked from their saddles, the rest had pulled up, wondering what to try next. The Roundheads had then launched a fresh cavalry regiment at them, bowled them straight back into the Royalists' lumbering main body, but had called them back before they pressed too far, repeating the enemy's mistake. Maurice and Hopton had called a brief council, decided to continue the advance under cover of a cavalry screen, one regiment leapfrogging the other. In this way the Royalists had reached Wells without further loss, only to see the enemy forces pour through the town like a brown tide, disappear into the hills beyond the safety of Waller's main army. Telling watched an officer gallop up the slope behind his troop, one hand clutched to his enormous black hat. Butler pulled up beside him, straightened his headgear with a flourish.

'Ah, there you are. I see you followed my advice, got yourself another horse? A fine mount, if somewhat feisty,' he observed as the big bay reared and stamped at the springy turf.

'The damned beast won't keep still,' Telling told him through gritted teeth, wrenching at the reins.

'Bit like that young strumpet last night. You would have imagined three men would have slowed her down a touch, wouldn't you?' Telling flushed, adjusted his hat. 'You needn't worry you know, she was well paid,' Butler said, amused at the youngster's obvious discomfort. 'Oh yes, you'd gone by then, hadn't you?'

'I was tired; the ride, you know.'

'Ah, what a ride! Still. This one might get you out of trouble if Waller turns sudden as he likes.'

'Yes,' Telling said glumly. 'He's got spirit, I'll say that for him.' He nodded, tugged at the prancing gelding. 'But I fear I may have made the King another enemy, his late owner wasn't particularly pleased to see him go.'

'He must know there's a war on.'

'He does now. I imagine he and his sons are ready to join Waller yonder,' Telling predicted gloomily.

'My God, you are a worrier!' Butler snorted. 'The fellow's probably hidden most of his animals away from us. You didn't take anything more from him than we did the whore last night. And besides,' he added, tapping his nose, 'it's better to have all our enemies in front of us now, where we can see them. We don't want to have to go back and forth across the country, fighting a new crop of rebels every year. Let them all line up now, and have done with it. Burying their heads in the sand with the don't knows, cah!'

Telling glanced at the dark features of the colonel, his weather-beaten, sun-creased complexion and jaunty black moustache which looked as if it had been painted in oils.

'If he's against us he should have retreated with Waller there. If he's for the King he should give up his animal in good grace.' Butler leaned out of the saddle, spat into the grass. 'I saw many like him in Germany, trying to be friend and ally to all. Let me tell you, in a civil war there can be no such creature. People like that simply prolong the dratted business. See how long the wars have gone on in Germany. Nigh on thirty years they've been at it, thirty years! We'll be in our fifties before we're done!'

Telling looked glum. He hadn't imagined he'd be soldiering for much more than six months, a year at the outside. Thirty years? A cannon on the slopes opposite boomed. The ball whistled toward them, crouched on their bucking horses peering into the drifting mists to guess its trajectory. The ball dipped into a copse half a mile ahead, started a blazing fire in the tinder-dry undergrowth.

'Not enough powder, damn them,' Butler commented, nodded down the slope toward a messenger, galloping up from the crowded lanes ahead. They watched him draw up in front of the general staff, grouped a little way along the creeping mole-infested hill. A dozen officers in silks and ribbons, dazzling velvet and glittering swords.

'Hullo. Trouble. I'd best get back to my lot before they go setting some barn on fire for a bit of fun. Be careful of yourself now, Telling, and cheer up! It might never happen!' Butler touched his hat, turned and cantered off down the slope toward the slow-moving hedgehogs of pikemen making their way forward along the road. Jacobs stood in his stirrups, peering toward the distant village.

'The Earl's in trouble,' he said in a told-you-so tone which annoyed Telling all over again. 'He's chased them too far and they've turned!'

'Thank you, Jacobs, I'll run along and inform Prince Maurice of your reading of the tactical situation,' Telling told him curtly, squinting through the thickening, reeking smokes drifting from the village. The mist which had seemed likely to blow away for good had been merely holding its breath. Now it writhed out of the willows and the rushes, swallowed the narrow heath all over again as if the simmering forces of nature had, for once, favoured the counter-attacking Roundheads. The dull slate roofs and strangled steeple of the village church glimmered wetly in the murk. Through its ragged fringes Telling could see a body of horse in blue pouring four abreast through the main street, picking up speed as they got out on to the misty heathland between the hill and the village. He could make out dark smudges moving swiftly along the hedges running parallel, hemming the shaken Royalists into the narrow lane, a killing zone for tired horses and terrified riders. Telling turned as Prince Maurice, a beefy doughboy in his plain buff coat, cantered down the ranks, drawing his sword.

'Prepare to charge!' he bellowed, his Life Guards closing in about him with his personal cornet flapping above them.

A bugler sounded the charge, and the whole hill lurched as hundreds of hoofs drummed the turf, demolished the scattered molehills. Telling glanced over his shoulder, saw Cady and Jacobs close up, their pinched faces and chalky features smeared with dirt. The regiment trotted down the hill and divided around the merrily burning copse like the sea breaking around a boulder. The Prince had spurred his enormous black Arab out ahead, his colour party bending over their horses' necks to keep up with him, the mist shredding as if it could not abide their frenzied faces. Other officers had been caught up in the excitement of the chase, spurted ahead with their swords flashing in the damp sunlight.

They crossed the rutted road and cantered over the flat grey heath beyond. Telling ducked low over the big bay's mane as it drew ahead from the inferior horseflesh behind, clods of earth flying about his head. Riderless horses careered by, stumbling men jumping out of the way or throwing themselves into the churned mud behind the scanty cover of furze or bramble outcrops. A sudden crowd of confused, sooty riders jabbering and pointing back the way they had come. What were they saying? Before he could register anything except the furious thumping of his heart, he came face to face with the enemy.

Two hundred yards ahead, trotting forward as if they were on a parade. Waller's cavalry had chased the young Earl of Caernarvon's regiment out of the village, and had formed up again, a chain of interlocking brown nuts and bolts. Ahead of them a skirmish line of dragoons took what cover they could, holding on grimly to their muskets, with every tenth man clutching a panicking herd of prancing ponies. The dragoons fired wildly, retrieved their mounts and spurred off into the hedges and willows to give their big brothers in the cavalry a clearer field of fire. Another flurry of hastily aimed pistol and carbine shots covered the field in acrid white smoke. Here and there a rider flung up his arms and slipped out of his saddle. The Royalist charge began to lose its momentum as the horses shied away from the formidable obstacle. Three troops of Roundhead horsemen. A terrible, segmented centipede with hundreds of legs, four ranks deep and three hundred yards long. No way through, no way past, no way out. Telling realized his mount had slowed down of its own accord, saw a dozen colourful officers surge past toward the overlapping enemy line. Maurice, Sandys and that insufferable bore Atkyns with his curly hair and tired eyes.

Where were his men? Would they follow? Was he on his own? He daren't look back.

Puffs of white smoke, a second later the harsh barks of their weapons as the trotting Roundheads emptied their pistols at the charging mob of Royalists. A rider alongside slumped over his high saddle bow, his sword dangling from his wrist strap, slipped out of the saddle to be destroyed by the thundering hoofs behind. Telling's bay had dropped to an ungainly canter, veered away from the noise and smoke toward the tidy gardens and rickety fences behind the houses on the outskirts of the village. He brought his sword up instinctively as a terrified Roundhead trotted into his path, his slower horse hoofed aside by Telling's thoroughly alarmed charger. He hacked out at the rider, who parried the blow with his smoking pistol, deflecting the blade on to his chest. His horse reared, stopped dead and he had to cling to its mane to stop himself being thrown out of the saddle. He had run into a milling crowd of russet-coated troopers, a great press of steaming horses and cursing men. He felt a sword jab into his back, under his backplate and through his coat. Terrified, he hacked about him with his own sword, knocking a Roundhead out of his saddle. Another trooper alongside gave him a backhander with his steel gauntlet, catching him in the mouth. He kicked at the cavalryman's thigh boot, slashed his sword across his lobster-pot helmet. The bay reared again as the enemy flowed past. He could taste blood in his mouth and feel liquid running down the crack of his buttocks, wetting his breeches. Horses and riders were dashing this way and that, ignoring him, pistols going off on all sides. A rush of air across his face, a louder crack, as a ball missed his nose by a few inches, buried itself in a post.

He kicked the bay into a fast trot, leapt a stone wall beside one of the outlying cottages. He hauled the reins back, turned the horse in circles over somebody's vegetable patch. A narrow lane ran alongside the far wall, and a squad of enemy cavalry had worked their way along hoping to outflank some of the madmen who had cut through their front ranks. One of them spotted Telling, at bay on a heap of turnip husks, aimed his pistol and fired. He ducked, the bullet hit the cottage, sparking on the stonework and sending a handful of razor shards over him. He felt the hot grit sting the back of his neck, wrenched his own pistol out and fired back. The shot went wild but the rest of the squad had trotted on past the lane, looking for easier kills.

He spotted Lieutenant Sandys just the other side of the wall, thrown from his horse and running around in circles as a rugged Roundhead hacked at him from the saddle, screaming for him to surrender. He eased a hand under his coat, felt gingerly for a wound. He thought about dismounting, hiding in the tumbledown cottage until the worst of this infernal whirlwind had passed. He had been hurt, it would be all right, he thought bleakly. Beyond the protecting wall hundreds of horsemen were locked in furious hand-to-hand combat in the misty field, the enemy line having swept round to engulf the entire regiment like a net of sardines.

He swallowed, his suddenly dry tongue glued to the top of his mouth. He knew he should spur his horse back out into the fight, but he knew he would be shot down before he'd cleared the gate. He watched the fight unfold, praying feverishly for the courage to charge once more.

Prince Maurice's party had become entangled with the enemy dragoons, the canny fighters using the cover provided by the hedges and ditches to work their way behind the slashing swords. The black Arab crashed to the ground and a mob of delighted dragoons doubled forward to finish off the struggling Prince. Atkyns' men had veered toward the village away from the captured Maurice, and were only called back by an alert groom, who twisted his horse around and spurred after the dismounted dragoons, hurrying back to their ditch with the dazed Prince staggering along between them. Two dragoons were slashed down, another, a cornet in a faded red Dutch coat, turned to escape, but was knocked out of the saddle by the groom, who leaned over and pulled the tawny guidon from his dazed fingers. Telling closed his eyes in silent thanks as the fearless Prince was surrounded by his cheering troopers.

Suddenly, another patter of shots pocked the cottage wall behind him. He turned his prancing horse again, struggling to hold on to the wild-eyed beast. Paralysed with fear, he watched the white-faced Sandys run toward the wall, shaking his hands above his head as if he was demonstrating some berserker dance. His Roundhead opponent spurred after him, shouting mad Gaelic oaths, and let fly with both pistols. Sandys screamed like a rabbit and fell down out of sight behind the wall. Another burst of shots and shouting from his left warned Telling more enemy forces were hastening up to join the furious mêlée. He peered round to see a second squad of enemy horse trotting along the dratted lane, emptying their pistols in turn as if he was a bottle in a shooting gallery. He turned the frantic horse again, put the bay to the small gate leading into the yard. He landed behind the Roundheads, who shouted and bawled at him but couldn't turn their mounts in the narrow alley. He felt the animal collide with the wall of the neighbouring cottage, stumble in pain and fear. He felt his wet groin explode with pain as he regained the saddle, tugged the reins up with his watery weak arms, coughed blood on to his sleeve. The bay slewed down the alley and into the main street, pawing the road as another troop of Roundheads trotted down toward him. They looked like ghosts, faces a white blur beneath their steel helmets. He looked to his right and realized why. Prince Maurice and his sadly reduced colour party were hurtling down the street toward them!

He urged the terrified horse toward the houses opposite as the Prince cantered by on a borrowed black nag, scattering the enemy horse which divided in front of him. Small groups of Royalists spurred their blown mounts after the impetuous commander, their swords chipped and bloody. Atkyns, his brown hair streaming behind him, slapped his sword over his bloody horse's haunches as he tried to keep up, called his men after him. Telling recognized Jacobs in the confused crush, a nasty cut above his glinting eye, a stream of blood running over his old coat.

'They'll never get out of here,' Jacobs said, nodding over the din of bawling men and screaming, steaming horses. Telling looked down the battered glass-strewn street, the inn signs swinging in the mad breeze they had whipped up. The Prince's charge had taken him straight through another body of enemy horse, but more and more russet-coated troops were trotting in from the other end of the village. He had driven almost all before him, and was now surrounded, at bay like a wild wolf, in his torn blue suit, his buff coat hanging in great yellow strips where he had been hacked and chopped by exasperated enemy troopers. The bugler and the cornet were knocked from their saddles, a couple of Roundheads barging forward after the drooping standard. Telling turned his horse, straightened his trembling arm and pointed his sword at the screaming throng. He spurred into the fray, catching the intent Roundheads by surprise. Jacobs cantered alongside, aiming his pistol. More Royalists had spotted his charge, hastened along the street to help. Telling's charge sent riders toppling from saddles, horses lost their balance and collapsed in the middle of the fray. Prince Maurice's black nag was thrown down, spilling its rider into a shop doorway. He spurred the big bay on, knocking a Roundhead's chestnut into a wall. The rider grabbed his smashed hand, lowering his guard, and Telling lunged with all his might. The sword seemed to skewer the rider as if he were a bag of laundry, the double-edged blade sinking up to the hilt beneath the man's new breastplate, a lucky gap between the overlapping edges of his yellow buff coat. He pulled back but the hungry sword wouldn't come. He let go but the handle was still looped to his wrist by a twist of leather. He wrenched his arm up and away, making the wounded Roundhead scream with pain as his horse squeezed by, practically wrenching his arm from its socket. The recovered sword was hanging bloody, twisting this way and that on its taut strap. He held the reins, got a grip on his weapon as a big Roundhead careered past, his horse's legs flailing about on a sheet of blood and broken glass. The collapsing horse spilled the rider through a window, his great leather boots kicking comically.

He risked a quick peek across the chaotic street. Atkyns' troopers were being surrounded and pressed back the way they had come. Their captain had pulled his tired horse about and was pointing to a bloody Roundhead officer steadying himself beside a broken-down doorway. Apparently infuriated by the man's continued resistance, Atkyns leapt from his saddle and barged through a whole mob of jeering enemy troopers. He pulled the offending officer round by his backplate and cuffed him across the face with his gauntlet.

'I've told you once,' he heard Atkyns shriek, 'will you take quarter or no?'

The Roundhead officer thrust the shouting captain back on his heels and raised his notched sword, but one of Atkyns' troopers parried the blow, thrust him back against the doorframe so hard the officer doubled up and dropped his weapon. The trooper caught him up by his crossbelts and ran him through in an instant, directing his blade under the enemy officer's unprotected armpit. Atkyns bawled something at the dying man, and pushed past him into the narrow hovel.

Telling spurred his horse through the press, pulled it around alongside the doorway where the Prince had taken refuge from his enthusiastic pursuers. He brought his bloody sword down across the back of another dismounted Roundhead's neck, snapping the man's helmet strap. The bareheaded trooper leapt out of the way, tripped over his fallen comrade and struck his head against the battered door post. He fell in a heap as Telling swung his boots over the saddle and slipped to the floor. The fighting, kicking, screaming mob disintegrated as more Royalists charged home, propelling the lurching Roundhead troopers back along the wrecked street and spilling Telling into the shop. He measured his length over splintered shelving, trampled vegetables, discarded equipment and scrambled to his feet to see three Roundheads grappling with the Prince. One of them brought his pistol down on the

Prince's dark head, making him shout in pain and redouble his efforts against the other two. Atkyns had upended a stool and was laying about him, forcing the enemy troopers to divert their attention to him. Another Roundhead kicked out at Telling's head, lost his balance on the rolling vegetables. Maurice heaved his broken sword into the man's face and he fell back, screaming. He elbowed the enemy trooper closing in on him, propelling him within range of Atkyns' stool. Telling grabbed the last man from behind, hurled him into a wall. He rebounded, turned and fled down the passage, hard on the heels of his bruised and bloodied colleagues.

He swayed from side to side, blinked at the Prince as he picked himself up and dusted the worst of the muck from his torn and bloody uniform. The Roundhead on the floor shrieked and gasped, his face a mass of blood and broken teeth. Maurice scowled at the man, nodded to Atkyns, breathing hard, and Telling, swaying drunkenly.

'Are you all right, sire?' Hugo asked shakily.

'Off cuss I am all right. Are you?'

Telling eased a hand behind him, felt his dripping breeches, fearing the worst. He was almost relieved when he examined his fingers, sticky with blood. He'd been stabbed in the arse? Maurice leaned over, looked down the trembling captain's back.

'You heff a cut on your back,' Maurice told him shortly, picking up a new sword from the clutter on the floor. 'Now let us get after them.'

Telling watched the Prince pick his way across the wrecked shop, stagger into the daylight. Atkyns dragged the badly wounded Roundhead officer back into the shop, laid him flat. The man was blinking his eyes, shutting them tight. 'He took quarter twice and then picked up a sword again,' he explained. 'They're either cowards or fanatics like this one,' he said in disgust. The Roundhead looked up at the three pitiless giants growing taller as he diminished on the bloody boards, blood bubbling from the side of his mouth. They heard him whisper 'Isobel' before he kicked once, and died.

They left him in the shop with the trampled vegetables. Telling limped after the two experienced cavalrymen as if he was being jabbed and harried by an army of demons armed with tiny needles. He leaned against the smashed doorway, focused with difficulty on the flamboyant Earl of Caernarvon, reining in on his foaming, soot-smeared white charger. He had lost his hat and his golden curls were speckled with gouts of blood and sticky grey fragments.

'You are safe my lord, thank God,' he called breathlessly.

The Prince scowled, pointed on down the road. 'Keep after them, but not too far, not too far,' he stressed in his accented English. He reached out and steadied Telling as he swooned, toppled away from the door-frame. Hugo opened his eyes, blinked at the Prince's frowning, pudgy face and slumped to the bloody paving stones.

BY
KILMERSDEN HALL
BONE HILL

SOMERSET, JUNE 11, 1643

The iron triangle had been hung by the fortified front door ready to warn of a sortie from the village, the long-expected attack on the last house in the hills which would still welcome its rightful King. They had heard the dull rumble of the guns throughout the previous afternoon, and Sir Marmaduke Ramsay was almost relieved to hear the furious clanging after enduring long months of tedious, agonized expectation. Either the enemy were upon them or their Sovereign had sent his faithful servants to deliver them from their arrogant entombment.

Ramsay had been in his drawing-room – complete with wicker-basket gun emplacement – gloomily examining the latest hopelessly dated dispatch, when Findlay, their game-keeping sergeant-major, had spotted the first movement on the lane. He had leaned over the fortified roof, bawled down to Bates, their corporal and former footman. The crusty old serving man had rattled a ladle around the iron triangle for all he was worth, bringing the rest of the casually besieged garrison running to the front of the house. Sir Marmaduke snatched up his loaded pistols and skidded into the hall, colliding with his fearsome wife Margaret who was already hurrying down the bare corridor with skirts bunched and ornamental halberd over her shoulder.

The squire, a lean, hollow-cheeked man of unguessable age sporting a neatly trimmed goatee beard, knew better than to get in Maggie Driscoll's way when she was on the warpath. A ferocious, unforgiving temper and near legendary stubbornness more than made up for her deficiency in height. She had never been a beauty, but her bold eye and scornful refusal to waste her time on the finer points of feminine endeavour had – at first – delighted young Marmaduke Ramsay, fresh back from the German wars. The malicious villagers and tenants claimed he'd never known what had hit him, that big Henry Driscoll's eldest daughter had frogmarched the poor boy to the altar and held him straight while the terrified bishop read the service. All the trimmings, if you please. None of your Puritan sackcloth and ashes sentiments the day the Ramsays wed.

The shocked congregation had glared in disbelief at the candles, the expensive gowns, the resplendent clerics in their tall hats. How the bells had clanged that day! Bewildered villagers had half expected to see the Pope himself carried down Chipping Marleward's muddy High Street in a red silk sedan. Not that many of the villagers had been invited, mind you. They waited behind the graveyard, a dirty flock of ragged jackdaws. Let them worship as they liked, up to their dirty knees in their pigsties if that's what they preferred. 'I won't presume to tell those dogs how to worship, so woe betide them if they presume to tell me,' the new Lady Margaret had snapped to her new husband, who had been anxious to keep the precarious, precious peace as long as possible.

She had been 'seeing things through', as she told her cronies, ever since they had married back in 1622. And she would see them through to penury and untold misery if she continued to have her way, Ramsay thought bitterly, striding behind her down their gloomy hall. All their paintings, expensive hangings and antique ornaments had been packed up safe in the cellar. The Elizabethan arsenal of old arquebuses, morion helmets and bills had been taken down and polished off, distributed to their loyal tenants along with a handful of modern muskets and some newly turned pikes.

Lady Ramsay advanced on their fortified front door, a skirted siege engine which had somehow rumbled inside the improvised fortress. The hall had been packed about with wicker baskets of earth, sacks of sand and diverse old cushions.

'What is it, are the rogues risking it at last?' she bayed, peering over Bates' hunched shoulder as he crouched behind the emplacement. Ramsay snatched up his glass, scanned the surrounding parkland, the barricaded gate.

'Some messenger from the village. Is it Jamie, Morrison's boy? All grown up now in his new buff coat.' Bates ran his knuckles into his eyes, a grey whiskered mole in ancient armour.

'Morrison's sent his boy up here? Whatever for?' Lady Ramsay snorted, snatching the glass from her husband.

'Under a flag of truce by the look of it, the treacherous snake! Findlay!' She leaned over the wicker wall, bawled up to the battlemented roof. 'Have an eye on him mind, drop the dog in his tracks if he tries anything!'

'He's brought a drummer and a white flag, my dove, we can't shoot him down in cold blood!' Ramsay said, horrified at his wife's impetuosity. 'You're not to shoot him,' he insisted.

Lady Ramsay blew a draught of air down her nose. 'He can't help his father, I suppose,' she allowed, grudgingly.

'I imagine he's drummed the whole lot of them into his blasted militia, including that flirt-gill of a daughter.'

Young Bella and her brother James had been frequent visitors to the hall before the war, despite their father's all too evident dislike of the 'penniless, superannuated squire', his 'howling harridan' of a wife and their feudal lifestyle. 'Hasn't that old bird heard of Magna Carta?' The squire, in his turn, had despised Morrison's shamelessly abrupt business manner, his cheerful dealings with all sorts of Fosseway riffraff. The man had climbed from the gutter and collected all sorts of rabid ideas along the way. Above all though, the squire detested Morrison's uncanny ability to rake in enormous incomes from the very hills he hunted. Their sour relationship had finally been severed with the war, and poor Anneliese, the Ramsays' spirited sixteen-year-old daughter, hadn't seen her old friend Bella since.

They watched the anxious messenger pass the sentries a small package. The detachment at the gate – six brawny tenants armed with ancient sidearms and long rifles, making up their lack of numbers with their reputed ability to be able to hit a mosquito between the eyes at three hundred yards – represented a quarter of their available manpower. Margaret had advised Ramsay to post them at key points rather than attempt to spread them around the wide open grounds. Besides, the fools down below were bound to assume every approach was equally manned. She had heard of hard-pressed garrisons playing similar tricks all over the country, and had boned up on other aspects of the art of war, devouring military tracts, the newsletters describing the recent bloodbaths in Germany.

Ramsay didn't need books to remind him, he'd battled

through blood enough in Bohemia. Streams of it running away from the smoky battlefields like the vile trails dribbling from the slaughter pens in the city. It was no use telling her. Lady Ramsay particularly admired Wallenstein, the Czech adventurer who had altered the whole course of the German wars, saving the Holy Roman Emperor from almost certain extinction on the swords of the ambitious Swedes and their Protestant allies. Wallenstein had recruited, trained and led vast armies, fed them and paid them into the bargain. All he had wanted in return was the odd duchy, the occasional princedom, anything he could get his hands on, until his untimely end in 1634. Wallenstein, in his heyday, had used every trick and stratagem he could come up with. He had marched his legions of camp followers in behind his veteran regiments, given them banners and flags to deceive the enemy into thinking they faced enormous odds. Ramsay had listened to his wife outline half a dozen similar schemes, tugging his weary beard in agitation.

'That's all very well, my dove. But Wallenstein was beaten by the Swedes and shot by his own side! You seem to forget, my dear, that I was there!'

'Nonsense. You were home by 1621. The war had hardly started by then!' He had closed his eyes, tamped his pipe and retired behind a smokescreen into the bare shelves of the study.

Lady Ramsay's dispositions were every bit as daring as her hero's, but they were fraught with dangers, leaving as they did large swaths of the estate's extensive parkland with little or no cover. An observant enemy, noting the shadowplay of troop movements around the gates, could get a regiment of foot and battery of guns into the grounds before the meagre garrison could even attempt to do anything about it. Miraculously, the gamble had paid off so far, and the lonely outpost had been left unmolested for over a year, a thorn in the side of the village and surrounding farms. The all too familiar militia seemed convinced the house sheltered a whole swarm of ferocious Cavaliers, just waiting to swoop down from the hills and burn their humble homes to the ground, and kept themselves well out of range.

Games, that's what they were playing. Desperately dangerous games which could end in blood and ruin for all of them, squire and shepherd alike. Sir Marmaduke had worried himself sick, a scurvy sailor beneath his fine buff coat and gold doublet, torn by doubts and questionable loyalties. He worried his teeth loose in his wet gums and fretted the grey hairs from his head. Lying abed wondering how long their daring pretence would remain unchallenged, what would happen to his family and home when it was finally, inevitably, put to the test. At least Findlay, their hawk-eyed gamekeeper, had kept them in the game, spotting the movement on the troubled slopes from his sandbagged eyrie on the roof.

Hadn't his family done enough already? It was no laughing matter, keeping a Royalist beacon burning on a range of hills positively lousy with Parliamentary sympathizers. True, most of the farmers thereabouts had owed their allegiance where they owed most of their money: to fat Morrison. But Sir Marmaduke knew the local Parliamentary commander – Sir William Waller – of old. He'd served with him and his old comrade Sir Ralph Hopton in the German wars. As soon as that wily devil had time, he'd be dropping in on his old friend's frail fortress, tumbling his walls down as if he was swatting flies from his horse's ears. Never mind old times' sake.

By God, they'd had times, though. Ramsay had been packed off to Germany by his formidable father, Sir Hector, to 'toughen the lad up a little' with a bit of rough service. He'd been toughened up all right, that brutal Christmas in Bohemia. The Catholic Imperialist forces of Count Tilly had invaded the province to punish the upstart Elector, Frederick, who had been talked into manoeuvring himself on to the vacant throne of Bohemia by the bickering Protestant princes. The princes had been happy to see Frederick cock a snook at the all-powerful Emperor in Vienna, but had been less forthcoming when it came to providing troops to help him maintain his new crown. Frederick's Bohemian rebels, allies and assorted hangers on had been cut to pieces at the Battle of the White Mountain in 1620. The 'Winter King' had been forced to flee his fine palace, the Vysehrad, high on a hill outside Prague, like a thief in the night.

Young Marmaduke Ramsay had been in Hopton's troop, one of the many English units which had been dispatched to prop up Frederick's naïve stab at glory, and had subsequently been detailed to help cover the panic-stricken retreat in the teeth of a biting snowstorm. The King's family had abandoned their new palace with such haste they had left their new-born son in his cot on the floor, and he had only been rescued at the last minute by an alert and unusually loyal nobleman.

The boy had grown up now, dark and dashing and cutting a fine name for himself over here, fighting for his troubled uncle, Charles Stuart. The boy was Prince Rupert. Ramsay took little comfort from the Prince's meteoric progress across England, bristled with irritation when his wife and daughter swooned at the very mention of his name. Why was he trumpeted by grateful Royalists from

Cornwall to the outer isles of Scotland? Why had this wretched mongrel Parliament nourished the monster with their slavish stories of his demonic, supernatural powers? Surely the truth, the dreadful reality of the German wars, was terrible enough to make an Englishman think before he took up his arms.

Was he alone in seeing the horrible bonds that connected this English conflict with that bloody carnage in Germany? Was he alone in seeing these vile creepers stretch and curl, bind and snag the King's counsels? He had been forced to walk through the carnage and the chaos because his horse had died of starvation and been eaten by his grateful comrades. He had seen the death, destruction and disease Rupert's wretched father had unleashed on Germany, and now he was to stand by and watch his boy unleash the same furies on their dear old England? Bohemia had been reduced to a smoking desert, its fine cities heaps of ashes where the unlucky living wailed over their roasted children, hid their ragged bodies away from roaming packs of wild-eyed cannibals. Saxony, the Rhineland, Pomerania, Westphalia and the rest had suffered the same and sometimes worse. Goblets of urine – the Swedish drink – were poured down prisoner's throats by beastly soldiers who made the winter wolf packs look like missionaries. At Magdeburg Tilly's troops, crazed by starvation, had clawed their way past the crazed defenders and put every man, woman and child to the sword. Danes, Swedes, Spaniards, Poles, Germans, Hungarians, Scots and French had been fed into the vast, bubbling maelstrom, and still, still the war went on. Frederick's matchstick tinderbox had whipped itself into a fire-storm which had devoured half of Europe, stopped the Renaissance in its tracks, demolished all the arts, ended the Enlightenment.

Dragged the whole bloody world back two centuries, into the dark ages of the Inquisition. And here was the fool's boy up to his father's tricks, stoking the flames in England! If Ramsay had had his way he would have gripped the King and this Pym fellow by the ears and cracked their heads together for even thinking of importing that killing craze to their own back yards.

Ramsay entertained these heresies while his wife bustled around the house fortifying kitchens, burying food and barricading unnecessary entrances, thinking up new ways of bombarding the upstart villagers while he thought up ways of getting them to see reason. He had locked himself in his study, penned heartbreaking letters to his old comrades Waller and Hopton, urging them in the name of God to call a truce. Once the western armies had been brought around a table, who knew what might happen. Ramsay even imagined a grand march on London, the respective armies – a combined band of brothers – carrying their King and their Pym to the conference table. Forcing them to sign a treaty at gunpoint, if it proved necessary. He had received affectionate replies from both generals, who regretted they could see no opportunity for such a course without exposing their persons to allegations of treachery to the cause they had, in all conscience, taken up. Sir Marmaduke had not given up his glimmering hopes for a negotiated peace. Surely there were other individuals around the country who felt as he did? His family had suffered already, but he had no thought of the revenge his wife craved. Thomas had been his boy as well as hers. He still was, the pitiful trembling scrap of him which remained, at any rate.

The war had been just weeks old when his son had ridden down the hill with eighteen of the best men on the estate, armed with an assortment of old swords and antique pistols, a fluttering, snapping pennant Anneliese had embroidered for them. Sir Marmaduke had had his doubts then, of course, but had hoped a short, decisive battle might stamp out the evil embers of civil war before they engulfed the whole country. Let the King beat his enemies, and treat them mercifully. Let the rebellion be a lesson to him, to change his ways and mend his courses. The tattered silk rag had returned that winter, wrapped around Thomas's lamentably burnt face.

The tiny troop had been hastily brigaded into the Prince of Wales's regiment, the chilly night before Edgehill. They had been stationed on the far flank of the King's army as it swept down the slope to face Essex's army on the flat farmlands beyond Radway village. Prince Rupert had led the cavalry wing in an irresistible charge which had scattered the opposing Parliamentarian horse. Thomas had galloped off the field after them, spurred his tired horse into the enemy camp, cutting down fugitives running for their poor lives. Carried away with the rest, he had come up against some Roundhead desperadoes at bay beside a convoy of stalled wagons. One of them, a crop-headed fanatic holding his dreadfully quartered face in one hand and a taper in the other, had screamed defiance through a hail of bloody spittle, thrust the lighted taper among the powder barrels.

The blast had torn Thomas's charger in half and set his hat and hair on fire. His attendants had rolled him in the trampled grass to extinguish the flames, stood back from the carnage of burnt horses and crisped men in helpless desperation. They had carried him home at last on a creaking cart, the trained bandsmen at the bottom of the hill parting respectfully, dragging their own barricades aside to let the bloody, unidentifiable boy get home to his horrified family. Sir Marmaduke had hurried them inside the house with their stinking stretcher, the cold nights having wrapped bandages of frost around his mutilated features. Lady Ramsay, demanding to know who had tried to stifle her son, went to snatch the tattered flag from his face. The broken boy had shrieked, clawed at her hands as if she was some grave-robbing looter, roaming the bloody field for trinkets. He had been carried to his room, the surgeons called from Bristol and Wells, to please examine the horrific injuries the army sawbones had refused even to look at.

'I don't care whose son he is. I can't give him a new face—' one of the surviving troopers told Ramsay what the army doctor had told him. The apologetic surgeons had at least agreed to dress the wounds, suggested ointments and poultices to reduce the vast, pustulating blisters which had erupted along the right side of his face. Between themselves, they agreed the boy would probably die before the Christmas week was out. For once, Ramsay had asserted his authority in his own house, closed the door on his crying womenfolk, insisting he would care for his son himself. He had nursed the boy from the pitiless brink, found some desperate reserve of courage from somewhere to sit alongside the delirious boy as he writhed in his fevers, held his arms by his sides as he tried to claw at his fearful injuries. By February, by some miracle, the danger had passed, but Thomas would need more than a miracle if he was ever to have a face again. They fed him on soups, poured the tepid liquors carefully between his blistered lips. The cook came up with possets, rich broths Ramsay spooned into his son as if stoking his inner fire. Thomas could walk, see and hear, but smoke and sparks had got in his throat and he would not talk. He stayed in his room, gazing out of the immense window at the rolling hills he had used to hunt, the trees he had climbed with his sister. Ramsay would sit with him every evening, describe the day's events in painstaking detail. It seemed to comfort him, a little.

Ramsay paused, thought of old Morrison's boy out there now in his brand new buff coat. He detested the merchant more than any other man in the world, yet he could not bring himself to wish his own boy's misery on Jamie, nor yet his own misery on Morrison. Lady Ramsay had noticed his expression, suddenly ghostlike features.

'For God's sake, Ramsay, it's only a letter,' she reported, as one of the guards by the gate trotted up the path and doubled up the steps to their fortified door. 'I can't understand why you insist on being such a defeatist.' He glanced sorrowfully at her, watched her features rearrange themselves as she read his mind. 'He was my boy as well as yours, I brought them into the world, God knows,' she whispered over Bates' balding head.

'And he is still, my dear, and he is still,' Ramsay said resignedly. His wife concealed her feelings under a barrage of rude questions, snatched the paper from the guard's outstretched hand.

'What? Does he expect a reply? Let the damned traitor wait, if he pleases.' She examined the letter, passed it to her husband.

'It's for you. He knows full well I wouldn't have any truck with that despicable rogue.'

Ramsay picked the seal and slid his fingers along the luxurious vellum – no expense spared – opening the letter. He straightened, walked along the bare corridor scanning Morrison's wild scrawl. Lady Ramsay sent the guards back to their posts, leaned her heavy halberd by the door and hurried after him.

'Well? Does he surrender? Throw himself on your mercy?' she called, peering over his shoulder. 'He'll get none, not even if he gets on that floor and polishes it with his red nose! That's the strength of it!' Ramsay finished reading, looked perplexed. 'Well?'

'There has been a fight, at Chewton.'

'Chewton. What? Not ten miles away! He's lost his nerve at last, then, the King's army so close, the guns we heard yesterday,' she cried.

Ramsay frowned. Could a man be as transparent as that? Morrison was far too crafty for such an obvious stratagem. Far too subtle for his own, or anybody else's, good.

'They are taking the wounded to the village. He suggests we put aside our complaints for now, show mercy to the poor soldiers . . .'

'Tend their wounded? Cut their treacherous throats I—'

'Of both sides,' Ramsay went on, flashing his wife a look. 'He says his daughter is already tearing her old skirts for bandages, and that they fear their own rude home will not be . . . what does that say . . . oh yes, commodious enough, to shelter all. Could we help our countrymen?'

'Tearing her skirts off, more like, the strumpet.'

Ramsay raised his pale eyebrows. 'She has expressed a wish to renew her acquaintance with her dear friends Anneliese and Thomas, and trusts they are well.'

'Trusts they are well? They must know how badly he was hurt,' Lady Ramsay said flatly. 'Don't they realize he has suffered, doing his duty to the King?' They looked up as Anneliese hurried down toward them, her robe wrapped about her, long black hair dripping.

'I was taking my bath . . . what has happened? Father?' she asked, blue eyes wide. Ramsay threw his arm about his daughter, as if he could protect her from harm and hardship, risked a small smile.

'Morrison says there has been a fight at Chewton. He gives us intelligence we would have otherwise have had to wait days to receive. The King's army is a few miles down the road.'

Anneliese clutched her face in astonished delight, glanced at her scowling mother. 'They have come for us? At last?'

'They're not here yet, dear,' Margaret responded, shooing the beaming girl away down the hall. 'Dress yourself, you shameless hussy. We're not Turks!'

Ramsay held the letter up, waved it after them.

'But what should I say? Will we help?'

'Help? Help who?' Anneliese wanted to know, slipping under her mother's arm and dashing back, wonderfully excited.

'We'll help, where we may, but if Morrison thinks he'll buy our silence when Ralph Hopton comes, he's got other things coming!'

Ramsay watched his wife bustle his daughter away up the broad staircase, turned into his study and snatched up his papers and quills. At last. A chance to do something. A chance to save something!

PART TWO

SKIRMISH

Sir Jacob Astley, lately slain at Gloucester,
desires to know was he slain with a musket
or cannon bullet

MERCURIUS AULICUS

BY
CHEWTON MENDIP

JUNE 13, 1643

The latrines had been dug on the far side of the trampled fields where Waller's rearguard had camped the night before. As usual the fastidious and methodical enemy forces had left the King's army nothing of any use, although the voracious camp followers had turned every barrel and biscuit box, run sticks through the heaps of fuming refuse in the hope of discovering something of value. The smoking rubbish of bloody bandages, broken-down boots and assorted papers and leaflets added to the fruity stink wafting over from the stand of willows, the pits which Waller had ordered dug the far side of a merry stream. Telling didn't need directions, although several of the camp whores curled their fingers at him, suggesting diversions into their stained canvas tents.

Matilda Dawkins, kneading the small of her aching back with her shapely hands, recognized the red-faced youngster from the colonel's tent, straightened up and pinched her cheeks hard as she saw him limping through the bustling camp. She had followed the army six months now, ever since the riotous Cornishmen had marched past her home town of Exeter. Life on the road with the noisy, rollicking westerners and their fine young officers had proved too much of a temptation for young Matilda, whose sober-minded father had obtained work for her in the kitchens of the Blue Boar. Why should she work her fine fingers raw scrubbing pewter plates and serving ale when she could follow the guns and see something of the world? They were marching all the way to Bristol, so they said.

By the time Hopton's army had rendezvoused with Maurice and Hertford at Chard, the cheerful, fresh-faced girl had become something of a favourite, and had already sewn dozens of gold coins into the hems of her skirts, more in a secret panel in her musical box, the only item she had brought from her old home by the river. Not that life on the road was a bowl of cherries, mind you. The men smelt like bears, unless it was raining in which case they smelt like so many damp dogs. The fine and dandy young officers weren't much better, and were usually drunk into the bargain. Matilda preferred them like that, they paid more and came quicker. The bumbling bloods thought they knew as much about women as they did their horses, but nine times out of ten Matilda would simply press their variously erect members between her young thighs, have it out of them before they had actually achieved penetration. Even if they suspected they had been tricked, they were normally too embarrassed to argue with her, especially if their jeering friends were waiting their turn. Lying beneath dirty men in a lake of mud didn't mean she had to behave like an old sow either. She kept bowls of clean water by her at all times, and had adopted, or had been adopted by – she wasn't quite sure which – an older woman well past her prime who had taught her various tricks of the trade, and took just a few pence a week for herself.

'A good douse of cold water, straight after mind, and don't touch no seamen or sailors, them's allus got summat nasty comin' out th'end. If it's seepin', leave 'em weeping, is what I allus sez,' Peggy Rake had advised. It was Peggy who had shown her how to grip the man between your legs, making him think he was hard inside. She looked after her when she was ill, darned the rents in her skirts, did her bits of shopping and spread the word around the camp about her charming young protégé.

'She'll fuck your hind legs off for a shillin',' was old Peg's proud boast. The direct approach was all very well, but some of these young bucks weren't quite the rams they made out. This one, for instance, with his tawny moustache and staring eyes. He had limped past her, avoiding her jade eyes, glaring at the guy ropes as if he was afraid he'd be tripped on his face in front of her. Wincing as he eased his leg over the stile on his way to the latrines. Matilda hurried after him, bunching her skirts up around her suntanned legs. He was squatting over the crossbeam, biting his lip, as she touched his arm and made him jump.

'You all right sir? Need a hand?' Matilda suppressed a giggle as the boy flushed deep red, stammered something about a call of nature. Calls of nature!

'Well, when you've finished there, drop into my tent and we'll have a cuddle. You'd like that, wouldn't you?' The boy looked like a flapping mackerel in the bottom of a boat, his eyes bulging as he stared at her powdered skin, rouged lips, wild rummaged mane of auburn hair. 'It's that one there, look, with the petticoats hanging up to dry.' Telling glanced over her shoulder, recognized her underwear, swallowed with difficulty. 'It's all right,' she encouraged, giving his thigh a powerful squeeze which damn near toppled him from his uncomfortable perch, straddled over the gate. Matilda flashed him a smile and walked as gracefully as she was able back to her tent. Telling looked up as one of the Cornish infantrymen strode up from the other direction, splashing in the mud (he hoped it was mud) and adjusting his voluminous breeches.

'You gon' be all day thar or what, me beaut?' he demanded, teeth the colour of old tobacco and reeking breath. Surely the girl didn't do it with creatures such as these? He thought for a moment of the wagon girl and her clown lover, rolling and tumbling in the wool sacks. 'Sir?' the surly devil added as an afterthought. Hugo picked his leg over the crossbeam, eased himself down into the muck as the musketeer lost what little patience he had, barged him aside. He found the pits easily enough, held his white hand to his nose and mouth as he picked his way carefully along the muddy rim of the trench. A simple rope had been hung between a series of stakes, to which various papers and leaflets had been thoughtfully nailed. He chose a relatively fresh spot, removed his belt, carefully picked up the tails of his shirt and eased his dirty breeches down. Jacobs had cleaned the wound in his lower back twice, but the deep cut was still seeping watery blood and pus into the rough dressing.

The dark-complexioned sawbones up at the dressing station had taken one look at it, asked Telling if he should cancel all his amputations, barked at him in his heavily accented English before breaking off into a flood of Italian. His mate, a grinning youth in a bloody overall, nodded him away. 'The gist of it is away and bandage it yourself. He's got too many stomach wounds and split skulls to worry about you.' Hugo, who had studied a little Latin, didn't imagine it had been an exact translation of the foreigner's furious speech, but he had got the message.

112

He had watched the Italian wipe his hands on a horse blanket, take a gulp from a flask as his assistant washed down the bloody butchering table with a bucket of water. Jacobs had done his best, but the blade which had pierced his lower right side just above his buttocks had been dirty and the wound wouldn't heal.

He squirmed round to take a look at the weeping cut, winced as he made himself as comfortable as possible on the rocking rope. He shut his eyes and finished, ripped a piece of paper from the sheaf which had been tacked to the rope post. One of those wretched broadsheets which seemed to acquire a life of their own, passed from hand to hand around the camps like some terrible disease. King's Wool Gatherer Foiled. What nonsense. He paused, read the first paragraph through a growing red mist which clouded his double vision.

'The bastard, impious lying creature!' Telling straightened with difficulty, tugged up his breeches as he read on. Brave troop of hand-picked Cavaliers, sent out to collect new undergarments for the Cornish foot, much given to shitting their breeches! A certain Captain Cautious Woolpicker, late of German wars where he was in charge of socks and handkerchiefs with Prince Bernard of Saxe-Weimar, charged with rectifying delinquents' deficiency. Brave captain spies unarmed caravan belonging to God-fearing merchant. Twenty (twenty?) fearless Cavaliers gallop in to attack to be worsted by farm hand, seventy-year-old driver and milkmaid. Under said fusillade Cavaliers obliged to bleat (bleat!) a retreat, last seen accosting sheep. God save the King's men's drawers!

Telling tore the hateful paper into confetti, felt his puckered wound tear as he shoved his shirt back into his baggy breeches. He winced, stepped back, lost his footing on the muddy bank. He grabbed for the filthy rope, thought better of it, and toppled, windmilling arms, into the pit.

Matilda had gotten fed up waiting for the young pup and wondered if he was avoiding her. She suspected he had taken the long way around the fields to get back to his tent, or had tried to sneak past while she adjusted her make-up in the small glass she'd been given by a grateful artillery officer after they had taken Taunton. She pulled the tent flap aside and peered out at the crowd of soldiers, beggars, hauliers, drivers, stockmen and hawkers, all shouting and bawling at the tops of their voices. Looking at the dirty throng, she imagined for a second what her mother and father, strict Puritans, would make of their language and gaudy colours. She spotted the Italian doctor she had heard about, picking his way between steaming heaps of horse dung in her direction. He was a small, dark-complexioned man with an oily forked beard and blazing eyes. His teeth, remarkably, were white, his hands neat and precise when they weren't stained to the wrists with blood. The Italian spotted her craning out of her tent, gave her an extravagant bow to the delight of the whores lounging beside their own bivouacs.

'Come on in, me deary.'

'Bow over my bum, if you've a mind.'

'Come on, sir, sixpence is all.'

'Thruppence!'

'Tuppence!'

''Ave it on the 'ouse, sir,' they shrieked delightedly as the fantastic foreigner in his well-made shoes picked his way along their canvas alley and arrived in front of

Matilda's tent. He took off his hat with a flourish of feathers, picked the corners of his expensive cloak from the mud and nodded to the younger girl.

'Madonna, they deed not lie,' he said in his exotic, outlandish accent. 'You are indeed, a princess of the air,' he went on expansively, in Italian, at length. There was a dull splash and a shout from beyond the willows. The Italian turned his head, wrinkled his nose. 'I 'ave come, to take you away from this feelth,' he suggested, ignoring the shouts and laughter from the far side of the stream. He stepped closer. Matilda could smell his luxurious oils and fragrances, see the tiny herringbone patterns in his expensive black suit. 'I am Ambrosio di Meola St Corelli, madam, I am at your service.' He bowed again.

'She'll be at his service, more like,' Matilda's red-faced neighbour called. Behind the flamboyant Italian the teeming crowd had coagulated around the stile, shouting and laughing. Naturally curious, Matilda peered over at the commotion. She saw a couple of cavalry troopers carrying some drunk between them through the jostling, laughing pack, realized with a start the drunk was none other than her young buck of a captain. She smiled shortly at the Italian, gathered up her skirts and dashed past.

'Another time, my darling,' she promised over her shoulder. The astonished surgeon watched the girl elbow her way through the crowd, which had already divided to let the grisly trio through. Matilda stood back holding a corner of her skirt over her nose.

'You'll have to wash him off,' she scolded the boy's reluctant supporters.

'Us? We got him out!' Cady snapped back.

'He'd fallen in the shit!' Jacobs added, rather unnecessarily.

Matilda peered over the bobbing red faces of the crowd, pointed them back to the stream.

'Set him down there, he can't go about like that!' she cried, surprised at how upset she felt, the sudden stab of anxiety on the boy's behalf. Feeling sorry for some young captain who couldn't hold his drink, Peg would have something to say about that. Jacobs and Cady about turned with the red-faced youngster, dragged him back through the dissolving crowd and eased him down beside one of the leaning willows. They stood back, rubbing their hands on the lush grass alongside the chattering stream, then on their breeches. Matilda bent down, peered at the groaning youth, his grey eyes flickering under his long lashes.

'What's up with 'un? Has he bashed his 'ead?'

Jacobs shrugged. 'That Italian friend of yours, 'e's the surgeon,' he said shortly. 'Oh no. He's gone,' he added, looking back over toward the mass of stained canvas, the ropes of damp washing.

'I'll see to him,' Matilda said shortly, holding her hand to the youth's damp forehead.

'If I were you, Tilly, I'd clean the bugger up first. You'll be smellin' worse than us, otherwise,' Cady advised, settling his red Montero hat back on his head. The two of them shambled off toward the horse lines, leaving the concerned girl bending over the reeking youth.

Telling, in his feverish delirium, was taking wonderful, deep lungfuls of air, inhaling the fragrant blossom drifting and blowing in vast pink clouds around the rectory orchard. Lying beneath the old apple tree gazing at the larks through a gentle snowstorm of blossom, a blizzard of softly blowing flakes. And here was his mother. No, not his mother, younger. Much younger. The beautiful goose-girl who had climbed down from the wagon, blown tufts of

116

stray wool from her long fingers as if she was blowing the seeds from a dandelion. He reached out, touched her apricot cheek.

'Careful now, Captain, don't go gettin' it all over me,' she scolded, gently, easing him forward so she could remove his coat, open his shirt. 'Yeuch! I'll fetch Peggy for these clothes. Come on now, there's nobody going to take any notice here.'

He held his arms up, drowsy, felt his shirt tugged from his back.

'Agh ... you've gone and cut yourself and all. Let's have a look.'

Telling rolled to one side, luxuriating in the fragrant quilt of pink apple blossom, laying his sleepy head on a curving root. Matilda stripped the stinking clothes from the unconscious youth, whistled Peg along to take them. The old woman peered over her protégé's shoulder, nodded approvingly.

'That's it, my chick, empty his pockets. Pissed as an old pot walloper, at this time o' day,' she snorted.

Matilda waved her away. 'He's not pissed, he's sick. Look at this cut on his back, it's all manky. He wants a clean poultice on it.'

Peg shoved the boy's clothes into her basket with the aid of a discarded stick, shook her old head.

'Your doctor friend, that Ambrosio bloke, went next door. You can't afford to lose custom like that,' Peg went on, straightening her baggy bonnet.

'I've custom enough, as well you know.'

'Well, 'e'll catch his death you leave him buck naked there.'

'I'm not going to leave him buck naked. Give us a hand to get him down into the stream.'

The grumbling old woman picked up her skirts, picked her way down the crumbling red bank and helped lift the semi-naked youngster down into the pool. Matilda bent over the stinking youth, hands beneath his armpits as she manoeuvred him down the slope, fed him into the stream. He thrashed like a fish as he felt the cold water, stared about him as if he had been captured by cannibals on some remote island. Peg dragged her bulk back up the bank, frowned at Matilda as she untied her bodice.

'Off bathin', you'll catch a chill and be on your back for weeks,' Peg scolded. Matilda hung her bodice on a bush, tugged down her skirts, and stepped down the bank in her plain ivory-coloured shift.

'Well, on me back's the best place for me,' she said over her shoulder. Peg watched the girl wade toward the gasping youth, sitting on his behind among the moss-covered rocks in obvious agitation. He couldn't stand up, with that woman staring down at him. He shivered in his soaking cotton drawers, splashed water over his throbbing back for something to do. Peg stomped off muttering, disappeared into the overhanging willows. Telling watched the girl's shift change colour as she knelt down in the green pool. He noticed her nipples were poking through the thin material, dark acorns with their stippled surround. The girl cupped her hands, splashed water over his head, making him yelp with the sudden chilling shock. His dark hair plastered to his head. Matilda crouched behind him, washed the filth from his shoulders, down his goose-pimpled arms. She laid her hand on his wet hair, pushed his head forward, and poured water over the seeping wound staining the stream with his thin blood.

'What's your name, then?' she asked at last.

'Hugo,' he husked.

'This needs dressing. It's full of dirt. It'll go bad,' she said, gently squeezing the reddened flaps of skin, releasing a dribble of smelly discharge.

'They haven't time for flesh wounds,' he growled.

'I heard they took most of the wounded up to the big house up the road. You should have gone with them.'

'I didn't like to make a fool of myself. 'Twas only a cut.'

She squeezed harder, felt his rigid white body tense with pain. 'We'll see if we can't mend you,' she whispered, her lips to his burning ear. She turned him slowly, gazed into his startled grey eyes, pulled the strings of her shift and eased the soaking cotton over her head. Telling licked his lips, gazed at her firm breasts, the dark nipples he hadn't been able to blink from his mind. Her underarm hair was thick and wild as his own, he noticed with childlike fascination. Matilda ducked her head, turning her wild auburn mane into so many ropes the colour of new tar, wet and slick now, hanging in great thick coils over her slim shoulders as she reclined into the deeper water, nodding him forward. He crawled into the pool after the bewitching harlot, this English lamia, and closed his trembling hands around her cold face. He leaned forward to kiss her red lips, blossom forgotten in his panting urgency. The stream, of a sudden, ran warm and silky over his bursting body. He could have sworn he could hear trumpets.

BY
CHIPPING MARLEWARD

JUNE 14, 1643

Mary Keziah, the eldest and sharpest daughter of former wagoner Gregory Pitt, wasn't about to see those fine skirts torn in strips to bind some fool's arm. She had brought every shift she possessed, and others besides, over to the Morrisons' town house headquarters. Bundled them into a basket which she had stowed beneath the dining table while Bella skipped upstairs to find more of her own clothing. By the time Bella had returned with another armful of shifts and sheets, Mary had swapped the bundles, reasoning that if the soldiers needed bandages, they wouldn't mind them stripped from her own ragged old skirts. No point in tearing up good linen.

Her flighty mistress stood on tiptoe at the window, watched her father's men loading the wagon with various chests and cases. They had been busy all day, emptying the outhouses and loading the plate.

'Confidential papers, business matters, my love. A few precautions, that's all. Don't you worry, we'll be safe enough here,' Sir Gilbert had reassured her. She didn't want to be in Chipping Marleward, safe or otherwise! The draughty old house her father seemed so anxious about was nothing but a prison hulk run aground on the hills, like Noah's Ark without the animals. Sir Gilbert seemed convinced their home was about to be invaded by marauding hordes, hell-bent on poking their noses into his private affairs. 'Christian charity towards a few wounded is one thing, but if they start nosing about the house, well, my dear . . .'

He had already sent a letter to the Ramsays along at the hall, informing them a convoy of wounded from the fight at Chewton would be on their way shortly. They had felt the guns beneath their slippered feet and seen the dishes tremble on the dresser, at once terrified and hopelessly excited that the war was coming their way at last. The girls had stood at the window the previous afternoon and watched files of sooty musketeers and weary pikemen with sloped arms trudge past their house. On their way to defend the Avon, so Sir Gilbert had said. They had watched the merchant, strapped into his best buff coat and sash, deliberate with a tall, bearded officer on a horse, point up and down the road, thrusting papers up at him which the officer signed hastily, thrust back at him. Her father had closed the door, leaned heavily against it, while Bella stood white faced in the hall, Mary Keziah peeking behind her.

'What is it? Are they going already?'

Sir Gilbert had recovered his composure, straightened his coat and enormous tawny sash. 'They've beaten the Royalists at Chewton,' he reported, fixing an unconvincing smile on his red face as he strode briskly toward the stairs.

'Then why are they running away?'

Sir Gilbert halted, spied Mary Keziah at the sitting-room door, whistling to herself. 'They are not running away, my dear. You know Waller, he's as full of tricks as a knife-grinder's monkey.' He glared significantly at Mary. 'He is merely straightening his front.'

'He means to abandon us to the King, then?'

Sir Gilbert had pulled his coat open, ran his hands through the closely cropped curls behind his red ears. 'No, no, my dear. He's given Hopton another bloody nose. There may be some wounded arriving, I've offered to do what we can here, for both sides. I've a letter from Waller, see.' He waved the scrap of paper, tucked it away safe inside his coat. Mary Keziah had raised her eyebrows, Bella had been pondering her father's unusual attack of charity ever since.

'Do you think the Ramsays will help tend the wounded, then?' Mary Keziah asked, busy tearing lengths of her own skirts into strips. Bella, typically bored by the mundane reality of this menial task, fiddled and folded an old shift, gazing into space.

'Father's offered a truce, while they're brought in. It would be nice to see Annie again. I've quite forgotten what she looks like.'

'Well, that's nothing. Zach and Mordecai and Eli have only been gone since yesterday, and I've quite forgotten what they look like already,' Mary said with a quick smile and a twinge of concern. The three eldest boys had joined Morrison's regiment of militia the previous morning, loudly proclaiming they would ruin the Cornish upstarts, invading their county like the papist pirates they were! The cheerful boys had found themselves ordered off with Waller's army that afternoon. Packing up what little bits of kit they could find, pulling on the short green coats they had been issued from Sir Gilbert's plentiful stocks. The farm boys had shaken their heads in wonder at the gorgeous hoard of clothing and equipment, been told to take their pick of coats, breeches, stockings, shirts and boots. Bella had waved Jamie off with them. Looking glum on his fine horse in his gleaming new equipment. Sir

Gilbert had assured his doubtful son he would be along after the regiment as soon as he had settled his affairs at home.

'I'll stay here with the rest of the battalion,' he had called. Jamie had frowned behind the unfamiliar iron bars of his helmet. Caged like a reluctant lion.

'The rest of the battalion? They're all here with me,' he had called down to his twitching father.

'The men'll come flocking in, once they realize the enemy are so close,' Sir Gilbert had told him. 'Why, we'll double our numbers before the week is out,' he added, hopefully.

Mary Keziah looked up as Bella dropped the bandage she had been rolling, dashed to the window at the sudden clatter of hoofs. She peered into the busy yard, deflated. 'Oh. It's only William,' she reported, turning back to her chore.

'What does he want? He must be brave, coming so close to the King's men with all that tittle-tattle he writes about them,' Mary observed. 'That pamphlet about you and poor father on the wagon' – she smiled, noticed Bella's flush – 'had me in stitches. Meaning no disrespect to Dad, of course.' They looked up as William Sparrow knocked softly on the door and walked in slipping his familiar sack from his shoulder.

'Hello, Will.' Mary Keziah raised her eyebrows and gave the tall man a crafty wink. Bella nodded at the table, hidden by an avalanche of snowy skirts.

'We've been tearing up bandages for the wounded,' she said.

Will nodded. 'I thought I'd have a scout down, see for myself,' he said casually, entering the room. 'Is Sir Gilbert still at home?'

'He's sorting his papers.'

I bet he is, Will thought, smiled winningly. He covered his mouth, gave a little cough. There was a boisterous snap as Mary Keziah tore another skirt down the middle.

'Mary, could you allow us a second?' Will asked with a short smile.

'A second what?' Mary asked cheekily, looked up at her mistress, who opened her mouth, then nodded absentmindedly. She sighed, bowed out of the door and closed it behind her, bent her dark head to listen.

'I've finished that draft for your father,' he began brightly. Bella stood by the window, gazing at the sweaty activity in the yard. Will's enormous black and white horse, which always attracted clouds of flies, swished his tail in the hazy afternoon heat. It turned its head, gazed back at her with its horrid white wall-eye. She shuddered.

'You didn't need to send Mary away, she'll not tell tales about you,' she said softly.

Will grasped at his hat, hot and uncomfortable in his best red suit with the slashed sleeves which revealed the creamy shirt beneath. He had folded the enormous collar as neatly as possible around the matching jacket.

'No, I'm not worried about that,' he said with a dismissive wave of his large hand. 'I've had an offer, from the Parliament. To go to London and write pamphlets in the capital.'

Bella looked startled. 'When are you leaving?'

He looked hurt, pulled at his red hat. 'I'm not. I said I'd have to think about it, and I have.'

'You're not staying in Bristol?'

'Well ... I've lots to keep me here. I can write as well here as up there. Your father has already said he'd commission me into his regiment,' Will said, playing his best card early. To his considerable irritation Bella dropped the curtain beading she'd been fiddling with, turned around and laughed.

'Father would give poor Gregory a commission in his regiment,' she scoffed. 'He's already made Jamie a captain, our Jamie! So I wouldn't set too much store by that.'

Will compressed his generous lips. 'It's time I did my little bit,' he said lamely, beginning to feel a little uneasy about refusing the commissioners' offer. Wouldn't be the first time she'd dashed his hopes.

'Well, I wouldn't let the loyalists catch you, if I was you, not after all those stories about how silly Prince Maurice is.'

Will strode across the room, made Bella jump a little as she caught the flashing look in the big man's eyes. 'They're Royalists! How many more times? Rrrrrroyalists!' he barked.

Bella compressed her lips, her honey-coloured skin paling in anger.

William closed his eyes and caught his breath. 'Look, Bella. I mean, Miss Morrison. I, that is, if, I mean if things go on as they are, I was wondering, possibly, that is to say to be in a position . . .' William, who could compose twenty stanza lyric poems about the bewitching creature in the safety of his own bed, found himself tongue-tied and tangled as he fidgeted in front of her.

'I mean, one day I may be able to say, professionally, no not . . .'

Sir Gilbert hurled the door open, crashed into the room like a cannon shot. 'What's Mary think she's up to, listening at keyholes? Ah, there you are, William.' He flung a wad of dockets and ledgers on top of the undergarments on the table, turned to his reddening daughter.

'Now then, Bella. I was thinking about what you said the other day, and I think it would be a grand idea for you to help out with the wounded up at the hall. See your old friend Anneliese and that handsome brother of hers.'

William glared at the merchant's fleshy face, wondering whether he had heard properly. 'Send her up to Kilmersden Hall?'

'They've more room for the wounded than we have. I'm told we can expect a dozen cartloads at least,' he said with a small shudder. A dozen cartloads of wounded, plus all the dead, and Popham, the colonel he'd spoken with the day before, said it had only been a skirmish. God help them if there was to be a battle. Sir Gilbert's flushed face brightened as he picked a letter from the bundle on the table, shook it at them.

'I have heard from Sir Marmaduke, a very pleasing letter, very pleasing indeed.'

'Pleasing? I imagine he's pleased enough, the King's army not ten mile off,' William snapped, losing his temper a little.

'I'll run and get ready, Father,' Bella interjected, giving William a short smile and hurrying from the room with the bandages they had already prepared.

'I'll see you before you go my dear, send Gregory and a few of the lads up there with you,' he called, shutting the door behind her.

'I still can't see—'

'William.' Sir Gilbert cut him short. 'There are many things you do not see. I am a man of the world, a self-made man, true, but a man of the world none the less. Now if at present I consider it politic to rebuild a few bridges with that old fox and his hateful wife, I'll consider myself free to do so, is that clear?' William opened his mouth, nodded glumly. 'Good. Now then, let's see your pamphlet.' He opened his sack, passed over another inky draft. Sir Gilbert held it up, scanned the leaflet.

'I thought I'd add something about Jamie joining the muster at Shepton Mallet,' he suggested, watching Sir Gilbert's crafty little eyes as they scanned the document.

'This is all very good, William, very good indeed. It's just . . .' He pulled at his thin lips.

'What?'

'It's just I think we ought to step back a little, consider the overall direction.'

William closed his eyes a moment. Was he going to sell him down river too? Pull the rug beneath his feet just as he was standing up for himself, putting old Greesham in his place? He'd have to gallop back to the shop and apologize, volunteer to polish the presses again.

'Oh, it's very good, mind you, very good indeed. It's just I feel we've taken this business about the town's regiment about as far as we can go.'

Town's regiment? William thought ruefully. It was Morrison's damned regiment, not Chipping Marleward's.

'I'm wondering whether it is fair on my family to maintain this rather high public profile at this particular moment in time.'

So that was it. The Royalists were on the march and Morrison was getting twitchy.

'We ought possibly to think about toning down some of the passages. This bit here about me, tower of strength, rock of the cause . . . excellent, excellent. Take it out.' William frowned. 'I don't think we need remind readers it was my wool, do you? And Jamie being cheered down the street by the population, perhaps, the regiment was cheered.'

'I can't see why we need to tone . . .'

'Well, let me put it this way,' Sir Gilbert sighed. 'How would you like your name and address at the bottom of this leaflet, eh? Precisely. It's a question of retrenching ourselves, you understand. Now, what of Bristol? Will it hold?'

William scratched his nose, pondered for a moment. He was worried about that great store of wool, shorn from just about every sheep in Somerset, baled up in his warehouse under the pitiless gaze of Master Algernon Starling. 'It might. Four thousand men, one hundred cannon.'

Sir Gilbert unpicked Ramsay's letter, reminded himself of the crucial last paragraph. 'You know, it might not come to that. Waller and Hopton are old friends, they could call a truce.'

Will snorted. 'A truce? Do you think those poor buggers at Chewton were negotiating a truce? Seventy dead, at least, so I'm told.'

'Yes, yes, they were fighting all right. But Ramsay here . . . well, never mind.'

Ramsay what? He would hold his hall until hell froze over or the King's men came to his rescue, that was clear enough to anyone. And here was Morrison about to send his only daughter up there? William narrowed his eyes, watched the merchant reading, his thin lips moving slowly over the page.

'There is just one other thing, sir,' William began shrewdly. Sir Gilbert looked up, half surprised to still see him there. 'I have some information which might be invaluable to your present situation,' he said carefully. The merchant frowned, nodded him to go on.

'Well, before I bore you with the details, perhaps we

can return to the matter we discussed the other week? My commission in your regiment.'

Sir Gilbert blustered, sorting his papers. 'Well, I can't go making every Tom, Dick and Harry an officer now, William, can I?'

'That would depend, sir, on their worth to your good self,' he answered. 'I believe we mentioned the rank of captain?'

Sir Gilbert replaced the ledgers on the table. 'If we mentioned a rank at all, it was ensign,' he said flatly.

'The information I have, with all respect, would be worth a little more, sir,' William said with a short smile.

'Well? Spit it out! What have you heard?'

'I feel I have so much to offer the regiment. Captain Jamie will need sound colleagues, sir,' William went on, holding his ground as Sir Gilbert growled and rolled his eyes alarmingly as if the pamphleteer was some dumb farmer up in the hills to be hornswoggled out of his produce for a few pennies.

'Let me understand you, sir. You require me to sign your commission, and you will give me your information.' William nodded. 'That Nathaniel Fiennes won't hold Bristol more than a week. There, that's your information, is it not?' William shook his head. 'Well, what, then? How do I know it is worth the price you ask?'

'The price I ask is your signature on a piece of paper. If you do not consider my information worthy of the rank, you may have it back at once and cast it into your fire.'

The fire hadn't been lit, but Sir Gilbert got the point.

'Very well.' He fetched a pot and quills from the heavy, otherwise empty sideboard, took a sheaf of paper from the table and scratched a few sentences on it. William took the commission, made sure the wily merchant had made it out correctly.

'A date, sir, if you would be so kind.'

Sir Gilbert muttered, added the date. 'Well? What's your information?'

'My information, Colonel, is this. I was at Bristol keep two days ago, where I met Masters Webster and Lyle, Commissioners for Parliament.' Sir Gilbert frowned, went to take the note back. William held it out of his way. 'They are very keen on visiting you and your fine regiment, and seeing what has become of the money you have been advanced for the recruitment and equipment of such a force.'

Sir Gilbert paled. 'Lyle and Webster? I've never heard of them,' he snorted.

'Well, sir, they have without doubt heard of you. They said they would be here in a matter of days.'

BY
KILMERSDEN HALL

JUNE 13, 1643

Sir Marmaduke Ramsay had been out of the saddle for months, and his buttocks were aching long before he and his small escort reached the bottom of the hill. He glanced at his son, riding equally stiffly alongside, his reins gripped in his white hands, his plumed hat pulled down low over the velvet mask. Findlay had ridden ahead, scouting the overgrown lane for enemy outposts. They had heard nothing since young Morrison's visit two days before, and the guns which had boomed all through that long afternoon had fallen silent. Where was Hopton? Where was Waller?

'And what's that snake Morrison up to, sending his boy up here to do his dirty work?' Lady Ramsay had demanded at their impromptu council of war that morning. 'For all we know Waller's beaten and the damned rogue has run off with him.' Ramsay had smiled painfully, wondering also. Had he been tricked by the cunning weasel once more? Morrison's letter had been a tissue of hopelessly divided excuse, opinion and exhortation. The merchant had offered to use all his reputedly enormous influence with Waller, if Ramsay would do the same with Hopton. They were old comrades, after all. The two of them may have had their slight differences of opinion in the past, but couldn't these difficulties be put aside,

131

might they not broker a truce between the warring parties?

Ramsay had glanced at his formidable wife, wondered how Morrison could have heard about young Thomas, or could have guessed his present state of mind. How had the damned merchant known his true heart, known he detested this war as much as any man alive? A spy then, but who? Ramsay pulled at his beard, mentally evaluated each and every member of his household. His family. Thomas, hiding away up in his room most of the time, refusing to endure anybody but his father; Anneliese, tugging her dresses out of their packing cases for the victory parade through Bristol. Her only thought was to reignite some kind of a social life. His daughter had been such good friends with Bella, had they kept in touch in spite of their fathers' wishes? Kept each other abreast of developments? Surely not.

'Ramsay? Whatever is the matter?' Margaret demanded, leaning over their simple map table. The house, its shadow defences and spider-web fortifications drawn in red. A black circle around the grounds, and beyond? Empty spaces. The unknown.

'I'm sorry my dove, I was . . .'

'Woolgathering, as usual. Findlay says he hasn't seen as much as a campfire for two days. Are we to sit here until the world remembers us, or are we to venture forth, take the miserable town back for the King?' The tall, rangy gamekeeper was leaning on his long rifle beside the table, nodding his grave head.

'True sir. They're either lyin' lower than a slow worm's belly or they'm off.' Off?

'Then we ought to ride out, all of us, and see for

ourselves,' Margaret decided, lifting her halberd from the chair where she had lain it. Ramsay bristled.

'All of us? You can't be serious, my dear. Findlay and I will make a reconnaisance toward the town, see what has happened.'

His wife frowned, nodded. 'Well, it's no time for half measures. Get all the horses we have left, they'll never guess we have emptied the whole house.'

Findlay had agreed with his wife's shrewd judgement of the tactical situation, and he had marched out to organize the horses, stabled in a fortified outhouse for most of the past year. Ramsay had made his way up to the first floor, knocked softly on Thomas's door. His son, as usual, was sitting up straight by the window, gazing out over his view of the park, the surrounding woodland. He had pulled his chair about, clutching the rigid carvings, silent as a statue in his baggy white shirt. Ramsay had warned him a dozen times about making himself such an easy target at the window. Why, any fool with a musket could risk a shot. His hair had grown on the left-hand side of his head, made up for the bald ruin on the right. The skin was puckered and dark about the still livid scars. The velvet hood he'd asked his daughter to sew lay on the bed, untouched. Ramsay paused, stepped over to the bed and picked the soft blue hood from the unmade quilt.

'Ah, there you are, boy,' he said, as if he expected him to be elsewhere. 'Looks as if our friends yonder have retreated, Hopton might be a mile down the road.' The youth glared at the window, Sir Marmaduke stepped around to his left side and made himself comfortable in the window seat so he was at eye level with his son. A vantage point from which he didn't have to look at the black and red ruin which had been the right side of his face. Thomas's lips seemed to have been shrunken by the blast, pulled back from the few teeth he had left giving him a grinning death's head.

'We have heard from old Morrison. He sends his greetings, and his daughter's. You remember young Bella, of course. Flighty little thing, always was.' His son's rigid blue eye remained fixed on the parkland, unblinking.

'We were wondering whether you wouldn't like to ride out with us?' Ramsay gazed at his son's deathly pale face for a moment. He sighed and got to his feet.

'Well, we'll let you know, whatever happens, when we get back,' he said. Ramsay had been halfway to the door when he had heard the scrape of the chair leg across the floor, looked round to see his son standing on his own.

'There. You'll feel better for some air, a change of scenery. You can't skulk up here you know, not for ever,' Ramsay said shortly, with a stab of guilt. Just how old Sir Hector would have treated him, shaken him out of this brooding limbo.

Findlay suddenly held his hand up, bent forward over his grey nag's head. Startled, Sir Marmaduke halted the rest of the ragged column, loosened the pistols in their holsters along his thighs. Ramsay tilted his head, heard the faint creak of wheels on the road ahead. The overhanging trees and bushes had formed a cathedral of interlocking boughs and branches, reducing their vision but funnelling the distant noises toward them. Findlay slipped his long leg over his horse, handed the reins to Bates. He checked the mechanism of his musket, straightened his equipment and doubled forward down the gloomy lane. Ramsay held his breath, listened for every sound. All he could hear was the creak of the wheels, the scrape of hoofs tugging a heavy load. He glanced at his son, who had eased his horse forward, to the head of their tiny troop.

'Artillery,' Ramsay hissed, beads of sweat breaking out along his upper lip, bristling his moustache. They were coming. One or two guns cleverly placed could reduce their home to a smouldering ruin in half an hour. They were trapped in this damned lane like rabbits in a run. They waited an age in the suddenly chill tunnel, fingering their weapons, until Findlay appeared, carrying his musket lazily as if he was stalking easy game. He waved. Ramsay closed his eyes, sighed with relief. Thomas spurred down toward the gamekeeper as the first lumbering wagon rounded the bend. The driver wore the ubiquitous cream smock and dark felt hat and sucked and chewed a barley stem in his toothless gums. He pulled his horse into the verge, glanced into the back. A dozen battered, ragged wounded stared up at him. He peered down the lane as the rest of the convoy rolled into view, the walking wounded staggering alongside the overloaded carts, tucking hanging arms and legs back over the blood-smeared boards. Ramsay backed his horse into the undergrowth as the convoy creaked past. A cavalry officer squatting beside the second driver, a bloody rag tied around his left eye, lifted his black hat in greeting.

'Captain Collins, sir, Earl of Caernarvon's horse. The colonel directed us to your home, sir.'

Ramsay frowned. 'What colonel?'

The captain was about to answer when there was a rude shout further down the narrow lane.

'Ramsay! Is that you?'

Sir Marmaduke looked up sharply and focused on the

rolypoly figure standing on the running board of the last wagon, waving his feathered hat. Findlay stepped along-side the squire's horse, nodded on down the slow-moving convoy.

'Morrison. Seems he was too fat to keep up with Waller. He's brought half his bloody household, by the look of it.'

Ramsay blinked in the dim, filtered sunlight, thought frantically what the cunning hound was up to. Allowing the wounded through the barricade was one thing, riding up with them as if they were off for a picnic on the top downs quite another.

'Where are his men?'

'He says they've gone. He wants to talk.' Findlay hawked and spat in the grass.

'They've abandoned their barricades? All gone?'

'All gone,' Findlay confirmed.

The portly merchant was already clambering down the wagon, helping his daughter as he went. Mary Keziah clawed her way down the splintered boards by herself, modestly straightened her bodice and hurried after her mistress with a loaded basket.

'By God, he's brought his girl.'

'Peace offerin'?' Findlay wondered aloud as the merchant blustered along the verge leading his blushing daughter. The bloody wounded in the creaking carts propped themselves on their elbows as she hurried past them, head bowed. They were cavalry mostly, blue-coated Royalists from Caernarvon's regiment which had taken the worst of the mauling at Chewton. There were also dragoons from both armies in a variety of civilian coats, making the best of things and sharing whatever they had. Water bottles, stale loaves, pipes of tobacco. Russet-coated Roundhead horsemen from Waller's or Burghill's regiments shared their own cart, remaining aloof from their less particular comrades. Most seemed lightly hurt about the arms, shoulders or head, sword cuts which could be cleaned and sewn. More unfortunate troopers had stopped a pistol ball at close range and winced and groaned at every bump in the badly made weed-grown track. The darker coated troopers belonging to the Parliamentary army had known enough to refuse the screaming youngster lying longways in their cart a sip of their water. He had received a terrible wound to the lower belly from which his blue and red entrails coiled and pulsed with every jolt. His bloody hands clutched and patted at the torn shirt his companions had used to try and staunch the dreadful slash. His taut skin was transparent as ice on a pond, his trembling lips as blue as frost. They sat and stared, wishing he would die. Three days he'd hung on, screaming and moaning and pleading with them, grating on their already frayed nerves. Wounds were one thing, death another, but this hanging on was worst of all.

'Put him aht his misery,' a crop-haired musketeer called from the next cart along. He and his comrades from the remains of one of Waller's London regiments had been inadvertently left behind when the army passed through Chewton. They had been busy about an urgent rearguard action of their own, ferrying bottles from an abandoned alehouse to a small dogcart, when they had found themselves caught up in the blistering mêlée. The sergeant of musketeers, a long and lean veteran with a bloody bandage tied around his neck where he had been clipped by a Royalist's blunted sword, elbowed his colleague in the ribs, making him holler with pain.

'Wodger do that for?' he snorted.

The sergeant closed his tired, sooty eyes. 'That bang on

the head addled your brain, Butcher? Let the man die in peace.'

'Swot I said, wunnit? Was smatter wiv you anyway?'

'You ought to have compassion for your brother in arms,' the third scolded, holding on to his dislocated shoulder. 'Rejoice that he will go unto the Lord having done his duty.'

The wounded trooper groaned, tried to prop himself up on his frail elbows. A burly, unshaven Royalist dragoon with a smashed knee tied up with lengths of horse blanket patted the lad's trembling leg, shook his head.

'Oh, here we go. Preachin' all the way to the Pearly Gates. Fuckin' Roundheads.'

'An' 'oo arsked you, straw 'ead?'

'All right, all right.' The sergeant waved his bloody paw as the wounded in the wagon exchanged insults and threats. 'Leave it out now, for pity's sake. You too, Gillingfeather.'

'Gillingfeather? What kind of a name be that?'

'Sis bleedin' name, awoight?'

'Butcher!'

'Butcher by name, butcher by nature,' one of Caernarvon's troopers sniffed, picking dried blood from his sleeve.

Ramsay, irritated to distraction by Morrison's blustering and hallooing, rounded on the bickering troops, rapped on the cart with the butt of his pistol. 'If you can't behave in a civil fashion you'll find no treatment in my house, no matter whose side you have chosen!' he bawled. 'Thomas, escort these wagons up to the house, have Anneliese organize the servants. We shall want hot water, bedding and bandages.' Thomas glared at his father through the embroidered eye slits in the velvet mask, pulled his horse on around.

''Ere, wos wrong wiv 'is face, then?' the irrepressible Butcher wanted to know. The sergeant, baptized Colston Muffet but usually known as Long Col, tilted his head and hissed something under his breath. 'Well, I was only arsking,' Butcher sulked, leaning behind the sergeant's arched back to peer at the noisy merchant's beautiful daughter.

'Excuse me, Sir Marmaduke,' the girl curtsied, 'my maid and I have prepared a basket of bandages, and would be delighted to help where we can.' She smiled encouragingly. 'Well, I . . . that is . . .'

'You run along and help Anneliese, child, her father and I have got so much catching up to do.' Sir Gilbert insisted, shooing the girls along the verge. Ramsay bristled on his horse, avoiding the eye contact the merchant was desperately trying to establish. Sir Gilbert had caught hold of the squire's bridle and held on to his prancing stallion like an overgrown groom.

'Praise the Lord, you received my letters,' Sir Gilbert panted.

Sir Marmaduke tugged his reins, staring at the bushes opposite.

'You are mistaken sir. I have received only one letter.'

'Only one? Why, that treacherous grasping snake! One? Why I've been sending you secret dispatches for the past six months. And paying the rascal to carry them through the lines!' Sir Gilbert swore and muttered to himself as Ramsay frowned.

'You mean to say you have been in touch with me before this week, sir?' Ramsay snorted.

'Each and every week! Well, that's why I'm here . . . but you wouldn't know that! You'll think I've merely run off or something awful! God's wounds, if I lay my hands on that messenger he'll rue the day he tricked Gilbert Morrison.'

The squire risked a look down at the apoplectic merchant who was stepping from one boot to the other in agitation.

'Are you saying you have not abandoned the cause you took up last year?' Ramsay asked disbelievingly. Morrison grasped his head as the last enormous wool wagon rumbled past, the hired driver from Bristol looking nervously about.

'Get along there man, keep up,' he scolded, then beamed up at the bewildered squire. 'Abandoned the cause? But of course ... you didn't see the letters. Sir, if you had you would have no need to ask any questions of me, you would know me to be as true to the King's cause as you are yourself!'

'The King's?' Ramsay spluttered. 'You raised a regiment for the Parliament, man!'

Sir Gilbert gave a hearty laugh, slapped Ramsay's horse in an irritatingly familiar manner. 'I raised a regiment for myself sir, with the hope that you would swoop down from the hill and unite with my men so we could throw out the ranters and the rogues I found myself saddled with. Oh yes, they're all long gone now of course,' he said scornfully, as if to himself. 'Troublemakers and busybodies sir. I do believe that scoundrel Fiennes sent them down from Bristol deliberately to undermine my men, godly, honest, sober men, sir. Infecting them with their damned rebel talk.' He broke off, clapped his hands to his sweating brow once more. 'But without the letters, the letters!' he wailed.

Findlay shook his head, watched Ramsay frown and scratch and pull at his beard.

'We had better get up to the house,' Ramsay decided at last. 'Where are these sober men of yours?'

'That's the thing sir, that's the thing. Men don't grow from seed, sir, as I'm sure you know. Gone, sir. Gone with Waller. The rogue marched every last one of them off with him just yesterday. If only you had swept down with all your men, you could have had him like a lame hare in a snare! Released all those boys up for true service with the King, cah!'

Ramsay bristled on his stamping stallion, beginning to imagine diverse unpleasant consequences from the unlikely scenario. He had kept his tiny troop tied up guarding his own hearth while the enemy straggled through the village. What would the King's generals make of that?

'One good charge, sir, you would have scattered his rearguard, scattered it, sir!' Sir Gilbert added, shaking his head at the abject failure, the lost opportunity.

'Findlay, take a couple of men and scout both ends of the village. I want to know where Hopton and Waller are.' The gamekeeper strode off to his tethered horse, cussing under his breath. 'Sir Gilbert, you had better come up to the house.' He paused, thought of something. 'By the way, I didn't see your son, Jamie?'

Sir Gilbert coloured, pulled at his nose. 'Well, sons don't grow from seed, squire, as I'm sure you know. You can't stake 'em out or prune 'em when they get too big for their breeches. I'll make no secret of it sir, I'll not hide it.'

'Hide what?' Ramsay asked patiently, turning his horse to follow the merchant as he strode up the lane.

'He's gone, sir, off with Waller. I tried to talk him into

staying behind, sir, but he wouldn't leave the men without an officer. Thought too much of them to allow some raving rogue from London to take them over. It's my Jamie all over, stubborn like. Anyway, he's gone now and there's nowt I can do about it.' He panted along beside the perplexed squire for a moment, said slyly: 'By the way now, Ramsay, I see your lad's back on his feet? Hurt at Edgehill, I hear.'

Ramsay nodded sourly.

'Some kind of facial injury, not too bad, one would hope.'

'One would hope.' Ramsay thought of his son riding out for the first time, taking a part once more in their topsy-turvy war. He was still brooding when he pulled up his horse beside the fortified front step. Lady Margaret was standing at bay on the barricade, arms akimbo. Ramsay would have rather charged a block of ready pikes dressed in his drawers than face the baleful gaze of his wife.

'Lady Ramsay,' Sir Gilbert purred mischievously. 'It's been so long!'

BY
KILMERSDEN HALL

JUNE 14, 1643

Margaret, Lady Ramsay was no stranger to her husband's eccentricities, his infuriating mannerisms and worrying tendency to see the good in people despite everything. He was quiet, dignified and thoughtful, a loyal husband and wonderful father of course, but he drove her to distraction with his subdued, reasoned arguments and naïve, misplaced generosity. The hurt looks he would give her when she had overturned all his childish fancies. Ramsay meant well, but he let himself be taken advantage of. He needed a strong hand at all times if he wasn't to be carried off by crafty gusts and dashed on the rocks. Crafty gusts blown by that whining windbag Morrison, for instance.

'He helped organize the care of the wounded, theirs and ours. Half those men would be dead by now, if he hadn't grabbed the bull by the horns and driven on up here. If he had been loyal to Waller he would have loaded his wagons and left with him,' Sir Marmaduke pointed out wearily, settling his nightcap on his grey thatch and wishing it was a steel bonnet.

'That, my dear, is all very well,' she declared, leaning over her dresser and attacking her hair with a brush. 'But only a complete fool would trust the scheming beggar.' They had eventually retired to bed at midnight where

Margaret, knowing it didn't do to shout a man down in front of his cronies, strove to set him straight. Before she had closed the door on her helpless husband she had detailed half a dozen guards to keep watch on the rooms they had allocated Sir Gilbert and his household. The merry merchant had helped himself to the Madeira, picked a capon quite clean and demolished the cheese as he spun out half a dozen anecdotes about life in the village during the past year, the scrapes he had gotten himself into.

'Riding two horses at once, not advisable, even if I remained true to the King throughout. You know, without those letters, some people will be all too quick to condemn me. Drat the fellow, taking my coin and failing to deliver my correspondence. Thank Heaven I decided to send my Jamie with the last one, otherwise you would never have believed me.' Sir Marmaduke had opened his mouth but the merchant hadn't finished. 'And I for one couldn't blame you. Why, I wager you'll find the whole hoard, all the evidence I would ever need to clear my name, hidden beneath some tree out on the estate there.' Sir Gilbert had chattered on incessantly as Lady Ramsay fumed and the squire nodded, reeling before the belching tornado.

Lady Ramsay had by now collected her breath and her thoughts, placed the brush on the dresser and turned to her errant husband.

'The thing is, Ramsay, it wouldn't be the first time Gilbert Morrison has pulled the wool over your eyes.'

That was true enough, he thought glumly. In all their dealings down the years the squire's hopes had always been dashed at the last minute, an apparently beneficial deal somehow falling foul of the small print, some overlooked subsidiary clause. Sir Gilbert had tied the squire in knots, bought cheap and sold dear. A stand of timber on the northern slope of the estate, the coal pit over at Dunstones, for instance. And here they were putting him up for Lord knows how long while he settled his tangled affairs.

'But surely he would have left with Waller,' Ramsay moaned, holding his aching head. 'What does he gain by staying?'

'He's changed his mind, turned his coat,' Lady Ramsay barked. 'He was as big for the Parliament as we were for the King, from the beginning. But Hopton's on his way and he's terrified he'll lose his house, his assets.'

'His assets would appear to be locked up in Bristol, my dove.'

'His assets are lying on our linen three doors down the hall,' Lady Ramsay observed, folding back the sheets and sliding into their ornate four-poster. Ramsay climbed into bed beside his wife, sat up against the pillow, shaking his head.

'Bella? I was thinking of . . .'

'Take it from me, he's thinking of a match. He's changed sides and his money's tied up in wool and what-not, he needs a sweetener to coat the taste of his medicine. Bella and Thomas, that's the match he has his eye on.'

Ramsay digested this shocking titbit. 'Well then, my dear,' he said thoughtfully, 'so long as Hopton takes Bristol and Morrison gets his wool back, he will still be the principal player in these parts.'

His wife snorted derisively. 'He will have the capital to provide a suitable dowry. It's coin we need now, my dear. The estate idle this twelvemonth, no income at all and a company of soldiers to keep from our savings.' She attacked the sheets in a passion.

'Are you suggesting we allow our Thomas to marry that slattern? You sound as if you regret we ever kept the house for the King.'

'No, dear, of course I don't.'

'Our Thomas and some tradesman's daughter, it won't do.'

'Our Thomas, dear, is not the catch he once was, meaning no disrespect to him,' Ramsay retorted. He was about to elaborate when he noticed the tears in his wife's eyes, her habitually well-resolved lip all a quiver.

'How can you say that?' she asked hoarsely. 'How can you write off your own son as if he was a lame gelding?'

'I haven't written him off,' he bridled. 'I'll tell you this, he's written himself off. Sitting by the window in a white shirt, riding out ahead of us all as if he was seeking a damned bullet.' He paused, realized he had said more than he had meant to. Lady Ramsay dabbed her eyes, grim faced now.

'Look here, Maggie,' Ramsay said, with all the decisiveness he could muster, 'that girl could put the heart back in any man. She's bags of spirit, a fine figure. If she could learn to accept him, accept his injuries . . .'

'Accept him? Accept him? You talk about your son as if he's a drooling idiot,' Lady Ramsay snapped.

'He's lost half of his face, woman!' Ramsay shrieked. 'He wants to die, can't you see it? He's had his life snuffed out of him, it's his ghost we're looking at, his damned ghost!' he cried, beating his fists on the counterpane. Lady Ramsay recoiled as her husband leapt out of bed, stood with head bowed by the guttering fire.

'He doesn't want to live,' he wailed, resting his grey head against the bare stone above the mantelpiece. 'He can't bear himself, he thinks he's a monster. If that girl,' he pointed a trembling finger at the opposite wall, 'can put a smile back on his face, for an hour and no more, then I would give them my blessing,' he said shakily.

Sir Gilbert Morrison couldn't sleep. His throat ached where he had damn near talked his tongue off. His eyes stung from sitting too near their smoky fire. Hadn't they heard of sweeps? The capon had been under-done and had soured his gut. He sat in the window, brooding, massaging his belly and thinking hard. Had they accepted his story? Time would tell. Certainly he had achieved the most difficult and immediate task, switching boats in midstream. He had half convinced the foolish old squire, if not his harridan of a wife. All he needed now was some ready cash. If he could only liquidize his assets, locked up tight in his warehouse in Bristol, he could sweeten his arrival a little more, if necessary. It was no secret that the King's army was chronically short of money. Troops needed pay, pay didn't grow on trees to be picked like pears along the way! Starling was a good man, trustworthy. He'd see the wool stayed where it was until the price hit the ceiling. Sell it to Parliament, sell it to the blasted King, Morrison didn't give two hoots. Sell it to the highest bidder. He could put a thousand pounds into Hopton's coffers to clear his conscience and settle their blasted suspicions, keep three for himself and keep his house into the bargain. It was a nerve-racking business, walking the tightrope between the two parties, but if anybody could pull it off, it would be him. And if he couldn't get his hands on ready cash at the moment, there was always Bella.

The Ramsays' broken-spirited son had hidden himself

back upstairs, hadn't stayed to dinner. Kept that mask on, so he obviously had a nasty facial wound. Well, as long as he was whole everywhere else, he could do his duty to Bella as a husband and heal the breach into the bargain. They needed money now, aye, as much as he did. Say five hundred for a dowry. That still left him two and a half thousand to the good. Ah, life. Life was good, if you could run with it, fence with it, he reflected. Stand by like the squire now, up to your eyes in sandbags and wool packs, and life simply passed you by.

Sir Gilbert sighed, hauled himself to his feet and tiptoed over to the cold bed. With Bella off his hands and Jamie up the other end of the country somewhere, he might even have time for a mistress. A fellow got lonely, climbing into cold, empty beds. A nice plump simple girl with good breasts. He rolled under the musty covers, fully clothed apart from his buff coat, hanging on a hook as if he had taken passage in some pirate's cabin. Yes, a nice plump girl with good breasts. They didn't grow from seed either. They had a price. Just the same as everybody else.

Anneliese slipped down the passage past the dozing guard, eased the door to Bella's room open a crack and crept inside. She peered at the unmade bed, looked up to the window and gave a little cry. Bella was standing, bathed in the moonlight, the strong silver beams shining through her as if she was a creature of the air and darkness. She turned, her shift shimmering, smiled. 'You startled me,' she scolded quietly.

They hadn't had much time for conversation, with all those wounded to help. Dirty cuts to daub with warm water, bloody scraps of cotton and leather to pick from

148

gaping flesh. Lady Ramsay had bustled in and out of the great hall where the injured had been laid in long lines, supervised their needs as she made her way between the broken rows. They had built up a considerable store of medications, everything from splints and poultices to a supply of maggots to fill the small muslin bags they would tie to rotten, gangrened limbs. Both the cook and the maid had sewn cuts before, and Findlay knew joints and tourniquets, but their combined medical experience didn't stretch to picking lead balls from pulped, purple flesh.

Lady Ramsay took a note as she passed along the bloody files, marking the men who would have to lose a limb. She came up with three legs and four arms. The belly shots she couldn't do anything about, so she had ordered the groaning men carried along to their small family chapel.

A pale Roundhead cavalryman had stared at the candles and velvet, the silver and the carved crucifix, and tried to prop himself up on an old door, his improvised stretcher. 'There lad, pay no heed to it now. No time to worry about a few candles, is it?' his comrade had told him, holding his frozen hand in his bloody paw. The boy had glared over his shoulder, through him.

'It's so cold in here, ain't it, Matty?'

The trooper had nodded his head, tugging the stitches he had received for the deep cut down his cheek.

'Why've they carried me out, Matty? They'll stitch me, won't they?'

'I dare say, I dare say.' Matty Culverhouse had seen the boy cut down, skewered by some upstart ensign in the crowded, madhouse main street of Chewton. The Royalist had hacked down hard, dragged his sword back as the boy's terrified horse had carried him past, his guts streaming over the crupper. He'd already left the dying boy for a moment, gone to talk with the bad-tempered lady of the house.

'Is there nothin' you can do then? For my mate there?'

Lady Ramsay had stared at the dirty, stinking cavalryman, the tawny sash which marked his allegiance speckled with blood.

'We've sent a rider back to the Lord Hopton to send his surgeons here,' she said shortly.

'Ah. Hopton's on his way, then.'

The woman frowned. 'As he and all the other generals serving the King are on their way,' she declared. 'To every corner of England, until the vile fires of this heinous rebellion are stamped out in deserved ruin,' she breathed dramatically.

The trooper pursed his lips and wiped his nose on the sleeve of his coat.

'Well, that may be my lady, that may be. But they're gon' need 'ellish lot of boots, 'cus I'll tell 'ee this. It's a big blaze the King's cooked isself, a real bonfire, all across England.'

Lady Ramsay had stalked off to attend to some of the lightly wounded dragoons. There was no point in arguing with these Roundhead fanatics. The girls were supposed to have been helping the cook with her needle and gut, but neither had managed to overcome their revulsion at piercing torn flesh, working the silk through slippery skin. Embroidery didn't bleed, cushions didn't quiver and jump or tug away from the needlepoint. Lady Ramsay had snatched the thread from their trembling fingers, steadied the bleeding ear against the dragoon's stubbled head, completed the operation without any further fuss.

Anneliese skipped over the cold room, slipped her arm around her old friend's narrow waist. 'I don't care what Mother says, we'll have plenty of time to rest tomorrow,' she said. The taller girl smiled, nodded on out over the park, many-threaded spider webs glowing silver in the long grass, swishing like young corn in the moonlight. Seven cloaked figures left trails of dragon breath as they marched across the overgrown lawn toward the trees. Anneliese squinted, made out Bates and one of the gardeners, gleaming weapons slung over their hunched shoulders.

'Why are they patrolling now? With the King's men coming on?' Anneliese asked, squeezing closer.

Bella shook her head, her fragrant hair tickling her friend's twitching nose. They aren't patrolling. They're off to dig graves.'

Anneliese shivered, looked again. 'Mother's sent the badly wounded to the chapel. Some of them made a dreadful fuss when they saw the altar cloths. I would have thought they would have been glad to be in the sight of God, wouldn't you? No matter how He's worshipped.' She sighed with perplexed irritation. 'Why do they make such a fuss? Why shouldn't we have candles and cloths? It's our chapel,' she said sulkily.

Bella nodded gravely. 'They'll fall out over anything. I heard some of our London men arguing with your horsemen over their silly names!'

'Ours? Yours? We're all one again now, Bell, aren't we?'

Bella nodded. 'Of course. It's just ... we've been for Parliament for a year and suddenly we're with the King.'

Anneliese stood back a little. 'Well, that's all right, isn't it? Now the King's winning again,' she reasoned. 'He'll drive the rebels back to London and then retake the capital and we can all get back to normal. I couldn't say in front of Mother and Father, but it's been awful up here. Especially since Thomas came back with his face all burnt.'

'Burnt? Is that why he wears that mask?' Anneliese nodded. 'Is it bad?' She turned away for a moment. Bella glanced at her thick black hair, squeezed her hand reassuringly.

'I walked in on him once, you know how we used to spend so much time together. I'd forgotten, Father had told us all to knock before we went in. He—' Anneliese broke off.

Bella felt her warm body racked with stifled sobs.

'Jamie's gone off too. And William, remember William?'

'Will Sparrow, the printer's boy?' Anneliese dried her glittering eyes on her sleeve, laughed softly.

'Everybody else has gone.'

'At least you could get around the town, go up to Bristol.' She took her friend's hand, pulled her over to the bed and sat down.

'Did I tell you about the captain that tried to ambush Father's wool?' Bella asked, leaning forward to whisper confidentially, her hazel eyes sparkling in the silver light.

The sun was already up over the hill, raising a curtain of mist over the quiet parkland, the silently steaming trees. The whole house seemed tense with expectation, the crumbling mortar and weathered stone shifting and sighing with imminent relief. Bella and Anneliese, who had chattered excitedly long into the small hours, were still wrapped up in their creased counterpane, fast asleep, and didn't hear the cock crowing lustily around his opened run. Three doors along the quiet corridor Lady Margaret had ordered Ramsay up early to check the guards and ensure the merchant hadn't made off with the plate.

'He would have had to dig about in the cellar to find the little bit we have left,' the squire complained, buttoning his shirt and slipping on his buff coat.

'I wouldn't put anything past that rogue,' she said, pursing her lips.

Ramsay had gone on downstairs, found the garrison troopers lounging over their breakfasts. Findlay was interrogating the hapless Bates.

'Well, you had your musket,' the gamekeeper told him, straightening up as the squire wandered into the room gnawing one of the few chicken legs the merchant hadn't stuffed the night before.

'What's happened?'

Findlay growled something, nodded disgustedly over his shoulder. 'The burial party gave us the slip. Four of them ran off into the woods as soon as they were away from the house.'

Ramsay shook his head, stared hard at the former footman. 'Well? You took Purvis and Hodges like I told you?'

The footman nodded awkwardly. 'We had 'em digging, then they wanted a rest. We didn't think they'd go far, they were all wounded.'

Bates muttered and gestured furiously. 'Did you not shoot after them?'

'They'd only gone for a piss, sir. They were all wounded, why would they have wanted to run?'

Ramsay closed his eyes, shook his head.

'Does that captain know? The one with the head wound who is supposed to be in charge?'

'He took funny last night and all. Said he had a headache, then he was seein' double,' Bates blustered.

'It was that horseman from Waller's gave her ladyship all the lip, and those mouthy buggers from London. None of 'em were badly hurt, a couple of stitches and a rest and they were as right as rain. Back with Waller by now, I'd wager.'

Ramsay frowned, wandered along the stony passage toward the great hall making way for a couple of servants carrying sacks of bloodied dressings. A good wash and they could be used again, no doubt. He looked in on the wounded, propped up on their blankets chatting quietly with their neighbours, or lying still as sarcophagi on their makeshift litters. A night's rest and a good meal to set them on their way. Is that all they needed? he wondered. Thomas would need more than a bed and a bite to set him right. He stared morosely at the closely packed wounded, some of whom nodded or raised their cups to him.

'Bless you, sir, for opening yer 'ouse,' a heavily bandaged dragoon called, earning a chorus of approval from around the room. Ramsay picked his way through the sprawled men and heaped clothing, the occasional pool of sticky blood. He made his way out of the small door next to the stairs, ducked into the dimly lit family chapel. The lingering smell of death held sway over the feebler odours of their inadequate medications, the oily stink of the candles and tapers. Three bodies had been tied up in old sheets in the silent cloister. They looked almost comic, immense steamed puddings ready for the pot. A small piece of paper had been tucked under the bindings around their blue feet recording their name and regiment. Ramsay picked over the first, read: Benjamin Cutler, truper, Burrells Horse. Killd at Chuton Menndip. Killed at Chewton Mendip although he hadn't actually died until three days afterward, twelve miles away. And Thomas? Had he been killed at Edgehill? Eight months before, a hundred and fifty miles north? A calico pudding in all but name?

Findlay coughed quietly at the door.

'More wounded arriving at the front gate sir, with the surgeons.'

Ramsay nodded, followed the gamekeeper out of the death hole.

'His mate stayed with the boy until he died,' Findlay said. 'Then he went off with those London buggers. We'll be seeing him again, no doubt,' he predicted, following Ramsay down the hall and out to the front door. They clambered over the makeshift barricade, watched more walking wounded stagger and limp along the overgrown path. A dozen lightly hurt soldiers who hadn't managed to shake off their injuries or had developed infections and discovered they were more seriously hurt than they had at first imagined. A young girl in a red gown was leading a tall bay, the rider slumped forward in the saddle. She smiled broadly at them, nodded over her bared shoulder at the unconscious youth. 'It's his back. S'all manky.'

Ramsay looked up at the pasty-faced youngster as Findlay took the reins.

'Your husband?'

The girl raised her painted eyebrows, gave the squire a broad wink. 'Now wouldn't that be tellin'? Not yet, sir, but he's as good as promised to make an honest woman out of me.'

The girl couldn't be more than a few weeks older than Anneliese, Ramsay thought with a small shudder. Would the war bring all girls to this? Baring herself for every ragged soldier to see? He'd seen plenty of young girls whoring in Germany a sight younger than either of them.

Findlay smirked, led the horse around the back of the house. The girl curtsied to the squire, skipped along behind her fallen idol. The next rider was considerably more aware of his situation, taking off his hat to admire the house, shake his dark head at the naïve fortifications. The rider wondered whether the fools were seriously proposing to defend such a pile. With the woods all around from which a single galloper gun could wreak mortal havoc without the least risk to the crew? These English, they were brave, fanatically so, but they knew as much about making war as they did about making love. The surgeon's sweating assistant trudging alongside carrying a leather portmanteau nudged the rider's leg as the squire marched up, nodded briskly. The swarthy surgeon finished admiring the architecture, bowed from the saddle.

'Ambrosio de Meola St Corelli, at your service, sir!'

Ramsay stood back as the Italian swung himself down, dusted himself off and bowed formally.

'Signor, you do us a great honour.' The squire shook the Italian's hand and showed him the way into the bustling house.

The girls, still in their shifts but protecting their modesty behind the curtains, peered down at the newcomer from their first-floor window.

'Who's that?'

'It's not him is it, Prince Rupert?' Bella gasped, noting his dark complexion, expensive black suit and flashing brown eyes. 'Or Maurice, at least,' she amended, deciding the stranger couldn't be much more than five feet tall. Everybody knew Prince Rupert was a towering six footer. Perhaps they would meet them all, on the victory parade through Bristol, and be allowed to go to the court when it was re-established in London. Well, it couldn't be long now, could it?

KILMERSDEN HALL

JUNE 16, 1643

Mary Keziah helped Bella into her dress, picked the ruckles from her satin sleeves and stood back to admire her mistress. She was staring at the mirror without registering her rather crumpled reflection and fly-away hair, which generally meant she was bored to distraction.

'Well, so much for living out of a trunk. It's this one or the blue, but that's still damp from yesterday. I told you to borrow one of my aprons.' Bella hardly heard Mary as she fussed and twittered behind her, arranging the few personal items she had been able to bring up from the house. Bella had craved excitement, a break from the punishing monotony of Chipping Marleward, but their sudden departure and brief flight up the hill had seemed a craven escape, a mean business for which everybody seemed to be blaming her. She had imagined they had been packing their essentials ready to follow Waller's army north, catch up with Jamie and William and the rest.

'Oh, they'll be all right,' her father had blustered that chaotic afternoon. 'They're safe away, it's us, girl, us who have left it too late.'

'Too late?'

'Hopton's men have cut the road, we're trapped.'

Trapped? Had the war caught up with her at last? She

had felt faint with delicious expectation, life in all its shapes and sizes hurrying up the road to whisk her away from her domestic drudgery. But it hadn't quite worked out like that. They had waited until everybody else in the county had been busy extricating themselves from Hopton's rumoured trap, and then fled across the green and up to the manor house, running against the swirling, sweaty tide, a cursing confusion of carts and cattle. Three days stuck up at the hall and Bella wondered why she had ever imagined life here could be more exciting than her own excruciating existence. The truth of it was Anneliese's fortress infirmary was as dull and boring as her own father's abandoned house down the hill. Bella had volunteered to help with the wounded, but although they were glad to leer and whisper as she hurried past they seemed to prefer Mary Keziah or one of the squire's serving women to stitch or clean them up. Did she appear that useless to everybody? It wasn't as if her maid had spent years working as a surgeon's mate before she joined the Morrison household. Perhaps she was more used to men's peculiarities, having been brought up with so many boisterous brothers. Whatever the reason, the wounded appeared to be happier screaming and bawling while Mary held their hands, and seemed to positively bite their lips bloody when Bella was in the room. It was quite ridiculous.

Lady Ramsay seemed to relish sewing ears back on, stitching flaps of skin together with her sharp red tongue clamped between her thin lips. She had always been a quick-tempered, unsmiling woman, and had never shown Bella any particular respect. Now she had extra cause to dislike her, her father being a turncoat as well as a tradesman. Aiming frosty stares in her direction as if she had been responsible for her family's earlier allegiances.

Anneliese had assured her she thought no such thing, but Bella knew daggers from butter knives. She left Mary Keziah scrubbing the blood from her blue gown, wandered through the house peering into musty rooms, nodding at the hobbling wounded as they made their painful way to the wash house. She arrived in the busy scullery, recoiled at the cloying smell. A heady combination of the cook's potent medicinal potions and her favoured staple, boiled cabbage.

'That'll put 'em back on their feet, and some 'airs on their chests an' all. Niver seen so many bare boys,' the cook had declared with a broad wink, picked a basket from a shelf and passed it to the bewildered girl.

'If you've a moment, miss, you could fetch us some more mint, crowsfoot, dandelions an' a 'andful of vetch while yer at it,' the woman asked, none too politely either. Bella frowned, but on second thoughts took the basket and hurried outside into the bright sunlight and fresh air, glad to get away from the bloody bustle of the hated house. How long would they be there? she wondered. Why hadn't they left earlier, gone north toward the river with Waller? Father had muttered something about tricky businesses and market pressures, the acceptance of military realities and avoidance of hasty decisions. By the time he had made up his mind they had had no choice but to make for their enemy's house! Some decision! And what about her future? Were they to run from pillar to post until the war was over? She tugged a handful of dandelions from the foot of an outhouse wall, threw them into the basket in disgust. Vetch, crowsfoot? She was supposed to be a young lady, not a goose-girl!

Bella snorted to herself, strode through the kitchen

garden gate and collided with a young man who had been limping in the opposite direction. He immediately lost his balance and toppled over a refuse heap, impaling himself on something to judge from his anguished howls. Bella dropped the basket, bent down over the wounded youth, who tore his hat straight and stared up at her, eyes blazing. The captain with the kingfisher coat! Here! She stood back from him as if he had risen from the dead grey ashes like a heron over a pool of minnows, watched him lever himself to his shaky feet.

'I'm so sorry . . . I wasn't looking where I was going . . . You're hurt,' she told him, reaching out as he steadied himself on the wall, swallowed painfully. He waved her away.

'It's all right . . . just a scratch,' he lied, wincing as he straightened his back. He had changed the exquisite turquoise coat for a plainer brown doublet, the same colour as his twitching moustache.

'Miss Pitt,' he growled, racked with embarrassment as he began energetically dusting the worst of the ashes from his breeches.

'Er . . . Miss Morrison.'

'Morrison?' he repeated. 'Not the Morrison?'

'Miss Pitt is my maid. She's helping with the wounded,' Bella said awkwardly, holding the basket behind her back as if it represented all the evidence of her family's doubtful allegiance, their uncertain place in an uncertain society. The captain looked up sharply, narrowed his eyes as if he suspected another trick.

'And where is your friend Starling? The courageous horse beater?' he asked, rather rudely, Bella thought.

'Will?'

'Billy,' Telling reminded her.

She stifled a giggle, compressed her glistening lips. 'Yes. Billy. He's gone with Waller.'

Telling's face flushed and paled as he reached gingerly under his shirt, ran a probing finger over his heavily bandaged wound. 'Well, it won't do him any good hiding behind Waller's skirts,' he snapped. 'Kicking a man's horse and then telling tales to some filthy news-sheet! I'll teach the blackguard to make a fool of me.' He flustered, frowned. 'That is . . . I don't think we have been properly introduced,' he growled, remembering his manners and snatching off his hat. 'Hugo Telling. Captain of Prince Maurice's horse.'

'Bella Morrison,' the girl smiled, curtsied cheekily.

Telling glanced up at the grey house, the squat fortified pile behind her. 'I hear Mr Morrison has lately decided to change his allegiance. Remembered his duty at last, no doubt.'

Bella's bright hazel eyes flashed, helpless and hurt. Hugo instantly regretted upsetting her.

'I've no influence over my father. Have you instructed your family which side to support? Do they take more notice of you than my father does of me?'

His family wouldn't have trusted him with a burnt-out match, if the truth was told. Ironic that he should be galloping around the country with pistols and sword, six thousand men at his back. That would make the rector and his weary wife and sober sons sit up and take notice. Telling smiled shortly, stole another look at her. He had seen her step down from the wagon that day as if she hadn't a care in the world, but now he would remember her like this: angry and passionate, her perfect creamy features flushed and set, her sweet mouth shaped into a cruel snare.

'I am quite sure he did not abandon our home without very serious consideration,' she said haughtily.

'I have no argument with you, Miss Morrison,' Telling said testily. 'I'm sorry if I upset you.'

Bella nodded, returned his bashful smile. 'It's I who should be apologizing, knocking you over like that. And I am sorry Will kicked your horse. He was convinced you would drag him away for the King's army,' she explained.

'Why should he fear doing his duty to his King?' Telling snorted.

'There are many men who see things differently to you,' she pointed out. He pursed his lips, shrugged. Bella looked over his thin shoulder, noticed his threadbare coat. Perhaps he had spent all his money on the one fine jacket and kept it for special occasions?

'Could I perhaps accompany you on your walk?' Telling asked. 'The surgeon said I was over the worst.'

'Worst?'

'My wound. It's only a scratch but it became infected and I caught a fever,' he went on, unaware of the change which had come over the girl. She touched his arm, bit her lip. Wounded? Wounded he was even less resistable than he had been before, her mysterious outlaw Cavalier! And he didn't even know it!

'You mean you're recovering from a wound, and I've knocked you flying?'

'There's no need to worry,' he said casually. 'I lost my balance, is all,' falling in behind her as she reddened, strode out of the kitchen garden and off across the overgrown paddock.

'I was in a fever for two days,' he went on, lengthening his stride as he tried to catch her up. 'I was brought here on my horse, quite unconscious.'

Bella stopped dead, thought for a moment. 'Oh yes. The girl with the red dress.' Which had evidently been three sizes too small for her. 'We saw her bring you in.'

'Matilda. She's taken rather a shine to me, it seems. Sat up all night bathing my brow and what have you. Pity she didn't see the rogue who stole my coat.'

'Your coat?' she asked quietly.

'Yes, my best coat, turquoise velvet, Spanish cut. It seems it was stolen while I slept.'

'And your friend,' Bella said shortly, 'never saw anything?'

'Nor the blasted thief who took my pistols.'

'Your pistols?'

'A pair of wheel-locks, finest workmanship you could find. Gone.'

'And how long did this girl look after you?'

'Two nights and two days, without a break,' Telling beamed.

'Well, at least she wasn't out of pocket,' Bella sniffed, made off over the dewy grass.

Telling stood smiling at her back. Frowned. Hurried after her. 'What do you mean by that?' he called.

KILMERSDEN HALL

JUNE 16, 1643

The ragged volley of carbine shots rebounded around the gloomy wood and scattered the black battalion of crows which had been murmuring their own guttural covenants above the hushed service. The indignant mourners cawed and flapped over the treetops, performed agitated caracoles as the sharp crackle of gunfire echoed back, punctuating the heartfelt amens from the congregation standing with heads bowed beside the open gravepits. Six oblong bundles had been laid carefully in the rich leafy mulch beneath the trees.

Bella shuddered, pulled her light shift about her shoulders as she stared at the anonymous bodies. Strapped and wrapped, robbed of their features and personalities. A length of grey tape knotted about their middles and ends serving as a grave sash. The young Roundhead trooper with the slashed belly lay alongside Captain Collins, who had seemed to be making a strong recovery until he had swooned over his dinner, fallen into a frozen sleep and died two hours later without a whimper. Cold bundles now, neighbours for better or worse, for ever. The reasons, causes, strategies and excuses which had brought them all to the bottom of a muddy ditch already forgotten. Some of the Roundhead dragoons, easy in their allegiance, had already agreed to change sides. They had abandoned their cause once and would probably do so again, the lucky survivors devaluing the sacrifice of their dead friends.

Telling slid alongside Bella, placed his hand over hers. He smiled slyly, gave her hand a gentle, reassuring squeeze. Lady Ramsay, squinting over her shoulder, spotted the gesture and shook her head. That girl! Could she not control her farmyard urges while they buried these poor men? Bella had missed her icy glare, and was alternately smiling weakly at the captain and dabbing her eyes dry on the lace trim of the shift. Anneliese and her mother linked arms and walked back toward the house, Sir Gilbert and Sir Marmaduke falling in behind them, conversing in strained undertones. The rest of the household and the soldiers who had recovered thanks to – or in spite of – their treatment, fell in behind them, settling their hats back on their bandaged heads. They limped back to the house leaving Bates and a squad of the turncoat dragoons to fill in the graves. Findlay stood alongside, keeping a beady eye on them as he leaned on his long rifle. The nervous diggers smiled, set about their task with all the enthusiasm their healing wounds allowed.

'You're all right there, matey, we're not goin' anywheres.'

'I'm here to make sure of that,' Findlay replied. 'Those horse boys of yours wouldn't have got out of my woods if I'd been there,' he said, casting a sour look at the hapless Bates.

'It's all right for them, they get better 'orses than us,' another dragoon piped up.

'I seem to remember those London boys went with them, on foot,' Findlay corrected.

'Ah well, they'm all mad an' all, with their preachin' and rantin'.'

'Just get those lads planted, and we'll see,' Findlay said.

Bella made to follow the quiet congregation back to the house but Telling held on to her hand, pulled her back.

'You've been avoiding me,' he accused in a determined whisper.

'You're hurting, let go. I've been busy up at the Hall, in case you hadn't noticed,' she simpered.

'I've been trying to speak to you without that Ramsay girl hanging on to our every word.'

'Our every word? Why should she not hear every word which passes between us? You are impertinent, sir.'

Telling narrowed his eyes, caught the tiny smile shaped by her full, red lips. 'It's either her or your father, and I'd not be responsible for what I say in front of him,' he said arrogantly.

'I haven't seen Anneliese for over a year, and Father's been busy helping Sir Marmaduke on the arrangments for the truce.'

Telling shook his head.

'Truce? On the basis General Hopton knew Waller in the German wars? Half the officers served in Germany. There's more at stake here than a few friendships,' he remarked casually.

'Yes, well, we've been busy trying to save some of these men, now you soldiers have finished your brave business,' she snapped back, annoyed. 'Father says the real battles will be many times worse than this. I can't imagine how they could be.' Telling could imagine well enough. The whole affair at Chewton, over and done in ten minutes, had left a hundred and more dead and wounded. Edgehill had gone on most of the day, the two armies had been locked together like baited bears. And the poor soldiers had hardly known their business back then. Hugo thought grimly the next battle must be worse still, and the next and the next and the next worse again. A soldier could not afford to dwell on his future, he reminded himself. A soldier must occupy himself with life, the moment, and not concern himself with the countless, unimaginable variations of his death. That Roundhead they had planted there, he had overheard the soldiers describe his wounds. His belly slashed open in the Chewton fight. He had in all probability killed him. Skewered him on his sword and gutted him getting it out. He didn't know his name. He had made a point of not catching it when Sir Marmaduke had read it out during the service earlier. He remembered one of the rolypoly sergeants back at Oxford schooling the enthusiastic students in the arts of war, telling them they were there to kill their enemies, not count or convert them.

'Don't ever walk the field after the battle, kind sirs. Don't ever go and look at what you've done. If you have pity, if you show remorse sirs, somebody'll be walking the field looking at your cold corpse, wondering who you were.'

'Look at your silly causes now,' Bella said, nodding at the bloated white chrysalids disappearing under shovelfuls of earth. 'It could be you down there, wrapped up in a sheet, and nobody would know who you were or what you'd done.'

Telling pondered her forceful speech for a moment, pulling his small moustache in agitation. 'It's not for strangers to know what I do,' he replied stiffly. 'I don't care for their opinions, whether they care for me or my cause. The King's struggle is my own,' he said piously, 'I am ready to die for it, even if I were all alone in the wide wastes of Asia.'

Bella snorted, walked on. He watched her slim figure shimmer beneath the rather grubby and creased dress, hurried after her.

'I could have hidden myself away, hidden in a house in Chewton,' he said, trying a different tack. 'Nobody would have noticed whether I did my duty or not, but I'd have known, don't you see?'

Bella frowned, shook her head dismissively. 'Yes, it's all right for you men, smug and safe with your causes. At least you know which side you're supposed to be on.'

'Well, your brother and your friend Starling the horse kicker seem clear on whom they serve.'

'They're young and foolish, the same as you. It's father's fault to be too clever, to see everything as if it were a business to be bought up and sold off.'

'Well, then, why are you snapping at me?' he demanded.

'Because I don't want every young man I know to end up down there in the dirt,' she snapped, pointing back over the dewy paddock. They had left broad trails through the thick wet grass, soaked their shoes and clothing as they wandered under the eaves of the rook-ruled wood.

'There has to be a better way for you to settle your arguments. What good is it if you've succeeded in killing each other?'

'It's not just my cause, it's everybody's cause,' Telling declared.

'And why must we wait at home ripping up bandages, making you better so you can go out and do the same all over again?' Bella went on, ignoring him.

'They've talked enough. Let all the King's enemies, all the ranters and the rogues, line up in front of us, once and for all. The truth of it, Bella,' he said as if he were a kindly old uncle, 'is that people like your father, playing one side off against the other, they're the ones prolonging the war, not the soldiers.'

Bella tossed her head, stalked off along the overgrown path between crowds of bluebells. Telling hurried after her once more, tugging her round.

'Will you ever tire of ragging me about my father's actions? I can't help what he gets up to.'

Telling steeled himself and then gripped her shoulders, held on to her as she tried to pull away. He bent his head over hers, fastened his mouth over her cries as if he would steal her sweet breath for ever. Bella pulled back and forth, opened her lips slyly, as he snaked his tongue into her mouth, between her neat white teeth.

'Ouch!' He jumped back, clutching his mouth. She had bitten his impudent tongue, drawing a bead of bright blood from the tip. 'What did you do that for?' he spluttered, spitting into the bluebells.

'How dare you treat me like one of your camp sluts! Go and find your red-headed friend if you want to play those piggish tricks!'

'Piggish tricks?'

'Kissing a girl as if you're licking the drips from a bowl of porridge!'

Telling opened his mouth, stumped. 'I thought . . .' he narrowed his eyes and bristled up again. 'Well, if you're the blushing virgin you claim to be how was it we caught you rolling on the wool sacks with that rogue Starling, eh?'

Bella's hazel eyes flashed alarmingly, she took a step forward as he threw his arms about her. 'Don't you dare accuse me of playing the—' She wriggled as he encircled her narrow waist with one arm, slid his free hand over her heaving shoulder to clamp her warm breast. They stood in paralysed, mutually astonished silence for a moment, as if his lust and her temper had fused them to the earth like stone idols. Bella recovered from her surprise first, gave a choked cry and writhed away from him. This time Telling bunched his fist in the loose material gathered at the base of her back, and held on to her, bobbing and ducking as he tried to kiss her. She beat at him with her fists as he forced his knee between hers, tipped her backwards so she would either stop struggling or fall back into the bluebells. He closed in on her, stifling her angry fists with his chest, smiling to himself as he sensed her demure surrender. Hugo covered her face and neck with starved kisses as she dropped her arms to her sides then closed them gently behind his back in sultry expectation.

'There,' he murmured into her fragrant ear. She lifted the tails of his old brown coat, ran her hand over his hot back. Telling groaned and closed his eyes as if his body had been filled up. Imagined his skin popping its seams and coming apart at any second. Bella was still, enjoying the peculiar sensation as if she were floating above the wood, gazing down on herself and her lover. He seemed to have changed his smell, his breathing was quick and shallow, bristly moustache trembling with delighted concentration.

She narrowed her eyes and dug her knuckles into the bulky dressing over his lower back.

'Bella, my . . . aaagggggggghhhh!' He leapt sideways like a scalded crab, doubled over in agony, grasping at a mossy tree trunk for support. His narrow face was purple, his lips compressed as he took short sharp breaths. 'For the love of Christ,' he gasped, straightening a little as she stood still, trembling.

'Your precious army has taught you how to fight, and how to rape and pillage as well, I see.'

'Rape you, rape you? I wouldn't rape you,' he moaned. 'I love you. I loved you the moment I saw you climb down from the wagon. Christ's wounds, you've ripped my stitches,' he gasped, stepping from one boot to the other. Bella adjusted her bodice, retied the strings Telling's thrusting hand had loosened.

'You shan't bully me one moment and love me the next,' she said spitefully. 'Treat your whore how you like, but you don't buy me for a shilling!'

'She's not my whore! She's everybody's whore! She's nothing to me!'

'She took time off to bring you here,' Bella argued, surprised to find herself in tears. 'You can run back to her now, if you like. I've no use for a schoolyard bully.' She turned, spotted his discarded hat and ground it into the dirt with her heel. She glared at him, gathered her skirts and strode out into the paddock, the rooks cawing and wheeling over the silent wood.

Telling staggered after her, watched her through the canopy of branches as his anger and pain faded to a dull ache. He picked up his crushed hat, pulled the crown straight and dusted the worst from the black felt. He settled it on his head, and limped back to the house where he spent ten minutes collecting up his kit and some of the lightly wounded. They were taking their ease in the kitchen, cadging food from the busy, red-faced cook while they played cards and smoked short clay pipes. Telling stood over them for a moment, tapping his foot on the cold stone.

'Are you intending to spend the rest of the war with your feet up, or will you come back with me?' he demanded.

'And who might you be, my little bantam?' a whiskery veteran asked him, the glowing pipe bobbing in his gap-toothed mouth.

'I'm the senior officer, with Captain Collins gone,' Telling replied, with some satisfaction. 'And either you will accompany me back to the army or I'll have the gamekeeper fellow shoot you all for desertion!'

The players exchanged glances, nodded and threw down their cards.

'I was losin' anyway,' the veteran chuckled.

Thomas Ramsay, back at his usual lookout post in his room now the excitement of the last few days had died down, had watched the silent service from a distance, his hated face reflected in the pitted glass. He stared through his own ruined features, watched Bella and the Telling character peel away from the rest of the congregation, cut grey trails into the gloomy wood. A few moments later he had spotted Bella hurrying back to the house, and a minute or two later Telling had reappeared, paused by the edge of the wood and limped back across the grass leaving a broad and rather uneven trail behind him. He guessed the lovers had fallen out, but the secret knowledge gave him little satisfaction. How could he be jealous of Telling, paying such devoted attention to his sister's best friend? The laughing, scolding, insolent beauty he had loved to distraction as a child, watching her run in the paddock, climb trees in the woods, and dance around the fire with Anneliese? He could not bring himself to find fault with the handsome captain, or covet his boyish good looks. There would be other battles for him, powder and pistol and round-shot and pikes and musket butts aplenty to ruin his fine features. If it hadn't been for his own monstrous injuries he would have had a rival for her wandering attention.

Thomas was older and wiser. He had grown up from the sickly, dull boy Bella had so obviously despised. He would not have chosen to pursue the girl like a lurcher after a lame hare. Bella was strong willed and clever, not afraid to speak her mind. His mother found her vulgar and ill bred, but Thomas had always been captivated by her cheek, her hopeless impetuosity. She must be courted with elegance, grace and assured, mature intelligence, not chased into the woods by a hungry man-wolf. He lifted his hand, traced the crisped, fractured scars on the side of his face, the horrifyingly puckered skin about his ears, the scorched tufts of hair. How could she ever abide him, even if he sewed his hated face into that hated mask, never let her see the full extent of his frightfulness?

He climbed to his feet, watched the sudden commotion in the yard: Telling ordering the groom to find his horse, the big bay he had left in the stables when he had arrived. No, sir, beggin' pardon, sir, the young lady took it, sir, threw her leg over and galloped off like a gypsy girl, the day you arrived, sir. He smiled slightly as he watched Telling stamp around the yard, throwing down his hat and cursing aloud. Half a dozen of the lightly injured troopers manhandled a cart from the outhouse, walked a pair of sturdy Welsh cobs between the shafts. Telling climbed up beside the driver as the men threw their bits of equipment into the back, clambered up on the cart. The glowering driver lifted the reins and flicked them over the horses' backs, turned the cart out of the yard and back to the bloody war.

He watched them get smaller and smaller on the lane, turned at the soft knock on the door. His father smiled weakly, nodded at him.

'Thomas. Glad to see you up and about. I wonder if you would care to come along to the study tomorrow. Sir Gilbert and I have been discussing a letter which we propose to forward to General Hopton.'

Thomas eyed his father, watched him attempt to hold his steady gaze. Sir Marmaduke's eyes flickered from the window to the bed, from his son's boots to the top of his head, but signally failed to hold his unearthly stare.

'He has assured me he discussed the matter with Waller, and is confident he can use his influence to bring him to a meeting. That's right,' he repeated as if he was addressing one of the spaniels. 'A peace conference, to end the war.' He waved his hand. 'Before we find ourselves slipping into the abyss,' he said darkly. 'It's why he broke ranks, came to us in the first place, he feels exactly as I do, do you see?'

Thomas looked blankly at him, disconcerting his father, who took refuge behind a barrage of *bonhomie*.

'He thinks I will make a perfect go-between, having served with both Waller and Hopton in Germany. If we can talk some sense into those two, we can talk some sense into the King and this mongrel Parliament.' He watched his son cross to his desk, scrawl something on a slip of paper, hand him the note which read: *I don't trust him. Nobody trusts him.*

Sir Marmaduke frowned, nodded his greying head. 'I'm sure you're right to be pessimistic, but remember he had plenty of opportunity to go north with Waller, back to

Bristol and his precious warehouse. It took courage for him to come here you know,' he said crossly. He paused, bowed his head. 'I thought . . . that is, I wondered, if you might like to, you know, take a hand again. Have a look at the letter, see what you think, go over some of the clauses we're proposing. You're a soldier, you know better than me how soldiers' minds work these days.' He frowned. 'It's what you need, shutting yourself up in here. You can't stay in here for ever, you know. You aren't the only one,' he said quietly, turning away. 'You aren't the only one who has lost, and you won't be the last, unless we can stop this wretched business before it's too late. Before they feed its fires with hatred and revenge. I saw it, my boy, I saw them do the same in Germany.'

Thomas looked at his father's anxious face, the tears springing in his tired eyes, and nodded his scarred head. He couldn't stay here for ever, after all.

By
CLAVERTON MANOR

NEAR BATH, JULY 2, 1643

William had already stripped off his buff coat and
was working in his sweaty shirt, throwing shovelfuls of dirt over his shoulder to build up the
muddy wall. Surely they could hire some of the townsfolk
for jobs like this, he thought crossly. It was all right for
them, sitting outside their alehouses laughing and jeering
at the newly raised troops. What if Bella rode by now, saw
him up to his waist in a trench? He didn't imagine the
Royalist generals made that spark of a captain dig holes.

'What's wrong then, Will? Too long since you put your
back into some real work,' Zachary Pitt called cheerfully
from the broad rampart they had thrown up on the island,
a tongue of land between the out-flung arm of the River
Avon and a narrow mill-stream.

'That's *Captain* Sparrow,' Will growled for the hundredth time. 'I'm supposed to be in charge!' Supposed to
be in charge was about the size of it, since those meddling
crows Lyle and Webster had launched their investigation
into Morrison's regiment of foot and its missing colonel.
Most of the ragged recruits had already copied their
commander and taken to their heels. If it was clear to
everyone Sir Gilbert had defected, surely it was equally
clear neither poor Jamie nor Will had had any prior
knowledge of his treacherous intentions. Will slumped

over his shovel, examined his blisters and wiped his brow. Well that was as maybe, but until the commissioners were completely satisfied Jamie would be detained at Bristol Keep and William Sparrow would stay with the sorry remnants of the village regiment.

They had been marched out of Bath and were presently building a redoubt for General Waller alongside his pontoon bridge over the Avon in the narrow Claverton valley. The Royalists had crossed the river at Bradford-on-Avon and were presently advancing towards Bath along the northern bank while Waller pestered them from his strong position on the southern downs. The rampart they were constructing would dominate the ford, the churned umbilicus connecting the main Roundhead army with a small ambush party the general had left to contest the enemy's progress. As usual, the Roundhead commander had chosen his ground with meticulous care. Just below Waller's lookout post at Claverton Manor the Avon curved and divided across its guardian water meadows. The busy flow was interrupted by beds of gravel and banks of rushes to create shallow channels a traveller might jump without getting too wet. The main force of the current had been diverted away along a narrow stream to feed an ancient mill, rejoining the main river two hundred yards downstream to create a flat, featureless island called Ham Meadow.

Featureless no longer. Now the narrow islet boasted a squat earthwork mounting a small gun and garrisoned by two hundred picked men. They were protected by the river to their front and the mill-stream to the rear. The ends of the wall had been banked and curved to protect the defenders from enfilading fire from the far side of the river. The newly dug dyke was admittedly dominated by the high ridge across the river to the north, but an enemy gun crew would have to spend hours digging flat platforms if they were to stop their piece rolling down the steep slope as soon as they risked a shot. Building the necessary emplacements and manoeuvring the heavy guns into position on the tricky hillside would slow the enemy advance along the ridge, giving Waller time to work out his deployments to defend Bath.

Will had no more idea what the general intended than the rest of the garrison, but as he intended to hang on to his questionable commission as long as possible he had made sure the men were working hard whenever Waller or his busy officers cantered by. Well, he thought it was Waller, anyway. They hadn't been introduced as yet. William realized his field promotion must have been Sir Gilbert Morrison's last official function before he had decided to change sides, and that the order, carefully folded in his tunic, might not be worth the paper it was written on.

'Get your backs into it, that wall's got to keep those Cornish weasels out!' Will stared at the crumbling earth rampart, wondered what would happen to the men behind if it didn't.

'Cheer up, Captain Sparrow,' Eli called. 'It'll be grand for some action, all this marchin' and drillin's fair worn me down!'

There was a chorus of approval from the busy, muddy men along the wall. Zack and his brothers were working bare chested, enjoying the sun and the vigorous labour down by the river. Building redoubts was something they could lend a hand to with confidence, after all these weeks of hopeless training. The commanding officers had quickly realized they would never make musketeers from such a clumsy set of clods, and had concentrated on trying to teach them the rudiments of the pike instead. All those jeering Gloucestershire and Welsh men making out they were country bumpkins, the townsfolk of Bristol watching their efforts with a mixture of scorn and apprehension. 'You point the sharp end forward, you great swede!' 'Why have they bothered givin' 'em 'elmets? Their skulls must be three inches thick!'

The garrison officers hadn't been overly impressed either, but it was the unit's lack of numbers rather than state of training which had been the principal concern. Nathaniel Fiennes had walked along the ragged ranks turning his bullet head from side to side, his senior officers and the black-suited commissioners a whispering coven behind him. Fiennes had already received a sheaf of letters from Waller urging him to spare more men from the Bristol garrison for service with his field army. Where was he to find replacements to man the walls? Waller in his turn had insisted that it was vital to strengthen his army as the port would not hold out long without his vigilant operations in the country thereabouts. Masters Lyle and Webster had been dispatched to the city to settle the squabble over strategic and tactical priorities. They had carried out a quick head count on the poor Somerset militia Jamie had brought in, compared the number against the estimate drawn up in their ledgers.

'Eighty-seven men? Where are the rest of them?' Lyle had demanded.

Jamie, who had marched the men up from Chipping Marleward, felt the collar of his buff coat come alive about his neck, throttle the life out of him as he blinked before the dreaded inquisitors.

'A few ran off on the way up, sir. Slipped away by night.

I thought I'd best get the remnant up here as soon as I could, rather than waste time looking for them,' he explained shakily.

Lyle pursed his thin lips, ran his inky finger along the columns of figures. 'You were supposed to be raising six hundred, you've barely brought six dozen!' he snorted. 'Where's your father?'

'Settling business at the house, sir, back at Chipping Marleward. He'll be along with the rest.'

'The rest?'

The rest had turned out to be William Sparrow, captain, on his broken-winded piebald, half a dozen vagabonds, thrown out of their work at Sir Gilbert's depot in the town, and an equal number of stragglers and Fosseway wanderers who had tagged along on the promise of a hot meal. Three days later, and in the middle of another perplexing training session under the castle walls, the furious commissioners had returned, pulled poor Jamie out of the ranks and disarmed him in front of the men.

'Your father has deserted the cause! Taken the regiment's pay with him, no doubt,' Lyle had accused.

'We feel you have a little explaining to do,' Webster had added. Jamie was led away, ashen faced, and William had found himself in charge of a hundred muttering, mutinous men. Luckily for him the Pitt brothers made up in bullying what they lacked in martial skill. They had kicked and cuffed their comrades back into some sort of order while their instructor, a one-legged veteran of the German wars, had hopped about explaining how to deploy your pike against cavalry. Much good his damned drill had done him. Poor old Jamie! He hadn't wanted to get involved in the first place. Sir Gilbert's only son had been about to go up to Oxford to read law when the gathering stormclouds had finally unleashed their pent-up energy and the war had broken out in earnest. Sir Gilbert had called him into his study, announced he was going to join Parliament's army. 'I've written to General Waller on your behalf. A commission in the cavalry, what do you say to that?' Jamie had been speechless, helpless with rage.

Interrogated for two hours by the cursed, insinuating commissioners, he had finally found a voice.

'My father volunteered me for this service, that's true enough, but he'll not volunteer my treachery. I had no idea, no idea whatsoever, what he was planning.' The commissioners kept their impertinent accusations to themselves for a moment, impressed by his energetic and sincere defence. 'And if you'll allow me to return to my troops, I'll prove it, to him and to you,' he said.

'Well, that's as may be,' Lyle argued. 'But your father has had coin and provision for six hundred men.'

'And we have brought you one hundred of them. If it's the money you are worried about, I'll serve without pay. There, sirs,' he rapped their open ledger with his white knuckle. 'Make a note of that! You can't expect me to account for every pound my father has had from you.'

Lyle held his gaze, nodded. 'We expect you or your father to account for every penny sir!' he barked, snapping the heavy book shut. Jamie had pulled his hand back just in time.

'Even so,' Lyle said in a gentler tone, 'Master Webster and I have been impressed by your mitigation, and will continue with our investigations before we decide whether a court martial is necessary.' Court martial? Jamie had covered his face with his hands, paced the dripping, mouldy cell below the waterline of the keep, waited for them to make up their Machiavellian minds.

Will, meanwhile, had turned his attention from the rampart to their narrow valley. He walked along the six-foot-high bank of earth peering over the top, enjoying the fresh breeze on his sunburnt face. The redoubt had been built along the northern bank of the island between great green meadows which stretched along either side of the river. Beyond Bath the Avon had cut a narrow, winding course through the steep wooded slopes, which were only suitable for grazing sheep. The rich earth of the valley floor however nourished acre after acre of standing corn, scored and trampled by Waller's army as it marched to and fro. A company of engineers and civilian labourers was busy alongside the hastily constructed redoubt, adding the finishing touches to the bridge. It was a pleasant spot, ideal for a little fishing and a refreshing swim. Zachary had wandered after his captain, shaded his eyes as he gazed back toward Bath.

'Which way d'you think they'll come, then?' the towering, black-haired youngster wanted to know.

Sparrow shrugged, nodded back over the gurgling mill-stream which secured their rear toward Claverton Manor, a pale stone mansion squatting comfortably in the folds and ridges of the hill. 'They were at Chewton, last I heard. That means they'll be coming that way.'

One of the sappers on the wall shook his head. 'Chewton? They're at Bradford on Avon now. They'll be coming that way.' He pointed a muddy finger downstream.

Bradford on Avon? That meant they had put themselves between Waller and the London road, didn't it? Sparrow struggled to fix the uncertain geography of the area in his mind's eye, digested the information in silence.

Zack nodded, frowned. 'Well, what happens if they get on top of that hill there?' He pointed to the dominating northern slope. 'If they get some guns up on the ridge, they'll be able to drop shots right in among us,' he pointed out.

The sapper took off his helmet, wiped his filthy face on his shirt. 'Old Will's thought of that, see,' he replied, to Sparrow's evident relief. 'He's put a strong guard out on the Monkton Farleigh road, just over the rise. So he's covering the south and north banks at once. Oh yes, you'd 'ave to go a long way to find a better chooser of ground than our Will. Look at this spot now, the King's men'll have water to cross, whichever way they get at us.' He paused, shaded his eyes and peered back to the south. A column of brown-coated cavalry cantering down the hill beside the manor, switching direction to cut across the standing corn and approach the squat stone bridge over the mill-race. Sparrow shielded his eyes to try and pick out their flapping cornet, wondering whose side they were on.

A party of rogue horse, working their way through the ragged lines to take the pontoon by surprise? Will stared about him as the men went about their sweaty tasks, taking little if any notice of the intruders. The other officers were lounging about in the centre of their open-ended fort, playing cards in the back of a wagon. How did they know the cavalry were friendly? Some kind of sixth sense? How would he ever learn the difference? He was still fretting about it when he recognized Archibald McNabb at the head of his troop clattering across the bridge. The efficient-looking troopers cheered him a little as he watched them dismount on the narrow island to water their sweating horses. William waved, saw the bow-legged officer peer up at him.

'Oh, it's yoursen,' McNabb called, rubbing his backside as he marched through the trampled grass, casting a critical eye over the earth walls. Sparrow jumped down beside him, glad to see a familiar face.

'I'd heard that fool Morrison had made you up to a captain. They haven't broken you down the ranks yet, then?'

'Not yet. They've arrested Jamie Morrison, they say they might court-martial him.'

'Oh, don't talk to me about court martials,' McNabb snapped, irritably. 'And what's this lot supposed to be?' the Scots officer scowled, peered over the improvised defences.

'It's a nice enough spot, bit of fresh air.'

'Fresh air? Oh, it'll be fresh enough all right,' McNabb snorted, clearly in one of his cantankerous Calvinist moods. 'Better than Bristol at any rate. The place is like a midden in this weather, and they say there've been more cases of plague.' He hawked and coughed into the trampled corn husks.

'You seem a little put out, Archie. What's happened?'

The red-faced Scotsman wiped his flat nose, nodded belligerently. 'I'll tell ye what's happened,' he snarled. 'I've been sent out to beef up the forlorn hope over your hill there.' He nodded his rusty stubbled head toward the northern ridge. 'Just because I shot some upstart from the Prince's regiment.'

'You shot someone?'

'In battle, laddie, in battle,' McNabb corrected him impatiently. 'Outside yon Chewton place. I had him off his horse and he wouldna surrender, so I gave him both barrels. The colonel was right cranky about it, they said he'd surrendered.'

'Surrendered?'

'He had his hands up, see you.' McNabb held his

gauntlets above his head. 'But he wouldna keep still so I shot him. Where's the harm in that, we shot sixty or more men that day!'

'I thought shooting them was the general idea,' Sparrow said, perplexed.

McNabb snorted. 'Oh aye, until they're related to somebody and such, then it's quarter and ransom. The colonel was so het up about it he sent his own doctor over to treat the scoundrel!' he said indignantly. 'Sends him over and yet we lost a good dozen ourselves! Can you see the sense in it?'

Sparrow admitted he couldn't. 'Well, at least they've had the sense to put our new-raised men behind a fortification,' he said, eager to display his new-found grasp of tactics. To his dismay McNabb roared with laughter.

'They've not got you in there for your protection, sonny,' he spluttered. 'It's to stop you running away when the King's men come! Can you not see it, you're penned in like cattle with that burn at your backs, you'll either fight or you'll die, aye, sure enough!' He slapped him on the shoulder, turned back to his men. Sparrow watched him rejoin his command, leap up on to his horse. McNabb was beaming as he led his troop past the redoubt, Sparrow at bay on the crumbling rampart.

'Well, I'm glad we've given you something to smile about,' he shouted. McNabb waved his gauntlet, led his men across the creaking pontoon and on up the hill into the trees.

CLAVERTON MANOR

JULY 3, 1643

The grumbling garrison stirred sluggishly, stumbled and stamped around their earthen hold as the sun rose slowly, silhouetting the jagged treeline along the ridge. Pale streamers of mist curled and coiled from the quiet river, enticed the men down to duck their heads among the crowded lily pads or check the long lines they had set the evening before. With half of the force drawn from the west country there was no shortage of experienced poachers or foragers. Half a dozen fat eels were soon sliced into a pan, their discarded black heads twisting stiffly in the trampled earth, wide mouths silently champing the dirt. The London contingent wandered back from their ablutions, watched the breakfast preparations with evident relish.

'Billy here's caught himself a perch,' their sergeant told Zachary, busy adding handfuls of roots to the bubbling cauldron. Billy Butcher, recovered from his injuries, proudly held the two-pounder which had fallen for his juicy lobworm. 'Trouble is, he don't know 'ow ter skin it.'

'Ah that's easy, me bab. Get yourself a good ball of this clay 'ere.' Muffet tilted his head, tried to understand the farm boy's unfamiliar accent. 'Rub t'all over yer stripey look, till 'e's covered 'bout two inches thick.'

'What's he on abaht?' Butcher wanted to know, lowering the fish to his side.

'When 'e's all wrapped, like, stick'n in the foyre and bake'n about two howers.'

Colston Muffet nodded, led his section back to their place on the wall.

'What was all that about wrapping it in shit and chuckin' it on the fire?' Butcher wanted to know. 'I reckon the bleedin' swede was havin' us on.'

Muffet shook his head. 'It's an old gypsy receipt for cooking hedgepigs. Wrap 'em in clay and bake 'em till the spines come off. Applies to perch just the same.'

Butcher examined his catch doubtfully. 'Wrap it in clay?'

'Like the man said,' Muffet told him, picking his musket from the side of the cart and examining the mechanism. The sergeant and his three comrades, Butcher, Gilling-feather and the cavalryman Culverhouse, had walked nearly twenty miles over difficult country to catch up with Waller's army as it took up positions on Claverton Down. Matty Culverhouse had suffered the most. He had been badly depressed by his young comrade's cruel death at the hall, and to add insult to injury had been forced to make the long hike over the hills in his thigh-length cavalry boots. He had limped the last few miles barefoot, unable to bear the harsh leather grating on his bleeding blisters. At least his unit was still in one piece, though. Waller's cavalry regiment was the kernel of his army and had been able to build up something of an *esprit de corps*. They had already fought through half a dozen western counties, assisted to varying degrees by a constantly fluctuating set of locally raised regiments of foot, who retained little if any pride in their units. Sir William had taken his fine brigade of horsemen from the south-east into Dorset, from there to Bristol. That March he had picked up two local units, Hungerford's and Thomas Essex's, stormed Malmesbury and installed the former as a garrison. He had then marched west, thrown his tiny army across the Severn at Framilode and routed a newly raised Royalist army at Highnam House near Gloucester. The bewildered Welshmen had surrendered almost to a man, with half of them enlisting in Waller's energetic army for the next stage of the campaign.

It was hardly surprising for Colston Muffet to find himself in the midst of another gang of total strangers babbling in half a dozen regional dialects. In the few days they had been away the last pathetic shreds of their original unit – Merrick's foot from the Earl of Essex's first army – had been brigaded into the remnants of regiments from Gloucester, Wiltshire, Somerset and Devon. The canny sergeant had no idea who was in command, although the big lad he'd seen earlier with the wall-eyed horse seemed to be doing more than his share of shouting. The officer had gone very quiet though when they had led his and the other horses away to the rear, over the mill bridge and up to the main camp. Thinking of running out on them, was he? The wall-eyed piebald had made a fuss and all, tossing and bucking as they tugged him over the busy mill-race.

'He don't like water,' the officer shouted in a strong local accent. Another Bristol boy, not sure what side he was on that morning, Colston thought bitterly.

'Hold your hands over his eyes!' the big officer advised.

'I'm not puttin' my 'ands anywhere near this un's gob,' the worried groom bawled back.

'Who's that, then?' Colston asked one of the locally

raised men, limping along the rampart with a homemade crutch under his arm.

'Sparrow. They roped him in down Shepton way, Chipping Marleward, d'you know it?'

'No, can't say as I do. Sparrow, you say? Looks more like a bleedin' turkey cock to me.'

'T'other fellow's been thrown in Bristol gaol, so they say. Father's scarpered with all the loot for the regimen' an' all,' the grey-haired veteran told him.

'Cah. You can't trust any bugger, can you? Been in long yourself?' Muffet asked him.

'Not long. My boys're there cookin', I came up to keep an eye on 'em as much as anything. And if I can catch 'old the bugger who did this,' he wiggled the badly wrapped stump, 'I shall be 'appy enough.'

'A right old bunch this time,' Muffet told him, opening his tobacco pouch and offering the old timer a good pinch.

'Obliged to 'ee.'

'I'll tell yer this,' Muffet said, pointing the clay stem at the militia herded into the earth fort, 'until such time as they gets this man's army sorted, we're all wastin' our time. Those Welsh buggers now. They'll be off first chance they get. There's hardly a man here who knows what he's about.'

Gillingfeather had fallen in alongside, resting his musket with his sergeant's. Muffet closed his eyes, sighed.

'You're right there, brother,' the preacher/soldier said piously. 'The Lord's work needs must have a sober, God-fearing army of honest men who know why they fight,' he called. 'Who knows why—' There was a muffled boom from over the hill.

'What was that?'

'That was the Lord agreein' with Gilly there,' Butcher laughed. Gillingfeather scowled, picked up his musket and strode along the line to find an easier audience. Gregory Pitt pulled at his gin-blossomed nose, asked the sergeant what he made of their position.

'Of our Lord's own righteous army or this 'ere mudpie? Well, it won't last five minutes. If I were you, uncle, I'd get myself back up the river with the horses there.'

'Ah, I was . . . hello . . . there it is again. Hear that?' Colston Muffet dropped to the dirt. For a second old Gregory thought he'd been hit, but the lean Londoner had placed his ear to the ground and was listening intently. He jumped to his feet as the dull thump of gunfire was punctuated by a sharper crackle of musketry.

'That'll be the ambush on the Monkton Farleigh road,' Gregory told him conversationally.

Muffet opened his sack, selected a coil of match and patted his powder horn. 'Well, it won't be long till we get our turn. Take care of yourself now, Uncle.'

'And you too, me lad.'

Nobody seemed to be moving apart from him. The other officers, a set of careless clods still reeling from the drink they had taken while their men threw up the redoubt, had stood up and run their perspective glasses over the hills, slumped back down to their damned cards again. Sparrow cursed them under his breath as he strode along to the banked earthwork overlooking the narrowest arm of the divided river, the chattering mill-stream which fed the wheel further along the island. Gregory Pitt was squatting on a barrel, passing the time of day with a set of surly looking Londoners.

'Have a care, Greggy, they're on their way.'

Greggy tipped his hat, nodded. 'Keepin' an eye on my boys there, Will,' he replied cheerfully, taking another puff at his pipe.

Sparrow looked up and down the defences in agitation. There was only one way off Ham Meadow without swimming for it, the mossy stone bridge by the mill there. He could well imagine the scene if they were forced back from the wall. Two hundred men trying to squeeze through a bolt-hole just wide enough for one rider at a time. As far as Sparrow could make out the engineers had left them to it, as good as sealed the militia within an open tomb.

'We'll never get out,' he muttered to himself, chewing his fingernail. He turned on the London section, calmly lighting their match, checking their bullet bags and broad leather bandoliers. Each belt carried a dozen blue-painted pots which the troops called the Twelve Apostles. Each pot carried a charge of powder sufficient for one shot. They had been taught the complex drill one step at a time. First they would take a pot and thumb the lid open, tip the contents down the barrel of their musket. The musketeers would then add their lead ball and some wadding and ram it down firmly with their scouring stick. If they were careless or panicked by the enemy and didn't ram it home firmly enough the ball would pop out of the barrel with all the force of an old cork. Musketeers kept both ends of their match cord burning in case one should be extinguished. The glowing end was clamped in the musket mechanism, above a pan filled with finely grained powder tipped from their horns. To fire, the musketeer aimed and pulled the trigger, snapping the jaw shut so the glowing match plunged into the pan and ignited the fine powder.

This in turn set off the main powder charge and so propelled the ball.

At least, that's how Sparrow thought it worked. He had been more concerned with mastering the rudiments of pike and protecting himself with a sword to worry about the complex machinery and manoeuvres musketry required. Would these lazy buggers bother firing off more than a few shots? Christ's wounds, he hoped they knew their drill better than he did.

'Something wrong, Cap'n?' the sergeant asked casually. 'We've left a bucket there if it's a piss you're needing.'

Sparrow smiled thinly, nodded at the dog cart loaded with the light engineering equipment they had man-handled inside the fort. 'We need that ladder by the stream there,' he snapped. 'We'll need another way over to the bridge in case we're over-run,' he added.

The sergeant pursed his whiskered lips. 'Could give 'em ideas, Cap'n. Seein' the back door ajar, so to speak.'

'Well, then, your men will stand by and keep them back, until the order is given,' Sparrow barked with all the resolution he could command. To his surprise the sergeant nodded in agreement.

'All right, then. But if they panic they'll be off, whether we're here or no,' he said.

Sparrow bit his lip, nodded, and strode back across the crowded, rubbish-strewn fort. Cooking fires were hastily stamped out, powder barrels dragged out from the stalled wagons. The other officers seemed to have roused them-selves at last, and had distributed themselves around the ragged perimeter. The gunfire went on for another half an hour, and then gave out with one final spiteful spatter of musketry. Sparrow, clutching his newly sharpened sword alongside the Chipping Marleward contingent, estimated it was about nine o'clock. He leaned over and looked along the double rank, checked the company for the hundredth time. A dozen of them had muskets although their efficacy was open to question. The rest had more straightforward implements: pikes, looted swords or various halberds and bills. A flock of crows rose from the cowering ashes and elms along the ridge, glided off down the suddenly quiet valley.

'There they are!' Eli Pitt, who prided himself on his peregrine falcon vision, pointed over the crumbling stockade to the west. A small company of foot led by mounted officers in dark clothing, making its way between the crowding hedges along the lush meadow on the northern bank of the river. Sparrow squinted, made out squads of musketeers and a small block of pikemen, ambling along as if they were on the way to a May market. There couldn't be more than fifty of them. Surely they weren't going to attack? Eli shouted again, pointed to the ridge directly ahead. There's more of them!' Sparrow looked up to the wooded hillside, tried to pick the pikes from the tangle of hedges, the bare branches of old oaks. He couldn't see any soldiers.

'That's our lot down the meadow,' somebody called.

'They'll be cut off if they don't hurry!' Sparrow stared back over the standing corn, the black-suited officers becoming clearer every step. Lyle and Webster! Leading a procession of ragged altar boys to the slaughter! He tilted his head, heard their faint voices intoning psalms. Why in the bowels of Christ didn't they hurry? Sparrow gripped the crumbling rampart, peered back up the hill. The bare branches had blossomed with bright flags. Colours and pennants flapped and snapped in the light breeze as the enemy infantry marched out of the protecting woodlands.

Sparrow swallowed hard as three massive columns swung out of the treeline, drummers and colours ahead of bunched pikemen, files of musketeers making their way down the slope toward the bridge. There must have been thousands of them.

'Come on! The enemy are upon you!' Sparrow saw one of the other officers standing on the rampart, frantically waving his arms above his head. Lyle and Webster rode on regardless, letting their tired nags pick a way through the well-grown corn. The enemy forces on the hill looked like so many ragged-hued hares in comparison, bounding down over creeping terraces, filtering through narrow hedges, dividing around bramble outcrops like some foul biblical flood. A plague of gaudy locusts driven on by the small number of horsemen trotting alongside the three-pronged trident of men. Sparrow gazed at the hated slopes, wondered where their dreaded horse had hidden themselves. The company in the meadow would be cut to pieces by their flashing blades. Slashed to their knees along with the corn. Somebody was whistling nervously, a thin, wailing note which seemed to get louder and louder and . . .

'DOWN!' The company toppled to the trampled earth, hugged the dirt as the ball whistled overhead and splashed into the muddy ditch with a pathetic plop. There was a half-hearted cheer from the London men at the rear of the fort. And then the boom. A ragged, rolling peal like thunder over a church spire. Another and another. Sparrow peeped between his fingers, saw clods of earth raining down on the terrified company.

'Stand to, stand to!' The officer had climbed down from the wall and hurried along the terrified ranks. Major Tobias Fulke, a jaunty, white-haired gentleman resplendent in businesslike black-lacquered armour. He doubled along the inner wall with surprising agility, thwacking the cowering soldiers with the flat of his sword.

'Back to your positions!' he barked. Sparrow pushed himself to his knees, stared at his trembling hand, clamping the hilt of the newly forged mortuary sword he had picked from Sir Gilbert's improvised armoury those few weeks before. He wondered where Bella was at that moment. Picking over her breakfast, he supposed. In the Royalist camp? The thought came back to him, pricked him all over again. Bella with the enemy. He pictured her watching the action from the quiet manor house across the river, up on the roof where she would enjoy an unrestricted view. For a second, he hated her with all his heart. Somewhere up there, beyond the silent manor house, high on the wooded down, was Waller himself. Watching to see if he was worth his commission, if he was worth anything at all.

The lost company had finally realized their danger, hurried over the juddering pontoon and on to the island. They clattered beneath the wall towards the bridge over the mill stream and the safety of the main army high on the downs. The black-suited commissioners were waving their hands, shouting slogans to the open-mouthed soldiers taking cover behind the rampart. Sparrow stared down at them as if they had arrived from the moon. Bellowing incantations and encouraging the garrison to do or die with bloodthirsty quotes from the Testaments.

'Let God arise, let his enemies . . .' The rest of Lyle's prayer was drowned out by a heavier shot which came bucketing in over the cornfields, buried itself into the sharpest angle of the ramparts. There was a hush and then a sudden burst of frenzied screaming. Sparrow stepped back, peered back along the line, but couldn't see what the commotion was about. A black shadow rose on the wall above him and he practically jumped out of his skin with fright. The man jumped down alongside, grinned broadly.

'Jamie, you candle-wasting whoreson . . . you could have stopped my heart!' William gasped.

Jamie Morrison grinned, straightened his felt hat and nodded to the sooty, sweating men from his long-lost company. 'What are you doing here?' he asked hoarsely.

'They've marched half of Popham's out to reinforce Waller. Those two hooded crows raised another company by emptying the prison and pressing sailors from the harbour alehouses! They needed every officer they had!' he said cheerfully.

Sparrow closed his eyes. 'You volunteered?'

'This looked the most dangerous spot. I have to prove I'm no traitor, so here I am!'

'They've cleared you, then?'

'Not yet. I'm still under arrest, but have given my word to attend the inquiry in a week's time. How are you, Zack? All right?'

'Glad to see you, sir. I should get your head down, though.' Jamie followed the tall farm boy's advice as another culverin shot ripped the air above the smoking redoubt like an old sheet.

The attackers had halted just out of musket range, let the cannons play on the fort. The Royalist gunners had clearly found a suitable slope to unlimber their pieces. One big culverin, to judge from the intervals between the loudest bangs, and a number of small galloper guns, which could be dragged round and set up practically anywhere. The few veterans among the defenders knew full well they wouldn't do much damage through six feet of earth, but the cowering, pop-eyed recruits had no idea what havoc they could wreak. They clawed and chewed what cover they could in the reeking, drifting smoke. The enemy commanders had taken stock of the island's improvised fortifications, pulled their men back up the slope so they would have a good run at the weak works. The last culverin shot sent up a fountain of earth alongside the wobbly pontoon and the guns fell silent. William had no idea how long they had been firing but he had only seen half a dozen men stagger out of the line, make their way to the rear clutching wounds. He closed his eyes, whispered a silent prayer of thanks that his colleagues had so far stood their ground. He had courage enough to stand and fight, or at least, he had convinced himself he wouldn't be the first to run away. But he was terrified the rest of them would abandon the works, leave him facing the enemy alone. Together, shoaled in their tight earth net, he was as safe, and as exposed as the rest of them. Zack and Eli, crouching alongside him, grinned nervously, but he couldn't make out what they were saying. They had all been deafened by the barrage and covered in sooty dust so they blinked like giant owls in the thinning mist. More time crawled by like the forgotten eel heads squirming in the dirt by the breakfast fires.

Sparrow peered over the rampart and was mortified to see the enemy troops were less than fifty yards off, mighty columns wreathed by pale serpents of smoke from the guns on the hill behind them. He was at once horrified and fascinated by their casual ferocity as they stamped the stalks and ground the husks as they came on. He could pick out their pinched white faces under their brightly coloured hats. Officers stuffed and spiked with feathers and bunting, lawn and lace. Ragged breeches and dirty knees, boots with flapping soles tied with string. One column had emerged on to the meadow and had followed the broad swath made by the pressed company, another had been flung out along the eastern flank and the third had formed up directly ahead of them, advanced with pikes levelled to clear the bridge approach, swamp the tiny, fortified island.

'Don't worry, stand your ground, you've got a wall and a river they haven't,' the black-armoured old major bawled over the clatter of the drums.

'Pick 'em off, they can't get you,' Sparrow shouted, warming to his theme.

'Hold your fire!' the red-faced officer roared in response. The company twitched and chattered, standing with heads ducked down and knees bent behind the rampart. The Royalist musketeers halted, fired a brief and ineffective volley and surged forward with the pikemen, bellowing and shouting. The enemy regiment trampled the corn as they swept over the last few yards to the narrow pontoon.

'Fire!' the major shouted. A gun captain lowered his linstock to the small drake they had rolled up into a wickerwork emplacement. The blast threw out a tongue of red fire and enveloped attackers and defenders alike in blinding, choking white smoke. Sparrow coughed, squinted into the razor-edged gloom. His ears popped and he could hear the enemy wounded screaming as their comrades hurried forward before the gun could be reloaded. The enemy infantry had divided, the musketeers into the shallows, the body of pikemen to the barricaded bridge.

Sparrow's company rose up raggedly, rested their

muskets over the wall and fired. There was a splutter of shots and another surge of stinking smoke. Half a dozen Cornish pikemen collapsed into the shallows, staining and stopping the feeble flow with their bodies. The rest dashed forward over the narrow bridge, poured on to the island. They worked their way around the defences, poking and prodding the defenders back from their works. The musketeers waded the narrow river or hopped from the stepping-stone sandbars, swarmed up the earth rampart on their hands and knees. Jabbed and gutted by the defending pikemen they drew their swords or upended their muskets to join the furious mêlée. Sparrow saw a woolly hat rise in front of his eyes, prodded it away with his sword point as if it were a giant yellow wasp. Somebody grabbed his arm and pulled him forward into the earth wall. He swallowed a mouthful and coughed, pulled his arm back as more enemy troopers clambered up on the rampart.

'Back! Back to the wall!'

'What wall?'

'Back where?'

The defenders gave ground, shoulder to shoulder as they stepped backwards across the wrecked fort. More and more enemy troops poured over the earthwork, hacked and jabbed at them as they retreated in good order. Sparrow sheathed his sword, snatched up a six-foot section from a broken pike, jabbed it in the faces of the enemy soldiers. They stepped back, shouting and roaring in their barely comprehensible English. The Roundhead troops caught up behind the struggling skirmish line had abandoned their posts, doubled back toward the bridge to escape the dreadful attack. Sparrow found himself trotting back on his heels to stay in line with the grim-faced

defenders. Zack and his brothers were ramming their
boots down in the dirt, digging miniature trenches as they
thrust their pikes at the howling Cornishmen.

'Take quarter, you bastards!' 'Grind 'em into the river!'
'Drown the rebel scum!' they roared and spat, redoubled
their efforts at the stubborn line. There was another volley
of musketry from overhead and the Cornish mob recoiled,
another half-dozen hit by hot musket balls. Sergeant
Muffet, true to his word, had ordered his file to stand on
the bridge, fire over the heads of the desperate defenders.

'Now then, Cap'n, over the river with you!' he shouted.
The defenders seemed to abandon the fort in the same
instant, turning on their heels and hurling themselves at
the mill-stream like horses at a steeplechase. Some managed to leap the fifteen-foot channel, others scrambled
down the bank and waded for their lives in the strong
current. Sparrow dropped his pike, spotted the Londoners
dashing back upstream, where the mill-race divided from
the main river. The water there was slowed by gravel banks
and stands of seven-foot rushes. Muffet and Butcher
doubled across, leapt the deeper channel and disappeared
into the thick bulrushes, scrambling and hacking their way
up the other side. Sparrow switched direction to follow
but was carried away in the mad stampede as the defenders
leapt into the mill-stream, took running jumps toward the
lurching lily pads. He was knocked into a deeper channel,
panicked as he felt the heavy bodies crush him beneath
the swiftly flowing bright green water. He flapped and
kicked in desperation, tugged himself free from the mob.
A youngster in an enormous morion helmet was splashing
his arms and screaming, drowning with panic in five feet
of water. Sparrow gripped him by his civilian coat, yanked
him on across the stream and into the boggy shallows. The

youth recovered in an instant, shot off up the muddy bank like a startled rabbit without a word.

William looked over his shoulder, could hardly believe the total, panic-stricken confusion as the garrison abandoned the fort with desperate, feverish haste. Two hundred militia reduced to a few dozen screaming refugees in less than six minutes. His clothes felt like three-inch armour as he scrambled up the bank, joined the frantic mob as they raced across the meadow. A troop of horse trotted across their front, picked up speed and cantered down toward the bridge, still blocked by struggling men. He paused, caught his breath. The Roundhead troop reined in a pistol shot away from the mill-race, covered the ragged survivors as they scrambled and crawled up the bank, made off toward the rest of the army up on the down. The Royalists were cheering and waving from the captured works, their musketeers helping themselves to the powder and ball they found loaded in the abandoned wagons. Their officers sorted the tangled companies and beat their men on over the smoking island to take the stone bridge. The exhausted Cornishmen eyed the wary Roundhead horsemen across the water, held their ground. For the moment, they had done enough.

Sparrow saw the black-armoured major who had braced the men on the wall stumble up the bank, dabbing his bleeding nose with a soaking wet handkerchief. He spotted the bedraggled captain and gave him a sour grin.

'Well, that went better than I expected,' he said.

KILMERSDEN HALL

JULY 3, 1643

Mary Keziah had peered and squinted over her mistress's bare shoulder, but hadn't been able to make out much of the letter save for the *Dearest Bella* at the top. She had fiddled with a loose hem of Bella's gown, taken a brush to her hair, whistled a jig at least an octave flat until she had practically run out of breath and still the girl hadn't volunteered any news. The dark-haired maid couldn't bear the suspense any longer.

'From Master William, up at Bristol?'

Bella folded the creased paper between her long fingers, offered it over her shoulder.

'I can't imagine why they think we're so interested in their silly doings,' she scowled at her reflection in the glass Mary had propped up on the narrow chest, studied her profile. Mary glanced at the letter, but she had never been a fluent reader and soon became entangled in Sparrow's enthusiastic description of army life. She looked up, canny enough otherwise.

'I can imagine very well, miss.' Bella didn't respond. 'To impress their sweethearts, miss,' she added.

Bella swung round on her, snatched the letter back in vague annoyance. 'Don't talk such nonsense, Mary. William and I were never sweethearts,' she said, colouring a little. Mary grinned.

'But he's a fine young man, everybody round here says so. Sensible with his money too.'

'Sensible? That's one way of describing it. It's a good job he took that uniform from Father's store while he did, I'll wager he'd still be wearing that awful red suit otherwise.'

Mary bristled a little, cross to hear her own true hero slandered in such an offhand manner. 'Well, he wasn't a rich man, miss' – although he was rich enough for her – 'Old Greesham only allowed him a few pence here and there.' Bella strode over to the window where Anneliese was busy with her watercolours, listening to their conversation with amusement. Bella caught her inquisitive look, frowned.

'I think you must have painted the view from every single window of the house,' she declared, forestalling any further comment on her stalled love life. Anneliese raised her eyebrows, studied the glistening painting. As usual, the background was on a slight tilt and the trees had leaked clouds of green ink over the massed rhododendrons.

'Oh, at least twice over,' she agreed. 'I'm afraid I haven't had any diversions up here for months.'

'I haven't had any diversions either,' Bella said indignantly. 'I hardly think that upstart of a captain could divert me,' she added. Anneliese and Mary glanced at each other. 'Treating me like one of his whores,' she said under her breath.

'What'd he do, again?' Mary wanted to know, crowding up to her mistress and passing William's letter to Anneliese.

'He behaved like a scoundrel,' Bella said haughtily. 'And I shall never speak to him again.'

'What, ever?'

Bella shook her head, studied the view over the trees. It was as dull and monotonous as the panorama from her room. She had walked out with Anneliese on the breezy battlements, gazed longingly at the towers and spires of Bristol shining invitingly like bars of silver and gold in the summer sun. But the grubby streets beneath the dreamy pinnacles weren't much better than open sewers. Steaming refuse heaps where ragged children coughed and sneezed and scratched and died. Gutters and sagging beams busy thoroughfares for the armies of rats, flourishing in the sad detritus of armies of men. The long sandy walls were pitted and stuck with gaping cannon, ready to reap and rake their crop of bodies. She sighed, listened as her friend read highlights from the letter to the grateful maid.

'Your rebel friend here says your brothers are doing fine, Mary, and that they have been picked for pikemen because they are so big and strong.'

'More like they'm too stupid to work a musket,' Mary retorted, waving her on.

'*Da de da de da* they're hoping to leave the city because of the plaque . . . sorry, plague . . .'

'Plague? They say they bury a dozen a day up there,' Mary said wretchedly. 'It's brought in from the ships in the harbour, so my old dad reckons.'

'Yes . . . well his leg's better anyway,' she said, reading on, 'he's keeping an eye on your brothers, helping prepare their food. Ah. He says it's terrible.'

Mary laughed, looked up to see her mistress gazing out of the window again. She'd never be satisfied, that one. All these men to pay her court and she moped around just like Mr Thomas along the hall there. The tall masked captain gave Mary the chills. A walking advertisement for war and battle, half his face chewed off, so they said below stairs. But at least he had something to be sorry about. Bella hadn't exactly suffered, no matter what she claimed to the contrary. If she could make her own letters she would write back to poor William, if her selfish mistress wouldn't.

'Why don't we write back, tell him what's gone on with us?' she asked enthusiastically.

Anneliese smiled shortly. 'I don't think we'd better tell your friend too much about our situation, Mary. He is after all our enemy now.'

Mary looked hurt. 'Not an enemy, miss, surely.'

'Well, he's not on our side, is he? Neither is Bella's Jamie nor your own brothers. If they've joined Waller's army, they can't be our friends, can they?'

'Well, they can and they can't, miss, is how I looks at it.'

Anneliese smiled patiently. 'Well, no matter. When Mr Sparrow and Jamie and your brothers have come to their senses, and please God they do soon, we can all be friends once more.'

Mary nodded, stared through the open window, following her mistress's wistful gaze. All of a sudden the horizon seemed a long way off. Damn Sir Gilbert, for making outcasts of them all.

Ramsay knew to the core of his heart he was in danger of being sucked into this tantalizing web of half truths and hearsay, of sentimental speculation. He knew all about Morrison's wiles, but it was difficult to remain unmoved by his generous devotion to his heartfelt cause: a lasting peace for all Englishmen. Lady Margaret had propped herself up in bed every night since the merchant's unexpected arrival, lectured him to be aware of Morrison's glib tongue.

'By the Lord, Ramsay, I swear he's swindling you all over. Never mind my previous opinion of William Waller, I am sure even he wouldn't stoop as low as to employ this lousy snake as an envoy. He's another one gifted with word spinning and tale telling, but at least he's open about it. You've read his letters, they're clear and to the point.'

'Yes, dear, but—'

'He cannot in true heart betray the cause he has taken up. He's wrong, but at least he's honestly wrong. This viper, this cutpurse, this blasphemy against creation . . .'

'He has a letter signed by Popham authorizing him to treat,' Ramsay had whined, smoothing the sheets over his thin thighs. 'I've seen it, signed mind you, with my own eyes.'

Lady Margaret had shaken her head. 'Well, Alexander Popham's no better than Waller, but I suppose you would have to call him a gentleman. Though I can't imagine a gentleman would have anything to do with Morrison,' she had insisted.

Ramsay picked and worried his calico skull cap, told himself off, warned himself off all over again. And here he was being taken in all once more.

Sir Gilbert leaned back from the crowded table, rubbed his whiskers. 'Ah, Ramsay, I see you still have reservations about the draft.'

'No reservations, sir, merely the . . . odd twinge. This offer' – he picked up their smeared manuscripts, studied the revised letter – 'is almost too good to ever imagine being agreed. It's not that . . .'

'But, Ramsay.' Sir Gilbert thumped the table in his

frustrated agitation. 'We've been over this a thousand times. Treaties don't grow from seed, as well you know. We can't wave our hands and make this damned war disappear,' he said wearily, with all too evident sincerity.

His wife was mistaken about the merchant. He might have been ill bred, but he was never the conniving hound and common trickster she accused him of being. They had sat up night after night preparing a document that they might present to Waller and Hopton. If they didn't hurry the war would have moved off to Gloucester or Nottingham or over the border into Scotland, for all they knew.

'Of course Waller couldn't come right out and say, "Gilbert my friend, get yourself off to my old comrade Sir Marmaduke and knock an offer up for me." It's no good imagining he would do that any more than your friend Hopton.'

Ramsay closed his tired eyes.

'What he has given me, through his lieutenant-general Popham, is a brief note, authorizing me to treat as I see fit,' Sir Gilbert insisted.

'Well, yes, I know that. But what it actually says is that you are authorized to treat for the proper care and comfort of the wounded. I can't help thinking there's a world of difference.'

'Splitting hairs, old man, splitting hairs. Treat. That's the word. That's the ground you have to anchor yourself on, as my old tutor Eli Organ of the Merchant Adventurers told me many a time. Treat, sir. I am to treat with Hopton, through you, sir. For the life of me I can't understand why you see fit to confuse yourself with finer meanings and small print. Treat I'm told, treat I will!'

Sir Marmaduke nodded wearily. 'I don't mean to delay

or hinder the process, sir, as you know.' Sir Gilbert pursed his generous lips. 'But we must be sure of what we do. These clauses ... I cannot imagine Waller would ever agree to—'

Sir Gilbert rapped the table with his knuckles. 'There you go again, sir! Clauses! Of course there are clauses! To be struck out or written in as the conference goes on. Bargaining points, sir. Here we say Hopton gets Taunton—'

'He's got Taunton already.'

'While Waller keeps Bath,' Sir Gilbert went on, ignoring him. 'And the gist of it, sir, the only clause you need worry about, Bristol is declared an open city. Trades where it will, with whom it will and no favours to either side. The armies can retire into laager, let the men get home for the harvest. And there'll be no more bloodshed, not while we've a hand in things.'

Ramsay could picture it easy enough, the armed camps dwindling on the hills as the men returned to their homes and hearths. The guns growing rusty on the unwatched walls. They could go back to living decently, put this damned war behind them once and for all. As soon as the rest of the country saw the example they had set, the King and Parliament would be forced to get back around the table, settle their differences like responsible adults rather than village bullies. It was too great an opportunity to be missed. Waller and Hopton must be approached again, they must be nagged and heckled and persuaded to the rightness of it. And Sir Gilbert here, he had a pretty tongue for that work. If any man could do it, it would be him. With Ramsay's help, of course.

'We're wasting time, sir, even as we sit here more men are being fed into the fires.'

Ramsay wavered over the scrawled document, picked up the pen.

'Why, another day's delay could mean another thousand men never see another dawn. What a burden, sir, God give us strength to carry it.'

'Amen!' Ramsay cried, scribbled his name beneath the list of clauses.

Sir Gilbert snatched up the quill, added his name below Ramsay's.

'Made this day, July the third in the year of our Lord sixteen hundred and forty-three, by Kilmersden Hall, Somerset. There, sir. Think of the learned masters up at Oxford in a hundred years from now. Two hundred. The peace of Chipping Marleward, a byword for all humanity sir.' Ramsay got to his feet, positively twitching with feverish excitement. 'We'll send this very night, sir. One to Waller, one to Hopton.'

'Indeed we will, sir.'

'But?' Sir Marmaduke asked, noticing the merchant's worried frown.

'But, sir, faithful messengers don't grow on trees, sir. I'd take it to Waller myself but he'd hang me as a traitor before I could make him see the truth, the gravity of our position tottering as we do on the very brink!'

'You're right, of course. Well, there's Findlay, and Bates . . .'

'Meaning no offence to your honest retainers, Ramsay, but I wouldn't trust the dogs as far as I could throw them. Remember that man of mine, sent up to the hall week in week out with my precious news for you, and what happened to it, sir? Hung on a bush, sir, I'll be bound.'

'Well then, who? I cannot ask my wife or daughter to set foot in the enemy camp.'

'No, no, no. Wouldn't hear of it. You must go yourself.'

'Me? Go to Waller?'

'It's the obvious choice, you are an excellent intermediary, knowing the general as you do. He'd respect you sir, where he wouldn't me.'

Ramsay saw the truth in the merchant's wise words. 'And what of Hopton? Who'll go to Hopton?'

'Well, you cannot overlook your own son's honour, sir. He would want as much of the glory as the rest of us, I'll wager! A fine lad, a fine lad. I've said so to Bella many a time. Stoic is the word I used, I believe. Yes, a true stoic, bearing his misfortunes with uncomplaining fortitude. I could only wish my own boy turns out as well.' Ramsay nodded, embarrassed by the merchant's heartfelt tribute. Morrison leaned forward, winked broadly. 'And I'm not the only one with a high opinion of him.'

'You're not?'

'I've said as much already, have I not? My Bella, sir! She worships the very ground he walks on!'

Ramsay was startled. According to Lady Ramsay the merchant's headstrong daughter had set her cap at one of the young captains they had been treating. The wounded had all gone now, of course, apart from the unfortunates lying cold under freshly dug mounds in the corner of the paddock. They'd not be going anywhere.

'Fine girl, all her dear mother's qualities, you know. They don't grow from seed, lookers like her.'

'Quite. I am not sure Thomas is recovered sufficiently to be particularly . . .'

'Ah, now, Ramsay, you haven't seen him look at her.

He positively delights in her, sir, every time he sees her.'

Ramsay couldn't remember an occasion when Thomas had given anyone more than a passing glance, but said nothing. He had obviously missed all this interplay, being so taken up with the war, the wounded and their treaty.

'Well ... I am sure ... if we can see our way clear, we can talk of this another time.'

'I think we might have to, Ramsay. My girl's not one to stand on ceremony long.' It was the truest word he'd uttered all evening, he reflected, but this doddering fool of an inbred buffoon wasn't to know that. Sir Gilbert smiled broadly. Ah, life. Sometimes it was too easy. Even if this wretched treaty was thrown on the nearest bonfire, as Sir Gilbert sensibly imagined would be the case, the very preparation of it would have helped secure his new position as an influential and trustworthy Royalist business-man. Who said? This stupid squire, that's who. He had received secret word from Starling in Bristol that his wool was sold, and for a handsome profit and all. The coins were hidden so far under the cellar those thrice-damned black-rogue commissioners would need to burrow halfway to hell to find it. Oh yes, they had already been round to the warehouse, turned it upside-down looking for contra-band goods and hoards of gold. The last shipment was already on its way to London, but whether it would get there was anybody's guess. The coastal seas were thick with Cornish pirates, the main road over the downs prey to Prince Rupert's dashing cavalry patrols. Sir Gilbert didn't care whether the wool got to Westminster, it had been paid for whether or not. He had been a little put out to hear the rascals had arrested Jamie, but then, he had had plenty of opportunities to desert as well. It was his stubborn fault, staying in Bristol while he manoeuvred down here. The boy would always be a few steps behind his father, he reflected ruefully. Perhaps, if Bella did refuse to marry Thomas, he could interest young Jamie in Ramsay's daughter. Fine-looking wench, no doubt about it.

PART THREE

BATTLE

O Lord, thou knowest how busy I must be this day.
If I forget thee, do not thou forget me.

SIR JACOB ASTLEY

BY
THE CITY OF BATH

JULY 4, 1643

William dreaded he would die of exposure, catch some horrible, unshakeable chill and be found the next morning as stiff as a new buff coat. What a glorious end to a brilliant military career! He would have his work cut out making a brave tale of this catalogue of miserable misadventures for the *Mercury*. Why in the name of God hadn't he stuck with what he knew, scribbling drivel for the newsletters? Was this to be the end of his great crusade, freezing beside a green ditch on a windy hill? A soggy bundle with blue paws held to his sunken chest? His stomach turned over in wretched sympathy. He hadn't eaten since the morning, if you could describe a hunk of bread and cheese washed down with cold river water as breakfast. If the cold didn't get him the hunger would. And if he did ever arrive back in Bristol he'd probably be so weak he'd catch the plague into the bargain, he thought pityingly.

His clothing, soaked through by his unexpected dip in the mill-stream, hung on his freezing frame like a suit of lead, weighing him down as he trudged along the muddy lane after the rapidly retreating army. He and a couple of hundred other stragglers from the ill-fated rearguard had climbed the stiff slopes of Claverton Down as the sun sank over the hill, only to find Waller had ordered the main force back into Bath. All their spare clothing, weapons and other equipment had been trundled off with the baggage, leaving the troops hungry, cold and miserable. William had looked over his shoulder so many times he thought he must have cricked his neck. Imagining he had seen a sudden swarm of enemy cavalry behind every bush. The whereabouts of Prince Maurice's horsemen had been the principal concern of the fugitives dragging themselves wearily to the windy summit. The only sign of the enemy had been the Royalist foot, busy as insects down in the valley. They had over-run the fort, made their way over the narrow river like a giant speckled lizard lumbering down to the water for a drink. The last survivors from the débâcle by the ford had caught up with the rearguards, brought news that the enemy had established a bridgehead on the southern bank but had last been seen marching back the way they had come. All that trouble for nothing! Why didn't Waller turn and snatch the crossing back, William wondered, flapping his arms around his sodden trunk. He trudged on, Eli, Mordecai and Zachary Pitt equally downcast alongside.

'He was away with the wounded,' Sparrow encouraged, shivering. 'Greggy would have been across the stream and long gone.' The brothers had searched high and low for their missing father, and were now fearing the worst.

'Well, if 'e was with us 'e'll 'ave caught 'is death,' Mordecai muttered. ''Ow's 'spect the old feller to cadge up with us with 'is leg 'n' all?'

Sparrow shrugged, ground his white hands together for warmth. The night had hurried up the hill faster than the Royalists, and the men shivered and coughed as they stumbled along in the army's muddy tracks. Major Fulke caught up with Sparrow and gave him a cheerful grin. He had stripped down to his soaking shirt and breeches and was carrying his lacquered armour slung on his bent back. He didn't seem bothered by their defeat, the cold or the fact the army had already run out on them.

'You'd do best to get that coat off, son,' he advised cheerfully. 'Let it dry out.'

'I'm damned near freezing already,' Sparrow moaned, his right foot squelching in his remaining shoe. The other must have come off in the mill-race.

'We'll catch up with the general soon enough,' the indomitable major told him, falling in alongside. 'Your first fight, was it? You always get funny after your first fight. It's your body reacting, you see, releasing all that built-up energy. Like waking up next to a randy lass after you've broken your duck, is how I always think of it.'

William frowned, wondered how by any stretch of the imagination that day's experience had been anything like a good rogering. 'Why has he retreated, though?' he asked, changing the subject. 'Why didn't he support us down in the fort?'

'No need. He put the ambush party across the river to hold Hopton up a while, not to fight him into the ground. Hopton's also used up another couple of barrels of powder, and we've a better supply line than he has,' the major pointed out. William hobbled on, completely flummoxed. So their function was simply to be lined up in front of the guns to use up Hopton's powder, was that it? He pulled at the knotted, waxy flax on his head, his curls stuck to his sunburnt scalp. He would have to get it cut, much more of this, he reflected. A true crop-eared Round-head, and what would Bella think of him then? Fulke had rattled on about feints and thrusts, passive and active defence and tried to explain the perplexities of terrain. Sparrow had been trudging on glumly, barely listening.

'Don't fret yourself. We held them up half the day, and I reckon we hurt them as much as they hurt us,' the white-haired veteran concluded gamely.

'But they kept their weapons, we've lost ours,' William pointed out.

'We kept ours, Cap'n!'

Sparrow peered into the gloom, recognized the London contingent and their rugged sergeant, carrying their muskets barrel down to keep the weather out.

'Well, you wouldn't leave the steam off your piss without a fight, would you, Muffet?' the major asked banteringly. The men roared with laughter, depressing Sparrow even further. How would he ever know how to lead these men, he wondered gloomily. When would they ever respect him as they evidently respected the major? He hadn't run, had he? He had stood his ground as long as the next man. What was the secret? A burst of shouting up ahead broke his concentration.

The bedraggled company halted at once in the misty gloaming, tilted their heads to listen to the sudden stamping and snorting. Sparrow felt the distinct rumble of hoofs through his dirty bare foot, turned to the major in alarm. There was nowhere to hide. The empty down fell away from the muddy track on either flank. Bramble and elder bushes which would have barely sheltered an undernourished fox let alone fifty scarecrow soldiers who had lost their arms. Even the gallant old major appeared disconcerted enough to throw his lacquered armour down into the trampled filth, ready to take to his heels. The terrified mob ahead of them scattered in all directions as the first

of the enemy cavalrymen cantered down the road, glory-
ing in the instant anarchy. Sparrow stepped from his bare
foot to his torn shoe, paralysed with indecision. His reeling
brain was working too slowly to register fear. The lumbering black and white beast churned the mud with its great
hoofs, snorting and rearing, tossing its wall-eyed head.
Sparrow squinted, stepped forward with his arms held
wide as the rest of the stragglers ran off over the open
slopes.

'Jasper! Whoa, lad! You four-legged fornicator!' The
immense cob slewed around, fixing its startling transparent eye on the bedraggled youth, its black ears twitching at the familiar voice. 'I told them, keep him away from
water! He don't like water,' Sparrow yelled, reaching up
to grab the loose reins. The sweating gelding stamped and
bucked as he slapped its foam-splattered neck. 'There boy,
whoa, steady, steady!'

Sergeant Muffet stepped out of the gloomy bramble
coils, his musket cradled in his arm, shook his lean head
sourly. 'If they had any sense they'd 'ave tied the bugger
up,' he growled.

'Over a spit,' Butcher called cheekily.

Sparrow glared at them, reassured the steaming beast.
To his amazement his snapsack had remained in place,
tied over the back of the cheap dragoon saddle. He kept a
spare shirt and breeches stowed inside with other items of
kit, and was soon delightedly dragging the clothing out.
Major Fulke watched him tear off his buff coat and arrange
it carefully over the horse's broad back. He stared at the
beast's peculiar wall-eye, a frosty bloodshot ball flecked
with pale blue and grey motes, shook his head in disbelief.

'I was going to say I ought to pull rank and requisition
the beast for myself, but I think I'll walk,' he said ironically.

Sparrow shivered in his drawers as he tried to locate the armholes in his shirt, tugged it down over his head with a broad grin. He tugged on his breeches and hauled himself up into the saddle. The worn leather seat felt like a velvet throne after the rigours of his first day's action. William nudged the piebald back along the muddy track, grinning at the shaken soldiers who had made way before him. Down in the vast scooped-out bowl of the hills the lights of Bath twinkled and glittered.

The depleted rearguard traipsed into the city by the Westgate, and followed their noses into the crowded yard of the Green Dragon Inn off Cheap Street. The boisterously noisy inn looked like a great squat lantern, standing a pistol shot from the open paddocks surrounding Bath Abbey. The neatly maintained gardens were already being grazed by several score of horses while their troopers made themselves comfortable indoors. Late arrivals had been sent back along Cheap Street where they had demanded free quarter from the terrified townsfolk, or tried their luck at the stale alehouse. The doors and shutters had been thrown open to clear the foul, smoky air, the sodden stink of a hundred and more men. A score of horses were tied up to the rail, to the wheels of the stalled wagons and to the overhanging branches of the big elm in the yard. Waller's cavalry had as usual picked the best billets for themselves, a dozen cloaked troopers stamping about ensuring the scoundrel foot didn't try to make off with any of their mounts. William had recovered some warmth and his customary good spirits by the time he pulled Jasper up under the swinging inn sign, peered into a first-floor window.

'Fugh off and find yer own billet!' a cavalry trooper growled in a broad Scots accent. He and his colleagues were lying on the floor and table and had even balanced themselves like logs between creaking chairs. A serving girl in a dirty apron was stepping between them slapping their roving hands away as she attempted to collect tankards and bottles from the snoring, moaning troopers. Sparrow nudged the piebald into the busy yard as Major Fulke forced a passage through the front door, evicting a great pall of smoke from the stinkhole snug. Zachary and his brothers peered over his shoulder glumly as the officer elicited a similarly unwelcoming response from the lucky occupants.

'I've a company of men here want feed and beer,' Fulke bawled to the apoplectic landlord.

'And coin to pay for it, same as these kind gen'lemen?' he asked snidely, running a wet hand over his shining bald head. 'We don't give free quarter 'ere,' he said belligerently.

The veteran bristled, and threw his armour down in the porch. The dozing dragoon in the corner swore, turned over like a hunting lodge hound.

'I'll sign a chit, pass it to the quartermaster in the morning,' Fulke offered.

'A cheque of credit? I've a whole deck of your damned chits. Do I look like that cracked up to you?' the landlord protested, squeezing his bulk through a room full of Popham's soldiery, sleeping where they stood packed in like sardines between the hearth and the bar. The Wiltshire men had been marching to and fro all day, but had managed to miss the action on either bank.

'All right, you damned piker, a gold guinea and I want 'em fed proper!'

'I'll see what we've got left. Cold shoulder'd be about right for this bloody mob.' The landlord shoved and elbowed his way toward the steaming kitchen.

Sparrow eased his leg over the saddle bow, made himself comfortable where he was. Jasper stood eyeing the taller, sleeker cavalry chargers tied along the rail. Muffet nodded to the officer, led his file of musketeers on a fruitless mission around the improvised laager. Every last space in the yard had been taken, every rafter, bale and bucket in the adjoining barn occupied by a fitfully dozing trooper.

'Ah, it won't trouble me,' Gillingfeather growled. 'You won't catch me wallowing in an alehouse with the gin blossoms and the bloats. Where's their officer, shoo 'em out is what I say!'

'Shut yer noise, you vinegar pisser!' one of the disturbed troopers shouted down from the crowded hayloft.

'Blasphemer! Do you dare call yourselves godly men? Is this how you go about the Lord's work, stinking of ale and interfering with serving wenches?'

'Aye, when we can!' a dragoon replied from the stables with a fruity chuckle.

'Pester someone else, you Puritan prick!'

The agitator flushed red, glared from side to side at the crowd of hostile, jeering faces.

Muffet pulled him back by his coat-tails. 'Let's off down the road a while, we're bound to find a billet somewhere.' His efforts to call his squad together were cut short by the awesome arrival of another troop of horse. His jaw dropped as they trotted along the main road, four abreast, their burnished armour glinting and flaring in the light from the torches they carried.

'My God, what are they?' he asked dumbfounded as the

cuirassiers clattered past. Every man was encased from head to toe in gleaming black or bronze armour, their faces and features invisible behind closed helmets. The horses were all sixteen hands plus, great sturdy beasts with shaven manes and jingling harness.

'By the Lord above, tell me they're on our side!'

'Are they men or beasts or what?' Butcher wanted to know, peering over Muffet's shoulder at the mighty troop as it escorted a party of officers down into the town.

'Aincher seen Haselrig's boys before?' one of the lighter equipped harquebusiers asked, nodding at the formidable troop which had been raised by the MP of that name. Sir Arthur Haselrig had been a leading figure in Parliament's increasingly bitter battle of wills with the stubborn monarch. He had been one of the five members Charles had attempted to seize from the House of Commons just before the outbreak of war. But the 'birds had flown' and the King's desperate bid to halt the growing tumult against his rule had pushed many doubtful MPs into clamouring for action. A persistent and resourceful opponent with a thick mane of dark hair and round, staring eyes, Haselrig had spent months recruiting and equipping his frightening force, each man well armed with pistols and carbines, mounted on a good horse and protected by segmented steel plating.

'Eight troops of Lobsters. Get in their way and you'll know it all right,' the trooper advised. The heavily protected horsemen were given a ragged cheer as the common soldiers lined the walls for a glimpse of the newcomers. The cornets bore light green guidons with a white cloud and descending anchor.

'What's that say? Only in Heaven?'

'Only in Heaven! There! God's own soldiers!' Gillingfeather rejoiced, spreading his hands as if he had been personally invited to review the regiment.

'At last, true crusaders for the cause, not a bunch of muck-raking pot wallopers!'

Muffet frowned, eyed each super-heavy rider as if he was a bronze statue. 'All very fine and dandy, as long as Prince Rupert keeps 'isself still for 'em,' he muttered.

Gillingfeather snorted, jabbed the sneering sergeant in the arm and pointed a trembling finger at the gaggle of officers crowding behind the armoured escort.

'Look! It's the general himself! God bless you sir!' Gillingfeather waved his arms as the bare-headed general trotted by, nodding at the mass of astonished troops. Sir William Waller sat tall and straight in his fortified cavalry saddle, a pale man with an immense misshapen beak of a nose with a fleshy, crooked bridge and flared nostrils. His thin brown hair was worn long, parted over his large skull. His prominent eyes were red and ringed with fatigue. Haselrig and Popham, both wearing black armour, rode alongside looking equally drawn and pale, but they managed a smile and a wave for the delighted troopers.

'I will lift up mine eyes unto the hills, from whence cometh my help. My help cometh from the Lord who made heaven and . . .'

'Shut your trap, preachpurse.' Gillingfeather turned on his heels and struck a dragoon across the mouth with his powder flask.

'Shut up yourself, you whore's melt.'

He turned back to the procession, watched Popham lean over in the saddle to confer with Major Fulke, who had emerged from the bustling inn leading the reluctant innkeeper and half a dozen serving girls carrying trays of bread, cheese and peas, flagons of frothing ale. The men closed in about them, scrambling and stretching for a mouthful. The general's party rode on, Major Fulke running a hand over his face. Sparrow, stuffing his face with a half-pound of cheese, nodded encouragingly. The veteran frowned up at him.

'Sir William's congratulations on holding the fort, but don't get too carried away. We're to join the army on Lansdown by dawn.'

'Whggaat?' Fulke looked away as Sparrow regurgitated most of his meal in a yellow, spit-licked fusillade.

The mill-wheel creaked and grated on its immense spindle, the ancient wooden paddles stuck firmly. John Clegg, the burly miller, had hidden his family and dependants away in the gloomy, dripping cellar all day. Out of harm's way while the battles raged on either side of the narrow island. They had emerged, blinking, into the last rays of the sun, to find the hated, unwelcome fort fuming quietly to itself, burial parties working over the trampled, littered mounds. A company of pickers and pokers had found the battlefield already and were flitting from corpse to corpse, rifling pockets and stealing boots if they were any good. The Royalist troopers seemed shod with rags and strips of bark rather than good leather boots, they found to their cursing disgust. Clegg, touring his delapidated mill for signs of damage or looting, had been thanking the Lord for his good fortune when one of his sons had run around the house reporting the immense oak wheel had stopped turning. Clegg had strode over to the stream, peered into the dark rush, pulled at the jammed mechanisms until the sweat started from his brow. The wheel wouldn't budge.

'It's jammed beneath, that's what,' his foreman Abraham Pinchbeek told him ruefully, nodding down at the deep stream.

'Well I don't pay 'ee to stand 'ere watching 'er, get on down there!' Clegg commanded.

Pinchbeek stripped to his drawers and called for the family to stand by with torches as he slipped gingerly down the bank and into the cold water. It wasn't deep but the current needs must be strong, and pulled at his slippery feet. The foreman held his breath, ducked under. He emerged, spluttering, a moment later and spat into the grass.

'There's a dead soldier up under,' he reported.

'Well, drag the bugger out,' Clegg called.

''E's half in an' half out. We won't budge 'un,' the foreman replied.

'Bugger will we,' Clegg replied, striding over to the yard for a length of rope. An hour later they stood back in silence as the great wheel churned again. Lying on the grass before them was a bloated blue man in civilian clothes, a rope tied around his bruised, bloodless ankle. Pinchbeek had been forced to knot the rope around the corpse's left foot as the poor old bugger was missing most of the right.

'They must be scrapin' the barrel, sending poor gaffers like 'im out to fight,' Clegg commented. The miller's simple statement was the only funeral oration the drowned man was likely to receive.

The burial party took him, after an argument, and threw him down with a dozen and more others into the trench they'd dug beneath a twisted, shot-blasted oak. Gregory Pitt the drover had smoked his last pipe.

BY
BATHEASTON VILLAGE

NEAR BATH, JULY 3, 1643

The tiny hamlet had been over-run by the Royalist cavalry just as effectively as William Sparrow's rude ramparts a few miles down the river had been demolished by their foot. Troopers and staff officers had tied their filthy, mud-splattered horses where they could, dashed up to every stone cottage and hovel chalking their names on the splintered doors to reserve the choicest billets for themselves or their commanders. Hugo, gradually adapting to the rough and tumble of army life, had learnt his lesson the hard way. He had already spent many a night squatting in the open, trying to coax a flicker of flame from a heap of damp sticks while cannier officers relaxed in the splendour of a warm house with a good fire and a hot meal. Now, Hugo knew if he wanted a good night's rest he needed a quick tongue, a ready purse and eyes in the back of his head. He didn't possess any of those gifts but he did have the next best thing in Cady and Jacobs. The experienced troopers were widely regarded – not least by themselves – as the foremost scroungers and foragers in the regiment. They had managed to requisition a damp room in a stonemason's hut on the northern fringe of Batheaston village. The narrow beds of vegetables and herbs at the rear were dwarfed and dominated by the three-mile ridge of Lansdown, just across the valley. Six horses had already made short work of the mason's vegetable crop, and the disconsolate man sat brooding in the smoky kitchen as Cady plucked and dropped his last fowl into the pot. Jacobs stood at the open window, looking out for the captain in the crowded lane and making sure rival units knew the hut was already spoken for.

'Telling's troop was 'ere first. Yes, and bugger yer uncle too, mate!' The inquisitive cornet from Caernarvon's horse shook his head, strode off along the lane to try his luck elsewhere. Jacobs presently spotted his commanding officer lost in a rainbow-hued logjam of latecomers, nodding and dipping in the saddle as his tired charger picked his way through the crowds. The trooper waved his dirty hand.

'Hola, Captain, over here! Captain Telling, sir!' he turned, chuckled over his shoulder.

'He's dozin' along again. That girl must be shaggin' 'is 'air straight, I tell yer.'

'I don't reckon 'e's worked out where to put it yet,' Cady replied, adding a handful of pulled carrots to the bubbling cauldron.

'Oh, he's worked it out all right, trouble is Tilly's workin' it out of 'im, every twenny minutes!'

They watched the bedraggled officer guide his horse through the open gate and past the huddle of troopers relaxing by the porch. Telling slid out of the saddle like a sack of honey, passed the reins to the Gloucester man who dragged the bay around the back of the cottage into their improvised corral. The captain paused at the door, looking around the drab room nervously.

'Evenin', sir!' Cady called cheerily, sipping the soup and licking his lips.

Telling smiled weakly, yawned. 'Matilda's not around

tonight, is she?' he asked, stepping into the snug and removing his hat. His long brown hair was waxy with dirt, his shirt sticking to his wiry frame, his breeches practically fused to his backside. The girl had attached herself to the captain since his return from convalescence at Kilmersden Hall, and had quickly exhausted his supply of shillings as well as his energy. She insisted on darning his shirts and collecting his rations, attending to his every need. When she wasn't working, that was. He had tried to persuade the girl to give up her day job, but she had smiled radiantly, shaken her tousled head and eased her pert breasts back inside her straining bodice.

'I can't be leechin' on you for ever,' she had told him sweetly. In other words, she'd had all his money and needed alternative incomes. She usually managed to return to his billet before midnight, however.

'Shaking the poor splinter awake for a session on the house,' as her old drab Peg said crudely.

'Haven't seen her since last night, sir. D'you want one of us to run along and fetch her?' Jacobs asked casually.

'Good God, no. I mean, that's all right.' Hugo studied the morose mason for a moment, threw his hat on to the dirty bunk pushed against the far wall. The middle-aged artisan didn't waste any breath protesting about the unwashed invasion. He was hoping the buggers would be off just as quick as the other lot had been the day before. Providing free quarter for a houseful of troopers could wash a man out. Waller's army had been to and fro a few times, but the mason's house was a good walk from the road, and he had kept his door shut until then. Now he had the King's men to contend with, rumoured to be the worst robbing rascals of all. They had marched and fought all day and needed to rest and regroup, attend to their assorted wounds. It was the misfortune of the poor country folk of Batheaston that the Royalist commanders had pinpointed their village as their rendezvous for the night.

The King's army had exhausted itself that day, marching a good ten miles, fighting two determined rearguard actions and mounting a vigorous pursuit across difficult, hilly country. They had set out at dawn from Bradford on Avon, advanced along the northern bank of the river toward Bath. The cavalry going ahead with the foot, artillery and baggage bringing up the rear. They had only been marching an hour or so when the scouts had wandered straight into one of Waller's fiendishly clever traps.

The Bradford road divided at the tiny crossroads of Farleigh Wick, with one lane leading north toward Monkton Farleigh and the southern track dropping away toward the river. The scouts quickly noted the enemy's earthwork alongside the ford, and anticipated Waller had thrown troops over the Avon to occupy Warleigh Hill, the heavily wooded ridge which dominated the crucial crossroads they could see ahead of them. If the army was to continue its march to Bath it would have to follow the narrow, overhung lane along the foot of the hill, exposed to an ambush or sudden charge out of the trees. A troop of dragoons had been ordered over the crossroads to clear the tangled undergrowth bounded by a dry-stone enclosure. The grumbling riders advanced in cautious leaps and bounds but had barely gone a hundred yards before the wood erupted with smoke and fire as the enemy troops concealed behind the wall sprang their trap. An overture of musketry heralded the dry crack of a small drake, knocking several of the dragoons from their cheap saddles.

Two were killed and six injured before the survivors spurred back to the main body.

A troop of horse had been dispatched to work around the enemy held enclosure, only to be charged in the flank by Roundhead cavalry on fresher horses from further up the slope. Annoyed at the delay, Hopton had leapfrogged musketeers from the main force stalled on the road to support the cavalry. They had worked their way forward firing from whatever cover they could find. Weight of numbers soon forced the Roundhead horsemen back, and seeing they were about to be surrounded the ambush party in the woods took to their heels up the steep slope, making off north towards the deserted village over the ridge. Deprived of their cover they had no choice but to run for their lives or be overtaken by the advancing Royalists. They had run all the way to Monkton Farleigh, working their way from one hedge to another with the enemy on their heels. Hurried and harried into Batheaston by noon, they hadn't drawn rein or breath before they arrived on Lansdown ridge that afternoon.

Back at the disputed crossroads Hopton was well aware of the dangers of allowing Waller to retain his pontoon bridge and guardian redoubt. If he was allowed to keep the bridgehead the wily Roundhead could hurl fresh units over the river to attack the exposed flank as the Royalists pressed on towards Bath. Hopton had sent the dour Prince Maurice swinging down the southern track to seize the crossing over the Avon. He had then spurred on after his cavalry, rounding up some of the enemy musketeers who hadn't managed to out-distance the pursuit. The general had allowed his horsemen to pursue the fugitives through Batheaston and then swing south, only ordering the recall at the foot of Lansdown. The long escarpment ran away west from Bath toward Bristol, the steep slopes and narrow hedges already manned by growing numbers of enemy troops. One good charge might have carried the ridge and denied Waller one of his precious hills, but the horses were blown and the regiments had fragmented during the exciting steeplechase from Warleigh Hill. In addition the exhausted Royalists could see Waller's army in battle order on the green downs across the valley, a large number of cavalry and several regiments of foot which looked like stacks of bricks in the lush fields. The Roundheads were leapfrogging units from Claverton Down to Lansdown to block the Royalists' surging advance. General Hopton, more than satisfied with the day's work, had decided to call the men back to Batheaston and wait for Prince Maurice to return with the bulk of the infantry from their fight at the ford. The trouble was, not all of the Cornishmen were quite ready to join him.

Colonel Maurice Butler's belligerent footsloggers had been first across the juddering pontoon, as eager as ever to get their paws on Waller's proverbially overloaded wagon train. The ragamuffin regiment had made short work of the defence, scrambling up the earthen embankment and turfing the panicked militia from their daft fort. They had endured ineffective volleys of musketry and one shot from a small drake which they had promptly captured and turned on the fleeing enemy, to demonstrate their superior gun drill as much as to inflict any casualties. They had left a few barrels of powder and a pile of neatly stacked balls, but precious little of interest to the sooty Cornishmen. Jethro Polruan had upended his musket, hammered and clubbed the lily-livered defenders out of the way as he led the mad charge through the ruined camp, turning wagons over, rifling pockets. The Roundhead cabbages had left nothing but wrecked weapons and broken kit. The powder supplies might be good news for the commanders up there on the ridge but Polruan's men weren't planning on loading themselves down with excess weight when there was loot to be had. Jethro kicked an empty basket into the mill-stream, eyed the troop of enemy horse Waller had sent down from the ridge to cover his retreat. He called his file to order, lined them up and began blazing away at the Roundheads, who jumped a little at the sudden volley but started laughing and jeering when their shots fell smoking into the trampled grass, well short of the mark.

'Stop your firing, men, you know damn well you wouldn't knock the skin from a milk pudding at that range!' Butler bawled, striding over the wrecked island and knocking their smoking muskets aside. Polruan wasn't about to be denied his chance to catch up with the enemy baggage train that easily. He leaned on his musket, scowled at the familiarly flushed features of his colonel.

'They'm get'n away up th'ill t'ward that house thar,' he protested, his pirate eyes smarting from the powder smoke. 'Those harseboys won't bide us long if we face 'em out a lick.'

'We're down to our last few barrels of powder and you fools go picking firefights with a beaten enemy!' Butler yelled, his moustaches quivering over his wet red mouth. 'Get your file together and prepare to defend the work,' he ordered, swinging his bloody sword around the trampled corn stocks for extra emphasis. The giant Cornishman hesitated to disobey a direct order, waited until Butler had strode off cursing to confer with Prince Maurice. The

Prince was walking his black horse around the wrecked earthwork in absentminded circles, as if he was amazed he could have ordered such whiplash destruction, unleashed such a fury of fire and death. Polruan thumbed his pocked nose, nodded at the pikemen who had collapsed into the trampled grass for a well-earned rest.

'Simon Shevick, you prickless clot, get those pikes over the bridge!' he called.

Shevick, idly picking a broken tooth from his bloody lantern jaw, leaned heavily on his pike and shook his head. He was as tall as the musketeer and twice as wide, his wild hair flattened by his badly dented morion helmet.

'I didn't 'ear 'im say anythin' 'bout crossin' the stream,' Shevick called back. His men had borne the brunt of the enemy fire, taken the enemy roundshot through the belly. Seven of them had been killed crossing the bridge, their comrades stripping them of buff coat, boots and baccy before rolling the blasted bodies into the bloody ditch surrounding the Roundhead position.

'Not first goin' off no, I grant yer,' Polruan growled. 'But there's a mill downstream and a big 'ouse up th'ill thar, fat as calves, they'll be, some Purton gentryfolk with a cellar full of coin, aye.'

The pikeman sat up, listened as the big musketeer strode through the tired ranks.

'North Zumzet's always been hot for the Parliament. Wily Will's been camped on this 'ill a fortnight, and you know's well as I they London Johnnies won't leave their mams without their creature comforts!' There was a chorus of agreement as Simon Shevick stood up and peered into the gathering gloom. Night was hurrying up the valley to blot the fire and the blood from view. Shevick could just make out the Roundhead cavalry's gleaming breastplates as they escorted the last of the fugitives away up the hill, so many shepherds at the sheep dip.

'They might turn nasty now, Jethro, them up slope an' all,' Shevick worried, adjusting his baggy breeches to relieve himself noisily.

'Those candle-wastin' bell-wethers? Get on with you! Cross the river and they'll be off like 'ares, and we can have a look round big 'ouse yonder.' Shevick pursed his lips, kicked his tired section to their feet.

'Ah now, 'ere we go,' Jethro cried, hastily reloading his musket.

'Judd, boy, you keep a match burning there, rest of us'll take light from yours if they get funny. We don't want to light ourselves up like whorehouse windows now, do we, lads?'

He whistled the rest of his men into order, formed up behind the pikemen as they followed the greasy, rutted track over the meadow and hurried over the mossy bridge. Further up the hill the Roundhead cavalry peeled off and cantered for the ridge, leaving the last of the fugitives from the ford to sprint for the cover of the woods. The Cornishmen yelled and catcalled, doubled up the slope towards the dimly lit manor house. They were practically at the door when Butler galloped up on his lathered horse, cursing them blind and thwacking his miscreant infantry with the flat of his sword.

'Back! Away from the house! Polruan, you sack-bloated bastard, I told you to hold the fort, not pursue them!'

Polruan, halted in his enormous broken-soled tracks, rolled his dark eyes and muttered hair-raising Cornish oaths under his feral breath.

'Mind your tongue, you forest ape, or I swear by all God's books I'll have it cut out of your foul mouth and fed to the dogs!' Butler called, walking his horse from side to side before the angry mob.

The giant Cornishman raised his musket toward the officer on the prancing horse, his generous mouth a twitching snare.

'Ah, that's it is it? Shoot, damn your eyes, if you dare draw a bead on me! But I've warned the Prince what you're about, and he'll have his cavalry ride your ape faces into the shit before you've done!'

Polruan glanced down the hill, the island barely visible now the last fuming fires had been stamped out. A couple of torches blazed by the earthwork, illuminated a huddle of staff officers studying a map over an upturned barrel.

'I don't see no harseboys, Colonel,' he said menacingly.

'Back to the river, haven't you spilled blood enough this day?' Butler scolded, sensing the tempestuous battalion had taken a step back from outright mutiny, and were their usual surly selves once more.

'If you can't keep still you can lend a hand with the burial parties. There's a dozen of theirs as well as ours to plant before we're done.'

Bury bodies when there was a King's ransom of loot just waiting at the treasure house over the hedge? Polruan's feet wouldn't move. The men were twitchy though, Simon Shevick grumbling on about securing bridgeheads and suchlike. What about their loot? The brigade needed some new blood, a real soldier giving the orders, not some jumped-up ninny of a squire's son. He cursed and grumbled as the men fell back from the manor, wandered back down the hill toward the bridge. Butler walked his horse around the back of them, herding the maybe mutineers back to the broken pen. They stacked arms and rolled their sleeves, traipsed off to help bury the stripped blue bodies.

'And Polruan,' Butler called, 'seeing as you're so fresh for action your section will mount guard duty tonight, and woe betide you if I catch you napping, you dozy bloat!' Butler held his burning gaze for a moment, turned his horse and spurred across the churned meadow. Polruan watched him disappear into the gathering gloom, running his thumb over the warm, sooty rim of his musket barrel.

They had been at it for days now. Drafting and amending their wishful petition. It was only right young Thomas should have a look at it. Sir Marmaduke Ramsay had followed the merchant's sensible advice, and gone upstairs to persuade his son to cast his soldier's eye over the inky object of their labours. Thomas had eventually been enticed from his lair having agreed to come downstairs and review the Domesday document his father had set such store by. He had read the treaty, wondered how Sir Marmaduke could have been so easily duped by the cunning serpent of a merchant. Sir Gilbert had stood back, watched from under his bushy brows as Thomas digested the list of clauses, each more outrageous than the last. It had been hard enough holding Morrison's loathsome stare, but he could not look at his father, nodding pathetically, willing his son to throw up his hands in mute wonder. How could Waller and Hopton reject these offers? How would they keep their faces straight, was more to the point. They had spent the last weeks scribbling this nonsense? They might as well have danced jigs in the kitchen, the good this wretched paper would do. Standing in his father's cold study, the shutters creaking over the hastily patched breaches in the walls, he had realized, accepted at last what he had fearfully suspected these past months. That his family, the great Ramsay clan which had held sway over the hills since the days of King John, would be blown away, rendered and reduced by these changing ages. Destroyed utterly by the revolution Charles Stuart was desperately staving off. How could they hold off the great flood of mercantile wealth, claw back the power their new wealth bought? The King could no more stop the flood than Canute could turn back the tides. Looking at Sir Gilbert's livid, greasy folds was to see the face of progress. Power and money in a grubby, blistered fist.

His father would have been horrified by his gnawing doubts. Cheerfully insisted their blood would run strong for generations yet. But here he was being hornswoggled by a backdoor tinker, a cheap trader with a quick eye and a sharp tongue. It wasn't the first time the merchant had outmanoeuvred his father, baffled him with his conjuring-trick dealings. Sir Marmaduke, terrified by his memories of the wars in Germany, gripped by his obsessive mission to stop the bloodshed at any cost, had allowed himself to be steered like a Judas goat by the damned rogue, played like a fish into the merchant's faultlessly knotted net.

'The beauty of it is it leaves so much alone, do you not see? All Waller has to do is draw the garrison from Bristol, leave the city be. He will in all probability jump at the chance to increase his field army, he was never one for sitting around or setting sieges, was William.' His father shook his head, over-ruled by his unreliable memories. 'The armies stay where they are. Melt away to their homes while their masters come to the table, come to their senses!' Sir Marmaduke declared, rattling the sheaf of papers in his trembling hand.

Sir Gilbert, gazing intently at the masked captain, read Thomas's thoughts. 'Ah, but your boy's canny sir. He's not convinced, I can see it in his eyes.' Well, he couldn't very well see it anywhere else, his features wrapped in the velvet bag. Sir Gilbert thanked his stars the boy was dumb, he would have had a tougher task talking the fool's whelp around to his line of thinking. But he could read the boy's glance, guess at the shallow oceans of his doubt. To know one was beaten, to know one's future was a worn stair carpet to nowhere, the merchant mused, stifling an ironic laugh. Ah, the lad wouldn't bear it. They had no spunk, these Ramsays. They had left their grit on a dozen bloody fields over the centuries, and now they were no more than dust wrapped in living skin. Shrouded ghosts like Sir Marmaduke. Sir Gilbert took the papers, shook his head.

'Thomas is right. We fool ourselves with our clauses and offers. They'll fight on to the end of everything, they'll tear every village and hamlet, every church and chapel to the ground before they put their damned pride and prejudices aside.'

Sir Marmaduke's gaunt features paled, as translucent as the racked wings of a cabbage white, a tiny dab of colour beneath each blinking eye.

'Sir Gilbert ... Thomas, you are mistaken. We have a duty to pass the treaty on, to save something, at least,' he reasoned, stung to his goodly core by the merchant's sudden change of heart. 'Sir Gilbert, you said yourself, peace will be harder to declare than the war proved to be. Surely we cannot pick up our swords again until we have worn out our pens, aye, and our tongues!' he said with feeling.

Thomas glanced at his father. A washed-out old hen-peck, just as the servants, the washerwomen, the children playing under the walls maintained. Despised by the village they had once owned. Dominated by a guttersnipe trader who only bothered to wash his hands because he had heard tell gentlemen did so. And here he was, the scion of that noble house. A weak, sickly boy who had found even his twin sister's rough and tumble games too trying. Who had run crying from Bella's scorning tongue a dozen times. The war had been a Godsend, for him. It could have turned him into a man, given him the strength and the knowledge to find a place in this turbulent and changing world. He could have ridden back from Edgehill with men at his back and a sword at his side. He could have made Bella an offer then, her father greedy for the connections their name would have lent his lowly born family. But that bastard on the wagon, defying him and the King to the very end of his miserable existence, had blotted out his hopes and dreams, stolen his future as effectively as if he had strolled up and put a bullet into his feeble brain. What son was he now? A scarred monster, a curious Caliban pacing his room afraid of his own shadow. Ashamed of his diminishing breed, unable to help in this damned war, his family, his people's last desperate struggle with the titanic forces of tomorrow. The Morrisons and the rest.

'Thomas,' his father pleaded, eyes welling with sincerely struck tears. But even his all too evident despair, his truly held conviction he was doing right, rang hollow in Thomas's scorched ears. Clanged discordantly playing Sir Gilbert's hatefully inventive, precocious new tunes.

'You mustn't give up hope,' his father implored him. 'Take the treaty to Hopton, I'll go to Waller. We'll bring the old buzzards together whether they like it or not!' he cried.

'Aye, what have we got to lose?' Sir Gilbert chimed in. 'At least we'll be able to say we tried, tried talking some sense to 'em. A body couldn't do less for his fellow man.'

Satisfied he had snared the squire with his quicksand confidences, Sir Gilbert decided it was time to launch a diversionary attack on his silent son. Thomas Ramsay was a damn sight sparkier than his father, and he would need a more subtle approach to bring the boy around to his way of thinking. Rather than trust his own powers of persuasion, he decided it was time to wheel up the heavy artillery to undermine the boy's scowling defences. In other words, if he couldn't beat him, he would join him – or at least be joined to him. By marriage. No more veiled insinuations, he decided as he strode purposefully down the hall towards his daughter's room. It was time to come right out with it.

Bella certainly hadn't felt up to her father's knockabout banter just then. She had been rummaging in her trunk when he knocked and let himself in. She watched him as he strode around the guest room, admiring fittings and the wonderful view from the window. She had been packing her clothes for the journey back down the hill to their deserted home, depressed by their pointless flight to Kilmersden Hall, exasperated by their virtual imprisonment, annoyed at Telling for stalking out on her. Back with his red-headed whore no doubt, drinking and wenching with the worst of them while she dawdled up here. She had been somewhat tearful that afternoon and had sent Mary away with Anneliese while she packed, glad of the time to think.

'Ah, fine spot they have here, nice bit of land if only

they had a manager with an ounce of sense instead of a gang of forelock-tugging buffoons,' Sir Gilbert began by way of a preamble.

Bella sighed. 'What have you got in mind, Father?'

'In mind? Me? Why, nothing, my dear. Leastways . . . that is, Ramsay and I have been talking. He's noticed the way young Thomas has been fawning after you.'

'Really? I can't say as I have,' she snorted.

'Reckons you've worked wonders for the boy, got him back out and about. Stopped him brooding. It's terrible, what with his burns and all, but he's not the only one to collect a scar or two and he won't be the last, will he now?'

'He might be, if the generals accept your treaty,' Bella said innocently. Sir Gilbert's eyes twinkled merrily. Ah, she was his daughter all right. A chip off the old block there, not like that blockhead Jamie, off with the militia in Bristol.

'What I mean to say is this. He's done his bit, nobody could ask more. You might have half a hundred fine young captains come calling on us now, but if the war goes on they're as likely to come home the same, if they come home at all.'

'Come to the point, Father,' Bella said flatly.

'Well, what do you think of the lad, Bella?' he asked at last. 'As upright a fellow as you could wish to meet. Pity about his head, obviously,' he went on, answering his own question.

'Obviously, Father,' she had breathed, warningly.

'But there again, a few scars and burns aren't hereditary, are they?'

'Spit it out, Father dear.'

'I'll spit nothing, my dear. Gentlemen don't spit these days. I was merely observing. You wouldn't have noticed but I've been watching him you know, keeping an eye on him and you.'

'Then you will know better than to tell tales. You have seen nothing pass between us which could have been interpreted in anything like the light you have,' she scolded.

Sir Gilbert held up his pudgy hands. 'Don't be so hasty, my dear. I wouldn't find fault if you had grown to admire the lad. Bears up very well, considering. Very noble. Of course, it's in the blood.'

'You've always said their blood was thinner than watered wine,' Bella corrected him, irritated by his ridiculously obvious approach. Why not come straight out and say 'you're to be married anyway' and have done with it?

'The point, my dear? Well, it's this, in a nutshell. Fine young men like Thomas don't grow from seed. Now he's back and his face is like as not messed up a bit, but he's his father's son and he'll inherit all this. With all my hard work and slaving, I'll finish this war as I started it, an honest merchant, comfortable enough, aye, but no prospects. Now once this war's done with the big houses will all be open again and the young bucks'll be out looking for a good lass. Now you might be prettier than most girls, but I can't see 'em coming to our door before they come up to places like this, can you?'

Bella had reddened, stared at her hands.

'I'm not knocking you, of course, just saying it like it is. These gentry, they stick together, see. They won't give the likes of us the time of day, once we've fought their damned war for them, put them back in their big houses.' Sir Gilbert had snorted with disgust. 'Can you imagine the Ramsays dropping in for the evening? Trying to hold a ball in our drawing-room, why you wouldn't get more than three couples around that ... what's wrong, my dear?' Bella had ground her lips together but hadn't been able to stem the flow of tears down her flushing cheeks. 'There now, girl, what have you gone and got yourself in a state for now?'

'Well, I might just as well court one of the Pitt boys, hadn't I, Zack's always been fond of me, I know!' she cried, wiping her wrist under her nose and tugging up the counterpane to dab at her puffy eyes.

'Zack? Who's talking about Zack? I haven't mentioned Zack!'

'Well, you've said as much, nobody else will want to visit us in that horrible house down there! I might as well marry William! He doesn't mind visiting.'

Sir Gilbert paused, wondered if his canny daughter was pouring vinegar in his wine deliberately. 'Pull yourself together, girl, I said no such thing. What I said was, young Thomas would be a fine match. He's here now and he's not likely to go away what with his face hanging off and all, and I know damn fine the Ramsays need a good marriage with some prospects, if they're to hang on to this place.' Bella was sobbing freely. Sir Gilbert wondered if he had gone too far, twisting her arm when she was down and all. 'And let's not beat around the bush: we need prospects too. Mrs Thomas Ramsay, mistress of all this! If that's not fine enough for you I've gone wrong somewhere!' he declared.

Bella frowned. She hadn't thought of things quite like that before. Bella Ramsay, mistress of Kilmersden Hall. She thought of Thomas in his blue mask, shook her head.

'I couldn't love him, with his face all burnt off,' she protested. 'I'm not sure I could even bear to see him, without it.'

'Well, you won't know that until you try, will you. Where's your Christian charity? You'll only marry some pretty boy Narcissus, is that it?'

'I'll marry who I like, not for you,' she retorted fiercely.

Sir Gilbert sat beside her on the bed, clutched her slim white hand in his great paw. 'Bella, Bella. My own Angel. Would I drive you to a loveless marriage? Well? No, of course I wouldn't. You'd grow to love him, same as your dear mother grew to love me, with all my faults. Good men don't grow from seed, is what I always say. Don't judge a book by its cover.'

'Better the devil you know,' she said simply.

'Better the devil you . . . what d'you mean by that?'

'Nothing, Father. It's academic anyway, as we're returning home tomorrow. I shall not have a chance to get to know your precious Thomas if he's riding out tonight, will I?'

'He's not my precious Thomas, Bella, and . . .' He slapped his pudgy hands on his thighs, got to his feet. 'Well, in any case, it's not my future we're talking about. I'll see you tomorrow,' he snapped, stomping out of her room in a huff.

Bella sat for an hour, brooding about what he had said, and what he hadn't said. He was right in one thing though. She would never know poor Thomas's worth unless she made an effort to get to know him a little more. He might not be so bad. Certainly he would love her to the ends of everything, for showing such selfless sacrifice, taking pity on him. He would worship her, endlessly indulge her idle fancies. She made up her mind. Adjusted her dress, checked her reflection, and hurried along the hall to his room.

*

Thomas had taken out his riding coat and eased his leather baldric over his shoulder. He drew the heavy sword from the leather scabbard and was examining the notched blade when there was a quiet knock at the door. He imagined it was his father, with some last store of good sense for him, but he was amazed and disconcerted to see Bella in the doorway, framed by the lamps in the hall.

'I'm sorry to trouble you, Thomas, but I didn't want to let you go, without a word.'

Without a word? What words would she have for him? He squirmed before her beautiful, awesome gaze as he had squirmed many times in the past. Startled by the bewitching apparition, he realized he had taken off his mask and quickly turned his back on her, snatched it up from the table. Bella stood like a Venus on the threshold, willing her features to ice. Willing her eyes and lips to stone. She had imagined he must be badly burnt, the way he scowled and scuttled with the velvet bag over his head. She was not prepared for the crisped black skin, the horrible tufts of hair around his grotesquely melted ears, nor the roasted, turkey skin of his neck. In a second he had snatched up the mask, tugged it over his abominable features. She couldn't speak. Apologies, tears, screams of horror piling up in her throat. She swallowed them down as if she was eating a hedgehog, even managed a tiny smile.

'I didn't mean to startle you,' she said, the barest tremor in her voice. 'I didn't realize ... do you mind if we talk for a moment? Without our fathers hanging on our every word. My every word,' she corrected, flushing. Her every word right enough. He could hardly exchange small talk with her now, could he? Bella watched him as he stepped from one boot to the other, flicking his sword

249

in agitation. She closed the door behind herself, stepped into his room. A bare box with a bed and a scattered heap of books. He moved to the window as if he was retreating from an advancing army, a superior, elemental force.

'Are you going soon?'

He nodded.

'We are going back to the house tomorrow, to see what they have left us,' she said wistfully. 'It was kind of your family to put us up, in all our troubles,' she said, wondering whether she should try and catch his eye or modestly look away, spare his blushes beneath the horrid mask. She thought suddenly of Hugo, his boisterous, nervous smile. Dumped on his behind in the refuse heap at the back of the house he had seemed like a silly boy, and then, in the wood, a wild-eyed goblin creature, tearing at her with his trembling lips and vile tongue. Hurrying in close, forcing himself at her as if he were putting a horse to a fence. She blushed, wondered how different Thomas would have been without the mask, without the wounds. How different he would have seemed if he had been in Hugo's shoes, under the dripping eaves of the wood. His wood. Would he have been the husband her father so desperately wished? Bella had thought about all the things she could say to him, how she would have to keep the conversation going. Now she realized with a start she had been staring into space for minutes, leaving him hopping by the window.

'It's still early days yet,' she encouraged quietly. 'For your injuries, I mean. They are bound to get better, in time.'

He stared blankly at her, picked his wide-brimmed

hat from the table and settled it over the close fitting mask.

Bella gathered it was time to leave.

Thomas Ramsay rode alone, as befitted one without hope. His life, his dreams had been burnt and scorched from his heart just as the exploding powder at Edgehill had eaten up his face. Eaten up his innocent, frail good looks and left him with this hideously knowing death's head. This loathsome mask Bella had recoiled from as if he was a troll from the underworld, a tattooed imp from Satan's hottest furnace. He had imagined the cunning old merchant had said his piece in his father's study, but the bastarding hound hadn't finished with him. Sir Gilbert had sent his damned daughter along to trample the last of his defences, to scour the garrison of his spirit, eat up his soul. At least he was away from Bella and Sir Gilbert and his nasty little schemes. How would he ever have the courage to face them again? He closed his eyes, forced himself to concentrate on his thankless mission. A day's ride should see him catch up with Hopton to present his pathetic petition. The various stragglers and travellers passing through the village had reported Waller at Claverton, Hopton at Bradford on Avon. He had ridden with his father as far as Odd Down, where they had gone their own ways to the respective camps. Thomas had ridden into Bradford on Avon, found broken-down wagons and occasional stragglers but no sign of the main army. The curious, resentful townsfolk had shaken their heads, pointed up the north road.

'Follow your nose, sir. You won't need a map to find 'em,' a red-faced trader had told him as he struggled up from his cellar with a crate of bottles. Thomas had wondered about finding an inn for the night and completing his journey the next day, but he had decided against it. Surely they couldn't be that far? Six or seven miles a day was generally reckoned to be good progress for an army on foot encumbered by baggage and artillery. And if Hopton had headed for Bath like this belligerent merchant had said, there would be a battle any day, tomorrow even. It was late afternoon and his horse was fresh. He could catch up with the army before nightfall. The fat trader dusted himself off, glanced up at the masked stranger.

'It's killing hot,' he said, wiping his brow. 'Will you not come in and take a glass, sir?' he asked, knowing full well the army had eaten him out of house and home for three days and he needed to make some cash back, as quickly as possible. 'The wife does a mutton pie you'd die for,' he offered. Thomas was hungry, but he couldn't eat with the mask on, and wasn't about to take it off in front of a room full of staring peasants. He shook his head, touched the brim of his hat and spurred the horse on down the cluttered street.

He took the high road over the hills, glad of the solitude of the empty, rolling downs. The sun was sinking slowly as he came down the hill to the crossroads at Farleigh Wick. His horse snorted, pulled to the left away from the trampled verge. Heaps of ragged clothing, scattered paper and broken weapons. The detritus of a battle. He halted, took off his hat and lifted the mask. He knew that smell. Brassy, sickly blood. A slaughterhouse stink. He urged the horse forward and spotted the carcasses. Three dead horses had been stripped and butchered, their gleaming bones and blue and red entrails knotted with clusters of feeding flies. The horse shied from the horrible heaped flesh, and Thomas looked up and around. A smashed gun carriage beside a broken-down enclosure wall. He looked down to the river, saw the abandoned pontoon and trampled rampart. Even in the gathering gloom he could see the fresh brown earth where they had buried the bodies.

Thomas replaced the mask, settled his hat and kicked the horse down to the river. He let it drink at the trampled ford, noting more broken weapons, discarded shoes. He rode over the creaking pontoon, around the partially demolished earthwork and on across the island. He crossed the bridge and paused once more, then trotted up to the lower Bath road. The track was heavily rutted, the verges trampled by hundreds of feet. He rode on. He paused at a dimly lit hovel on Claverton Down, noticing three ragged horses tied up to a gnarled apple tree in the tiny garden. Poor cavalry mounts, but whose? He was debating whether to ride on or risk shouting when the door opened releasing a rectangle of yellow light and a tottering old woman dragging a bucket. She straightened slowly, tipped the bucket over the broken-down wall. There was a series of excited snorts and grunts as the pigs found the foul food. Human blood and scraps of tissue she had snipped from the Roundhead dragoon indoors. He and his colleagues had been attached to Major Dowet's ambush party. Finding themselves out-distanced by the better mounted Royalist cavalry, they had abandoned the road and ridden into the woods, hidden themselves as best they could until the enemy had ridden on. The dragoon had taken a pistol ball in the thigh, but the lead bullet had missed his femoral artery. He might limp, but he'd live. The old woman gave a small cry as she spotted the masked stranger.

'Heavens protect us, it's a warlock!' she exclaimed. Thomas dragged his pistol from its leather boot, aimed it behind her as the other dragoons hurried out to see what the commotion was about. They froze in the doorway, squinted up at him.

'Where's Hopton's army?' Thomas shouted, his muffled, unearthly voice alarming them even further.

'Over the river! All the way to Bristol b'now, sir!' a greyhaired, grizzled veteran told him shakily. Thomas cursed under his breath. All the dragoons could see was the plume of breath in the chill evening air. He backed away, keeping the pistol on the cowering men, turned his horse and spurred back the way they had come.

'What on God's earth was that?' the old woman asked.

'Wood demon,' was the grizzled dragoon's fearfully considered opinion.

Night had fallen fast. Thomas had barely been able to find the bridge and had taken off his mask to listen for the gurgling stream. He dismounted, led the horse over the bridge, back across the trampled meadow and down to the pontoon. He found the road once more, urged his horse along the rutted track to the crossroads. He paused to get his bearings, cantered on along the northern track. The lights of Monkton Farleigh twinkled behind splintered shutters at the top of the hill, guided him past the village. He followed the road down the slope between stands of oaks and birch trees, owls gliding by on silent wings. At the bottom of the hill more lights, the quiet hamlet of Batheaston, recovering from its Royal ordeal. He spurred down the main street, meeting hurrying townsfolk and furtive deserters and stragglers. Surely they couldn't have gone much further? He paused at the western end of the hamlet, saw the line of glowing campfires along the invisible ridge of Lansdown. A surly wagoner dozing on his cart called him back as he was about to take the narrow lane toward Charlcombe.

'They went that way but came on back,' the drover told him, scratching his flaxen mop of hair as he realized the stranger appeared to have painted his face blue. He pointed nervously down the dark lane toward Bristol. 'That's the road you want, sir. The general's trying to race t'other lot round the ridge. My guess'd be Swainswick then Cold Ashton, but I wouldn't risk it in the dark, sir, if you'll pardon me. Not if you don't know these parts.' Thomas frowned, peered up at the invisible ridge to the south. A thousand twinkling bonfires silhouetted the tall trees along the summit.

'Pretty sight, ain't it? From 'ere like. Not so funny close up. This mornin' he was over Charlcombe way, on top th'ill there, but then they started racin' each other t'wards Freezin' 'Ill. Niver seen nuthin' like it, sir, I ain't.'

Damn this darkness, Thomas thought. He couldn't find his way through these damned valleys by night. But if the armies were a few fields away from each other they were bound to clash soon. By dawn they might be at each other's throats. The damnable treaty wasn't worth the paper it had been scribbled on, Hopton would use it to light his pipe, if he was any judge. But he had taken the papers up in good faith, he couldn't just dump them in

255

the nearest marlpit. His hot face itched like fury beneath the hated mask. He was tired and hungry. A doubting messenger, a reluctant Mercury.

'Stay an' 'ave a bite sir, they ain't goin' nowheres now. They'll be there this mornin',' the driver offered, reassured by the stranger's obvious doubts.

Thomas raised his fingers to his mouth, tapped his lips and made a cutting gesture with the flat of his hand.

'Keep quiet, sir? Why ... ah, ye've no words.' The alarmed carter breathed an inward sigh of relief, wondering for a moment if the blue-faced stranger had been miming his own imminent murder.

'Well, I'll tell 'ee what, sir, have my lantern sir, and return it to me in camp this mornin', 'ow's that?' Thomas nodded, waited while the driver picked the pitted metal canister from its nail on the running-board. 'Don't 'ee go 'urrying mind, or 'e'll blow out.'

Thomas took the dim lantern, a tiny flame glowing behind a portcullis mantle, held it up. The driver smiled nervously at the hideous apparition.

'Mind 'ow thee goes now, sir, and don't forget me lamp, sir.'

Thomas turned his tired horse, trotted into the night.

Jethro Polruan turned on his heel, stamped back along the trampled lane he had created in the wheat field. He could see a cluster of tents in the next field, the long, low-lying main street of Marshfield village beyond that. A chilling, mournful wind worried the wheat, picked and pried at his tattered clothing as he mounted guard along the eastern end of the Cornish camp. He paused, listened to his colleagues laughing and shouting over the wall, watched a soldier in his bright white shirt stagger to the stones and relieve himself. Jethro growled a Cornish curse, releasing a cloud of vapour into the chill air, groped for his water bottle. He had filled it with the last of the brandy his section had borrowed from a merchant's house in Somerton. The fiery liquor burnt his throat and warmed his bowels. He wiped his mouth and stoppered the bottle, checked his match was still burning. Wind like this could blow it out and then where would he be?

He gazed up at the stars, a bright cascade of tiny eyes from one horizon to the other. My God, there were a lot of 'em. Shining bright all over the wheat field. A star for every soldier's soul, they said. Lord Jesus, there would be a few more up there this time tomorrow, he thought. The armies had shadowed each other all day. Waller on top of the hill, Hopton at the bottom, at a considerable disadvantage. He was a canny bugger, that Roundhead. Leap-frogged his men along the ridge while the Cornishmen toiled in the narrow, stuffy valleys, funnelled by the lanes, steered between patches of damp ground and bubbling springs. They'd have a crack tomorrow though, that milksop Butler had said so, anyway. Jethro paused, tilted his massive head. Had he heard something or was it just another noise from the camp? He looked over his shoulder. Acres of wheat swishing this way and that. A fine crop on this chalky soil. A rider on the road, making his way furtively toward the camp. A bliddy spy, at this time of night! Jethro ducked down into the wheat, doubled back along the track he'd stamped. He paused, checked his match, cupping his hand over the glowing point. The rider was creeping along behind a low wall, a large hat pulled down over his ... Lord Jesus. A blue man! A woad-faced troll on a black horse, come to scythe souls at midnight.

Jethro blinked, stared at the strange rider, urging his horse on now, seeing the lights at the end of the dark tunnel lane. The rider bent low and blew out his lamp. An imp, a warlock and his familiars, spidering up on a field of men. Jethro lifted the musket, squinted along the gleaming barrel. The rider was cantering now, toward the campfires. Jethro pulled the trigger. He closed his eyes against the dancing sparks, the cloud of white smoke. The retort rolled backwards and forwards over the windy plateau, brought men running from the nearest tents and shelters. Jethro stood up, reloaded his musket like an automaton. He blinked his eyes, tried to focus in the gloom, stepped forward. A dozen men were hurrying down the narrow lane, holding their arms out to catch the terrified horse. Jethro grinned, hurried through the wheat and came up to the dry-stone wall. He peered over into the rutted track, saw the demon stretched out in the dirt, his blue face plain to see. Plain to see he had pulled his montero down over his face to keep out the cold. Cut eyeholes in the velvet. Three of them. Jethro threw his leg over the wall, aimed the barrel at the groaning demon. Soldiers and wives from the camp had formed a circle around him, stared down at the stranger.

'What's he got on his 'ead?'

'Who fired there?'

'Is he one of theirs?'

Jethro barged the curious onlookers aside, knelt beside his victim. He was a man from his shoulders down, at any rate. His ball had caught the stranger below the nose. Streams of blood were running from beneath his velvet mask, staining the chalky track. Jethro eased the mask off, stood back with a gasp of horror. The women cried and looked away, the men stared at the ruined face, the bulging eyes. His mouth was a bubbling red ruin, shards of white teeth and bone twitched and splintered as he tried to speak, swallowed throatfuls of his own lifeblood.

'Good God above, what is it you've shot?'

'What's he sayin'?'

'Who shot 'un?'

Jethro swallowed hard, stared at the ruined features, the old wound crisp and black alongside the spouting crater where his ball had struck home. The man tore at his coat, buttons popped and rolled over the dirt.

'He's got a pocket pistol mind!'

'Shoot 'un again, Jethro!' The giant Cornishman towered over the drowning victim, watched him tug a sheaf of papers from under his coat.

'What's he got there?'

'Who's here who can read?'

The stranger balled his fist, crushing the paper into a tattered club. He beat at the dusty track, raising tiny clouds of dust. They watched him beat the earth, beat time until he died.

BY
LANSDOWN HILL

JULY 5, 1643

'I should have stayed in Bristol. Out of the frying pan and into the fire,' William moaned, gripping the piebald's reins in white-knuckled hands as the horse bucked and reared at the unfamiliar reeks on the ridge, the unnerving streamers of smoke drifting over the hill. He felt a sudden yearning for the narrow, familiar world he'd left behind. Greesham's stuffy little workshop, the trays of type, sticky brushes and pots of ink, the constant, hellish bubbling of the molten lead. He'd get hot metal and more, sitting on this damned wide-open ridge while McNabb picked his nose, as carefree as a squire's son out coursing with his cronies. Thank God those cannon were pointing in the other direction, across the narrow valley.

'Cheer up, laddie. You don't want to spend the war trying to remember the butt from the sharp end of a pike. See, it's not you,' he cried cheerfully.

William didn't want anything to do with anybody, at that particularly uncomfortable juncture of his brief existence. He had always imagined he lived life at his own pace, that he could decide the when, where, why and who. Working on the pamphlets back at Greesham's guttersnipe den he had been allowed to choose what he should include and what he should leave out, select the right tone

260

for a whole chapter. Writing scurrilous sermons on the rotten behaviour of the dreaded enemy he could change time and place, rewrite endings as often as he liked. It struck him how ironic it was that he should have lost all these godlike privileges now he had actually made his decision to take a hand in the wretched war.

The more he saw of it, the less he controlled. The more he heard, the less he understood. He tried to assert himself, to shape events in the field as he had on paper, and they turned on him like a snapping dog. War was wildly unpredictable, an elemental force preying one moment on the simplest fishing smack, the next on the bravest treasure galleon. A hateful hawk bred from fire and tempest which man could unleash easily enough but never be sure of calling back. A dead-eyed pike lying up in the shallows, reviewing its roach-mouthed victims as they flickered by on the tide. William was one of the little fishes washed along with the rest, shoaled tight with ten thousand anonymous others, caught up in a smoky net which tightened every moment, brought him ever closer to war's razor-toothed jaws. Causes and motives and reasons and excuses hardly seemed important when you were striking complete strangers over the heads with your sword. Did all these ten thousand marching men feel as he did?

Now he sat brooding while the endless manoeuvres continued on the hill opposite and the steep valley below. As far as William could see Waller and Hopton were taking it in turns wearing their men out with pointless marches, as if they were intent on wearying them of war before they had begun. Up and down the lanes, in and out like the convulsions of some marine creature washed up on the rocks. The bright banners and hedges of pike points its groping tentacles and poisoned spines.

The battle had been predicted for days. An intense, expectant excitement that seemed to vibrate down the very horse lines and along the dirty rope fixed above the latrine pits, setting the pennants above Waller's marquee cracking and snapping in the sharpening breeze. The Roundhead army had been unceremoniously turfed out of two strong positions and yet their morale had strengthened rather than suffered. The men had been especially cheered by the arrival of new regiments of foot from Gloucester and Haselrig's awesome Lobsters. Their segmented armour was allegedly proof from pistol ball and sword thrust. The only hope an enemy might have at close quarters would be to work a blade up underneath them, stab them in their unprotected buttocks or the backs of their thighs. The cuirassiers had been issued with strong and heavily buttressed saddles with a stuffed seat and high pommel. They had been trained to ride with legs outstretched and toes pointing upwards, so even this avenue of attack would be next to impossible, according to the army's increasing number of experts.

The regiments had marched out of Bath accompanied by the warbling whistle of the fifers and the doom-laden beat of a dozen drums, and taken up new positions on the windy Landsdown plateau. Unassailable on their ridge they had watched the Royalist army coil and pulse along the narrow lanes below, unable to deploy because of the patchwork of enclosures and ribbons of formidable hedgerows. They had marched west, shadowing the enemy host and keeping them in constant fear of a sudden swoop from the high ground. Furious skylarks tumbled and sang overhead, annoyed at the sudden interruption of their solitude. A dirty brown mass of men and equipment, singing psalms at the tops of their voices as they trundled across the butterfly glad fields.

The tired but cheerful Parliamentarian troops had swung through Bath and toiled up on to Lansdown plateau, straightened their backs and dressed their sweating ranks as they marched past the entire Roundhead officer corps. Haselrig buttoned and strapped into his armour, Popham in lacquered black, Waller nodding and pointing as he conferred with his unexpected visitor, a last-minute emissary from Hopton.

Sir Marmaduke Ramsay had ridden into Bath early that morning with Bates the faithful footman walking ahead. The weary old retainer had alternated between beating a nervous tattoo on his borrowed drum and furiously waving a white flag. Although the long if not strictly rigorous siege of Kilmersden Hall had kept the squire from the front line of the fight for the best part of a year, he hadn't forgotten the treatment meted out to spies and agents. He knew full well anyone caught within an enemy camp without a flag of truce or under a drum would be hanged from the nearest branch, and had ordered poor Bates to make suitable preparations. He had parted company from his son at Odd Down the previous afternoon, Thomas heading for Bradford on Avon while Sir Marmaduke sought out his old companion William Waller at Bath. Sir Marmaduke hoped his son's journey to Hopton's headquarters would be as uneventful as his own ride up the Fosseway. They had taken what passed for a good road and had made good time. The squire had pulled at his beard as he rode, pondered the course of the conversation. Fretted at the more difficult clauses which could become obstacles to the peace they all sought. He had uttered silent prayers, called on God to bless his counsels. Surely Waller, a sound if misled man, would see the sense of his and Sir Gilbert's sincere petition? The country must be brought back from the brink, set back on the road to peace.

The Royalist envoys had been discouraged by the greeting they had received at the town gate, where they had been treated with disbelieving derision by a party of Roundhead dragoons. The ragged horsemen had been stationed just outside the Westgate, deliberately left behind to ensure all stragglers and deserters attempting to slip out of the town were returned to their units on Lansdown as soon as possible. The tatty troop, most of them still in the civilian coats they had arrived in, had been expecting to detain Parliamentarian deserters, not Royalist gentry clutching allegedly vital correspondence for their general-in-chief.

'It is essential I see Sir William. We were in Germany together, he'll remember me,' Ramsay had scolded the impudent dragoon captain as he scanned his flimsy papers in evident bewilderment. 'I bear letters from General Hopton which I do not propose to discuss with anybody other than your commanding officer,' the squire added stoutly.

The dragoon captain decided discretion was the best policy, and ordered four of his men to take 'this yer squire feller an' all' on through the town and up to Waller's highly mobile headquarters. It had been another hour before the envoys and their escort had arrived on the ridge and tracked the general and his staff down to the shade of a lone oak from which they had been reviewing the troops. Sir William had barely recognized his undernourished comrade in arms from the German wars, and had concealed his initial embarrassment behind a show of familiarity, much to the suspicion of Masters Lyle and Webster.

The whispering commissioners had attached themselves to the general's immediate entourage the previous evening. Sceptical old crows in black broadcloth who hovered like vultures at Waller's elbow, deeply alarmed at his apparent friendship with notorious malignants. They were increasingly disturbed by tales of his reputed refusal to regard General Hopton as a true and bloody enemy. Rash rumours were meat and drink to Webster and Lyle, who had been specifically sent to the west to ensure the commanders Parliament had appointed were entirely behind their righteous cause. They had been suspicious of Nathaniel Fiennes in Bristol, and now it seemed they could not fully trust their principal officer in the field. Writing letters to the enemy? Receiving their misguided ambassadors with open arms?

The commissioners had already driven the general to distraction with their viper advice and reptilian fanaticism. They had wasted little time, bringing their baleful influence to bear at the candlelit council of war Waller had called in Bath the previous evening. Webster had listened grimly as the senior officers debated the tactical situation, his pinched features souring by the second. He had shaken his narrow head, urged an immediate attack on Hopton's positions around Batheaston.

'Sure the enemy is below you, sir, and tired from his long march across the country,' Webster had insinuated in his unblinking impudence. 'He has been stopped in his vile tracks twice, and reels like a punch-drunk boxer. Strike him, sir, bury the snake!'

'My colleague speaks true, sir. This is no time to let any lingering affection for your Mr Hopton impair your unquestioned military judgement. They must be destroyed sir, every man Jack of them!' Lyle had added with a maniacal leer.

Colonel Popham and Sir Arthur Haselrig had blanched at their unbelievable accusations, their utter want of tact. Both officers had been in arms since the beginning of the war, and had already seen half a dozen valued comrades throw down their commissions and join the King after similar slights. Young Chudleigh, for instance, one of the best young Roundhead officers in the west country, had been made the scapegoat for the disaster at Stratton the previous year. Ralph Hopton's Cornishmen had taken on and destroyed an army of twice their size, pushed Parliament's Devon and Dorset forces from the great west road. Chudleigh, the only commander worthy of the name that day, had been accused of cowardice and had immediately transferred his allegiance to the King. Popham, a dark-featured, serious-minded young nobleman who had been at the forefront of Parliamentary resistance in the west, had been particularly stung by the commissioners' sneering tone.

'Sir William's high personal regard for Sir Ralph Hopton is understood and shared by all gentlemen presently in attendance,' he snapped, furious. 'Indeed, if the King had more Ralph Hoptons in his immediate retinue it is highly doubtful the country would be in its present straits,' he added.

Webster and Lyle studied him coldly. Inquisitors taking the bloody confession from some self-declared heretic could hardly have been more intrigued by these alarming developments. Commanding officers who made no secret of their warm correspondence with their opposite numbers, lieutenant-generals who dared question the will of Parliament's own appointed commissioners. They had held their tongues as the red-faced commanders had returned to their debates, left them lurking in the shadows where the feeble candle glimmer barely lit their hooded features.

Sir Marmaduke had shaken hands with his erstwhile companion Waller, bowed to Haselrig and greeted the uncomfortable Popham as an old friend.

'I am here on your encouragement, sir!' Sir Marmaduke had announced to the immediate astonishment of that officer and the further suspicion of the commissioners.

'On my encouragement, sir?' Popham had replied uneasily.

The Royalist squire, who had reputedly held his formidable manor house for the king these past twelve months, nodded delightedly. 'You will recall your letter to Sir Gilbert Morrison, sir?'

'Morrison?' the commissioners crowed knowingly.

Ramsay turned, acknowledged the commissioners with an eager nod.

'The merchant of Chipping Marleward, sir, you will recall you gave him permission to treat with me, sir!'

Popham paled, glanced nervously at Waller. 'I remember the man ... I signed a chit for him.' The commissioners eyed him. 'To care for the wounded as he saw fit ... after the fight at Chewton,' he recalled with some feeling.

'You gave Sir Gilbert rather more than that, sir, if I am not mistaken?' Sir Marmaduke queried.

Popham ground his lips, shook his dark head. 'Indeed, sir, you are mistaken. I signed a note authorizing the man to treat for the care of the wounded, and nothing more!'

Sir Marmaduke's smile slipped as he looked back to Waller. 'I fear I have been misled by my colleague's impetuosity. He gave me reason to believe Colonel Popham had given him full powers to treat with me, and that we should act as intermediaries with General Hopton.'

'Indeed,' Webster said menacingly.

'You are evidently unaware, sir, that Parliament has drawn up and signed an indictment against Sir Gilbert, and that he is currently lingering under sentence of death for high treason?' Lyle enquired.

'High treason? Who dares speak of high treason here?' Sir Marmaduke snorted, losing his temper a little as he turned his aristocratic gaze over the shabby ranters cowering behind the general. Waller held up his hand, stared sternly from the commissioners to Sir Marmaduke.

'Your pardon, sirs, there appears to have been some mistake in intention between the parties. Much as I desire to get to the bottom of this conundrum, you will remember I am in command of an army which stands not half a mile from its enemy. I must beg leave to return to my position at the head of my men.'

'Sir William, please, the petition requires . . .'

'Time I do not have at the moment sir,' the general grated. Waller waited a moment, turned his horse and spurred off along the ridge, Popham and Haselrig falling in behind.

'And now, sir, perhaps we can get to the bottom of this, what did the general call it, sir?' Webster asked, turning his vile attention to the nervous squire.

'A conundrum, sir.'

'A conundrum indeed, Master Lyle. A conundrum indeed.'

William Sparrow had caught up with McNabb on Lansdown that dawn.

'Hah, laddie, you're still a captain, then!' The red-haired Scot had been attached to Major Dowet's ambush party at Monkton Farleigh, and had been in the thick of the cavalry scrap around the smoky woods. Sometime during their last furious charge against the massed enemy horsemen he had lost his cornet, and been obliged to gallop off the field without him.

'That wee Sassenach Cooper, aye. I didna see what happened.' He shook his stubbly head in annoyance. 'He got whacked from his horse right enough, Thomas says he was on his feet when he took the colour from him, ah, who knows, eh?'

William had been shaking his head in sympathy when he had caught the Scot's crafty stare.

'We lost men as well as you,' he countered quickly.

McNabb gave him a rueful grin. 'I'll not say you didna. But whether yon Cooper's taken a whack or hidden himself away, I'm still short a cornet.'

'Well?'

'Well, do I have to spell it out for you, man? A great laddie like yourself and yon bleary-eyed beastie there? Will you not take service with me?'

'With you?' William spluttered.

'Aye, I can fix it up with the colonel. Are you up for it? My cornet?'

'Cornet? With Jamie waiting on his inquiry I'm in charge of this lot,' he protested, nodding on down the slope where the remains of the Chipping Marleward contingent were busy digging earthworks around a battery of guns. McNabb shook his head, taking his water bottle from his saddle and taking a quick swig.

'Aye, for now. Your boys are to be brigaded in with the Gloucester men there. They've plenty of officers with a mickle bit more experience than ye have yourself, if you'll take my meaning,' McNabb encouraged. 'You've come so far with them, they'll thank you for it. But when it comes to push o' pike, they'll want a proper captain, not a beginner. Take my word, laddie, you'll do better here with me, I'll straighten it with headquarters.' Sparrow slumped in his saddle, thinking it over. 'Well, don't do me any favours, laddie, there's never a shortage of volunteers for the cavalry!'

'I did all right at the fort back there,' Sparrow retorted, stung by the burly Scot's apparent criticism of his command capabilities.

'D'ye want to spend the war walking around up to your britches in mud?'

'You reckon you can swing it for me? A transfer?' Sparrow remembered his ill-gotten commission, wondered how much longer he was likely to retain his rank. Surely the commissioners would snatch it back, once they had gotten to the bottom of old Morrison's turncoat dealings? And if they didn't, there was always Jamie. If they decided he hadn't known of his father's impending treachery he would have more claim to the company than he had. He rubbed his bristly chin, nodded.

'There y'are! Welcome to Waller's horse!' McNabb had been as good as his word, and had ridden off to arrange his posting with his busy superiors. He had wandered around the busy headquarters while messengers hurried in with fresh reports, hurried out with new orders. McNabb had returned with his field commission as a cornet scribbled on a slip of paper, and taken him along to the quartermaster who had eventually been persuaded to hand over a brand new lobster-pot helmet, back- and breastplates to go over his buff coat and a pair of new pistols. Sparrow had stood admiring the weapons, wondered how they were loaded.

'Och, never mind all that nonsense now, there's no time. If we get to grips get your sword out and defend yoursen, don't go botherin' yer heed trying to skewer anybody. Keep that great beastie of yours trotting, when in doubt, gallop.'

Sparrow hadn't time for any more instructions, and by ten o'clock he had found himself riding over the hills at McNabb's elbow, the big piebald labouring, as he tried to keep up with the major and memorize the commands at the same time. Left wheel, right wheel, charge. 'Not that left laddie, the other left, eh!' It was as much as he could do to stay in the damned saddle at all at that speed, let alone turn the lathered gelding where he wanted. The troop had finally been ordered out to the western tip of the long ridge. Sparrow could see Bristol away in the distance.

'Hanging Hill, now there's an omen for ye,' McNabb called cheerily as the newest cornet in the army caught his breath, eased a sore hand under his flaming buttocks. William frowned, gazed longingly at his home town away over the lush patchwork of fields and narrow enclosures. He should have stayed at the shop, working the pulleys that tipped the molten lead into the narrow gutters of the hungry press, proof-reading warm galleys until his eyes watered. His eyes were watering all right, in this damned heat on this damned hill in this damned wind. He should have stayed with the militia, taking their ease in the pits down the slope. War was unfamiliar enough without having to master the art of staying on a frightened horse into the bargain. He should have stayed with his friends, instead he had walked out on them with hardly a word. The Pitt brothers, convinced their father was dead, had barely nodded as he had told them. The Londoners had raised their eyebrows as if he had announced his imminent departure to the Americas. Will slumped on the wheezing piebald, grinned good naturedly at his new colleagues.

'Does that windbag always make that bloody noise?' one of the riders wanted to know.

The armies had skirmished for the past weeks, two torn dogs in a pit, hemmed in by the winding lanes and steep, windblown gorges of north-eastern Somerset. The generals had probed and jabbed, trying to avoid a frontal assault and the inevitable bloodbath this would entail. But as the deadlock continued and the two armies remained in contact, the prospect of a big no holds barred battle looked ever more likely to the veterans on either side. Noon on a sultry summer's day. Cavalry patrols were being thrown out far and wide, galloping along the treacherous lanes locked in combat like mating snakes, pulling away to

trot back to their armies. Not even the enormously experienced McNabb knew who was getting the better of who.

'Well, we're nearer your precious Bristol than we were,
but there'll be no shifting us from the ridge,' he said, as
their troop was ordered into line at last, stirrup to stirrup
behind one of the low walls which ran the length of the
windy plateau. Below them and to their right great blocks
of pikemen were filing into spaces between the guns. The
artillerymen had been busy all morning, blasting shot at
their counterparts sweating about their pieces on Freezing
Hill. Peering down into the drifting smoke they could see
brown-coated dragoons exchanging potshots over the
cramped hedges while every tenth man held on to their
panicked nags. Now, the bulk of the enemy forces had
withdrawn over the hill, a giant sea anemone hurrying
back into its sheltering pool. Sparrow sighed with relief.
'Is that it, then?'

'No, it's not it, ye whining poltroon!' McNabb barked,
pointing his gauntlet away to the right flank where six
black lines of horsemen had detached themselves from
the army and were trotting downhill across the churned
fields. Why couldn't they leave well enough alone? The
buggers had retreated, hadn't they?

'There's yon Burghill, and the big laddies behind
Haselrig and his Lobsters. Aye, all very fine and dandy, as
long as our friends opposite don't turn and bloody their
noses,' McNabb commented drily.

Six hundred of the cavalry backed by a regiment of
lighter horse moved across the green hill like a summer
thundercloud, picking up speed as they reached the
bottom of the valley and pounding along the lanes after
disorganized parties of enemy horse and dismounted
dragoons who clambered into the hedges to get away from

their flashing blades. Waller had ordered his dragoons to redouble their efforts to clear them away, winkling them out one by one as they made their way along the brambled verges, ducking and hiding like so many duck hunters. The hideous blacksmith clattering built up and gave out suddenly. McNabb stood in his stirrups, stared into the ragged, breath-tangling fog. Another flurry of shots, brief spatters of musketry and the Parliamentary cavalry reappeared, dozens of riderless horses galloping this way and that, small groups of horsemen working their way back to their lines.

'What's wrong now?' Sparrow protested.

'Did I not tell ye? They're damn fine on a chess board, but not a field of battle.'

'We seemed to be winning, though. Their cavalry ran like hares,' William pointed out, unhappy at the apparent fallibility of their left flank.

McNabb snorted, gathered his bay horse which had begun pawing at the earth in agitation. 'Damn this waiting. Send us all in or none at all,' he muttered.

'Old Waller knows what he's doing,' Captain Hunt chimed in, nodding over his shoulder to the cluster of staff officers and their milling attendants further along the ridge.

What did they know about it? Could they see through a hill or an enormous mushroom cloud of smoke any more than the poor creatures dug into the earth below? William closed his eyes, opened them again as the ground vibrated and the last of the cavalry streamed back to their starting lines, officers bawling as they tried to get their men to stand in some kind of formation.

'Now what?' McNabb asked, peering over the summit opposite. Bright banners blossomed on Freezing Hill followed by blocks of pikemen, files of musketeers, pea-cock officers on prancing chargers. The foot-soldiers breasted the ridge, rolled down the lush slopes once more. They seemed to move lazily, taking their time, as if they were deliberately prolonging the hateful waiting about, undermining the nerve of their enemy on the ridge. Thousands of them, closer every moment. Thousands more than the thousands William had seen at the ford. He remembered with a shudder how long they had resisted the enemy there!

His nervous imaginings were silenced by the breathtak-ing roar of the cannon. Culverins and sakers belched brimstone, sent angry gusts of smoke and flames rushing through the man-packed hedgerows. A screaming Royalist musketeer dashed into the field, beating at his chest as a spark set off the charges hanging from his bandolier. He rolled over the turf, shrieking like a banshee as the blue flames crackled around his coat, burnt the hair from his crisped black head in an instant. More guns were dragged about to stoke the furious cannonade. Red-hot metal scissored through the smoke, lanced whole files of men who collapsed awkwardly on to growing heaps of smashed equipment, maimed men and lamed horses. The enemy soldiers seemed to have run aground in the black fog, stuck fast on the chaotic lower slopes. More minutes dragged by.

Hopton had gathered several hundred of his scattered cavalry and sent them bowling back down the slope to support his foot. They were toiling up the hill now, musketeers ducking behind hedges, taking what cover they could as the mass of pikemen in the centre ground uphill in the teeth of a storm of shot, volley after volley of musketry from the hidden Roundhead positions. Sparrow slowly realized this was different from the fight at the ford. This was ten, twenty times bigger than that sideshow. Suddenly, the real battle had started in earnest. The long summer's campaign in the west was about to be decided.

McNabb slapped his thigh, gave a loud whoop. 'This is it, boys, they're coming on now, coming on smart!'

Sparrow blinked, clutched the piebald's soft mane as the drifting smoke stung his face, dried his tongue to the roof of his mouth.

'They'll be slaughtered, we'll ride 'em down like stubble!' McNabb called, exultantly.

'I can't see a thing,' William moaned, wiping the stinging grit from his eyes. 'We'll charge our own if we're not careful.'

'Och, it wouldn't be the first time, or the last,' McNabb shrieked back, blue eyes bright, bared teeth shining white against his smoky demonic face. He drew his sword with a flourish, lifted it high above his head. He bawled something to his troop but all Sparrow could see were the strings of pale spit in his open mouth, all he could hear a constant roar that seemed to throb through the ground and up his horse's uncertain legs. He realized it was the drummers, out in front. *Brum, dum dum, brum dum dum.* Keeping manic time with his heart, thumping wildly inside his breastplate like a clapper to a brass bell.

BY
FREEZING HILL

LANSDOWN, JULY 5, 1643

'We'll fetch 'em off quick enough!'

'Let's fetch down those cannon!'

'We've suffered enough from them, let's up!'

Colonel Butler eyed his bawling, sooty pikemen, shouting like drunks at some chimney sweeps' convention. Oh yes, they were fine soldiers, right enough. Brave and reckless as rabid beasts, now the enemy were within spitting distance. He gripped a pair of pistols he'd lifted from a dead cavalryman, one of the many half-looted corpses that littered the lane. The broken, splintered debris left by the pitiless, senseless hurricane of war. His company dashed on down the hill, their ranks disintegrating as they hurried after Grenvile's regiment, which was taking the brunt of the enemy fire further up the smoke-clogged slopes. He waved his enormous black hat, bawled himself hoarse trying to bring them to stand in the dead ground at the foot of the hill, a gale-lashed island crowded with lost and wounded men, shipwrecked survivors of the broken-backed regiments foundering on the rocks of Waller's entrenchments. He lashed about, beat the ragged soldiers into line with blows from his pistols, vicious kicks. The damned savages didn't seem to register pain any more than they would pity. Suffering like bullocks penned beside a slaughterhouse. Never expecting quarter nor giving any either. Butler was sent sprawling by the mob of jeering soldiers, clambered to his feet as Polruan led his musketeers forwards. The mountainous mutineer gave him a triumphant grin, his strong teeth the colour of old rope. Standing defiant at the head of his bawling company, the jabbering apes waiting on his accursed word. His fierce dull beast eyes glittering with defiance. Butler would have been happy enough seeing the bastard sack kneel before the executioner's axe after the murderous outrage the night before. How he would have delighted to hold up that hateful head and let his vile blood splash and soak the chalky soil. Given his chance he would have hacked it from the giant's troll shoulders himself, paraded his grisly prize around the camp as a dire warning to the others. Let all the surly soldiery gaze one last time on their beloved champion, their homicidal spokesman.

Butler had been asleep in his tent, resting for the battle which must surely come with the dawn. He leapt to his feet at the sudden dry crack of a musket, raced out over the trampled wheat fields in search of the alarm. He wasn't in the least surprised to discover his own regiment had been responsible for yet another unnecessary death. Standing around the dead stranger in the road, crossing themselves like the Dark Age peasants they were.

'Downderry ... Polruan, you again!' he exclaimed, catching sight of the surly giant as he attempted to hide his vast bulk behind a muttering gang of his idiot cronies. A curl of smoke was still rising from the sooty barrel of his musket. Butler shoved his companions aside, bristled beneath the enormous musketeer. For once, Polruan seemed to have had some idea of what he had done.

'He nivver said a word, rode up on me blind side and made off fast t'wards the camp when I called 'un,' he said truculently. 'And when I caught sight of his face ... all bound up blue like, well, was 'speck I to do but shoot 'un?' His belligerent confession was greeted with a chorus of approval by the rest, who had been attracted from all corners of the camp by the gunfire.

'You shot him down like a dog, it's written all over your face!' Butler screamed, fists clenching about the walnut stock of the pistol he had snatched up on his way over. 'You've crossed me once too often, Polruan, and by God I'll see you pay this time!'

'Weren't Jethro's fault, Colonel,' Downderry piped up. 'Here's his mask, look, frightenin' folk with his mummery.'

Butler turned from the sulking musketeer to his colleague, fearfully holding up the bloody blue bag. 'Who is he?' he demanded, snatching the velvet from the musketeer. 'You don't even know who you've killed!'

'He rode on when I challenged 'un. Asked for it, he did!' The giant Cornishman's childish defiance ate away the last shreds of the colonel's frayed temper.

Butler swung the walnut pistol butt towards the brute's clay-featured face. The musketeer brought his heavily muscled arm up to shield his head, took the furious blow on his wrist and howled in agony. The mob surged forward, froze in their tracks as Butler brandished the loaded weapon in their faces.

'You don't care what you do, or who to,' he breathed. 'Who heard you challenge him?'

'I did.'

'Aye, I heard him. "Hoy, who goes there," 's what he said right enough,' Simon Shevick improvised.

Butler stared at the tightening ring of hostile faces

flared and shadowed by the spluttering torches they carried. He could feel the tension crackle in the still night air. He knelt beside the dead man as they twitched and muttered, closed about him. Turned the smashed face into the light to examine the horrific burns about his face and neck, the bubbling ruin where Polruan's ball had flattened against his face. The dead man's upper lip had been torn apart along with his nostrils. His upper jaw and teeth a mass of splintered white fragments showing up bright against the red. It must surely be obvious even to these vicious clods their victim had been badly burned before he ever set foot in the wretched lane.

'He couldn't speak,' Butler concluded. 'He wore the mask to hide the burns, I saw men do the same in Germany.' The colonel's icy accusation sent the mob into another convulsion of boot-scraping mutters. 'He couldn't cry out and you shot him down like a dog!' he snarled, levering himself to his feet.

'He didn't speak because he was too busy ridin' into th' camp!'

'One man against six thousand? Did you ever see a more conspicuous spy? He's more than likely a messenger for the general!'

'I 'eard Jethro challenge him, "Speak the password," he said, "or I'll shoot!"' Judd Downderry insisted stubbornly.

'You kept him a while then,' Butler said snidely, 'before you decided you'd shoot him anyway. Where's his satchel, where's his purse?'

'Purse? I nivver saw no purse nor papers neither,' Simon Shevick volunteered, shaking his ragged head. The gap-toothed pikeman had spotted the officer's furious approach before the rest of the curious mob, and had had the sense to dispose of the damning documents before

Butler had stuck his nose in. Even as the colonel ranted and raved an old bawd from the camp hobbled on out to the latrine pit over the wall, tore the top sheet of Sir Marmaduke Ramsay's precious petition from the nail where Shevick had hastily impaled it. The meticulous, closely written pages flapping in the breeze by the reeking trench. The old bawd, bent double with the bloody flux, had squinted at the writing, made nothing of it, and torn it into more useful strips.

Butler wheeled round on the giant musketeer who was nervously fingering his bruised wrist. 'Don't you dare imagine you'll get away with this,' he swore, barging his way through the angry battalion cuffing the surliest soldiers out of his path. 'I'm off to the general. You'd best shoot me down now, Polruan,' he called over his shoulder, back to the murderous rogue. 'Sergeant-Major Rice?'

'Here, sir.'

'Get that body over to my tent, and ensure none of these bastard's whelps touches it.'

Downderry nudged his brooding companion. 'Go on, Jethro, knock 'un down now. Nobody'd know.'

Polruan growled, nodded at the cavalry patrol edging along the wall behind them. Some young buck of a captain out walking the perimeter who had been attracted by the commotion.

'I cassn't shoot 'un down, with them horse boys a-lookin' on,' he hissed.

Butler had known Polruan had overstepped the mark at last, and gleefully anticipated watching the damned savage hang that dawn. Instead he fumed and glared, watched the rogue and his grinning cronies march down the hill with the jaunty confidence of some latter day Robin Hoods, untouchable poachers carrying off slaughtered deer. He marched straight to Sir Bevil Grenvile's tent, and told the commander of the Cornish infantry contingent exactly what had happened. He had been describing the murder in some detail when their heated debate had been drowned out by the growing tumult outside. They had ducked out of the tent to find themselves surrounded by an angry mob, confronted on all sides by threats and shouts. The best part of five regiments had mutinied, rushed to the defence of their assaulted champion.

'You mutinous scum!' Butler bawled as Sir Bevil placed a restraining hand on his pistol arm. 'It's like this, is it?'

'Release Polruan!' the demented mob roared back.

'He's right there, you bloody oafs!'

'Well, drop the charges then! We'll not fight your bloody battles else!'

Sir Bevil tilted his lean head toward the apoplectic colonel. 'Butler, I really feel we ought to . . .'

'Drop the charges? I'll drop the shit-sack from the end of a rope!'

The tumult had by then attracted General Hopton and Prince Maurice from their quarters in the village. The mutinous chorus fell silent as they strode between the smoky mob and the hesitant officers.

'What's the trouble here? Have we not enemies enough across the valley without brawling amongst ourselves?'

Sir Bevil had explained what had happened while Hopton nodded his head sagely.

Had he ordered an immediate execution to make an example of the damned savage? Forced the grumbling ringleaders to run the gauntlet past their shamed colleagues? Not a bit of it. Hopton had lectured the throng as if they were wayward children he had caught stealing apples from his orchard. His soothing voice and reasonable manner had carried his words through the mob like bushfire, burnt the wildness out of them faster than any furious threat or gunpoint growl. They had drifted back to their tents, satisfied by Hopton's promise to look into the whole business when they had more time. They had muttered and cursed until the dawn while Butler had accosted his commander, urged Grenvile to stand up to the trigger-happy devils.

'Well, that's just it, isn't it? These trigger-happy devils as you call them are all that stand between our sovereign King and dishonourable ruin.'

'He shot a man down in cold blood without a word of warning. What was the damned fool thinking of, riding up to an armed camp by night?'

'Well, quite so. We go picking Polruan out for shooting strangers and we'll lose half our foot this night. We'll be ordering them to march straight into hell on the morrow and here you are trying to lynch them! It's just not on, is it?'

'I would rather charge Waller alone than fight beside scoundrels and murderers,' Butler bit back.

Sir Bevil gave him a sardonic grin. 'I rather think not,' he said gently. 'You weren't up here last year, you won't know what it was like. Sir Ralph had his Commission of Array from the King, *carte blanche* to raise the western counties for the Crown. We had a few hundred horse, the gentlemen yonder mustered twelve thousand on Mendip Hill and we had no choice but to get out of there, damned quick!'

Butler fumed, pulled at his black moustache in agitation.

'Here we are again, and we've evened the odds a little. If it wasn't for this set of scoundrels, as you call them, we would be blocked up in some castle out west while the enemy ran rampage!'

They were running rampage right enough. Grenvile's realistic predictions had come to pass, his softly spoken words of wisdom hammered into Butler's head with each rib-crushing crescendo of the guns, every furious pop and splutter of musketry. The Cornish had taken cover in the dead ground to regain their ragged breath. Muttering and cursing and breaking into obscene shouting which had the whole lot of them stepping out again. Butler realized it was hopeless trying to hold them back. He waved the pistols toward the thickest smoke, ordered the charge seconds before the leaders dashed away like hungry hounds, pikes and muskets held like farm implements.

The maddened bushfire flock surged ahead over heaps of fellow Cornishmen, blasted and tumbled during half a dozen earlier attacks. Splintered equipment and cast-off clothing, looted sacks and a scattered pack of greasy cards. Butler shouldered his way past dazed and wounded, staggering back the way they had come looking for aid that wasn't there. He squinted into the darkness, the rolling smoke which had filled in, jammed the narrow defile. Get to the ridge, at least he'd breathe again, sweet air not this choking dragon-belch wind. A furious whistling and a sheet of flame, and he went down with the rest of them, dead and wounded piled haphazardly with the deaf and dazed. He heaved himself up, scrambled for his pistols in the logjam of bodies and litter of junk as his battered company steadied itself, went forward again in ones and twos to join the ragged, disintegrating rear of Grenvile's hotheads. The mighty phalanx had been shredded by heavy guns, constantly sniped by the enemy musketeers hidden in the smoke-shrouded trees. Bodies fell out and were trampled down on all sides, but the fresh impetus lent by Butler's company pushed the front ranks over the summit and into the gun emplacements like a swelling tide.

The cannon fell silent as the exhausted gunners grappled with the red-eyed fanatics, ran for cover to the pike blocks waiting in support. The Cornish attack dissolved into a mass of single combats up and down the lines, hacking and spitting, skewering and clubbing. The wavering Roundhead infantry were rolled back from their guns, over the summit on to the plateau. Half of the Royalist officers were already dead, the shell-shocked survivors taking up colours which had been reduced to splintered sticks of sooty rags. They stood fast while cautious sentinels crept higher up the slopes, through drifting curtains of choking smoke and tumbling smuts to reconnoitre the hard-won position. The exhausted Cornish looked up in alarm as the scouts came pelting back, shoving their way through the great mob of bloody men as if a host of demons were after them. The officers, half blinded by the smokes and deafened by the cannonade, cupped their ears to catch the scouts' bawled warnings. They bustled about their cruelly reduced companies, furiously pulling the men together as the word was passed along the bloody front.

'Have a care! Charge for horse!'

The pikemen lowered their bloody spears, the few musketeers who had threaded their way through the carnage rushing to their aid. The enemy infantry drew off into the sliding, dragon-breathing murk, scrambled to reform behind the low wall along the ridge. The firing died away, the smoke shredded and the surviving Cornishmen felt the ground rumble and slide beneath their ragged boots. Horsemen, from three directions at once. Haselrig's Lobsters, armoured from head to toe. A thousand cuirassiers from Waller and Burghill's regiments in back and breast, hundreds of dragoons on tired nags beating their mounts with their carbines. The enormous attack swamped their precarious foothold on the top of the hill, rolled and surged around the tattered stands of pikemen. The Royalists were ground back twenty yards by sheer weight of men and horses bearing down on them. They clawed the earth, dug in their heels, rear rankers raking their boots in the mud as they dropped their weapons and simply pushed their comrades in front. A wild scrummage of screaming, heaving hate-crazed men brought the attack to a juddering halt. The enraged horsemen flailed about them, emptied their pistols at point-blank range, hacked at the hedge of pikes until their swords snapped in shards. The speared horses whinnied and reared, legs kicking convulsively in the agonized faces of the wounded sprawled helplessly beneath.

Just when it seemed the human boulders must be carried away by the flood of horses, a blare of trumpets called Waller's cavalry away and the exhausted Cornish slumped over their broken weapons and slaughtered comrades. Butler clutched his eye, examined his bloody hand. He'd been hit by something but couldn't begin to guess what. He was seeing double, treble, from his left eye, nothing from the right. He shook his head to clear the fumes, picked at the sticky mess on his cheek, ran a fragile finger into the empty socket. The remains of his mutinous company, Polruan, Downderry, Shevick, Thrush, Sergeant-Major Rice and the rest were blooded, baited bears. Captain Porthcurn cradling his arm, creased by a hot ball. A dazed ensign clutched the snapped halves of their standard.

'Here they come!' The shout was taken up by a thousand hoarse throats, the brigades forming hollow rings with the last of the musketeers taking cover inside. The broken hill lurched, the ridge bucked and writhed as the Roundhead horse came in again, left and right. Butler felt as if he was clawing at the lip of a volcano, hanging on for grim death while torrents of lava swept everything away. He'd found a broken pike, wedged the shaft under his boot and levelled the bloody point toward the advancing horse. Closed his streaming eye and gritted his teeth. The cavalry swirled up out of the mists like a legion of ghosts, emptied their pistols, hacked at the newly grown forest. Riders toppling out of the saddle impaled themselves on the bloody points, dragged the pikes to the ground in their miserable ruin. Three or four others would spur their horses toward the gap, hacking at exposed arms and faces before the hedgehog could right itself, renew its defences.

Ten minutes of carnage and they gave up once again. In the respite Hopton sent up dismounted cavalry, dragoons, gunners, carters, sappers, engineers, anybody who could hold a broken pike. Musketeers were streaming down the hill, turning bodies and emptying sacks to find powder and ball. Chronically short of ammunition, he left his post on Freezing Hill – he hadn't been able to penetrate the rolling smoke for a quarter of an hour or more anyway – and rode to the rear to find his lost supplies. He ordered the terrified civilian drivers up to the ridge with a torrent of threats. He spurred on ahead of the lumbering carts, their feverish drivers flinching with every blast, every muzzle flash from the hidden guns. The general met a ragged mass of wounded, shocked and dazed survivors hurrying back from the hellish hilltop. He glanced around his staff, reduced now to a trumpeter without a hat and a frightened old gentleman on a broken-winded stallion. His aides had long since been sent galloping over the fields for one thing and another.

The general chewed the forked tip of his beard, cursed the upstart Prince who seemed to have disappeared after his scattered horsemen. One good charge now and Waller would be finished. One good charge from Waller and his old comrade Hopton was finished. 'Get those wagons moving there!' he bellowed through the smoke. He daren't imagine how many he'd lost already. Hundreds, possibly thousands of his fine army wasted on a worthless hill. He gripped his reins, scanned the terrible ridge with his spyglass. The rumble of a thousand sets of hoofs vibrated through the bones of the hill, making his own mount stamp and snort in alarm. On the ridge, the din of battle intensified as Waller's never say die horsemen charged in again.

LANSDOWN HILL

JULY 5, 1643

McNabb was bawling instructions but Sparrow couldn't for the life of him make out what they were. The Scot had lapsed into Gaelic and his fine bay charger had opened several lengths' lead on William's wheezing piebald. Ashley Thomas spurred past him with the troop's flag, a black fist on a tawny ground. The youngster had joined Waller's horse on its formation, and McNabb had wisely decided to let him have the honour of carrying it in place of his new cornet.

'Ye'll have more than enough to do without botherin' your heed with the colour, laddie,' the sweating Scot had told him as he adjusted the bars of his battered black lobster-pot helmet. Their troop had already been ordered back twice, and had retired one hundred yards to find better ground from which to charge the advancing Royalists. The Cornish musketeers had infested the trees along the western spur of the hill and had been taking optimistic potshots at the Roundhead cavalry straining at the leash on the windy plateau. Protected by their sporadic covering fire a party of enemy horse had advanced in support of the pikemen bearing the brunt of the struggle in the centre.

McNabb had been standing in his stirrups, peering through the rolling smoke and biting his lips bloody at the delay.

'Why do they not send us in? Are they all women back there?' he yelled at Sparrow, blinking and trembling on the stamping piebald. A messenger had galloped up to the impatient major, frantically jabbed his finger down the slope. McNabb had whooped with delight, turned to his men.

'Right then, you sad Sassenach scumbuckets, down the hill and on to Oxford! I'll shoot the first man I see drawing rein! After me!' He waved his sword above his head, yanked on his reins and spurred the terrified bay down the steep slope.

Sparrow swallowed, gripped his sword until he was in grave danger of splitting the hilt. All he could see was the lip of the hellish chasm, a black crater spewing smoke and showers of orange sparks. Specks of ash tumbled in the foul slipstream, the guttural belching of the guns further along the choking valley. He spurred the piebald forward, the heavy beast lumbering behind as the front rank disappeared over the edge of the blind precipice. Sparrow felt hollow, a scooped-out shell of all too fragile skin and muscle. Blown about on the choking gusts as if his shirt had been tied around a bag of air. His stiff leather helmet strap tied tightly around his dandelion-seed head, ready to be blown away with one gentle puff from the spouting, spiralling smoke. Before he could think Jasper had crowned the ridge and was stretching his muddy legs after the rest of the troop down the rutted, creeping slope. Sparrow was hurled forward over the pommel, his helmet biting into the piebald's dusty mane. The beast's black ears protruded through his helmet bars as he instinctively clutched at the saddle and steadied himself. The sweaty velveteen tips of the gelding's ears tickled his nose for a moment, reminding him of slower rides across sultry meadows. He jerked upright and clutched the reins as Jasper veered towards the trees along the western flank.

He could see puffs of white smoke blossom along the edge of the dark-eaved wood, and realized with horror they were shooting at him. He yanked the reins to his right, pulled the beast back after the rest of the troop, bunched around McNabb fifty yards ahead. There was a deafening clang as a spent ball ricocheted off his helmet. He blinked to clear the tears stinging his eyes, wondered where the God-damned beast was taking him. The Round-head troop had cut across the hill, plunged into the disorganized enemy horse struggling to kick their horses up the steep broken slope. There was a flurry of pistol shots as the battered, disadvantaged Royalists defended themselves as best they could. McNabb rode through the swarm of angry lead wasps as if it was a welcome shower of summer rain, flicked his charger's reins to bring his horse alongside a terrified Royalist cornet. The bearded ensign clutched the Scot's blade in his dirty glove but was dragged backwards out of his saddle by the force of the impact. He dropped the broken-shafted colour and was dead before he hit the floor, head first.

McNabb's charge carried him into the middle of the milling Royalists, who hacked at him in absolute panic. The Scot's sword had been dragged from his hand with the wrenching force of his first blow, and he was forced to hold up his armoured elbow gauntlet to protect himself. He ducked one vicious blow, dragged the pistol from his holster and shot his opponent in the neck. The trooper dropped his sword, clamped his hands around his ruined windpipe. The rest of the Roundhead troop collided with the panicked enemy horse, their unstoppable charge knocking half a dozen of them out of the saddle. William hauled back on his reins, watched one of the craftier enemy horsemen spur out of the way of the russet avalanche and off towards the welcoming woods. He didn't know whether to cut him off or get behind the enemy horseman, and was still trying to make up his mind when the Royalist flashed by holding the point of his sword towards him. Sparrow leaned back in his saddle, the lumbering piebald stumbled and the enemy rider was gone. Sparrow recovered, turned the wheezing gelding and looked up.

To his astonishment and horror the enemy horseman had frantically reined his mount around and had drawn his pistol. Before Sparrow could move he had raised the weapon and fired. A cloud of smoke and a splutter of sparks and the enemy rider dropped the misfiring weapon with a curse. Sparrow reached for his own pistols, realized they hadn't been loaded. The Royalist spurred toward him, sword outstretched. Sparrow held his own sword up, hacked despairingly at the razor blade. The man cursed, brought his fist back for a slashing stroke. William kicked out with all his might, seconding the Royalist's momentum as he leaned back in the saddle for the *coup de grâce*. The rider clawed at the bay's mane but he had slipped too far to recover and found himself dangling like a flour sack along his horse's lathered flank. William grabbed Jasper's reins, walked the horse in a tight circle as the big bay trotted by, snorting and rearing as the rider was dragged along, half in and half out of the saddle. William beat the gelding with the flat of his sword, dug his spurs into the beast's heaving flanks with all his might. He turned the animal around the terrified bay, hacked down at the rider's arm as he tore and grasped at his tangled stirrup leathers. The leather parted with a sudden snap depositing the rider into the trampled grass and knocking what little wind he had left out of him. His hat bounced off down the slope after his unburdened horse. The broken-winded piebald lumbered to a halt as Sparrow leaned over his gasping victim, recognized the thin face and twitching brown moustache. The Royal Wool Gatherer himself! The brave captain who had tried to steal Morrison's wool all those long weeks before. He remembered himself, peered anxiously around him. The enemy troop had disintegrated, taken to their heels or sprinted for the covering trees. McNabb had turned his steaming horse, called his exultant troopers off. He knew well enough his men were now as defenceless as the enemy horsemen had been, isolated from their support at the bottom of the slope on blown horses. One good charge would scatter them just as they had scattered the ad-hoc Royalist formation.

'Back up the hill! Regroup, regroup!' he roared over the din. He turned his horse in circles around Sparrow and his breathless victim, aimed his second pistol at the cheesy-featured Royalist lying prostrate on the grass. Sparrow couldn't speak, couldn't think or hear. He watched the Scot's mad expression flicker between fear and anger, re-form itself somewhere between the two.

'Och now, on your feet my bonny lad,' he growled.

The winded prisoner elbowed himself up, glared at his captors. 'I'll leave you lying here, if it's the crows you're after courting,' he breathed. The Royalist levered himself up, fell in with the half dozen others the troop had rounded up. Sparrow peered up the slope through the drifting, stinging smoke. He couldn't see the ridge. Another flurry of shots and one of the Royalist prisoners collapsed into the grass and rolled down the hill.

A couple of dozen Cornish musketeers had left the

cover of the smoky woods, doubled forward to pick off the tired riders as they tried to climb for the safety of the windy heights. A black horse was hit in the chest and collapsed with a frightful bellow of bloody-lunged agony. The rider picked himself up and ran off like a startled hare. Ashley Thomas caught a ball in the hand which split his palm, filled his worn gauntlet with blood. He dropped the colour to the grass, reeled in his saddle as if he was drunk. McNabb swore, turned his horse around to go to his aid as more enemy gunners closed in for easy kills.

Sparrow watched them reloading, frantic demons coughing smoke and sparks. Musket drill was just as time consuming for them as it had been for the Chipping Marleward men back at the fort! They had fired and missed, and now they were practically defenceless, he reasoned, light headed with the excitement and the smoke. He dug his spurs into the panting piebald once again, ducked down behind Jasper's foam-flecked neck and held his sword out as steadily as he could. The blown piebald broke into an unsteady canter as the nearest knot of musketeers scoured their smoking muzzles. A shot went wild as Sparrow closed in on the sweating men. A bare-headed youngster snapped his musket to his shoulder and pulled the trigger, but the impetuous youth hadn't rammed the ball sufficiently far down the barrel and the bullet smacked against Sparrow's boot. It jarred the bone and made him flinch with pain but didn't break the leather let alone his skin.

His lumbering impact bowled the Cornishmen aside. One gave up trying to load his weapon, turned it upside-down to swing at him with the wickedly curved butt. The blow went wild, caught the piebald across his enormous rear. Sparrow slashed at the man but the horse reared past his intended target, caught the bareheaded youth instead. Jasper's great dinner-plate of a hoof connected with the sweaty temple and he fell to the ground, pole-axed. The older musketeer twisted around for another blow, but the piebald had cantered through the disorganized ranks taking Sparrow out of his range. A giant musketeer in a red suit grabbed at the gelding's reins, yanked Jasper's head down. Sparrow brought the sword round in a whistling arc, chopped through the pirate's greasy montero cap. The Cornishman cursed, released the reins and grabbed at his bleeding wound. A sudden shout and the Royalist foot scattered for the trees as a troop of Roundhead dragoons trotted along the wood, swinging swords and aiming carbines over their crossed arms. They covered McNabb's exhausted troop as they hobbled back the way they had come. Sparrow was wild eyed with exultation, his heart pounding fit to burst as he recovered his breath and his wits. Three of the riders had lost horses and were making their way back up the trampled hill on foot, dragging their dropped colour and pushing their surly prisoners. McNabb was wheezing as loudly as Jasper, but nodded encouragement.

'There, laddie, you looked right handy, back there! Charging a passel of the devils y'sen!'

William was too astonished with his own survival to speak, nodded dumbly as they kicked their broken horses over the ridge and out on to the plateau. The troop limped in behind Major Dowet's men, the black-armoured officer nodding in appreciation.

'Well done, McNabb. Get your men behind that wall there.' He gestured behind him to the low-lying dry-stone barricade which ran behind the main road over the hill. Roundhead musketeers had already lined the rampart, great stands of pike silhouetted bleakly against the red, flaring smoke. Tattered colours were being waved from the top of the wall as ensigns tried to re-organize their units, the scattered defenders hurrying away from the bloody ridge. McNabb took the situation in at a glance, shook his smoke-clogged head.

'Ah, they've given ground, see you? We've done it all for nothing, if they'll let them keep the hill!'

Sparrow, wretchedly tired, slumped on Jasper's heaving back, blinked his eyes at the mass of movement in the murk. The tactical situation was no clearer now than it had been three hours ago. Up and down, round and round. He shook his head, still in shock, as McNabb raved.

'Send us in again! One more push and we're there!' he cried.

But the hard-pressed infantry in the centre, turfed out of their gunpits and winkled out of the trees by their fearsome opponents, had had enough for today. General Waller, poised just behind the gun positions, guessed they would break within minutes, and ordered the retreat to the formidably built wall which he had scouted that morning. The tattered companies which had disputed the ridge hurried back through the tangled trees and burning wreckage, over heaps of dead, groaning wounded. Sergeant Muffet was out of powder, Gillingfeather had caught a spent round on the chin and was still spitting blood and chipped teeth. Butcher had taken a firelock musket from a dead artillery guard and was picking at the unfamiliar mechanism with careless curiosity. Further along the burning ridge Zachary and Eli had thrown their arms around Mordecai's jumping shoulders, helped him back up out of the killing zone. He had been speared through the thigh by a wild one-eyed Cornish officer who had raced ahead of his men toward the pit full of frightened Roundheads. The colonel had turned to urge his men on, but the sooty devils had seemed awed by the defences, hung back just out of range. The cursing officer had gone on, leapt in among the jabbing pikes and swinging butts, and been cut down like a dog for his trouble.

Sir Bevil Grenvile had led the ragged remains of his regiment between the hellish gunpits and a stand of timber, stamped himself into the mulch at the top of the hill while the Roundhead horse pounded and roared and charged and ebbed. He had laid the human foundations of the Cornish castle. Screaming defiance, he had been shot in the head and cut down by a pole axe. Hopton, shocked by the slaughter of his officers and men, had ordered his musketeers to raid the dead and dying for ammunition. Practically out of powder they kept up a one-sided firefight with the Roundheads behind their unassailable wall. His horse had scattered all over Somerset and Wiltshire while Waller had kept several fresh cavalry units waiting in the rear. One more determined attack would swat his army from its precarious hold on the ridge like ants from a rolling log. Hopton ran his glass this way and that over the smoking heights, squinted into the gathering gloom and prayed for the night.

BY
LANSDOWN HILL

JULY 6, 1643

Their lighted match glowed like the glimmering eyes of night beasts, moths and flies and flutterbys dancing and flaring above the guttering fires the Roundhead troops had thrown up behind their walls. Now, in the night chill, the exhausted Royalist troops could hear the burning boughs pop and crack in wretched harmony with the yelps and cries of the wounded. Lost souls in the midnight darkness. Butler's leaderless regiment squatted and relaxed around meagre fires in the abandoned Roundhead entrenchments. They had ranged over the dark hill, voraciously looting the dead and dying of both sides. Now they tried on new boots for size, cleaned worn weapons and smoked pipes. Jethro Polruan winced and cursed as Gideon Wooly jabbed and prodded at his flapping ear.

'Gah darn you kill-calf bloat, can you keep that needle steady?' he growled as the Penzance fisherman tried his knots on the bloody gash.

'If'n 'ee'll keep still an' let a body 'ave a crack 't it,' Wooly hissed, giving up in disgust. The ear was hanging from a strip of dirty skin, exposing shattered swirls and truncated whirls of muscle and drum. Jethro pushed him away in furious agitation.

'Get away with you, pollack breath. Here,' he grabbed

the offending organ, raised his dagger and slit the fleshy connection, tossed the ear into the flames. 'I'll not sit and fidget like a wailin' widow while you dirty your breeches, fisherman,' he vowed.

'Well, I've mortal eyes not goblin gimlets, thees can't 'spect I pin your damn lug'ole on for 'ee in this dark!'

Polruan clamped a dirty neckerchief to the oozing wound, snarled an assortment of hair-raising oaths. He turned to his whispering colleagues, eyed their flared faces.

'What's that y'say, you damn bloats? Stick mutterin' behind me back!'

'I've that blue divil's velvy bag, if you wants 'un, Jethro,' Judd Downderry offered with a wink. The giant Cornishman tilted his head, growled into his beard.

The mutilated ear throbbed and popped, he dabbed it cautiously with his neckerchief, shook his tangled head to clear the peculiar chiming sound from his bruised skull. He would usually have been the first to reach for his musket, but he missed the snap of branches which announced the approach of a party of officers. An ensign was holding a guttering torch above his head, lighting the way for General Hopton and the pitifully few staff officers who remained in attendance. The Cornishmen struggled to their feet as he clambered down amongst them, looked up and down the filthy, fire-red faces.

'Gentlemen, a hard fight,' he said briefly. The ragged soldiers nodded and coughed as the general stepped between them, levered himself up the far wall of their dugout. He raised his glass and spied the silent wall, the steady glow of the insect-eyed match cords. He frowned, listened. What was Waller up to now? The one-sided firefight had continued past midnight, ending in one deafening volley from the black mass of the dry-stone wall. Since then, silence. Only the glowing match points remained. It was too much to hope Waller had retired. Drawn his battered army off the damned hill? Hopton stepped down, turned to the shaggy scarecrows gathered about the fire.

'I've a shilling for the man who'll run to the wall, see what's become of our neighbours,' he said crisply, fishing in his purse for a coin.

'What? What he say?' Polruan whispered.

Downderry ignored him, stepped forward. 'I'm your man sir, Judd Downderry of Newlyn, sir.'

'Ahh yes.' Hopton nodded, handed the coin over.

Downderry bit it between his teeth, grinned and hopped up the wall like a monkey.

'Where's he off to?' Polruan snorted. The dugout fell silent as the intent officers watched the shadowy figure flit through the trees, disappear into the darkness. He returned a few moments later, jumped in amongst the waiting men.

'Scarpered. The whole passel of 'em. They've left match cords burning on broken pikes, the canny buggers.'

Hopton closed his eyes, breathed a heartfelt sigh of relief. 'Thank the Lord for that,' he murmured. The army was down to its last few barrels of powder. If Waller had renewed the attack his surviving soldiers would have been reduced to throwing stones.

'And I tell you sir, Bath is to our right!' Webster hissed into the inky darkness after Master Lyle's practically invisible shadow. The taller commissioner halted, tilted his long pale head this way and that. His broad-beaked nose twitched as he sampled the unseen smoke, picked out the unmistakable brassy tang of blood. He frowned, looked over his stooped shoulder at Webster, whose long years poring over tracts and meticulously written reports had reduced his eyesight to the efficacy of a particularly myopic mole. Despite his shortcomings the shorter man had insisted he knew the road, and had led the way through the eerily dripping woods towards the Roundhead lines on the ridge. The commissioners and their precious prisoner – the enemy agent and unrepentant malignant Sir Marmaduke Ramsay – had already managed to lose their scowling escort, the four dragoons who had led the squire up the hill in the first place. They had tried to remain in touch with the general so that he might benefit from their experienced advice and clear grasp of the tactical realities.

'Let them come on, sir, only a fool would attack a well-entrenched position such as this,' Webster had advised the glowering commander.

'So long as the men have the heart to hold it,' Lyle had qualified.

'The men have the heart, sir, I assure you,' Waller had breathed dangerously.

'Then we are assured of victory,' Webster had concluded.

Sir Marmaduke, banished to the rear of the party and the fidgeting dragoons, had peered over their black shoulders, tried to catch his erstwhile comrade's tired eye. 'Sir, I cannot imagine how Sir Ralph Hopton, a man whose worth you all know well, could ever have intended to throw lives away in such a reckless enterprise,' he called to their bowed backs. 'I implore you sir, to pause a moment and consider the document I have negotiated with Morrison.'

Waller closed his eyes for a moment, took a lungful of smoky breath. The commissioners wheeled around, waved the squire back.

'Sergeant, if the rogue volunteers any more treacheries you will escort him to the rear with the rest of our prisoners,' Webster squawked. Sir Marmaduke, in a passion, had spurred his horse forward, brandished his petition like a pole axe. The dragoon guards leaned over and snatched up his reins, brought his horse around. Waller looked over his armoured shoulder, caught the squire's wretched stare.

'Sir William, in the name of God stop this while you have it within your power! In the name of—'

'Enough! Sergeant, to the rear with him!'

'William! Please!'

'You'll retire, sir, or walk with the rest of the wretches!' Webster snarled, pointing out the column of prisoners shuffling back up the hill. A hundred and more had been captured in the furious hedge-to-hedge fire-fight at the foot of the hill, the desperate cavalry mêlées which followed. They were being herded to the rear by squads of relieved musketeers, anxious to distance themselves from the impending doom on the ridge.

Hugo Telling, lamentably lost in their wearied ranks, felt light headed and slightly sick. Unhorsed for the second time by that hulking oaf Starling! He hadn't recognized him at first in the calamitous cut and thrust at the foot of the hill. He had been more intent on escape than gaining his revenge on some upstart apprentice. Intercepted by a black and white berserker of a horse carrying off its terrified rider, he had at first intended to ride straight by and gain the cover of the woods. The horseman had obviously been new to the saddle, pushing with his backside and flapping the reins as if he was beating washing. The poor brute of a horse had stamped and reared its hideous patchwork face, rolled its wall-eye as it lumbered deliberately into his path. He recognized the beast before the bastard on its back. The monstrous cob he had last seen tied to Morrison's cursed wool wagon! He had focused on his despised rival's fearful face as he contorted himself in the saddle trying to turn the clumsy cart horse. He recognized at once the heavy, furrowed features of his enemy and pulled his horse around to teach him his lesson at last. How was it he could have been beaten to the floor by such a bumbling idiot? A crop-headed dolt from the hills? What terrible sin had he committed, that God should punish him so?

Hugo blinked, remembering several of his sessions with the vivacious Matilda. The girl had drained him like a lemon, sucked the very marrow from his bones! The debauched Delilah had eaten up all his manly energies, left him staggering like a drunken man, dozing in the saddle when he should have been as formidable as Prince Rupert himself! Hah! Rupert didn't dally with the doxies every night. He pored over maps and practised his sword strokes. God's wounds, what had he done?

Mortified with shame and eaten out with anger at his contemptible end, he looked up at the sudden altercation on the hill and recognized the squire as he remonstrated with the enemy officers. He seethed with frustration to see a loyal officer dragged away from the command post as if he was trying to sell stale pies at market. God damn these rebels, these upstarts, these posturing pot wallopers. Is this how the Roundhead masters would treat with a true-hearted nobleman if, God forbid, they ever held on to their monstrous power? He saw Waller cringe with embarrassment as his fellow officer was dragged off by a couple of bandits on blown nags, the black-crow commissioners closing in behind as if they would shield their general from such outrageous influences.

'Away with you, sir, we'll not stand by while you attempt to subvert the Lord's purposes this day!'

'Subvert the Lord's purposes? Me? It is your damned serpents who—'

'Enough!' Webster had barked. 'To the rear with you, sir!' The commissioners had hurried him away, arguing and shouting as he went.

The commissioners and their dragoon escort had shepherded the squire back to the windy ridge, pulled him aside and watched the prisoners marched off down the rutted tracks toward Bath, mingling with the fugitives. There were hundreds of walking wounded clutching bloody bandages, dozens more masquerading as injured and others who had simply slipped away to their homes down the far side of the trembling hill. The commissioners had reined in, studied the fragile position along the ridge like black-coated Caesars.

'Will he fight, Master Webster? Are we to trust our general?' Lyle had enquired, when the dragoons were safely out of earshot.

Sir Marmaduke, white with anger, couldn't believe his own ears. 'You doubt your own commander?' he asked incredulously. 'How such a man of honour ever allowed himself to be caught up with you spiders and your vile webs, I'll never understand,' he snorted furiously.

Webster ignored his outburst, peered back over the hill. Thick grey smoke was welling up out of the valley, coils and columns swallowed by the encroaching darkness, swept away by the scudding clouds. The commissioner squinted at the sky, shook his head.

'He'll hold the centre as long as he is able, but the flanks, sir, I fear they'll buckle before nightfall.'

Lyle rose in his saddle, nodded. 'The open flank, sir. One last charge could mean the end of everything,' he fretted.

Webster chewed his lip, nodded. They had called the dragoons back, trotted over towards the western end of the ridge. The commissioners had found the situation confused but apparently stable, Haselrig's Lobsters a formidable reserve behind the bloodied troops of Waller's and Burghill's regiments. Webster had decided to return to the centre, but night was falling fast and they had been diverted by the steep-sided quarry pits, a series of hazardous obstacles behind the main Roundhead position.

Belching guns, screaming horses, choking smoke. Great gaping pits in the earth flared with fire and sulphurous fumes. Sir Marmaduke had ridden on through his own private excruciating hell, imagined he was in Bohemia all over again. A twisted land of fire and blood. He slumped in the saddle, sick to his stomach, sick at heart. The fuming commissioners peered into the flaring gloom, looked behind them to see what had become of their escort. The dragoons had fallen behind and then slipped away into the darkness. Where was the army? Five thousand men didn't just vanish into the night! They walked in circles around the treacherous pits and came across bands of soldiers hurrying along with sloped arms. The commissioners watched them make their way to the rear in tolerably good order. They had seen a fair few routs before, and knew the difference between men who had been ordered back and those who were running for their lives from a furious pursuit. Somebody must have ordered a retreat! An army didn't march in time when it took to its heels. There could be only one answer to this new riddle. Waller had presented their hard-held ground to the enemy. The centre they had imagined would hold all night had buckled if not broken.

'Where are you going?' Webster demanded, reaching down in his distraction to grab a sooty musketeer by his ragged coat. The man shook himself free, eyed the black-suited commissioner with supernatural suspicion.

'Off this ridge,' the soldier growled, hurried after his company.

'Are they advancing or retreating?' Lyle wanted to know.

Webster squinted at his fearful colleague. 'Retreat? Why on earth should the army retreat? We were winning, sir!' he cried indignantly. There was a shout of laughter from the darkness.

'Who was winning? Tell us who was winning!' a shadowy stranger called from the far side of one of the quarry pits. The commissioners spurred on as fast as they could through the chaos, carried along blindly in the flotsam and jetsam of the slow but sure retreat. They wondered what manner of disaster could have befallen the well-entrenched army. What sinister order could have under-mined their brave stand?

'To your right, sir, to the right lies Bath,' Webster intoned, urging his horse through the mass of frightened fugitives, across the wild path of the retreat.

'Horse!' The startled cry was taken up from the flank, passed on by a dozen increasingly anxious fugitives.

'Horse? Whose horse?' Webster snorted, turning his

exhausted cob in its tracks once again. 'The enemy are scattered! They must be ours!' He peered into the gloom, drew his heavy carbine from beneath his coat and squinted at it, trying to ensure it was properly primed.

'I believe escape might be advisable, Master Webster,' Lyle suggested.

'Escape? From our own rearguards? You saw our flanks, sir, as sound as a barrel!'

'A holed barrel, apparently,' Lyle muttered doubtfully. The jingle of harness and the ragged breath of a dozen horses. Shouts and catcalls on all sides.

'Master Webster, I think we ought to—'

'Hola, gentlemen!' A ragamuffin Cavalier on a lathered horse loomed out of the drifting smoke, his rich suit scorched with powder and shredded by shot and sword. He had crammed his black hat over his hastily bandaged head, his thick black hair matted with dark blood. The captain held a pistol in his right hand, menaced the furious prisoners while his men trotted around either flank. One of the few hundred horsemen Hopton had managed to round up from the choked valleys below, and hurled up onto the newly won ridge. Webster twitched right and left, but every way he looked he saw a dirty scarecrow soldier. Hostile stares, gimlet eyes ringed with soot and grime.

'Don't shoot! You have kinsmen here!' Sir Marmaduke, overcoming his wretched grief for a moment, called out despairingly. 'Don't shoot!' he cried piteously.

Dawn came over the mutilated ridge by fits and starts, as if it could hardly bear to light the frightful carnage. As if the heaps of dead, the crawling wounded, the fuming pits of broken equipment belonged to the witch realm of night. Feeble grey smoke recoiled over the smouldering debris, the trampled gunpits and smashed fortifications. There were more dead horses than they could eat, and burial parties from both armies toiled ceaselessly from the bloody ridge to the quarry pits, rolling pale naked bodies into the open graves. Hopton's few surviving senior commanders moved from one heap of corpses to another, pointing out their brother officers. The Royalist soldiers, stretching beside their hasty bivouacs on the hill, imagined at first they were gazing at the sorry remains of Waller's army. Closer inspection of the shot-riddled, piked and trampled corpses revealed the true extent of their disastrous victory. The fanatically brave Cornish had carpeted the hill with their dead. Splintered pikes and smashed muskets, rifled snapsacks and discarded helmets and hats littered the fouled slopes. Further down the hill, tangled in the tattered hedges, were dozens of out-sniped dragoons, cavalry troopers who hadn't managed to spur out of the way of Waller's regiments. More corpses had lain all night in the corn field on Tog Hill. They had crawled into the corn to escape the vicious fighting and bled to death during the night, hidden by the husks and stalks to all but the wheeling, croaking crows who flew in with the sunrise.

General Hopton rode the hills and the steep valleys, paling visibly as the full extent of the disaster dawned on him. Waller had suffered, of course. Hundreds of his miscellaneous infantry had lain where they fell defending their earthworks. The corpses of his well-equipped cavalry had been picked clean by the roving looters. But he had drawn off in good order into Bath where he could expect reinforcements and replenishment. Hopton's army, shorn of a third of its strength and most of its experienced officers, was little more than a hungry, belligerent mob. A gang of bandits who had temporarily taken over a wind-blown hill. They could no more hold this ground than they could plant banners on the pale morning stars. He rode along the ridge in silence, his attendants keeping a discreet distance. Their dozens of light carts and heavy wagons had been drawn up in one of the enclosures, the chattering camp followers and shouting cooks and scream-ing whores seemingly oblivious to the catastrophe. Those with loved ones on the field had been out through the night, tipping corpses and rifling pockets. The occasional shrill, broken wail announcing another dreaded discovery. The motley gang of prisoners lounging about the lightly laden powder wagon seemed awed by the destruction, nervously expecting to be made to pay for the all too evident Royalist misfortunes. A sorry squire in a torn coat and a pair of scowling, black-suited crows for company.

'My Lord! Sir Ralph!' Hopton glanced up at the run-ning-board, saw a bedraggled officer in a fancy red suit, loaded with lawn and lace. The reluctant Roundhead looked vaguely familiar.

'Sir Ralph Hopton, do you not remember me? Marma-duke Ramsay, sir, from Bohemia!'

Bohemia? Ah yes. Hopton smiled faintly, reined in beside the great wagon. The squire clambered down from his perch with the prisoners, quietly smoking while they watched the Royalists exchange uncertain greetings.

'You have had word, sir, from my son Thomas? I sent him to you with correspondence, sir, with a petition agreed by General Waller's headquarters.'

General Hopton nodded ruefully over the devastated slopes. 'General Waller would appear to have sent petition-ers of his own, sir.'

'I have talked with the merchant, Morrison. He has connections with the enemy high command, sir, and a note to treat with me as intermediary,' Ramsay insisted.

The black-coated jackals on the wagon leaned over, whispered secrets. Hopton glanced back at the wretched squire, his face lined and creased with powder and soot, his eyes as red as every common soldier's.

'Your son, sir? Your son was here?'

'He would have arrived before the battle, the night before last, sir.' Ramsay stared anxiously at the bewildered general, who turned in the saddle to confer with his officers.

'I have received no such petition, sir. Is it possible your son was delayed by the enemy?'

'I decided to go to General Waller, sir, with the same petition. Thomas should have reached you by now!' Ramsay exclaimed, tugging at his beard, wondering what could have happened to the boy. He had taken the safer road, surely, riding direct to the Royalist camp? He looked up as Hopton conversed with one of his attendants, a dark-complexioned man wearing an expensive black cassock and matching suit lined with rich red velvet. The general turned back to him, nodded gravely.

'Your son, sir, would he have carried distinguishing marks?' Ramsay's heart leapt as his blood ran chill through his sorry veins. Distinguishing marks? The smartly dressed attendant climbed down from his horse, a black-suited angel of death. Ramsay regarded him as if he clutched handfuls of vipers.

'Sir,' he began in his heavily accented English. 'I am Ambrosio di Meola St Corelli, I am a surgeon, serving with the Generale,' he said, his black eyes flickering. 'The night you refer to, I was called to the tent of the Colonel Butler,

310

now sadly among *i morti*. He had been called out by his men, sir.'

Ramsay could hardly hear the Italian, over the furious rushing in his ears.

'I am sorry to say, sir, his men had shot a messenger, a dreadful mistake. The messenger,' he paused, held his dark-skinned hand, encrusted with rings, to his olive face. 'He was a badly burn, his face, scars here.' Ramsay closed his eyes. The surgeon stepped back in silent respect, reading the squire's grief from his trembling lips, compressed into a thin white crease.

'Sir, I can only offer my humblest apologies that such a hideous accident could have occurred under my command,' General Hopton said stiffly. 'What was that, sir?'

'The petition,' Ramsay breathed. 'The treaty, sir. You saw the proposals my son carried with him?' He looked up, blinked through his tears as they exchanged glances.

'Colonel Butler ... his men were on watch that night ... has been killed. Perhaps among his personal papers ... we may find your petition, sir.' He looked awkward, bowed his head.

Ramsay watched the general turn his horse, pick his way along the trampled tracks. He felt the hill slide under his boots, as if hell itself would pick him out of the chaos. There was a sudden movement behind him, like the beating of a giant raven's wings. He saw a flash of black out of the corner of his brimming eye as his erstwhile captors, the fanatical, snarling commissioners, leapt from the wagon like naughty children. The bewildered squire turned, held his hand out as the rest of the prisoners, realizing what the gleeful agents had done, jumped for their lives.

Ramsay opened his mouth to shout a warning but the

cry was swallowed up by the enormous, ear-splitting roar as the carelessly dropped match ignited spilled powder, detonated the ten stacked barrels. The last of Hopton's preciously hoarded store. The massive explosion echoed around the hills, startling men and horses half a mile away. Prince Maurice, who had been riding to and fro trying to patch together a few troops of horse from the weary remains of his cavalry, had almost fallen off as the massive retort rolled over the hill. The great tongue of flame and belching smoke climbed into the clearing sky, scattering the crows and ravens wheeling overhead. The Prince ducked over his horse's mane, held his hands over his head as a shower of splinters and twisted metal from the wrecked wagon rained down over the slopes. The shock wave knocked the wind from him, he crouched, coughing and wretching over his terrified stallion's neck. Next instant he had tugged himself up and spurred off toward the calamity.

Astonished soldiers, dazed prisoners and screaming carters staggered by with singed hair and staring eyes. An officer rolled on the ground crying the flames had got into his breeches. Another had lost his luxurious beard and flowing locks in the agonized blink of his eye. Maurice pulled up before the massive tower of boiling flame and smoke, felt the heat crisp his cheeks. Hopton had been caught by the full force of the blast, and was lying groaning among the smouldering wreckage of charred men and leather horses. His clothes were in tatters, what was left of his beard blackened stubble. He was clutching at his face, rolling in agony. Thank God he had not been killed, the Prince thought, ducked down beside him. The Italian surgeon tottered in the smoky chaos, tangling his expensive boots. His horse had shielded him from the worst of the blast. The General's shell-shocked aides dashed forward and dragged their roasted commander from the flames, laid him out on the cool grass a hundred yards from the boiling maelstrom. Hopton blinked his eyes, clutched the earth.

'I can't see! I can't see!'

Maurice hurried up, knelt alongside. 'My Lord, you are hurt,' he said with his usual lightning intuition.

Hopton thrashed his scorched arms about him, tried to sit up. 'The powder! The powder gone!' he wailed, tiny wisps of smoke escaping from his blackened, cracked lips.

Master Ignatius Webster, skin blackened the colour of his customary coat, tottered out of the wreckage, walked in circles before collapsing to his ashen knees. He clutched his skeletal hands, burnt skin peeling and cracking from the white bones, stared unseeing at the silent pall of smoke. His face had been burnt like cork, his staring eyes reduced to strings of sizzling fluid and mucus, running over the pitted parchment of his face. His scorched mouth moved stiffly in a prayer his sealed ears couldn't hear.

'. . . And Samson called unto the Lord, and said O Lord God remember me, I pray thee, and strengthen me, I pray thee, only this once, O God, that I may be at once avenged of the Philistines for my two eyes.'

He toppled into the grass, thought at the last, so shall God turn defeat into victory. Victory.

PART FOUR

VICTORY?

*'Had he been victualled as well as fortified,
he might have endured a siege of seven years'*

KING CHARLES I COMMENTING ON
SIR ARTHUR HASELRIG'S
CONTRIBUTION AFTER THE BATTLE
OF ROUNDWAY DOWN

HAM MEADOW

JULY 7, 1643

John Clegg the miller had watched from his hayloft as the strangers explored the devastated meadow. Three days since the fight and the armies had moved on, but they had left more than enough refuse to bring the looters from as far afield as Bristol and Bradford, eager to poke through the rubble and the rushes in case something had been missed. A discarded shoe, a bent dagger. He climbed down the ladder, shaking his head. The damned tinkers would take anything the troops had dropped; maybe they would like to replant the field of standing corn he'd lost, mend the fences the armies had broken down. The heavy-set miller strode out of the yard and down the path as the strangers gathered around the freshly turned gravepits. God above, would they stoop as low as that?

'Hoy! This is private land, what d'you think you're doing there?' he called. The cloaked strangers turned, lowered their hoods. The miller stamped to a halt, eyed the two girls and the callow youth they had brought with them. The taller girl was strikingly handsome, with a mass of fine auburn hair pulled back from her forehead. She returned his stare, a flash of irritation animating her bold green eyes. The other girl was sobbing, running her nose over her sleeve.

'What are you doing here?' the miller asked, moderating his tone slightly. 'This is private land, whether they've fought over it or not,' he said indignantly.

The elder girl tilted her head, frowned. 'Don't you dare lecture me as if you've caught us after your apples!' she exclaimed. The other girl held her arm, nodded.

'It's all right, miss.' She looked up, smiled wearily at the red-faced miller with his wire-wool hair and crisp red cheeks. 'We're looking after me father, sir. We heard the army was here,' she explained hoarsely.

The miller nodded grimly. 'Oh, they were here right enough,' he said. 'You're looking at the mess they left behind 'em.'

'We were told up the hill the Bristol men were here, in the fort,' the elder girl said sharply, nodding at the crumbling earthworks along the far side of the meadow.

'Bristol men, Gloucester men, London men, all sorts, by all accounts,' the miller replied.

'We're looking for Gregory Pitt, the drover from Chipping Marleward.'

The miller had never heard of the place. 'Well, there's none here now,' he began, pulling at his broad nose. 'Leastways . . .'

The servant girl covered her face, looked away while the elder girl straightened, compressed her lips.

'The dead were buried here, is that right?'

'Roundabouts,' the miller agreed. 'Though we hardly knew 'em from Adam, as you'll appreciate, miss,' he added.

'Mr Pitt was an older man, and he walked with a limp . . .'

'His foot was off, just here,' the boy, Gregory's fourth son Jeremiah, lifted his holed boot and shook it for emphasis.

Clegg wiped his mouth, shook his head. 'I don't rightly

recall,' he mumbled. 'There were a good few of 'em,' he said doubtfully. The old gaffer they'd dragged from the mill-wheel had been crippled though, hadn't he? Dragged out like a dead sheep and rolled in with the rest, right where they were standing. They were near enough. Clegg, as superstitious as any of his narrow-minded neighbours, didn't want folks bawling and crying over his crops, wasn't lucky. He stuck his thumbs under his waistcoat, nodded back up toward Claverton Down.

'They took a barrow load on up to the churchyard,' he said sternly. 'You'd best go there and ask the reverend.' The elder girl scowled, said they would do just that. She linked arms with the sobbing girl, led her back over the bridge and up the muddy path to the small dog cart they had driven down from the hills. And good riddance, Clegg thought, watching the boy steer the cart around and clatter back up the lane.

'You heard the man, Mary,' Bella encouraged the distraught maid. 'He would have recognized your father, from the description we gave.'

Mary Keziah roughly wiped her eyes, her pretty chin trembling. 'There might have been dozens with their feets shot off,' she wailed. 'What am I to tell Mother?'

Gregory had been expected back two days before. He had set out on the eleven-mile journey to the river to deliver a large basket of provisions for his three elder boys working on Waller's redoubt. His wife had anticipated he would stay the night, but not a week. Gwen Pitt's joy on seeing her daughter Mary return safely from the big house on the hill had been tempered with anxiety for her old man.

'He would have cadged a lift off one of his cronies, all right, but what good is he to a marchin' army, 'obbling on one leg?' Gwen had cried bitterly.

Mary Keziah had begged Bella to excuse her while she took a buggy out after her father, but her mistress wouldn't hear of her going alone. This time, Bella had decided it might be politic to ask her father's permission before she went off.

Sir Gilbert had decided they had worn out what little welcome they had up at the hall. He judged the time was right to risk returning to their home in the High Street, especially after Sir Marmaduke and young Thomas had set off with their precious petitions. Left to his own devices, Findlay had been increasingly insolent, while Lady Ramsay seemed to regard the gamekeeper as a lieutenant rather than a hireling. Sir Gilbert bade the scowling Lady Ramsay a fond farewell, thanking her profusely for 'opening their house in their moment of desperate need'. Desperate need? The formidable woman watched them pack their wretched wagons, drive off down the hill to their abandoned town house. She was glad enough to be rid of them, she had worries of her own with Ramsay and Thomas away.

The Morrison party had driven in to Chipping Marleward, attracting half the village into the street. The merchant waved and nodded to the grim-faced villagers as if he had just returned from a drive in the hills. Bella stared straight ahead, half expecting to see their old home pulled down to the ground by the neighbours they had abandoned with such reckless haste. She was almost disappointed to see the house standing four-square as usual in the main street. A few windows had been put out by naughty children or deserters making their way through the village, the outhouses had been broken into and picked clean, but otherwise the merchant's home was still his castle. He stood on the steps, rubbed his hands and sent a boy running around the village to hire a few odd-job men. 'Get the place cleaned up, you know,' he said.

Bella had idly picked at her cases, back in the same room she had hurried away from those weeks before. Time had stood still. No, worse than that, it had whisked her back in some sort of infernal loop, deposited her back at the beginning all over again. She had been gazing at the all too familiar view from her narrow window when Mary Keziah had knocked on the door, brought the news about her missing father. Sir Gilbert, rushing about the house with piles of papers under his arm, had set his load down on the table, shaken his head after Bella had asked permission to accompany her maid on her search.

'Bath? Bradford on Avon? Whatever makes you think I'll allow you off on such a fool's errand? Our name's Morrison, girl, not Ramsay,' he said, unable to restrain himself from crowing about his masterful handling of the tomfool squire and his son. Bella had sulked, thrown her shoulders out.

'Well, at least I asked this time,' she snapped, paused a moment to summon up her most winning, mischievous grin. 'Besides, the armies are long gone, Father, you know that. Jeremiah will drive us as far as the river, we'll be there and back by evening.'

'With half the country up in arms, girl? Have you lost your sense?'

'Father, I've been in worse scrapes with you lately. You can't coop me up here for the rest of my life,' she exclaimed. Sir Gilbert drummed his fingers on the dusty sideboard, nodded in distraction.

'You seem to think I'm old enough to be married off, and yet you keep me close here like a six-year-old!' Bella accused.

Her father held his breath for a moment, secretly delighted at her marvellously cunning arguments. She knew damn fine he wanted her to marry young Thomas – when he had gotten back from his wild-goose chase to Hopton, that is. It would be the perfect match, linking his burgeoning fortunes with the Ramsays' pitifully declining line. My, she could play her cards as well as he could. Sir Gilbert had relented, nodded his head. He had an enormous amount of work to do in any case, now the balance of power had shifted so dramatically. A new place to establish in a rapidly fluctuating society. He had accounts to settle and letters to write and clerks away in Bristol to harry. It wouldn't do any harm if young Bella was out of the way for an hour or two.

'All right, then, but just make sure you're back by nightfall. There's all sorts of folk coming up and down the Fosseway now, as well you know.'

Bella gave Mary an encouraging hug as Jeremiah steered the buggy up the steep hill toward the main Bath road. He clicked the reins over the pony's broad back, looked down the slope toward the shiny tiled roofs and spires of Bath. Bella shielded her eyes, followed his gaze. She felt the familiar tug of the city, the busy streets and bustling markets, the Roman baths which still attracted the enthusiastic if unwashed crowds. The place was teeming with people getting on with their lives while here she sat in a dog cart with a couple of servants. A ride out into the country for the sake of something to break the tedium of her existence.

'Uh-oh, miss,' Jeremiah said, nodding his tousled head to the main road. Bella looked round, followed his pointing finger. A troop of cavalry were pounding along the rutted road under a fluttering cornet. She squinted at the tawny colour to try and identify their allegiance but gave up in disgust. What point was there in discovering whose side they were on when she no longer knew what side she was on? Bella told the boy to pull in, and watched the horsemen canter closer. She picked out the detail of their dark coats and dull armour, their orange sashes and sweating horses.

'I must have died and gone tw'eaven, lookit 'er, Michael.'

'Grouar Davey, would oi?'

Bella primly straightened her skirts as the rude cavalry cantered by shouting ribald comments. They were followed by another troop and then another riding through the dust cloud they had kicked up.

Mary stood up, waved at the cheerful troopers. 'Miss look, it's Jasper!'

Jasper? Bella didn't know any Jaspers. The girls watched the third troop ride up, the officers drawing rein beside their buggy. Bella recognized Major McSomething, wondered at the identity of the grinning stranger riding William's lumbering piebald. William with the cavalry? Surely not. He had a ten-day growth of beard, and the combination of army rations and twenty-mile rides across hard country had redefined his features. He seemed taller, his tanned face older and wiser. No longer a grinning youth with a mass of curls and boyishly rosy cheeks. He pulled his hat from his cropped head, nodded at her.

'Bella – Miss Morrison, Mary,' he said.

McNabb gave them an exaggerated bow from the saddle. 'Aye, it's himself. I take all the credit for the change, mind ye,' he said good naturedly.

Sparrow asked what they were doing, out and about so far from home.

'We're looking for Gregory,' Bella answered for her blushing maid.

'He went to take the extra vittles for Zack and the boys, but he ain't come home,' Mary added tearfully.

Sparrow nodded, glanced at his commanding officer. The Scot shook his head, dragged his horse's head up from the lush grass it was busily cropping. 'The war won't wait for ye, laddie. Five minutes, or I'll shoot you for a deserter mysen,' he growled, touched his helmet and rode on after the formidable-looking troop.

'We haven't seen old Gregory since the fight on the island,' Sparrow reported, climbing down from the sweating cob. 'But I'm sure he'll turn up somewhere. I've been transferred to the cavalry, but Zack and Eli are fine, Mordecai's hurt his thigh but he'll be up and about in a day or so. Jamie's got his company back, he's with Waller . . .' Sparrow trailed off, grinned awkwardly. Bella realized he must have thought he was giving secrets away to the enemy, just by talking to her. The turncoat's daughter. She felt a stab of angry resentment. Must she walk in this limbo for the rest of her life? Damn their war! Mary Keziah was blinking as she digested the sudden onslaught of news, young Jeremiah beamed. It had been worth the long drive down from the hills to see the fine soldiers riding by. He cursed his mother for keeping him home, away from all the nerve-tingling excitement.

'That's fine, ain't it, Mary? They been in a fight, 'ave they, Mr Sparrow?'

The officer grinned, looked down at his worn buff coat and dull breastplate as if following their curious gaze. 'I'm a cornet now, a proper cornet,' he said proudly. 'But I'll be a captain again by the time we finish Hopton. Running away faster than they came,' he said, unable to temper his enthusiasm. He pulled at Jasper's reins as the big horse headed for a patch of dandelions, nodded on up the dusty road.

'I can't stop and chatter, much as I'd like. Why don't you follow us on to Bradford, we can talk there?'

Mary glanced at Bella.

'Bradford? The Royalists are at Bradford,' Bella said uneasily.

William waved his hand dismissively. 'They're long gone,' he said casually. 'The rest of the army will be passing that way, you might see Zack and the boys.'

'Could we, miss? Father might have caught up again by then.'

'I don't see what harm it can do,' Bella allowed, secretly delighted at the prospect of prolonging their adventure.

William threw his leg back over the big piebald's saddle, pulled its head from the grass. Jeremiah turned the cart on to the track, flicked the reins over the pony's back as Sparrow fell in alongside, pushing his hat to the back of his head to describe his recent adventures. Mary Keziah beamed at him, looking so proud in his uniform and all. If she had the chance at Bradford, she would take the bull by the horns and ask him straight out. The great ninny needed a push now and again, to get him thinking. Thinking it was time he took a wife. The pretty brown-haired servant girl gazed at her hero, listened attentively while he talked. Bella, meanwhile, adjusted her skirts and gazed at the woods across the far side of the valley with studied indifference.

The creaking dog cart and its dusty escort caught up with the cavalry outside Bradford on Avon. Scouts had been sent in to the small mill town to ensure the enemy had abandoned the bridge, joined the general retreat to the east. The Roundhead reconnaissance force had dismounted in a meadow beneath a stand of chestnut trees, watered their horses at a small pond. Jeremiah drove the cart along the horse lines, waving at the troopers who stopped whatever they were doing to wave back.

'Here she is, then!'

'Over here, me chick!'

Sparrow rode alongside the wagon, waving the excitable soldiers out of the way. He jumped down from the lathered piebald as the swarming gnats and flies abandoned the other horses and made straight for the black and white beast. Jasper stamped, flicked his tail in annoyance as the buzzing clouds settled over his heaving flanks. Sparrow took off his gauntlets, helped Bella down from the wagon. Mary Keziah waited for him to help her down as well, but the sunburnt officer had merely leaned forward over the running-board to whisper to her.

'Give us a moment, Mary, can you?' He smiled shortly, turned his back on her and strode off after Bella. Mary sat still, watched them walk into the shade of the massive trees, out of earshot.

'I'm glad to see you're safe,' she said simply.

Sparrow nodded. 'I heard about your father, changing sides I mean,' he said awkwardly.

Bella blushed beneath the green hood of her cloak, lips set. 'Is that why you were being so vague about the whereabouts of the army? Afraid of me giving away all your secrets as if I'm a spy for my father?'

'Of course not,' he scoffed, reddening.

'He can change his sides as he will, it's my lot to be dragged along with him like a sack of washing,' she said with feeling. 'They didn't want us up there, at the Hall I mean. I hadn't realized Father was planning to . . .' She waved her hand, balled it into a fist. 'Lady Margaret treated me as if I were a common whore.' Bella coloured, frowning as she swept the overhanging branches out of her face. She paused in the dappled sunlight, chuckled. 'Well, we're back at home now, as if nothing ever happened,' she reported.

'Well, I'm just glad you're safe,' he said with a sigh. 'How far were you planning to come with us? We're moving quickly and it'll be no place for women when we catch up with them.' Bella wandered off around the great gnarled trunk, Sparrow ducking his head as he followed her. 'You ought to be going along now, if you want to be back at Chipping Marleward tonight.'

'I don't want to go back to Chipping Marleward tonight; to be honest with you, I don't want to go back at all. There!' she said, flashing him a dangerous look. 'I don't care if I never set eyes on the place again!'

Sparrow paused then hurried after her, noticed she was crying freely. He touched her arm. 'Bella . . . you're better off there, until we've finished this business. It's no secret Hopton won't last the summer. It doesn't matter who

327

knows it. He may have pushed us off the ridge but he lost a third of his army and used up all his powder! They're reduced to throwing rocks at us now!' He eased his arm around her waist, pushed her gently against the trunk of the chestnut sunshade. She rested her head against his buff coat and he closed his eyes, transported by her sunshine fragrance. They could stop the war now, leave him under the tree with her for ever.

'Go home to your father, and when we come back . . . we'll see,' he said obscurely.

'I don't want to go back to Father. He's going to marry me off to Thomas Ramsay, if he can. You remember Crybaby Tom? Crybaby no longer,' she sniffed. 'He was hurt at Edgehill and he has to wear a mask! Father wouldn't care if he had no legs or arms either, as long as he could . . . you know.'

Sparrow blinked away the beads of perspiration rolling down his face. 'I remember him, yes,' he stammered, taken aback by the unexpected twist. Would Sir Gilbert stop at nothing to gain his end? Marry her off to the squire's boy to cement his new position? Knowing the merchant as well as he did, there could only be one answer. He held her stiffly against his stiff leather coat and dull steel breasplate. Clamped her to him as if he could protect her from the war, the elements, her own damned rogue of a father. Her breath left tiny blooms of vapour over the pitted steel plate, reflected her cool apricot features. If Bella had been wearing armour he would have seen himself, a sweaty red oaf.

'I'll stay with you,' she whispered, interrupting his reverie. William swallowed, as much at a loss as he had been on Lansdown two days before when Telling had turned his horse and charged him. Hah! How he'd scowled, marching into Bath with the rest of the prisoners while William rode past with McNabb's triumphant troop. He had grinned broadly at the mortified youth, raised his hat in cheeky greeting.

'Captain Woolpicker, well met! That's the second time I've had the better of you!'

'Get down from that overstuffed armchair on legs and try a third, you scoundrel!' Telling had called belligerently. McNabb, riding alongside the delighted Sparrow, had taken off his dented helmet, guffawed.

'I'll give you a beating any time you want my fine wee laddie, but enough's enough for one day. Away and cool your heels, ye candle-wasting whoreson, ye!' Telling had turned purple as the laughing riders had spurred ahead of the shuffling column, hurrying to join the celebrations in Bath.

Reinforced and replenished, Waller's beaten army had practically charged out of the town after the unhappy victors, chased the Royalist rearguards off Lansdown and through Marshfield. Hopton's army was now scurrying off toward Chippenham like a beaten cur with its tail well and truly between its legs. As soon as Waller caught up with them, the war in the west would be over and done! The thought had buoyed Sparrow as it buoyed the rest of the army. He had never seen such enthusiasm in all his long weeks with the colours.

He had fought and survived, and here was Bella, his true sweetheart, offering to run away with him! He could hardly believe his ears. God's wounds, they wouldn't allow her to play the whore around their camp though. He frowned. They would have to marry, aye, that night! That wretched ranter Gillingfeather, he could perform the ceremony. He could wear the expensive sword he'd taken from the flabbergasted Telling! Perhaps he ought to invite the upstart along to witness his final triumph! He smiled to himself, glanced down at the gorgeous girl, realized with a start he had missed five minutes of her hesitant speech.

'Well? What should I tell Mary?' she asked, looking up at his delighted face.

'Oh, tell her anything you like! We'll be married tonight, what does it matter?'

'Married?' she squawked, pulling away from him. 'Married?' she repeated incredulously, peering out from their secluded bower in case any of the rude soldiers had eavesdropped on their heated conversation.

Sparrow grinned nervously. 'Well, of course,' he explained. 'Our army does not allow ... unmarried women in the camp.' Bella frowned, eyes flashing as she thought hard. Sparrow felt a familiar surge of uncertainty through his overloaded system. 'Why shouldn't we be married? You said you wanted to come away with me,' he pointed out, leaning over to nuzzle her bare neck, closing his eyes to savour her sweet scents.

'Well, yes ... but married. I mean, Father wanted me to marry Thomas,' she explained clumsily.

Sparrow clicked his tongue. 'So I'm not good enough for you, is that it?'

'I didn't say that. You're not listening,' she snapped.

'Well, I've got to go,' he said stonily, pulling on his gauntlets. 'Are you coming or not?'

'William ...'

'Ride up behind me, we'll cross the river and rejoin the main army tonight. We can be married by morning,' he said.

Bella felt trapped. Trapped and pulled about like a fox

cornered by the hounds. Run away with William now, or trot on back to her father and her prison home. She strode out from under the drooping boughs of the tired chestnut, gazed at the green river glittering over the meadow. A Rubicon of her very own, right in front of her. All she had to do was summon the courage, the conviction to cross it. She felt a twinge of excitement, knotted and tangled with doubts. Marry William?

'What about Mary? I can't leave her now,' she hissed, as Sparrow thrashed his way through the branches and stamped out beside her. His troopers looked round, nudged each other and muttered their own ribald commentaries.

'A lady needs a maid. She'll come with us, we can drop young Jerry off when we may. Well?'

'I'll come,' she said faintly.

CHIPPING MARLEWARD

JULY 8, 1643

Sir Gilbert Morrison strode up and down his sparsely furnished study in furious agitation, not sure which of his pressing problems he should worry about first. As usual, Bella's erratic behaviour gave most cause for concern. Damn the girl, taking off in a dog cart with a couple of servants for company. She could be anywhere, she could be lying in a ditch! Why hadn't he ordered her to her room, tried to interest her in some gentle art more fitting to her station in life? Embroidery or watercolours for instance, charming pastimes. Ramsay's daughter spent hours stitching and darning, sketching the surrounding grounds. If only Jamie had half his sister's drive he would have been here at home where he was needed, sharing the burden of running the business which put a roof over their heads. He'd spoilt 'em, that was it. Good help didn't grow from seed, it had to be nurtured like a hothouse fruit tree, brought on carefully until the fruit was ripe enough to pick and pack. Not that Jamie would understand. No head for commerce, that boy. Bella would have made them a fortune, if she'd set the family interests above her own damned amusements! He'd been too slack, too indulgent.

Where had she got to? Sir Gilbert paused, rose on tiptoe to squint out of the tiny barred window. The yard was quiet and the outhouses were empty. The last decent horses he hadn't sold off or lent out had been driven off by one side or the other. No use fretting, he thought, idly reckoning the cost of replacing the animals. Wasn't much point in getting hold of any beasts until he had some burdens sorted for them. But he had hardly a bean left to his name, what with war and wool and worry. Fair cleaned him out, it had. With luck Starling had managed to hide his gold from the greedy Bristol garrison, but he could hardly ride into the town to collect it, could he? Not while the city was held for the Parliament, at any rate.

He ran his finger through the grimy webs in the corner of the strong-room window, wondered how he could organize himself some additional credit in the mean time. The best bankers were in London, taking no risks with their lives while they took risks with their money. Their lesser brethren in Bristol wouldn't be ready to risk any venture capital, not with the armies fighting it out like a couple of tom cats in their own backyards. They would have already transferred the bulk of their fortunes on board their ships, run the gauntlet of the Bristol Channel and slipped up the western approaches to London. Willing enough to risk the Royalist privateers which were taking such a toll of Parliament's shipping in order to get their cash to the city. The damned cowards wouldn't spare him a penny piece! The merchant stroked his greasy chins, wondered about selling up altogether. Sell the house while the armies marched to and fro? He wouldn't get a hundred pounds for it. The place was mortgaged to the hilt as it was. He had borrowed heavily to raise the cash to pick up the deeds to several of the properties round about. It had seemed like a sensible investment, back in the boom years of the late thirties and early forties. But what good was property when he had nobody to oversee it, let alone forces to defend it? He had even signed papers for that simple-minded squire, after he had succeeded in fleecing him rotten over some purchase or other, left the interbred idiot short of ready cash. He must look the notes out when he had a moment, see exactly how much old Ramsay was in for.

Sir Gilbert chuckled to himself. Hard times, right enough, and high time he was seeing a return, picking up some of these promissory notes. He could just picture the old squire's face when he asked him to honour his markers. Morrison's wasn't a damned alms house, after all. He owed Jack Randall fifty pounds for milk and groceries alone. It was a good job Bella and Jamie were away, he'd not be able to feed 'em else! The serving girls had gone home for lack of wages and the surly workmen had bridled when he'd told them they would be labouring a month in arrears. Damn this war, giving folk airs and graces. Get more serving with Waller, could they? Go and earn it then, you rascals. What a fix. He shook his head, relishing the diverse but interlocking problems which beset him. Something would turn up. Fortunes didn't grow from seed, after all.

Armies didn't grow from seed either, but to read Sir William Waller's increasingly sarcastic letters, you would have been forgiven for imagining they did. Nathaniel Fiennes, with God's grace Governor of Bristol, had inherited a surly city, ill disposed to the Parliament, and five miles of tumbledown walls ill disposed to standing up. He needed every last man he could lay his hands on to hold the place, and yet Waller had taken going on two thousand men out of the gates already! His company commanders, understandably reluctant to lead their men out of their comfortable billets at the local inns, had drawn lots to decide which units should march out to join the field army. His Highness King William Waller had bombarded him with cantankerous correspondence on the subject. Drawing lots? He would have imagined the brave captains would have been clamouring to volunteer for the service! It was all right for Waller, dashing about the countryside with an army at his back. All he had were some half-hearted volunteers who couldn't decide whether to get up in the morning, let alone which side they were on. True, he did have a powerful artillery arm. There were close on a hundred guns of all calibres mounted at the gates and in the string of strongpoint forts, but where were the experienced gunners to man them? Where was the money to keep the men at the colours? The skinflint city fathers weren't exactly forthcoming when it came to paying their trained bandsmen either. The aldermen could only afford to finance the militia's drummers, fifers and sergeants. The rank and file volunteers they were relying on went unpaid. Little wonder there were barely four companies of them! It was no good looking to Bristol's wealthy merchants. To listen to their heart-breaking tales of hardship and woe it was amazing any of them had the price of a decent breakfast.

Fiennes had been forced to sign over the best elements of the reluctant garrison to the field army. Half his own regiment of foot had marched out with the last of Popham's to support Waller's enthusiastic drive to the east. And God help Bristol if anything happened to them. The stocky cavalryman watched from the draughty battlements as the short-straw soldiery shambled out under

Lawford's Gate, took the London road out of the subdued city. Put some life into it, he thought furiously. They looked like prisoners condemned to the galleys shuffling along like shackled scarecrows rather than fighting men. A sad convoy of carts and wagons rumbled out behind the troops with extra provisions and powder for the field army. A gang of street urchins ran alongside, shouting at the tops of their voices and running sticks between the wagon wheels. An irate driver flicked his whip at the dirty tykes and they responded with a volley of muddy stones and debris. By Bristol's sorry standards it was a formidable barrage indeed, he thought ruefully.

Algernon Starling found the wagon's worn running-board as uncomfortable as ever. Splashed and splattered with mud and squinting through a painful and rather livid black eye, he cursed under his breath and endured the childish barrage with his usual sceptical stoicism. Let the brats shout and bawl, they were distracting the guards and aiding his escape. If their wretched fathers knew what he had hidden under the bales and bodies in the back of the cart he would have had a rather more formidable gauntlet to run, aye, and some stiff questions to answer and all. Where did he think he was going, carrying enough coin to pay the garrison into the middle of the next decade? He chuckled mirthlessly, flicked the whip over the back of the broken-down nags. Starling had picked the two least likely beasts in Bristol to pull the precious load, on the grounds that no hard-pressed artillery officer would ever bother requisitioning such obvious and overdue candidates for the knacker's yard. He had hired a couple of roughs to sit alongside, but hadn't trusted them with the reins, let alone the pair of pistols he had wedged beneath the splintered seat.

The muttering clerk followed the weary regiments out of the sprawling Bristol suburbs and out along the Chippenham road. He whipped the labouring horses up the long hill to Warmley village, paused at the crossroads while the reluctant companies shuffled on up the left-hand lane and off towards Marshfield. He presented the surly postilions with their shillings and turned them off the heavy wagon, took the right fork and headed down the hill towards the broad water meadows along the Avon. Starling pulled up on the bluffs overlooking the river, looked out for the dragoon patrols. A couple of troops had been billeted at Keynsham and Whitchurch to watch Bristol's southern approaches, and they could be expected to be keeping an eye on the vital bridge.

Starling tied his neckerchief over his mouth, climbed into the back and pulled the filthy sacking from the stiff yellow limbs of the old couple they had picked up that morning. The plague had scratched and breathed its way into their vile hovel in the Marsh, clamped its roseate rings around their thin arms and undernourished legs. The poor were dying at the rate of a dozen a day now, especially in the filthy flats down by the muddy rat-run of a river. Nobody had minded Starling taking the forgotten corpses off for a decent burial. The clerk fastidiously wiped his hands on his coat-tails, clambered back on to the running-board and resumed his seat. The wagon creaked and groaned down the slope, rumbled toward the bridge. Starling spotted five ragged skewbald nags, typical dragoon mounts, tied up under the shade of the bushes along the northern approach. Their owners were lounging on the parapet and enjoying a quiet pipe. They blew contented smoke rings, watched the morose clerk drive alongside.

'Afternoon, Father! Anything for us?' a lackadaisical sergeant enquired, nodding his cropped head at the hidden load.

Starling looked up mournfully, covered his mouth as he was racked by a razorbacked cough. 'Plague!' he spluttered eventually. 'Bring out your dead!'

'Plague?' the astonished sergeant snorted, peering on tiptoe into the back of the cart. 'There's no plague here! What you up to bringin' bodies out this far? Burn 'em your own side of the river!'

'There's plague at Pensford, sir. I'm to collect Mr Jones the candle maker and all his kin!' Starling improvised. The dragoons, edging away from the horror load, dragged their shirts out of their breeches and held them over their mouths, waved the wretched wagon past. Starling allowed himself a crafty smile as he whipped the horses up the hill into Keynsham, drove through the busy village to pick up the Wellsway. With a little luck and no further interruptions, he would be back at Chipping Marleward before nightfall.

Bella hadn't returned but Algernon Starling's unexpected arrival had to some extent eased Sir Gilbert's understandable anxieties. The clerk was dozing on the running-board of a wickedly creaking wagon, a witch's familiar in his weather-worn cloak and tall black hat. Sir Gilbert peered out of his window, watched him draw rein in the empty yard. He was about to take a stick to him for venturing out at night without a couple of good clubmen for company.

Driving down the High Street in front of every stray beggar and starving deserter. What had he brought that couldn't wait till morning?

'Three thousand pounds, sir, and I'll take it straight back, sir, if you've a mind,' Starling snorted. The dour clerk stepped back from Sir Gilbert's door, imagining the delighted merchant was about to throw his arms about him and crush him to death for his troubles.

'Starling! You've brought the gold, you say!' Sir Gilbert bellowed down the street.

Algernon Starling raised his nonexistent eyebrows, tilted his narrow head in silent warning. The merchant had pushed him aside, trotted down the steps and out into the gloomy yard. He had peered over the back of the wagon before the clerk could utter a warning, leapt back in revulsion at the frightful passengers lying cold on the worn boards. Starling's glimmering lantern had attracted a velvet battalion of fat moths which flickered and flapped over the ghoulishly illuminated occupants. A ghostly host weighed down by the ragged souls of the dead couple. The mottled corpses were waxy and gaunt, pocked and bruised with purple buboes the size of a man's palm. Tell-tale signs clearly visible on their sunken chests and swollen, empty bellies.

Sir Gilbert covered his mouth, backed away from the hideous cart. 'What knavery is this? You tell me you've brought my gold, and scare a body out of his wits playing tricks with corpse candles!' he spluttered. 'D'you plan to kill us all with the fevers?'

'The rest of the load, sir, is beneath,' Starling hissed into the gathering darkness. 'I had to ensure they would not search beneath the bales.'

Sir Gilbert studied his clerk with revulsion, modified

his features into a sickly grin. 'Ah, good thinking, Starling. There's a pound more in your wage packet this week, my man!'

'A pound sir, a whole pound,' Starling remarked with a sniff.

Sir Gilbert rubbed his mouth, eyed the deserted yard. 'It's no good here, what with these robbing armies prowling the streets disturbing honest folks,' he concluded.

Starling allowed him a withering glance. 'You sent word I was to get the gold to you, by whatever means necessary. My journey has not been without considerable personal risk,' he said levelly.

'Never said it wasn't, Starling, never said it wasn't. You've done very well.'

'Thank you, sir,' he grated.

The merchant stepped from one boot to the other, racked his brains for a suitable hiding place. 'I have it. Of course. Ramsay! We've lodged there once, we'll do so again!'

Starling studied the grinning merchant even more sourly than usual. 'Then you have not heard of the events on Lansdown,' he remarked.

Sir Gilbert narrowed his eyes.

'Well, I heard the gist of it,' he blustered.

'Ramsay's dead and Hopton's as good as. I met a musketeer on the Wellsway making his way home, who claims he saw the whole thing.'

'Dead?' Sir Gilbert snorted, eyeing his pale clerk. 'Who says dead? Some damned deserter?'

Starling shook his head. 'He swore to me on his children's lives he saw it. The Royalist magazine blew up in front of his eyes the day after the battle itself. He heard afterwards half a dozen prisoners had been killed along with several senior officers, including Sir Marmaduke Ramsay. Hopton has been blinded and they're carrying him off on a litter to . . .'

The merchant swallowed hard, possibilities detonating the powder keg of ideas he had stored in his head. A chain reaction of schemes and deals set off in sympathy with the explosive news. 'Dead? Dead, you say? What appalling news!'

THE RIVER AVON

CHIPPENHAM, JULY 8, 1643

William cantered into the crowded camp, soldiers and their assorted followers jumping out of the way of his alarming black and white horse. He ignored the usual ribald comments about his broad-rumped mount, trotted up and down the tangled horse lines before he found his own troop. He climbed down from the saddle, straightened with a wince.

'Gah, we'll make a fine horseman of ye yet, William,' Buchanan, a grey-headed veteran called cheerily, watching the new cornet knead the small of his back. Sparrow took off his helmet, ran his dirty hand through his sweaty stubble. Was this any state to go courting? Stinking like a tanner? Where was the girl anyway? He ordered one of the horse boys to attend to the reeking piebald, limped on through the checkerboard ranks of closely fastened tents and jumbled assortment of carts and wagons which made up the army's bivouac. As usual, the mass of unwashed humanity and its tail of lowing livestock had turned every acre of greensward round about into a lagoon of bubbling mud. The women's skirts soaked up the filthy moisture, darkening their multi-layered garments. The officers stamped around the camp unconcernedly, the mud sucking at their rolled-top leather boots. The humbler soldier and camp follower made do with low-cut shoes or agricultural ankle boots they had brought from home or looted from the fields. They would try and pick their way from one dry patch to another but eventually gave up in disgust and stamped on through the dark puddles like everyone else, trailing filth through every street and lane, into every inn and mean hovel.

William hadn't seen Bella since the previous evening. Plenty of time for the wretched girl to have changed her mind and driven on home without a by your leave, left the army to its dirty laundry. After his breathless liaison with the merchant's daughter Sparrow's reinforced reconnaissance party had ridden into Bradford on Avon, the last Royalist stragglers having taken to the high road after the rest of their army. The Roundhead cavalry had crossed the river and rejoined Waller's main force as it rumbled along in enthusiastic pursuit, rounding up fugitives and deserters, picking over frequently abandoned loot along the well-trampled road. William had been in the saddle all day, and hadn't had a chance to ride back down the columns of men and equipment to ensure his sweetheart had kept her promise and tagged along. He had tried to imagine Bella lifting her skirts to wade through the filthy detritus of the camp carrying buckets of water for her toilet. Wrapping herself in her shawl while she queued at the latrine pits in the morning mist. Squatting on a biscuit barrel around a cheerful campfire while she gnawed at a raw turnip. Bella?

'Bella!' he bawled, turning on his heels and peering over the calico tents and sailcloth awnings. Where had she got to? Home, that's where. A nice warm bed and good hot food and Mary Keziah to run all her errands. He barged his way between the crowding traders, the hawkers and tinkers and villagers who offered everything from alleged virgins to rusted swords they had picked from the river at some fight or other.

'Bella!'

'Could you spare a penny for a wounded soldier, sir?'

A crippled beggar held his twisted palm in front of his liver-spotted face. Sparrow knocked him aside and strode up to the regimental canteen. An enormous covered wagon with a brood of smoking stoves and spits. He paused, his belly rumbling like a culverin at the savoury smells. He hadn't eaten more than a crust of bread and the odd chicken wing all day.

The army had poured down the hill towards Chippenham in heady expectation of Royalist loot and good ale. The cavalry had divided about the town to the north and south, negotiated vegetable gardens and pig pens while the footsore infantry followed the main road through the town. The Royalist army had clearly spent the morning drinking and gorging from well-stocked larders before continuing their retreat over the Avon, but had then drawn up in battle array on the opposite bank. The armies had come face to face once again, divided by a sturdy stone bridge and fifteen yards of reed-lined river, studying each other's lines with the usual mix of scorn, fascination and fear. The bulk of the infantry, the wagons, camp followers and creaking artillery had hurried up after the enthusiastic vanguard, concertinaed into the stalled forces by the bridge. The officers and sergeants, seeing the Royalist army ready for a fight across the water, had run themselves ragged trying to sort their units from the tangled, shouting mobs, but it was already late into the afternoon and neither army seemed keen to get to grips. The regiments had stood to for a few hours and had then been allowed to disperse to their camps and billets.

Sparrow sighed, stared morosely at the closely packed humanity. It would be dark soon and he'd never find her, even if she was here, which he doubted. He was about to return to his own troop's mean quarters when he heard his name called, turned to see Mary Keziah hurrying through the crowds, skirts hoicked out of the trampled mud.

'William! Here you are!' she cried, tugging dark strands of hair from her flushed face.

Sparrow strode over to her, caught her up by the arm as if he would save her from the milling hawkers, the servants hurrying along with trays of food and ale held above their heads out of the crush.

'I've been looking everywhere for you,' he said shortly. 'I thought you'd gone home.'

The girl looked hurt, smiled weakly. 'I'd not do that,' she said simply.

'I know you wouldn't, but you don't give the orders, do you?' He was about to elaborate on the character of Mary's wayward mistress, thought better of it. 'Where is she anyway? I've traipsed miles looking for her.'

Mary frowned, nodded over her shoulder. She had pulled Bella's green cloak about her against the evening chill, her rich curls brimming from the enormous hood.

'We've taken rooms at the Barrel, just off the High Street. The landlord knows her father.'

Sparrow snorted. 'I couldn't imagine Bella out here, in all this lot,' he said, slipping his arm through hers to walk her back the way she had come.

'I haven't seen Zack or Eli. D'you think they're here?'

'Around somewhere. I'll make some enquiries for you.'

She turned, smiled up at him. 'She's sent word to her father where she is. She means to stay, for now,' she said.

William paused in the middle of the bustling High Street, eyed her. 'What d'you mean, for now? She's made up her mind, hasn't she?' he asked, with more assurance than he actually felt.

Mary bit her lip. 'I shouldn't like to say.'

'Well, that'll be a first,' he snorted, tugging her along towards Bella's alleged lair.

Mary stood still, pulled him back. 'You know what I mean, Will,' she said, agitated. 'I'll say as shouldn't, I know, but it's no good, letting you think she . . .' She turned awkwardly away, the velvet mantle falling over her face.

William squeezed her arm gently, stepped in front of her. 'Letting me think what?' he asked, colouring.

'I can't say. If I do it looks as if I'm . . . you know, trying to come between you. I don't want you to think that,' Mary insisted, dark eyes watering.

Sparrow gave her a reassuring squeeze, smiled down at her. 'She's gone, hasn't she? Or she means to go tomorrow.' He had known it all along but he had pushed the thought away, banished the truth to the outer marches of his conscience. Buried his doubts about Bella's likely fidelity with the rest of his fears and anxieties about the tiny part he played in this great drama. He could get shot or piked or fall from his horse or catch a fever or suffer half a hundred equally vile deaths. The world would go on, the war would go on without him. Bella would manage just as well with somebody else. Pick another from her love-crazed battalion of devoted fools. He couldn't, he mustn't think of such things.

Mary Keziah wiped her nose in her handkerchief, shook her head. 'She's there. She means to stay, all right. But it's to spite her father as much as anything else. You'll not thank me for saying it, but she would have gone off with that captain the same as she would you. She couldn't stop thinking about him after he walked out of the Hall and all. Sir Gilbert wants to marry her off to Master Ramsay, and she don't want that no matter what.' The maid turned away from him, sobbing. Sparrow closed his eyes for a moment, felt the girl trembling in his arms. 'There! I knew you'd blame me,' she said quietly when she had recovered her voice.

Sparrow sighed. 'Of course I don't blame you. I've known her long enough, I know what she's like.'

'But she's changed, though, Will. I know I shouldn't say but she thinks ... it's like she and Master Jamie were mixed up when they were babes. She wants to chase about and fight the same as you, and poor Jamie wants to sit by the fire and read his books. She wants to get out and see all the world around, all this, it's like a game to her,' she said with some feeling.

'Jamie's doing well enough,' he said, deliberately evading the point. 'You make her sound like a child,' he said stonily.

Mary dabbed her eyes on Bella's cloak, her pretty chin trembling. She had said too much and she knew it. Let the great swede chase after her mistress, see where it would get him. She tugged her arm back, strode off along the cobbles towards the inn, hidden down a narrow alley. Sparrow hurried after her.

'Well, of course I'm here,' Bella snapped, tugging her brush through the tangled knots in her auburn hair. She regarded him in the mirror, standing as stiff as a parson in his jingle-jangle equipment and travel-stained buff coat.

He could have made himself presentable, at least. She had heard him stamping up the narrow stairs, felt his heavy footfalls vibrate through the worn, polished beams. If it had been anybody but William, good old dependable William, she would have felt a delicious thrill of alarm. The woody ring of the determined steps coming for her down the creaking, crooked-timbered hall. The landlord had managed to find her a room at the back of the inn, overlooking the stables. It was all he had left, the officers needing billets. Mary and young Jeremiah would have to make do with a blanket in the hayloft along with a dozen other menials from the camp. William glared sourly at the tightly bound back of her bodice. It seemed she had stringed herself up, tightened her clothing against his rude intrusion.

'I'm delighted to see you and all,' he said from the side of his mouth.

Bella paused, caught his green eyes reflected in her glass. She smiled, turned around and put the brush on the chest of drawers. 'Come here. You're not usually as bashful as this,' she said huskily. William felt stifled by the dark narrow surroundings, his own uncomfortable clothing. His skin itched and flared beneath layers of heavy wool, calico and his greasy leather buff coat. Before he could think, he was standing in front of her, lanced by her mocking, hazel stare. Her freshly brushed hair framed her sweet face like one of Sir Gilbert's copied Italian paintings. What was the artist's name? Titian. Sir Gilbert had been especially fond of him. Perhaps through him the merchant's daughter had inherited some spark of the serene beauty the painter had captured on canvas. A glory of flesh and blood to admire in open-mouthed wonder.

Bella stepped forward, pulled his stubbled head down and slowly kissed him. Sparrow closed his eyes, overcome by the subtle fragrances which charged and routed his reeling senses. He stretched a hand to the dresser, steadied himself and brought his right leg forward into the warm hollow between her thighs. Bella broke off, leaned away from his superheated and rather feral breath. He ducked under her chin, clamped his mouth to her slim neck, alternately biting and kissing her taut, honied skin.

'William,' she breathed. 'What tricks they've taught you here.'

He looked up, watched her browny green eyes twinkle mischievously. Was it love, looking like that? Did she truly want him?

'You smell like a bear!' she protested.

'I'll go and douse myself in the horse trough, if you've a mind,' he growled. The great iron pommel of his sword ground into her upper thigh, she reached down and pushed the hilt aside.

'You could do me an injury with that great thing,' she said, still mocking. He took her hand, guided it back to the mass of ruckled clothing around their waists. Her eyes changed colour, the dancing motes of black and brown stilled with expectant surprise. Her moist red lips parted slowly as he bent his head to kiss her again, driving her back against the dresser hard enough to knock the glass flat. She mumbled something under his searching mouth, twining her arms about his leather back. He reached down, came up for air as he tugged the heavy sword and scabbard up over his head and tossed it on the washed-out counterpane. His fingers trembled over the knotted strings of her bodice, unpicked the strands to release her trapped breasts. Bella pulled the fastenings open as he pirouetted her around the small room and lowered her over the end of the lumpy bed.

There was a cautious knock at the door. William hardly heard it as he buried his face in the girl's warm neck. Bella froze, tapped him on the back.

'Ignore them,' he croaked.

'Miss Bella . . . Miss Bella?'

Bella heaved him up, glared at his flushed features. 'What is it?' she asked, feigning disinterest.

'It's Mr Sparrow, miss, he's wanted by his officer, the Scotsman,' Mary Keziah hissed.

William groaned, rolled off the bewitching creature and hauled himself to his feet. Bella straightened her bodice, patted her hair.

'Go and tell him William will be down shortly.'

'Down shortly? I'll down him if he's not careful,' William muttered, dragging his sword back on.

Mary Keziah straightened up at the door, gave the worn oak panels a secret smile and tiptoed away down the creaking passage.

ROWDE FORD

Wㅤilliam stood up in his stirrups and attempted to pick his breeches from his backside while holding on to the troop's heavy standard with his right hand. Sparrow had finally inherited the heavy pole and its flapping banner from Ashley Thomas, who had been left to recover from his wounds in Bath. He was a veteran now – so they said – and had earned the right to carry the colour. Sparrow hadn't exactly relished the honour. He had barely mastered the art of holding on to the reins while brandishing a sword, let alone a six-foot ash lance with a fringed silk square which seemed designed to flap in your face in the easiest breeze. He could barely see where he was going half the time. He tucked the heavy pole behind his knee and shook his numb hand to free it from an attack of pins and needles. Pins and needles? It would be swords and pole axes next. Look at poor Ashley, shot through the hand at point-blank range. He'd never hold a fork again, let alone carry a colour. Sparrow had got the job until he earned another promotion or fell wounded or worse. What a charming prospect that was! He frowned, settled himself as best he could and turned his baleful eye on McNabb, slumped in the saddle at the head of their sweating troop. The Scot, peering unconcernedly down the hill, caught his sour glance and grinned back at him.

'You're not still mad at me, laddie?' he chuckled. 'Saving ye from that honey blob Bella?' The Scots officer wiped a bead of perspiration from his eye, examined his greasy gauntlet. 'She's as smart as a whip for you boy, d'you think she'll not lie backwards for every other fellow that happens along?'

'If I hadn't been dragged off on this fool's errand I'd have made an honest woman of her,' William growled.

McNabb snorted with laughter, turned his back on the glowering youth to study the enemy's movements away over the river. The last of the Royalist army's carts and baggage had trundled over the shallow ford and hurried on through the tiny hamlet beyond. If the foot he had been promised had hurried along he would have been over and at them already. The baggage train had fouled itself in the narrow village street, concertinaed by some obstruction or other. If he had only had some support he could have bagged the bloody lot. As it was, the enemy wagons had cleared the blockage and disappeared over the nearest hill. The rearguard, a mixed unit of foot and dragoons, as far as McNabb could see, had been ordered to hold the crossing while they got safely away. The alert officer had noted the rushing water had only come halfway up to the wheel hubs of the wagons, the knees of the anxious camp followers as they waded the busy stream. No more than a foot deep then, the Scot calculated. He scanned the ridge behind the hamlet, a shadowy hillock, a stepping stone compared to the great chalk downs which reared away to the east of the village. Silhouetted on the skyline a mile or so off McNabb could see half a dozen dark blocks. Troops of Royalist horse posted between the

rearguard and the main army, lumbering off toward
Devizes a few miles down the road. The sun glinted on
their breastplates and helmets, as if they were sending
bright messages to their counterparts across the lush green
valley. Get off the hill you bastards, and we'll see what
your rearguard's made of, the Scot thought grimly.

William, slumped alongside the expectant officer,
didn't give a fig for the wagons or rearguards. He'd
cornered his sweetheart at last, pinned Bella to the bed
just as Waller had pinned Hopton's army behind the
stream there, and what had happened? He'd been whistled
up like some hound to rejoin the sweaty pursuit halfway
across Wiltshire. Sparrow had no idea where they were.
He had never been further east than Chippenham in his
entire life, and these apparently infinite white downs and
great chalky escarpments were unknown territory as far as
he was concerned. You could lose an entire army on these
windy plateaux or down the frequent yawning chasms
between the diverging ridges of skull-white debris. The
farm hands and countrymen among McNabb's troop
might be singing the praises of the slopes and soil; as far
as William could see it was a soulless, desolate wilderness
of green, dissected by thin white track lines which looked
as if they had been scraped in the landscape by some giant
stick. The generous geography was almost beyond William's reckoning, stretching away to unguessed horizons,
unforeseen ends.

He slumped on the panting piebald, which had as usual
attracted whole squadrons of flies and insects. He waved
them away from his stubbly red face. It didn't seem as if
he was going to get to know Bella any better either, the
way things were going. They were taking it in turns to
deny him his pleasure, he thought furiously. He had been

pulled from his sweetheart by that candle-wasting captain when he had cornered her in the wool wagon that time. All these weeks later and he had finally come within range of her delicious defences only to be dragged off by Mary Keziah's whispered messages. 'You're wanted back at the camp.' William swore she and the damned Scot had been conspiring against them. Deliberately keeping them apart for their own selfish reasons. It was all very flattering, having a good-looking and sensible girl like Mary after you, but nobody could blame him for concentrating his amorous intentions on her weathervane of a mistress, could they? Mary was like a loaf of good, fresh-baked bread. She smelled lovely and she'd do you for a good few days. But who would make do with bread when they could have a bite at a tasty bit of cake like Bella? He'd smelled her close, tasted her cherry lips. A man couldn't just ride away from a kiss like . . .

'Sparrow! Are all these games you're playing going to y'heed? Bothering y'sen jobbing some flirt-gill while there's a job in hand right now?' The Scot slapped him over the forearm with his gauntlet, pointed over the peaceful valley towards the green slopes beyond the village. The dark smudges McNabb had pointed out to him five minutes earlier had gone, leaving the lush slopes bare. Sparrow watched the subtle changes of colour as the breeze shifted the long grass this way and that.

'Have a care, man!' the major growled, twisted in his saddle to watch a large party of dismounted dragoons and musketeers hurry up alongside their enclosure and make their way down the rutted lane toward the quiet ford. The infantry support he had been promised was here at last, an hour late as always. Officers and sergeants with halberds and drawn swords out ahead, bent double to conceal themselves as long as possible from the twitchy Royalist rearguards under the drooping willows by the ford. Further along the hill William spotted a gaggle of staff officers emerge from a small wood, aim their spyglasses on the unsuspecting enemy. He had been in the army long enough now to recognize trouble when he saw it. He blinked, turned to his energetic commander.

'Well, don't sit there gawping, laddie, we're on,' the major growled, turning his horse to trot along the expectant ranks, jerking his thumb over his shoulder and calling his captains closer for an impromptu briefing. Alone for a moment at the head of the column, Sparrow felt the hot and cold surge of battle creep over his rigid body. He swallowed, jerked the flag forwards and backwards to straighten the silk colour the troop would use as a rallying point in the confusing swirl of the fight. He felt peculiar: not scared, more like stretched. As if his stomach muscles had been pulled tight like a lady's girdle and then slackened off, leaving him feeling loose and light. A statue of air, wrapped in sweaty leather and itchy breeches. McNabb trotted back along the line, the buff-coated riders drawing swords as he passed. Sparrow fastened his helmet as tightly as he was able, watched the red-faced Scot ride alongside.

'Let the footsloggers get stuck in, draw 'em out a wee bit, then we go in, full gallop. Are ye all right with the colour, laddie?'

Sparrow nodded grimly.

'Ye won't let it go, now?'

William turned to him, his generous lips compressed. 'No, I won't let it go,' he grated.

The Scot nodded, wiped his nose and watched the fight at the ford unfold.

The Roundhead skirmishers had stayed in cover as long

as possible, running along the hedges, slinking between the willows and reeds to get as close to the stream as they could before they were inevitably detected. The Royalist sentinels had been sniffing the breeze for the hot stink of burning match, straining their hearing to detect the tell-tale clink of powder pots or the rattle of horseshoes on the lane. The rest of their comrades in Lord Mohun's regiment had been drawn up fifty yards to the rear, on a rather exposed slope. They would make excellent targets for the guns being eased into position above the ford. Sweaty gunners were struggling in silence with their creaking and clumsy weapons. A muffled splash from the fidgeting rushes on the far bank brought a sharp-eyed musketeer from Lord Mohun's regiment out of his cover like a demon duck hunter. He brought his weapon to his shoulder and snapped off a deafeningly loud shot, destroying the fragile tranquillity in an instant. A noisy dragoon, cursing under his breath as he stumbled in the reeds on the opposite bank, threw up his arms, his carbine splashing into the river. His colleagues leapt from their cover, drew a bead on the sniper as he peered through the cloud of powder smoke to see whether his shot had hit the target. The inquisitive musketeer was hit three times in quick succession, jerking like a badly slaughtered lamb before collapsing into his reedy bower.

The hidden Roundhead skirmishers broke cover, leapt into the stream with their loaded muskets and glowing match held above their heads well away from the water. The dragoons opened a furious fusillade against the enemy-held river-bank, forcing the defenders to keep their heads down while the musketeers and the sergeants waded the fast stream, scrambled up the crumbling bank and threw themselves on the startled Royalists. Taken by surprise by the ferocity of the assault a company of defenders was forced to abandon the reeds and the willows and take cover behind a broken-down wall and an abandoned wagon. The heavy vehicle had been manhandled out of the road after one of the horses in the exhausted team had collapsed, blocking the exit from the tiny hamlet. The dead horse slumped between the shafts had attracted a cloud of flies which rose like smoke from the animal's mud-caked hide as stray balls slapped into the beast's senseless flesh.

Their officers clubbed the terrified men back to the defences, stopped the imminent rout in its tracks. A tall captain was shot through the chest as he attempted to rally a body of wavering pikemen. A ball clipped the top two feet from one Cornishman's pike, the jarred soldier dropping his weapon in shock. The musketeers threw themselves down behind what cover they could find, leaving the wilting pikemen standing amongst a bloody ring of their fallen comrades. They reloaded furiously, ramming their scouring rods down the hot barrels, pouring in a charge of powder and scrabbling for another ball from their leather pouches. The veteran marksmen from Lord Mohun's regiment held their fire, waited for the over-confident enemy to emerge from the willows.

The exultant enemy musketeers did just that, doubling forward into an immediate hail of well-aimed shots which dropped three of them in their tracks and sent the rest scurrying for cover. They fired back, the shots going wide or knocking splinters from the broken-down wagon. Slingsby, the colonel in command of the rearguard, dashed along from his comfortable bivouac in an over-grown orchard and quickly re-ordered his defence. He sent parties of musketeers right and left to prevent any outflanking move and put himself at the head of his dwindling band of pikemen, cruelly exposed on the barren slope above the ford. They were kneeling down to avoid the angry exchange of shots, peering up anxiously under the rusted brims of their helmets at the fireworks across the river.

Bright flashes and balls of white smoke heralded a sudden cacophony, and another volley of lead. The Roundhead gunners were working like demons now, slaughtering the packed ranks with frantic haste. Killing while they could. The veterans amongst them muttered to their mates over the din. They knew they should have been moved, leapfrogged back over the hill after the rest of the army. A fearful young soldier collapsed to his knees, his morion helmet slipping from his tousled black curls, clutching a spurting wound in the side of his neck. Ricochets thudded into the trees, brought showers of leaves toppling from the higher branches.

A brazen blare on a trumpet and a thunder of hoofs brought the pikemen to their feet in an instant. Parliamentary cavalry had cantered down the lane across the far side of the river and divided around the obstructed ford like a herd of crazed cattle.

'Charge for horse!' the barrel-chested colonel roared, shouldering his way into the pikeblock brandishing a steel-headed halberd. The front ranks jammed their pikes into the ground at a forty-five-degree angle, stamped their right feet over the butts and braced themselves to receive the charging cavalry. The russet-coated horsemen spurred up the shallow bank and through the sparse undergrowth, flushing occasional stragglers from the brambles who ran off like hares toward the improvised defences. A spatter of shots killed one horse instantly and sent its rider plunging over its bloody neck to collide with a tree stump. The cavalryman's lobster-pot helmet sailed on through the air and clanked against the dry-stone wall, its owner's neck broken like a twig. The Roundhead horse divided around the makeshift barricades, the pikeblock upping sticks and hurrying to the flank to defend the tumble-down wall. The cursing cavalry hacked at the re-formed hedgehog of wickedly tipped spears but didn't dare come to blows. They were driven off towards another stand of trees. The horsemen on the other flank had cantered around the overturned wagon, got in amongst the musketeers who were flailing about with their musket butts.

William clenched the heavy cornet in his right hand and Jasper's greasy reins in his left, spurred the piebald straight at the scurrying defenders. The wall-eyed beast had shied away from the rushing stream, forcing its terrified rider to jam his spurs deep into the gelding's mud-splattered black and white hide. Jasper had reared and whinnied, crashed through the hated water in a series of spectacular rabbit jumps which had damn near knocked William from the saddle before he had reached the other side. He held on, panting into the beast's filthy mane, directing the angry horse after the rest of the troop. The enormous piebald, flaring pink nostrils running with mucus and horrible transparent eyes starting from his head, cantered straight at the milling infantry. He sent two of them flying, brought his great hoof down on the tattered boot of a third, who dropped his musket and howled in agony. McNabb spurred past, leaning back in the saddle to bring his sword around in a vicious arc which bared the defenceless musketeer's windpipe. The man grasped his spouting throat, collapsed over a wounded pikeman. The rest of the Roundhead cavalry swirled by, giving William precious seconds to straighten the colour, streaked as it was by spots of the Cornishman's ruby-bright blood. A wild-eyed sergeant jabbed at Jasper's broad hindquarters, making the frantic horse rear in pain and tipping William forward into its sweaty mane again.

The piebald leapt forward, the stubble-headed Cornishman lumbering after him like a rabid bear. William clenched his fist in the thick mane, held on for his life as Jasper tore into the middle of the meadow. The cornet dipped as he regained his balance, dragged the horse to a halt. Two more Cornishmen ran at him, holding their muskets by the hot barrels. Sparrow stuck the fringed silk under his armpit and jabbed the butt at the first man, catching him square between the eyes. The second attacker brought his brass-bound musket butt down on Sparrow's knee, making him yell in agony. He clutched his leg as the piebald stamped circles in the trampled grass, forced the wary musketeer to back off.

'Get off that cart horse, you Roundhead bastard!' the man bawled, his eyes stinging red from the smoke. William brought the flag around to his left side, jabbed the man away. The Royalist fended the blow away with the butt of his musket, ducked underneath and tugged the flapping colour from William's hands. Sparrow toppled out of the saddle and crashed to the uneven ground, the wind knocked out of him. The sky looked ridiculously blue, fleecy clouds chasing the sun west as he watched the Royalist raise his musket above his head to finish him off. He rolled away just in time, the brass butt thudding into the trodden turf. The man tugged the weapon free as Sparrow prised himself to his knees, watched Buchanan canter up on his dappled grey mare, prick the intent musketeer in the neck. Skewered like a turnip, the furious musketeer ran on tiptoe as he frenziedly tore at the pitiless blade piercing his spine. Buchanan pulled the blade back and the man collapsed to the grass. Sparrow watched, breathless and terrified, as a young officer with a bloody bandage tied around his head ran up to grab the discarded colour. Buchanan feinted to the right, corrected to the left, and brought the bloody sword down on the man's already fractured skull. The veteran horseman turned his horse, looked down concernedly at Sparrow.

'Pick up the fuckin' colour, boy,' he shouted, pointing the sword at the trampled cornet.

Sparrow gathered it up as if it was a babe in arms, jammed the butt into the bloody ground and levered himself to his feet. Buchanan trotted back with his grunting piebald, held the reins out to him. Sparrow took them in his trembling fist, coughed a mouthful of acid-tasting vomit into the grass, felt his body racked by tremors as if he had been stranded in some Arctic blizzard. The first Royalist musketeer was hobbling away holding his face. Sparrow watched Buchanan lift one of his pistols from his saddle and aim the weapon at the man's bent back.

'Richard Dashfield. Oy, Dickie!' Buchanan urged the horse after the ragged fugitive, who glanced over his shoulder at the sound of his name, blinked between the rivulets of blood flowing around his broken nose. The Cornishman squinted up at the rider as he was silhouetted by the blood-red sun, looked about the broken field nervously.

'It's me, you damn jobbernowl, Davey Buchanan of Bideford. Don't you know your own wife's cousin?'

The wounded musketeer pointed a bloody finger at the

cavalryman, who had tugged his lobster-pot helmet from his head to reveal his greasy grey hair and waxy whiskers. 'Davey the netsman? From over the water?'

'The same!' the rider said, bringing his horse alongside the bleeding fugitive and leaning out of the saddle to study his wound. Sparrow shook his head, steadied the panting piebald as the long lost relations studied each other.

'I'm surprised to see you so far from your boat now, Dickie,' Buchanan said, handing his erstwhile enemy his water bottle. The Cornishman took the drink, poured some down his parched throat and over his grimy necker-chief. He handed the bottle back and dabbed at the nasty cut between his eyes which was leaking runnels of blood either side of his broad nose.

'Ah, your man caught me a beaut boy. You remember Hugh Kew from Bude, though? Well that's him lyin' there,' the wounded man said ruefully, pointing over the untidy field.

The Devon cavalryman rubbed the smeared sleeve of his buff coat over his forehead, shook his head.

'Little Hugh, Old Sylvester's boy? Ah, it's a bad business, Dick. I didn't know him from Adam in that blue coat.'

The musketeer shrugged his thin shoulders. 'You mustn't blame yourself, Davey, I had a bead on you but me powder must have taken damp. I wouldn't have known you on that horse either. What happened to that chestnut you 'ad then?'

'He took a ball at Stratton. You weren't at Stratton, were you?'

'Hah, indeed I was, my old mudlark. We 'ad the better of it that day though!'

'And you can say that again, boy. What a race we had getting off that bliddy hill!'

Away over the meadow the Cornish rearguard was retreating in good order, the pikemen having formed a hollow square shielding their musketeers who were dragging their wounded with them. The Parliamentarian foot were hurrying up to take possession of the abandoned wall and splintered wagon, the milling cavalry re-forming in the open meadow to their left. Sparrow felt giddy, and could hardly haul himself into the saddle. Buchanan waved him off.

'I'll see to my mate, 'ere, and be back shortly,' Buchanan said. Sparrow didn't have the breath or inclination left to argue, urged the heaving horse after his fellows.

'And 'ow's old Gertie then, still poppin' em out is she?'

'A reg'lar company, Davey.'

'Ah, make sure they don't follow you this far, Dickie. No good'll come of it.'

William straightened himself and the banner as he rejoined the re-formed troop, spied McNabb spurring down the ranks towards him. The Scots officer pulled up, shook his fist at his absent cornet.

'Where in the name of all the furies have you been? If they'd formed on you they'd be over the bloody meadow b'now!'

'I got knocked off . . .'

'You get back on and get back to me, laddie, go gallavanting over the country by y'sen!' the angry major shouted, cutting Sparrow's feeble protests short. 'You stay by my side, d'you hear me now?'

Sparrow nodded dumbly, watched the red-faced officer spur back to the head of the waiting troop. Buchanan cantered up from the far side of the meadow having taken his leave of his old friend. The wounded fugitive had clambered down into a duckweed ditch, rejoined his retreating colleagues as they struggled over the hillock to their main body. The Aberdeen herring fisherman turned Bideford boatman turned Parliamentarian cavalryman wiped his nose thoughtfully, shook his head at the pale cornet.

'Ah, it's a bad business, son, when you cut down your own kin and don't even know it.'

BY
DEVIZES TOWN

JULY 10, 1643

Scipio Porthcurn stumbled out of the Royalist army's headquarters, blinked in the sudden watery sunlight as his fellow officers brushed past him to return to their units, scattered in various strongpoints around the besieged town of Devizes. The continual crackle of enemy musketry was punctuated by the occasional muffled crump of a larger gun, the litter of broken slates in the narrow street evidence of the efficiency of the enemy fire. The squat grey and red houses subjected to the extravagant bombardment seemed to have hunched their shoulders and furrowed their casemented brows. Flexing their creaking beams as if intent on presenting as insignificant a target as possible to Waller's culverins and sakers up on the surrounding escarpments. The solid and sober homes were as practical and down-to-earth as their temporarily absent owners, the well-to-do wool factors and hard-headed merchants who had brought the first trappings of wealth to the small market town, huddled in the lap of the rampant southern downs. The merchants hadn't waited for the war to come to them. They had dispersed to Bristol or London, or taken refuge in the remote villages while the armies marched through their jealously cherished but inadequately defended empires.

Colonel Nicholas Slanning, commander of one of the

veteran Cornish infantry regiments, paused to congratulate the swarthy yeoman as he stared at the unfamiliar shutters. The hostile faces of the residents who had remained behind peering out at him as if he had brought all these horrors down on them with some kind of supernatural malice. Slanning slapped him on the back with rather forced good humour, broke his melancholic reverie. 'Captain to lieutenant-colonel in one afternoon. You'll be a prince of the blood by the end of the week,' the weary warrior told him.

Porthcurn, a black-bearded brawler from north Cornwall, gave the colonel a feeble grin. As far as he could see it was highly unlikely many of them would be alive by the end of the week, let alone have the opportunity to distribute any more meaningless titles. As blunt as any of his tough tenant farmers back home, Porthcurn knew full well he hadn't been promoted because they liked the cut of his coat. He had only inherited the remains of Maurice Butler's regiment because both the two senior captains and the major had joined the commander at the bottom of one of Lansdown's many chalky gravepits. The clumsy and ill-mannered farmer's son had joined the army as an ensign at the beginning of the war, and had clawed his way up to command a company by the time the Royalist forces had assembled at Chard back in June. He wasn't used to being addressed by high-ranking Cornish legends like Sir Nicholas Slanning, and felt himself colouring under the formidable colonel's hawk-eyed scrutiny.

'Don't fret yourself, lad,' Slanning said, quickly interpreting his obvious discomfort. 'We've brought fighters up from home with us, they don't have any time for these Oxford dandy types.' Porthcurn caught the colonel's sharp grey eye, nodded. 'We don't care whether you eat your peas on your knife or pick 'em off one by one with your fork. Lead 'em from the front and keep the knaves in order, they'll not be interested in your damned table manners.' The colonel adjusted his wide-brimmed hat unconcernedly as another ball whistled overhead towards the tumbledown Devizes Castle, and strode off down the busy street to find his blue-coated crew.

Porthcurn was about to shout his thanks for the colonel's friendly welcome, but thought better of it. He had never been a great one for words and he was still reeling from his unexpected promotion, casually announced at the opening of the gloomy council of war held at General Hopton's sickbed headquarters that noon. The scorched, smoke-singed commander had been carried into the town on a litter, stretchered into his lodgings by his devoted bodyguards and propped up in bed so he could chair the dismal discussions. The more senior ranks had secured seats around the grievously wounded general's bedside, the rest had packed in around them or listened attentively from the cramped hallway. Porthcurn, squatting on a trunk halfway along the badly lit landing, had damn near toppled over the banisters in surprise when he heard his name mentioned. Appointed to the temporary command of Butler's notorious rascals.

Hopton's staff had drawn up a long list of similar brevet promotions, necessitated by the shocking carnage on Lansdown ridge five days before. The western army officer corps had been decimated by the long climb up the hill, the chaotic struggle on the ridge. Captain Bluett and half a dozen lieutenants and ensigns from the rearguard had been added to the calamitous casualty list at Rowde Ford the day before, further exacerbating the urgent shortage of good officers. The subdued discussion had moved from one crisis to another. The dire shortage of powder and chronic lack of crucial supplies for the musketeers had been the principal concern. Captain Mark Pope, in charge of Hopton's ordnance, had leaned over the general's bed to report the army was down to the last hundred and fifty pounds of match cord. The officers eyed one another, knowing full well such a meagre supply would be burnt out ten minutes into the first real firefight. The Royalist army had improvised barricades, organized defences in key houses in every street and turned garden and vegetable plots into formidable fortresses. But the men couldn't hope to hold on if they were reduced to throwing stones at their lavishly equipped enemies, pressing into the town from the north and west. They might still outnumber Waller's infantry, but they couldn't shoot back at them.

Sir Ralph Hopton may have been horribly disfigured, racked by agonizing headaches and unable even to read the grim reports placed before him, but his grasp of the tactical situation was as sharp as ever. His trembling hand, scorched and scarred and swathed in bandages as a result of the horrifying explosion on the ridge, moved over the creased counterpane like a blackened crab. His officers watched in bewilderment as he reached up, grasped the heavy hangings above the ancient four-poster bed and twisted his fingers around the cord sewn along the seams.

'Send guards to every house in the town,' he croaked. 'Have them take down all the bed cord and boil it in resin. It'll do, needs must, until our supplies arrive.' The general's incisive answer brought a loud murmur of appreciation from his admiring officers. Prince Maurice, squat as a frog as he slumped in his greasy buff coat in a straight-backed chair to Hopton's immediate right, slapped his broad hands on his thighs.

'Crawford's coming from Oxford with our ammunition,' he said flatly, unmoved by the commander's fanciful schemes. 'If Waller gets his men over the Oxford road Lord Crawford won't get through,' he said in his deliberate, heavily accented English. The room fell silent as the officers pondered the implications of such a move. Hopton winced as he straightened himself against the puffed pillows.

'The bed cord will make good our match,' Captain Pope retorted, irritated by the German Prince's glum summary of their prospects.

'My cavalry can't fight in towns. They are wasted shut up in narrow streets,' the Prince insisted in the same bland monotone.

Hopton held up his hand, nodded weakly. 'His Highness Prince Maurice is right, gentlemen,' he whispered over the sudden buzz of conversation. 'He should leave tonight, before our friend Waller completes his siege lines.'

'He has a third of the army, sire,' one of the Cornish colonels protested, the old rivalry between the constituent parts of the diverse force boiling to the surface all over again.

Prince Maurice was widely reckoned to have even less tact than his tempestuous elder brother, and completely lacked Rupert's dwindling hoard of flustered charm. The dour Prince glanced around the room at his accuser, shrugged his broad shoulders. 'We can't fight in towns, too many walls, too many barricades,' he said, a buff-coated automaton.

'Prince Maurice will leave tonight and gather reinforce-ments from Oxford. We will hold the town until he returns,' Hopton insisted, straining his burnt throat to win his point. The clique of experienced Cornish officers stared glumly at their wounded general, anxious not to upset his frail health by continual argument. Slanning coughed, eyed his nervous colleagues.

'With all due respect to the Prince, sire, I cannot imagine he could be back in less than a week. If he was to place his cavalry across our rear we might be able to punch our way out,' he suggested.

Hopton shifted on his sickbed, waved his blackened hand dismissively. 'The men have marched as far as they can. It would take them a further three days to get to Oxford. Gentlemen, I am afraid you must hold the town until Prince Maurice returns.'

'We won't hold Waller that long, now he's got the wind behind him.'

'I will return by Thursday, you must hold till then,' Maurice stated coldly.

'Thursday? What will you do, issue your men with flying carpets?' Slanning growled.

The newly promoted commander of Butler's regiment picked his way down the narrow streets, stepping over piles of refuse and broken tiles, occasional pools of bright blood. Wounded soldiers were being helped back to the dressing stations in the centre of the town, wheeled on borrowed barrows by anxious comrades. Lord Mohun's regiment had brought back seventeen wounded men from the fight at the ford the day before, of which no less than thirteen had already succumbed to their wounds. Porthcurn watched one of his giant musketeers stagger along the bullet-scarred street, an injured man slung over his shoulder like a sack of meal.

'You there, Polrickets, whatever your name is,' Porthcurn called, stepping into his path.

The musketeer looked up angrily, peered at the officer. 'What's that ye say?' Polruan snorted, tilting his bandaged head to make out what the officer was saying. He could still hear that damned chiming in the twisted stump of his left ear, and he had to turn to the right to be able to pick up people's conversation.

'You're with Butler's men, aren't you?' Porthcurn asked, raising his voice as another ball whistled toward the rear of the suburban hovels where the Cornish troops had taken cover.

'We wuz,' the giant agreed. 'Till he jumped in a pit of Round'eads up on Lansdown,' he added, raising his straw eyebrows and settling the wounded man on his broad shoulder. The injured musketeer coughed something over Jethro's coat as Porthcurn squared up in front of the eighteen-stone samaritan.

'Where's the rest of them? The rest of the men?' he repeated as the surly soldier glowered at him.

'Over yonder, by those sties. You'd best keep yer 'ead down though, they've a few sharp boys over that 'edge.'

Porthcurn nodded, stepped aside as the huge musketeer strode off down the street with his groaning load. He held his hand over his hat, ducked down a short muddy bank to the rear of the battered terrace. He found himself in a tangled no-man's-land of trampled vegetable plots and dry-stone enclosures. Empty pens where the residents had kept their goats and pigs. Rickety tool sheds which had been stripped of tools, buckets and anything of use.

The desperate musketeers had pulled lead piping from the mossy walls, melted it down to make much-needed bullets. For the most part, however, the demoralized troops were taking what cover they could, crouched behind walls, peering out of fortified windows. Porthcurn dashed through a back door and found himself in a damp and dingy pantry, lit by a roaring fire. A couple of soldiers were busy chopping up the household furniture, adding splintered table legs to the merry blaze. The rest of the file were squatting on the cold stone flags playing cards, and hardly gave the newcomer a second look. An old bawd in a dirty bonnet propped up against the scullery door gave him a more discerning glance, arranged her skirts and flashed him a gap-toothed smile.

'She'll be free in ten minutes sir, if you've a mind,' the old crone cackled, nodding over her shoulder at the narrow staircase. 'Best fuck this side of the Channel, sir, and she's yours for sixpence.'

Porthcurn took off his hat and tugged his fingers through his greasy black hair. The drooping moustaches and dark eyes gave him a piratical, Latin appearance which clashed strangely with his thick Cornish accent. Peggy Rake squinted at the enigmatic newcomer, nodded enthusiastically.

'Officers only, she won't touch no common serving man,' she encouraged.

Simon Shevick the pikeman snorted with laughter, threw his hand on to the pile of assorted cards and heaps of pennies on the floor. 'In that case I must be a general.'

'And I'm Prince Rupert,' Isaac Thrush added with a laugh.

'And I'm King Charles hisself,' Gideon Wooly chipped in, beaming up at the dark-eyed captain.

Porthcurn gave the players a menacing smile. 'Well, I'm a lieutenant-colonel, and I haven't time for jobbing doxies. Who's in charge here?'

Sergeant Rice, a rolypoly butcher from Penzance, struggled to his feet, straightened his bulging buffcoat as the men fidgeted in agitation. What bliddy fool had made young Poor-cunt colonel?

'I am, sir,' Rice said nervously, knowing Porthcurn's reputation as a hard man. He was reputed to have taken on all comers from his company and beaten them senseless, one after the other. Not a man to mess about with, by all accounts.

'I want to see you, the company clerk, the ensign and any officers who remain in here in ten minutes. Is that clear?'

'Company clerk, sir? I don't think we have one of them,' Rice muttered, tipping his morion helmet back to scratch his flattened brown curls.

'How many here know their letters?' Porthcurn snarled.

Gideon Wooly held up a dirty finger. 'I know most, sir. Savin' me Ps and Qs like.'

'Right, then. I want a muster list of all the men in each company, and the acting commanders. Is that clear?' Gideon nodded.

'That won't take long sir, we've suffered these last weeks, there bain't more than three hunnerd of us left out of goin' on five.'

William Butcher's sixth shot brought the total down to two hundred and ninety-nine. The ball ricocheted off the red brickwork and struck a lanky Cornish pikeman above the right eye as he relieved himself beside a coal-house door.

He tottered back, still gripping his spouting member, fell over a dirty step, stone dead. Butcher gave a gleeful yell, passed the smoking firelock back to Colston Muffet, who had crawled up beside the patient youngster to see how he was getting on with the looted weapon. The Londoners had chosen an overgrown orchard to snipe at the enemy soldiers trapped in the battered suburbs of Devizes, safe in the knowledge the Cornish sharpshooters had run out of ammunition and couldn't fire back.

'I tell you what, mate, at this rate we ain't ever goin' ter 'af ter get in 'and-to-'and with 'em,' Butcher predicted.

Long Col wasn't so sure. 'There's plenty more where he came from,' the greying veteran said, examining the firelock's sooty mechanism.

Butcher raised his head slightly, peered back down the tangled slopes to the gloomy row of holed houses. He could see frightened Royalist soldiers scuttling for whatever cover they could find. A fat sergeant in an enormous buff coat pointing over the hedgerows and shouting at his terrified troops.

''Ave some of that, yer Corny bastards!' Butcher yelled.

Muffet tapped his shoulder, nodded him back to the rest of the brigade dug in behind a formidable manor-house wall a hundred yards to the rear. The pair of them loped back, threading their way through tottering canes and strings of shrivelled beans. The Pitt brothers waved them in through the breach, swapped their hot muskets for stone jars of cider they had looted from the kitchens of the big house near by. The burly farmhands had waited anxiously for their return, eager to get to grips with the faltering foe. The rest of the company were taking their ease in the sun, backs to the cool stone wall.

'How many d'yer get, then?' Eli Pitt asked as Butcher

held the bottle away from his pudgy lips and poured the colourless contents into his pink mouth.

'One maybe, one definite,' Muffet told him, handing his bottle back.

'Shall we go on, then?' Zachary wanted to know, reaching for his pike from the stand by the breach.

Muffet waved his grubby hand. 'There's plenty of time, lad,' the veteran told him. 'They've put a battery over by that 'ill there, the whole town'll be reduced to ruins this time tomorrer,' he predicted.

Zachary frowned through the gaping breach, the pock-marked hovels across the field. Damn all this waiting about, he thought. The quicker they got in and at them, the sooner they finished the damn business and got home. He straightened up as Jamie Morrison doubled down the wall, picking his way over the outstretched boots of his resting company.

The youth pulled his hat off, nodded at the cockney veterans who had attached themselves to his command after the battle on Lansdown. Jamie needed their advice and experience just as much as his raw farm boys. The old sweats had been distributed around the newly raised regiments to stiffen up the green recruits, steady their shaky nerves ready for the final assault. Hereward Gilling-feather went among the men with his Testament in one hand and a pile of pamphlets in the other, stirring them up with his brimstone and treacle preaching and endless diatribes against the forces of the Antichrist. The pitiful, cowering King and his papist harlot of a wife, plotting to bring murdering Irish rogues over the sea to butcher and devour their kin in their own homes! Gillingfeather's relentless lectures had turned feckless recruits and even the enemy deserters in their ranks into loud and self-righteous Puritans. Jamie had squatted around the camp-fire to listen to Gillingfeather's hair-raising speeches, expecting to be amused by his naïve and blinkered reasoning. Instead, he had found himself clutching the pommel of his sword, itching to lead the forlorn hope into the town and get to grips with this rabble of cut-throats and pillaging beasts. How dare they invade their county?

Jamie had finished his rounds and was about to take his place by the fire for another evening of lively debate when the joyous news arrived from the scattered siege lines to the east of the town: Prince Maurice had broken out of Devizes with all his cavalry and had galloped off towards Oxford as if all the furies from the uttermost pits of hell were at his heels. The despised Royalist cavalry had run away, abandoning the rotten Cornish bandits to their miserable fate! The cheering soldiers climbed up on the walls, shouted and waved from their entrenchments as the news spread along the siege lines like wildfire. Stand to, prepare the assault! This time, there would be no retreat, no mistake. The King's western army would be utterly crushed. For once and for all.

KILMERSDEN HALL

SOMERSET, JULY 10, 1643

Good horses must be as hard to get hold of as decent help, judging by the knock-kneed nags Sir Gilbert's loyal clerk had selected to pull their lumbering wagon up the long hill to Kilmersden Hall for the second time in a month.

'They'll go no faster not now nor nivver,' Algernon Starling croaked through his misty muffler. 'That's why I picked 'em,' he added.

'I still say you took a risk with those bodies,' the merchant moaned, lifting his own scarf around his busy mouth. 'You're sure you never touched 'em with your own hands, now?'

Starling shook his narrow head. 'D'you think I'm cracked up, taking risks like that? Everyone knows you don't touch a plagued man's buboes. The pestilent humours will have you else,' the clerk said, nodding his head for emphasis.

'Or drink water from the same cup, or piss in their slop bucket,' the merchant added knowingly.

'There you are, then. I had those toughs I told you about load 'em on, and I pitched 'em off myself.'

'And covered them in lime like I said?'

'Half a sack, sir,' Starling agreed.

'Half a sack? Good quicklime don't grow from seed,

man!' the merchant spluttered. 'Ah, well. They won't do no harm now, if you've followed my orders and planted 'em deep.'

The wily merchant had locked the doors to his deserted home and kept a loaded pistol at his elbow as he counted the fortune Starling had delivered from his besieged warehouse. He had bitten into each newly minted coin to make sure they weren't some cheapjack forgery, a gutter-snipe makeweight. He had stayed with the money while the long-suffering clerk disposed of the bodies which had accompanied Sir Gilbert's precious hoard down from Bristol. The rogue had even had the audacity to ask for extra money into the bargain!

'Drivers might well get an extra shilling a day carrying stiffs up in Bristol. Everybody knows the plague's that much stronger near water,' he had snapped. 'I've already said, haven't I, you'll have an extra pound in your wage packet. You'll get no more from me, Master Starling, why I'll plant the buggers myself, if I have to!'

Starling had given the merchant a withering scowl but had been forced to give in and accept the unhealthy mission.

'That's better now. We've enough rebels to worry about without you getting uppity over hauling a few corpses.'

The muttering clerk had driven a short distance out of the sleeping village, furiously pitched the stiff yellow corpses into the refuse pits by the pond. The rusty points of the fork had released trails of evil-smelling liquid from the unfortunate couple's purple-ringed trunks. The cold clerk had tied his scarf tighter around his mouth and nose, sprinkled the waxy bodies with lime and heaped a few shovelfuls of dirt over them for good measure. He had hurried back to the merchant's gloomy garret and been obliged to tap on the door for ten minutes before prising Sir Gilbert away from his precious pounds. He followed the gloomy glimmer of the merchant's guttering lamp into the smoky counting room.

'You've dropped your passengers, then?'

'I have, sir.'

'And you're sure you weren't seen?' the merchant had enquired anxiously. Starling had shaken his head while he wiped his dirty hands on a dishcloth, squinted suspiciously at the small chest Sir Gilbert had opened on the counting-room table.

'I think it's time we paid Lady Ramsay a visit,' he had said. 'To pay our condolences,' he added with a leer.

A lesser man than Sir Gilbert Morrison might have felt somewhat daunted by the prospect of renewing his rather brittle relationship with Lady Ramsay. The fire-breathing harridan had hardly kept a light burning in the window for the blustering merchant, and the grim news he bore wasn't likely to endear him to her now. The barrel-chested merchant squatted on the running-board of the creaking wagon, pulled at his fleshy lip as if warming his mouth up for the oratorical ordeal to come. He had no doubt the looming showdown with Lady Ramsay would be the most trying test of his silver-tongued talents. The old dragon had never made any attempt to disguise her contempt for Sir Gilbert or his family, and had been downright rude during their recent stay at Kilmersden Hall. Poor old Ramsay had been a pushover compared with his doubting Thomas of a son, but Sir Gilbert would have rather negotiated with the scar-faced mute than his firebrand of a mother. What did she know about anything anyway? She was only a woman. The henpecked fool had indulged his wife as he had indulged young Bella. Oh, yes, he had seen her, snorting with derision and shaking her suspicious head at their wide-eyed schemes. She had gone out of her way to undermine his delicately poised plans, his marvellously convoluted strategies. Sir Gilbert had been obliged to employ every ounce of his cunning and skill to counteract her baleful influence. He had stretched his imagination to convince the dithering squire that his dear wife was mistaken, and that their preposterous petition could possibly succeed in bringing the generals around a conference table.

Sir Gilbert hadn't got on without developing something of a thick skin. He didn't mind the fact the Ramsays had despised his mean manners and humble birth. He was a commercial crocodile, and the slings and arrows of some upstart squire and his snobbish wife wouldn't trouble him. Let her snap and simmer and scowl, he held a marker in his pocket which her late husband had signed back in the bountiful years before the war. In those days Ramsay had been desperate to finance his foolish speculations, find the ready cash for a series of ever more disastrous business ventures. The merchant had played the old fool like a fat trout, milked him of all he was worth. Sir Gilbert had mortgaged every scrap he had, risked everything for his chance to put the surrounding squires and local lordlings in his debt. Get hold of their land and they would have to sit up and take notice of him. They seemed to despise money, refrained from handling hard cash unless it was absolutely necessary. Perhaps deep down they recognized their own commercial shortcomings. Left the sharp end of their doubtful deals to guttersnipe rogues like Sir Gilbert while they strolled around their precious parks and wasted time hunting and hawking. The merchant didn't mind their pretentious promenades. Why, he would wager King Charles himself had found time for an hour or two's hunting this very week. His kingdom balanced on a sword edge and you could bet their serene sovereign would be trotting round some wood with a squawking bird on his wrist. Hah! You wouldn't find Gilbert Morrison sitting on his arse while the warriors ran rings around him! Taking his ease while the country tore itself in two. The merchant hadn't even had the time to track down his flighty minx of a daughter yet, his own flesh and blood!

He had received a breezy note from the wretched girl, announcing she intended to stay with friends in Chippenham. As far as he knew the Morrisons didn't have any friends in Chippenham, or anywhere else for that matter. Bella had written to say she was safe and well and enjoying the change of air and waters, and could he please see his way clear to sending up her blue dress, her mother of pearl gown, assorted undergarments and ten pounds for expenses by return. She trusted he wouldn't mind her taking a holiday, especially as she would only be in the way at home, what with all his business concerns and so on. Well, that was true enough, he thought with an annoyed grunt. The merchant had carried out his daughter's imperious instructions, sent the messenger off with a trunk full of clothes and a sternly worded letter for the ungrateful little strumpet. God forbid the war would ever interfere with her precious schedules! As soon as they were finished at the Hall he would send Starling after her, fetch the wretched girl back home whether she liked it or not. In the mean time Bella could enjoy her holiday while he put the family business back on its feet, saw to their fluctuating fortune. The crucial thing now was to show no mercy. No mercy to any of them.

Death on the battlefield might have saved Sir Marmaduke Ramsay the humiliation of making a penniless apology, an excruciating admission that he couldn't pay the merchant what he owed. Sir Gilbert held his marker though, and how he relished the chance of presenting it to the old fool's cantankerous widow. He pictured the look on her face as she studied the marker, the promissory note her dotard husband had signed. Now he was dead so his family must pay, it was the law of the land. The law of the land he had died to defend. He felt and immediately quashed a tiny pang of guilt. War was war and business was business, after all. The Ramsays had never looked out for him or his kin, in fact they had treated him with the utmost contempt and scorn. Well, their days were numbered the same as the stubborn King's. He saw no reason why he should favour the Ramsays, treat them as anything but rivals to be driven out and despised. He was sorry the old fool had got himself killed, but there it was.

The merchant chuckled to himself, startling the clerk dozing beside him on the running-board.

'Ah, Starling,' he told his frozen assistant. 'You know the old tosspot actually extended his credit, the last time we were up here?'

'Indeed, sir? Then you weren't the only one to have over-extended himself,' the clerk observed waspishly.

Sir Gilbert overlooked his impudence, grinned broadly. 'I always keep a little back in case of eventualities, you know that,' he replied.

The naïve squire's most pressing thought had been for his men. He had told the merchant he had barely enough money left to settle his garrison's arrears of pay, and had tearfully admitted he probably wouldn't hold them through the summer. Sir Gilbert had thanked his lucky stars he carried a hundred pounds in gold guineas for just such an emergency. He had insisted the squire take the ready cash, pay off his loyal retainers.

'Just add the sum to what you owe me, old man! What's a few hundred between friends like us?' Sir Marmaduke had wavered, aye, just for a moment. Then he had signed up for the extra hundred, taken the sack of coins as if it had fallen from heaven.

Let Her Royal Highness, her captivating magnificence Margaret Ramsay, rant and rave and show him the door. There was only one way she would ever meet the debt now: by selling everything. Sir Gilbert glanced up at the stars, a glittering canopy of precious stones set in a velvet box. Another dose of Lady Margaret's bitter bile would sweeten his commercial triumph, underscore his own formidable skills. He clapped his hands at the prospect, urged Starling to whip the horses on up the darkened hillside toward the unsuspecting Hall and its tyrannical toad of a mistress.

The tired team toiled in the chill air, blew ragged plumes of vapour into the night. Sir Gilbert held the lantern above his head, squinted at the weirdly illuminated bushes whispering and shivering along the dark path. Where was the damned gate?

'You've got some nerve, showing your face here,' Findlay growled, stepping out of the undergrowth with his fowling piece cradled in his arm. The undernourished nags tossed their heads in alarm at the ghostly apparition.

Starling recovered from the shock first, groped under the running-board for the pistol. Sir Gilbert nudged him in the ribs, hissed a warning.

'He'd shoot you down before you could draw a bead, man. Leave your pistol be.' He scowled at the lanky gamekeeper as he stepped out on to the overgrown track into the dim glow of the lantern.

'Come to gloat, have you?' Findlay sneered. 'Now the master's dead?'

Sir Gilbert held his grey gaze for a moment, smiled wanly. 'I'll not bandy words with you, Findlay. I have business with your mistress whether you like it or not. Is her ladyship at home?'

'With her daughter, aye. Where else would they be, a time like this?'

Sir Gilbert could have imagined half a dozen locations, but he nodded on through the trees to the shadowy Hall, just visible beyond the shimmering silver lawns. Findlay shrugged, shouldered his long musket and led the way up the path and under the deserted gatepost.

'Am I to understand your mistress has been told of Sir Marmaduke's death?' the merchant called to his lean back.

'Aye. You'll not be the first.'

'Terrible business.'

'For some.' Sir Gilbert ignored the gibe, climbed down from the wagon outside the gloomily lit Hall. Nobody at the door either, he noted. The garrison had taken either to their beds or their heels. Morrison squinted up at the fortified roof, behind the wickerwork emplacements which had been thrown up beside the front entrance. Findlay pushed the formidably studded doors aside, led them into the gloomy hallway.

'You stay here, I'll see if the mistress'll see you.'

Morrison held on to the gamekeeper's dewy sleeve. 'She won't want to, but it would be better for us all if she did,' he warned.

Findlay tugged his arm back, frowned. What was the fat buzzard doing crawling up here all over again? Hadn't he done enough damage, talking the squire into drawing up the daft treaty? The canny gamekeeper knew the merchant must have realized he couldn't expect a welcome here any more, and yet here he was, as bold as brass and twice as slippery. What was the bastard knave up to now?

'I'll tell her you're here,' he allowed.

The merchant and his scowling clerk waited in the quiet hallway as the gamekeeper went in search of his grieving mistress.

'He's paid his men and they've buggered off while the going was good,' Sir Gilbert whispered, taking the situation in in an instant. 'They only stayed to collect their wages. If he'd kept 'em in arrears like everybody else he'd have kept 'em till Doomsday,' he snorted. The merchant looked up as Lady Ramsay swept into the hall like a sea squall on a fishing boat. She wore her widow's weeds as if they were a suit of armour, a challenge to a cruel world as much as a mark of her own unutterable grief. Her heavy features seemed to have been chipped from some monolith, her glaring red eyes ringed by dark smudges. Morrison swept off his hat, bowed as deeply as he could. When he straightened his eyes were dewy with tears.

'Lady Ramsay. I hurried here as soon as I heard the terrible news. Allow me to extend my sincerest sympathy to you and your children.'

The gamekeeper twisted his head to stare at the merchant. Sir Gilbert missed his glance as he wiped his face on his sleeve in a deliberately menial gesture. Lady Ramsay kept a storehouse of scorn for the grovelling tradesman, but somehow the supply had caught up in her throat. She willed herself still, throttled her feelings. The canny merchant eyed the woman, noted the clenched muscles of her neck, the rigid defences of her lips.

'The country, the world has lost a great man. A beacon of hope in these uncertain times. Unhappy King Charles, to have lost such a faithful servant. Your husband, madam, was a prince among his fellows, an example to us all. I won't need to tell you the whole village is shattered by his death.'

'Yes,' Lady Margaret grated. 'I am sure it is.'

'I know there is nothing I can say to ease your terrible burden, suffice to say I am at your service, madam. If there is anything I can do to be of assistance, please do not hesitate to instruct me.'

Even Findlay looked impressed by his heartfelt sympathy. Lady Ramsay, deprived of the opportunity of venting her spleen on the despised merchant, stood like a statue, bitter tears streaming down her cheeks. Morrison was momentarily unnerved by her unguarded emotion, felt a twinge of sympathy for the woman. No mercy!

'You have not heard about my son. About Thomas,' she said in a strangled undertone.

'Thomas? He is making a full recovery, one would hope.'

'I have lost my son as well as my husband,' she cried, steadying herself against the empty weapon rack. Morrison stepped forward as if he would stop her from swooning, held his pudgy hands out in mute sympathy. Thomas dead? He turned from Findlay to Starling as if he would read the details of the disaster from their shocked faces.

Lady Ramsay breathed deeply, collected herself. Findlay stood by awkwardly, mumbled encouragements to his stricken mistress.

'Thomas dead? He was to ride to Hopton!' Morrison cried, taken aback by this twist. Where was the danger in that?

'They shot him down riding into the camp,' Findlay reported gruffly. 'Bates had it all from the surgeon fellow as was here the other week. He didn't answer when they challenged him.'

'He couldn't!' Lady Ramsay wailed.

'The murderous rogues!'

For the first time in memory the lean gamekeeper found himself agreeing with the merchant's spluttered summary. 'King's men or no, I'll shoot the dogs that did it,' he vowed under his breath.

Sir Gilbert swallowed loudly, held a hand to his mouth as he quickly revised his options. The old man and boy both gone? He'd never get Bella up to the manor house now, he thought with a curse. Still, there wasn't ever going to be a shortage of suitors for that little madam, he consoled himself. Thank the Lord he had a son. Young Jamie would do just as well, marrying into the stricken family, diluting their precious blood and sharing their blasted titles.

'Anneliese . . . your poor daughter. How is she taking it?' he asked at last.

BY

CHIPPENHAM TOWN

JULY 12, 1643

Mary Keziah lifted the heavy bundle of sodden underclothing from the soapy tub, hurled the hateful laundry back into the water with all her might. Her fellow washerwomen shrieked in annoyance and covered their faces against the flying droplets, turned to stare at the red-faced girl.

'Have a care there, you'll drench us all!' an old drab called, shaking her gnarled fist along the crowded bank.

Cows and cattle had already turned the shallow bay into a wallow, drenching the women's skirts and soaking them to the knees. Mary had been obliged to wade out with the rest, elbow herself a place among the early rising camp followers to wash Bella's drawers and shift. Her mistress was still in bed back at the inn, of course. Taking it easy while she worked herself ragged. When she had finished the washing she would have to try and persuade the busy cooks to allow her to dry the clothing out in the kitchens, then find a space to get the fine linen aired and ironed. She had already been up since five, and wouldn't expect to finish her chores until seven at least, when Bella would dismiss her from the crowded snug with a wave of her hand. Make room for her beau for the evening. On Monday it had been Cobbett, the major of dragoons, Tuesday Captain Lynch from Haselrig's regiment, complete with his comically creaking armour. Not that those gentlemen had managed to secure Bella's wandering attention for the entire evening. Half a dozen noisy officers seemed to appear from nowhere, pack in around her as soon as she stepped down from her room overlooking the stables. Mary Keziah wondered Waller had any men left to give the orders, with distractions like Miss Morrison holding court just down the road. They rode in from their lonely bivouacs as often as they could, found any excuse to gallop back to the quiet town. The armies had passed by and the cautious remains of the local gentry had made a tentative return to the battered High Street and the soldier-shocked hostelries. As well as the absent officers there were well-to-do traders and minor lordlings and blushing clergymen's sons with plenty of money but very little sense. Jolly farmers and well-off weavers, eager to spend a few shillings and eye the pretty rich girl. Most of them had heard of old Morrison, the roguish merchant from Chipping Marleward, and although they might shake their heads and spit in the fire at the mention of his name, the opportunity of marrying one of their idiot sons off to his precocious daughter was too good to miss.

Mary wrung the last few drops from Bella's underclothing, threw it into the basket she had borrowed from the wash house. Was this all she was good for? Following in her mother's footsteps? Mary had been doing a deal of thinking recently. It was plain her mistress had no real interest in William. Why, she hadn't even mentioned him these last few days. Too busy fluttering her colourless eyelashes at the succession of red-faced admirers who had somehow squeezed themselves into the snug. No wonder Mr Sheldon, the scowling landlord, had let Miss Morrison have the room for a song. She was good for business, bringing in every eligible (and thirsty) bachelor from all over Wiltshire. The serving girl stared at her blotchy red hands. She was no stranger to hard work, she'd toiled up at the Morrison's house in the village High Street since she was six years old. It was just . . . she wasn't the only one who had ambitions to make something of herself. She may have been born the wrong end of the rutted main street but it didn't mean she had to settle on some hulking farm boy, did it?

Mary Keziah wiped her face in the hem of her apron, straightened up with the heavy basket clutched under her arm. She toiled up the muddy bank as more camp followers hurried down for their morning ablutions. If William had as much sense as his wall-eyed horse he would have realized Bella was no good for him. She played him like a roach in the shallows while she cast her nets for the salmon and sea trout further out. He'd admitted as much on half a dozen occasions, and yet he still trailed after her like a forgotten hound, a pariah. Well, you could keep the pack, she'd settle for Sparrow. He was good looking in a youthful, wide eyed kind of way, although this army life had stripped his jowls quick enough, left him somewhat leaner. A few more weeks of wretched war would strip the boyishness right out of him, she thought, biting her lip as she imagined the other alterations in his character.

He was honest enough and wasn't scared of a bit of graft; a girl could do a sight worse than William. They had flirted and kissed often enough, back in the old days when he had delivered his pamphlets and picked up the master's orders. He had time then, time for her. She had laughed with the rest, held her sides as he brought the servants up to date with the city gossip, regaled them with off-colour jokes about the princes, imitated their stuttering King or

Sir Gilbert's blustering boasts. It would be funny, kissing him now, with his face all thin and stubbly. God keep him from harm, she closed her eyes tight, prayed hard for his safety.

The road was busy with heavy carts lumbering in off the downs and hills, a succession of mud-splashed riders hurrying about their or the army's business. She would have to watch her step as she hurried back to her Turkish minx of a mistress or the precious washing would end up filthier than ever. Mary hoicked the basket under her arm, started off down the busy street. The foot soldiers jostling in front didn't seem in much of a hurry, shuffling along through the liquid mud as if they were off to the galleys. She tilted her hood back, peered closer. None of them had any weapons. Some even went barefoot, their poor legs red to the knees. Half a dozen drowsy dragoons were escorting the prisoners into the town, jeering them along through the filthy gutters. Mary Keziah wondered how you were to tell the difference between these poor boys and their cruel gaolers. One set of soldiers looked (and smelled) the same as the other lot, as far as she could see. A burly rider with a ragged red beard leaned over his horse to get a better look at her, offered Mary a toothy grin.

''Ello, me darlin', fancy cuttin' one of 'em out, do you?' he asked in a strong London accent. Mary shook her head as the dragoon peered down her generous cleavage, shown off to advantage as she struggled with the heavy basket.

'Cut 'em all out, the poor splinters. They look to me as if they need a good rest.'

The chubby rider winked coarsely. 'I bet you'd tire 'em out quick enough. I'll risk a hand or two though, if you're willing,' he suggested. Mary blushed, tugged her mistress's cloak about her shoulders. The dragoon glanced at the shuffling prisoners, who had peered over their shoulders at the object of his bludgeoning loveplay. 'You don't want to worry your head with these sacks,' he called loudly. 'Ask 'em where they're from and how they got themselves captured?'

'Get off that nag and try another fall then, lardguts,' an anonymous prisoner called from the ranks. The dragoon sneered back at the tousled heads and sweaty backs.

'Trying to get an ammunition convoy into Devizes by night. Hah! Your precious lead's bein' shot off at your friends even now,' the fat dragoon boasted. 'It saved us the trouble of bringing supplies of our own up though, I'll say that for yah.' The rider called out to his mates for confirmation of his version of the ambush. 'Abandoned the bloody lot they did, miss. Scared off by a few troops of horse!'

'It took two bliddy regiments of your 'orseboys to round up half-dozen wagons,' one of the irate prisoners called. 'Running round like chickens with thems 'eads chopped off, they were, miss.'

'Oy, fuck off and get your own miss, you blasted coxcomb! Keep your nose out of it or I'll shorten it for you!'

'Sergeant Dowling! Get those men moving there!' the bearded rider's officer called from the front of the column. 'Leave that woman be!' The captain spurred his coughing nag back along the road, waved the muttering crowd on towards the town. Satisfied his martial display must have had a devastating effect on the blushing beauty, he fell in beside her in place of his scowling sergeant. Mary Keziah bristled under his frank scrutiny, eyed him malevolently.

'I know you, don't I?'

'I should think you did by now,' she snapped, hurrying along with her laundry under her outstretched arm.

The middle-aged captain smiled apologetically. 'Miss Morrison's maid, isn't it?'

Miss Morrison's maid? Bella's creature? She had a good mind to throw her bloody drawers in the nosy old bugger's face, only he looked too kindly for that. She smiled wanly, nodded. 'I thought so. I was up at the Hall.' He lowered his voice conspiratorially. 'With the wounded, you remember?'

Mary Keziah studied the man, shook her head. 'There were lots of wounded up there,' she said. 'I can't remember every one of them.'

'I came in with the captain fellow, the one that took the shine to your mistress,' he added.

He would have to be a little more specific than that, unless he meant . . . 'Captain Telling? The pasty-faced one with the funny moustache?' Mary asked.

The captain coughed, looked up and down the files of shuffling prisoners. 'That's the man,' he whispered. 'I've er . . . taken a commission with Sandbagg's dragoons.'

'You mean you've changed sides?' she asked loudly. The captain shook his head warningly, grinned at his muttering men.

'It's a long story,' he hissed.

'I bet it is. Anyway, I've got washing to dry,' she said dismissively.

'You heard he was taken, did you?' the captain asked, changing the subject as quickly as he could.

'Who?'

'Telling. The rector's boy. Got knocked off his horse at Lansdown. We escorted 'em back to Bath.'

Mary Keziah reached out, grabbed the captain's stirrup leather in agitation. 'Prisoner? Captain Telling?'

'Oh, he was all right,' the turncoat dragoon said, mistaking her sudden concern. 'Bang on the head and cacked himself, I imagine,' he added, more for the benefit of his eavesdropping troopers than anything else.

'Taken to Bath? You're sure?'

'They've all gone to Bath. They don't trust 'em at Bristol, seemingly. Too many friends ready to spring 'em out, I shouldn't wonder.' The captain watched the girl dash off along the muddy verge, her basket swinging from side to side toppling Bella's wet washing.

'Wait for me, darlin'!'

'Take me with 'ee, elf locks, I've a shillin' for 'ee!'

Mary Keziah, hurrying back to her mistress, had no time to ignore their rude offers.

'Ah, there you are, Mary. There's no need to worry about my things, Father's sent more down from home.'

'It's—'

'Just in time too, you'll never guess who's coming to dinner tonight?' Bella looked up from the glass, held the brush out to her red-faced maid. Mary Keziah caught her breath, waved the ivory handle aside.

'He's taken, miss! They've captured him with all the others!'

Bella pursed her lips disapprovingly. 'Well, I told him not to go trotting off, didn't I, but he won't listen to me,' she simpered.

Mary wiped her face on a discarded towel, shook her head. 'No, miss. Not William. Captain Hugo.'

Bella looked round, startled. 'Hugo? Captain Telling?' she corrected herself.

Mary Keziah nodded. 'Taken at Lansdown and

marched off to Bath with the rest of them, miss. Chained like a galley slave from the Roman times,' she added mischievously.

Bella stood still, points of colour glowing under her sparkling eyes. 'They'll have thrown him in the deepest dungeon, of course, with all his uppity manners and all.'

'He wasn't uppity!' Bella protested, colouring rapidly now. 'Chained with the prisoners?'

'I had it from one of the dragoons up at the Hall, you remember the one with the salt and pepper hair that wouldn't let you touch his . . .'

'Yes, yes, I remember him,' Bella hurried her dithering maid on to the point.

'Well, he was there, if you see what I mean, miss. Lansdown, I mean. Rounded him up and marched him along like a poor sambo off the boat in Bristol,' Mary Keziah improvised colourfully. Bella clutched her mouth in wretched sympathy, picturing the handsome Cavalier as he bloodily defied his captors to do their worst. That would be just like him, of course.

'Bath, you say? You're sure?'

'Bath it was, miss. They don't dare cage 'em up in Bristol as the people are too hot for the King, see?'

Bella saw. In horrifying detail. 'Well, then . . . I must go . . . I must go back to Father at once,' she faltered. 'He'll know what to do.'

'Yes, miss.'

William had borrowed McNabb's full-blooded bay for the ten-mile gallop back to the town, and was astonished at the difference in their respective mounts. Jasper would have carried him back at his usual lumbering trot. Argyll, the Scot's snorting charger, covered the distance in an hour, lashing the road with his hoofs, sending showers of filth over wandering files of weary pikemen and grumbling musketeers.

'Where's he off to in sich 'urry?'

'Looks loik that Prince Ruppit feller's on 'is 'eels.'

Sparrow didn't have time for their ribald commentaries. He had persuaded McNabb to let him have the night off, promising on all God's books to be back by the dawn reveille.

'They're shut up tighter than a bull's arse down there,' William had argued, pointing over the lark-crowned downs to the besieged town fuming at the foot of the hills. It could only be a matter of time before Waller's army cracked the nut, broke all Hopton's shaggy army in so many pieces. Prince Maurice and his precious cavalry had long since galloped off over the rolling moors and his isolated infantry were practically out of ammunition. Their last hope, a convoy of powder and ball which had been sent down from Oxford under Lord Crawford, had been intercepted in a rather hit and miss ambush late on Sunday night. Without supplies the town would surely fall by the end of the week. The final assaults would be entrusted to the west country foot regiments who had thrown such a tight ring around the smoking suburbs. The cavalry would simply hang about to do the mopping up.

'They might risk a sortie, they're that desperate,' McNabb had countered.

'Come on, Archie, she's holed up in an inn with half the bloody army breathing down her neck. If I don't get to her quick she'll have married some whoremonger from the baggage train!'

The red-haired Scot had snorted, shaken his stubbled head. 'You've not much faith in the lass!' he cried.

'I'll have faith enough when she's properly mine,' Sparrow said coldly.

'That honey blob'll need a ball and chain, mark my words, laddie.'

William ignored the Calvinist's experienced advice. 'With your permission, sir?'

'Aye, go along then, you damned rascal.'

'Thank you, Archie. What about your horse?'

'What about my horse? You don't think I'd swap my mount for that howling beastie of yours, do ye?'

William gripped the gelding's reins, touched his spurs to the beast's heaving flanks. The dark horse leapt out, racing the clouds to the cheerily lit houses built up in the slow bend of the Avon. He pulled the barely sweating horse back to a brisk trot, ducked under the swinging inn signs as he searched out his wayward mistress's lair. The locals eyed him suspiciously as he rode along the busy street, turned into a narrow alley and jumped off outside the Barrel. A boy ran for his horse, tugged at the reins as the tricky beast tossed his head.

'See that he's fed and watered. I want him saddled and ready to go by half four,' Sparrow ordered, handing the youth a sixpence.

'Yes, sir!'

He had swept off his hat and strode toward the busy inn, a good crowd judging by the welcoming yellow lantern light and friendly banter pouring out of the open windows. It was a fine summer's night, and the smoke drifted out from under the black beams as if it was flexing its misty muscles. He watched it flicker and whisper into the starry sky, smiled at the hunter's moon. My God, he thought, swallowing with difficulty. The ride had dried his tongue to the roof of his mouth. A beer first, and then upstairs to Bella. He'd make sure he locked the door this time, and all.

'William! William!'

The heavy cornet threw his cloak over his shoulders, turned toward the stables. Mary Keziah hurried out from the dimly lit barn, her rich curls springing out from her haphazard bonnet. William smiled as she leapt up the steps, charged straight at him and flung her arms behind him.

'What the devil's the matter with you?' he snorted, alarmed. 'She's not gone off again?' It couldn't be true. Not tonight!

'Off after her captain! I told you, Will, I told you she didn't care for you!'

Mary cried, careful not to look too horribly distraught. William froze, drummed his chilled fingers against the girl's warm back.

'She's gone back to her father's to get him to do something! I told you, Will, but you wouldn't listen.'

Sparrow felt hollow, emptied. He had told himself off for even imagining what he would do if Bella hadn't been at the inn. He hadn't dared consider the possibility she would let him down again. Mary Keziah rested her head against his pulsing chest, felt his heart thump behind his warm coat.

'I did tell you, Will, I did warn you she'd do this,' she insisted, sensing his turmoil. She looked up tearfully at his rugged, moonlit features, knew she would have him now.

'I'd never run out on you, you know that too,' she

breathed. 'If you'd only admit it for a moment. I love you more than she ever could. I've loved you for ages, you great pudding,' she scolded, thumping her fist against his chest. He was gazing out over her shoulder, breathing heavily.

'She's back to Sir Gilbert and never a word for you. I said I'd stay and look for Father, but I wanted to see you, don't you see?' the girl insisted, unable to control her tears now. He wouldn't throw me off now, she thought. He couldn't.

'What can you think of me, Mary, chasing around after your mistress all this time?' he said thickly.

Mary shook her head slowly, felt his body grate against her thigh.

'I don't mind any of that now.' She thought for a moment, jabbed her finger into his shoulder. 'As long as you leave her be. I'll not play second fiddle to her any longer,' she vowed.

Sparrow studied the swinging sign, the cracked amber window panes and the large yellow dog snoring noisily beside a splintered table. Anything but catch the girl's moist eyes.

'I feel such a fool,' he said simply.

'Don't be a fool any longer, Will. Marry me. Marry me tomorrow,' she breathed under his twitching chin, forcing her thigh back against his uncomfortably constricted crotch. She closed her mouth over the fluttering veins in his neck, making him blink in agitated surprise. His arms came to life of their own accord, tightening his grip around her slim, warm waist. He tilted his head to the right as she looked up at him, thrust his nose into the fragrant hollow behind her pretty ear. Mary Keziah pulled away, wound her fingers around his dirty fist.

'Come on, we'll catch our deaths out here all night,' she whispered, tugged him stumbling across the narrow courtyard. He felt drunk, registering snatches of his gloomy surroundings as he ducked under the worn beams into the stuffed straw cloisters of the stable. His careless elbow knocked a set of reins to the floor, tangling his boots as the girl tore the cloak from her neck, threw it down over the loose bales piled against the wall. Sparrow swung under the stall, forcing her back against the dusty wooden panels, gulping the kisses from her searching lips. She tugged at her bodice while he ran his hands over her formidable piled skirts, seaching for openings in the heavy wool. Mary reclined on the bale, propped her soiled shoe against a stable post as her husky hero manoeuvred himself between the layers of her skirts, tugging the material up over her heaving belly. William could barely see her in the creaking, rustling darkness, groping for her as he smothered her mouth and eyes with blistering kisses. She bit back at him, hands tearing at his waxy breeches. With one final heave, one broken-backed thrust, William crushed her against the prickly straw. She cried out, bracing her leg against the stall while she wound her bare foot behind his bare buttocks. The stall rocked and quivered in splintered sympathy as Sparrow bundled the prone girl up in his arms, smothered her in his panting embrace. A set of rusty stirrups clanged tonelessly against the creaking stall, the tired nail working loose in the straw-storm of dust and fragments. Old webs stretched and parted adding partially decomposed insects to the hazy blizzard. William stifled a sneeze, his red face contorted with determined, feverish pleasure. The stirrups broke free at last and clattered over his back, followed by half a dozen forgotten horseshoes.

'Ouch!' He felt as if a regiment of Cavaliers had galloped across his bucking body.

'Never mind,' Mary grated, holding him into her. 'Never mind any of them now!'

Sparrow wondered fleetingly who she was talking about.

ROUNDWAY DOWN

JULY 13, 1643

Archibald McNabb screwed his fists into his red-rimmed eyes and peered across the rolling valley at the swift black shadows he had imagined moving over the green ridge. It was difficult country to keep watch on with plenty of cover for a wary enemy. The chalky escarpment was scored by deep white ravines, windy plateaux which suddenly fell away into treacherous hollows. Small hump-backed hills and prehistoric tumuli reared eerily above shadowed vales and shallow canyons. Creeping soil slopes which stretched as far as a man could see, and then, in the hazy distance, gave out over juddering white cliffs pocked and holed by flocks of whistling martins, scoured by wheeling choughs and harsh-throated ravens. McNabb shielded his eyes, sure he had seen a square shape detach itself from the mossy ridge of the Wansdyke, drop into one of the invisible hollows like a sail rising and falling on a choppy sea. He could make out the skeletal tendon of the Marlborough road, a white ribbon laid over the undulating down which hugged each dip and curve of the windblown wilderness. He closed his left eye, stared harder. There it was again, a dark mass studded with needlepoint flashes of light emerging from a dip between two outflung arms of the ancient earthen dyke.

'CAVALRY!' he shrieked to the dozing troop taking

their ease in the morning sunshine, the horses flicking their tails against the wind-blown flutterbys as they cropped the thick, springy grass.

'Mount up! Hurry up, you sad-sack Sassenach bastards!' McNabb tugged his helmet over his sunburnt head, snatched the piebald's reins from the runny-nosed recruit he'd left guarding the horse lines.

Captain Hunt flung his booted leg over his pommel and yanked his saddle girth tighter, nodded at the troop cornet which had been speared into the lush turf.

'Buchanan, you take the colour! Culverhouse, you watch his back!' Hunt snapped, straightening his leg and spurring the black horse to the head of the assembled riders.

McNabb's troop, still missing its absent cornet, had been camped out in the middle of the downs beneath the whispering arms of a sentinel elm tree. Waller had placed a string of cavalry picquets over the rolling hills in case the enemy dared risk raiding his skilfully laid siege lines around Devizes. The cavalry would have little else to keep them busy in the fiercely contested suburbs, where his foot soldiers had inched their way forward, sniping and harrying the defenders all week long. Hopton had tried to waste time with a pointless truce, but Waller had known full well he had no intention of surrendering his battered army just yet. The general had been putting the finishing touches to his orders for the final assault on the crumbling defences when a breathless dragoon had spurred up to his windy marquee with the desperate news: two thousand enemy cavalry on the Marlborough road, heading this way. Cavalry? What cavalry was he jabbering about?

'You damned rogue, they must be from my Lord Essex's army!' Waller had snapped, snatching up his maps and flinging a heap of laconic dispatches aside. 'He has my letter and he hurries to guard my flanks!'

The Roundhead general tugged at his fleshy nose in agitation, gnawed with sudden bowel-loosening doubts. He had written a lengthy report for the Earl just the day before, urging Essex to keep the main Royalist force at Oxford occupied while he finished off Hopton's bloody Cornishmen. There was no way on this earth Essex could have dispatched troops this far west in that time! Waller held his broad forehead between his heavy hands as if he could compress his racing thoughts, straighten the strategic situation in his mind. The Earl could have sent them marching a few days before, anticipating the enemy might attempt to relieve the town with a force of flying cavalry. Anticipate the enemy, Essex? He had hardly shifted his army in six months, complaining his men went unpaid and unclothed and had been ravaged by bouts of camp fever. Surely the reluctant general-in-chief of Parliament's forces hadn't allowed a relief force to ride away from Oxford and fall on his own rear? Waller snatched up his helmet and strode out into the bright sunshine.

'What are we doing now?' Billy Butcher wanted to know, hurrying along after his long-legged sergeant. 'We've got the buggers beat!' the Rye Lane apprentice whined, settling the firelock over his shoulder. Long Col had ground his shapeless felt hat over his greasy strands of dark hair, pursed his lips.

'Commotion up on the downs, according to the cap'n,' Muffet reported, waving his file of musketeers out of the trampled gardens and livestock pens and on up the road. Jamie Morrison had run from hedge to hedge, leapt heaps of rhubarb and pits of fuming refuse as he raced around the western suburbs of Devizes, assembling his widely scattered company. They had crawled and ducked and doubled their way through the tangled plots and narrow orchards behind the leaning hovels. Taken what cover they could in attics, sculleries or tumbledown outhouses and now they were being called off. The Cornishmen barely shot off ten rounds a day while they had maintained a relentless, chattering, hammering fusillade against the enemy strongpoints, picking off man after man as they belatedly ducked down behind their makeshift defences.

'Hurry up, come on! We've got to be on the hill in half an hour!' Jamie bawled to his snipers, anxious to finish off the despised invaders from the far west once and for all. The Cornish fighters didn't have enough powder for a good-sized firework, let alone a few thousand greedy muskets.

'What are we going up there for? Let's get in and flush 'em out,' the unwashed musketeers complained as they climbed over the broken-down walls, fell in behind their surly brothers trailing pikes along the trampled lanes behind the houses.

'The whole army's to assemble, double quick, on the top there, that's all they told me,' Jamie replied, pushing them into line.

'It's a bloody parade for some bigwig from Whitehall,' Butcher protested. 'Wants to hear us all give him a huzzah for his troubles.' There was a ragged chorus of agreement, punctuated by two muffled bangs.

'Silly buggers shooting from that far away, get their guns right up here with us, s'what we want,' the sharp-shooter observed, spitting into a discarded helmet.

'That wasn't our guns, you jobberknol,' Muffet

snapped, striding over a dead horse which had been partially butchered by the hungry soldiers. 'It's theirs.'

'Theirs? What d'yer mean, theirs? What they playin' at with guns up on the top?'

'It's Waller, playing tricks again,' Scipio Porthcurn called down to the huddle of dispirited troops in the narrow yard. The newly promoted commander had climbed a twisted apple tree, stepped across to the slippery, sloping roof of one of the strongpoint hovels to get a better view of the surrounding downs.

He could see dark blocks of cavalry moving over the haphazard horizons, long files of infantry smearing the neat white roads etched into the chalky topsoil. Individual soldiers hurrying after their units reminded him of so many scurrying ants. Something had stirred them up all right.

'Is it the King come from Oxford?' one of the hopeful ragamuffins called up from the rubble-strewn courtyard. Porthcurn could make out small splashes of colour, blood reds and bright yellows, but he couldn't hope to pick out the banner detail from a mile and more away. He shook his head.

'It's Waller making a show for us, wants to save himself the bother of a storm,' he concluded, picking his way down the slippery slates and swinging himself back into the gnarled arms of the apple tree. He wiped the mouldy green moss from his hands on the back of his breeches.

'He's trying to lure us out after him. He's a clever bugger, you'd have to admit it.'

*

Major McNabb's troop trotted over the springy turf as if they were on a Sunday morning parade in the capital and not the last unit on the farthest point of a non-existent flank. The wily Scot was alternately calming his panicked troopers and cursing Sparrow's hulking horse. Where was that damned cunny hunter? The Scot cursed in Gaelic, steadied his remaining troopers' nerves as they gradually opened their ranks.

'Spread out ... three paces ... steady there, that's enough! Get on, you brute.' He had ordered his men to stretch their formation to trick the approaching enemy into thinking they were twice as strong as they were. God help them if the King's horsemen rode straight in at them. McNabb scoured the downs for the hidden vales and folds which could conceal hundreds of Royalist cavalry, watched for the sudden charge which could scatter his dangerously exposed formation. He guessed they were heading north, towards the mossy ridge of the Wansdyke. His men had ridden down the gentle slope of Bagdon Hill, the downs rearing and falling in front of them and to either flank. Another mile to the left and they would be over the massive chalk cliffs of Beacon Hill. A mile to their front the steep and craggy Morgan's Hill reared out of the green sea like a monstrous ox head. McNabb turned to the right, squinted at the long hog's back of Roughridge Hill. The Wansdyke ran from one to the other, linking the formidable heights. The old earthworks had been worn away by centuries of sheep herders and hurrying travellers who had opened wide breaches in the grassy walls.

There. There they were. Neat blocks of enemy cavalry. Twenty, thirty, forty troops at least, each brown and black and chestnut block topped with blue- or red- or green-coated riders and sprouting a gaudy pennant. The enemy cavalry were streaming through one of the breaches heading west, urging their beasts down the slope toward the great gladiatorial arena in front of them. Devil take it, his poor troop was almost at right angles to the colourful cavalcade! Where was the bloody army? He peered over his armoured shoulder, blinked with relief. A bright red flag with a small cross of St George in the top left-hand corner appeared over the ridge his troop had just vacated. He watched a tide of men flow over the lush grass, hoist the flag higher over the eggshell horizon. Thank the Lord for the infantry. As he watched a horde of russet riders surged past the army coagulating on the hill, followed his forlorn troop into the quiet valley. Individual riders spurred ahead of the rest, hurrying to deliver hastily scribbled orders or to call back some of the hopelessly lost patrols.

'Right wheel, close up!' McNabb bawled. The loosely ordered riders tugged their reins to the right, eased their horses closer to their neighbours as the troop swung around to face the rapidly approaching enemy. The experienced Scot could pick out their faces now, white smudges under dark hats. Less than a mile off and picking up speed as they came. Please God Waller had turned his army round in time to face them. He leaned forward over the piebald's matted mane and glanced down the front rank of his sixty-man troop, nodded in satisfaction. They had closed ranks until their boots touched their neighbours', their horses snorting and rearing in agitation. McNabb had stationed himself on their left, the last man in the last formation on Waller's open flank. The gap between the supporting troops was disappearing fast as Waller's regiment formed up behind, Burghill's coming down the hill behind them. Five hundred, seven hundred, a thousand of them at least. Forming ranks as they trotted down to shore up Waller's northern flank. The Scot tipped his helmet back, brought the troop to a slow walk. Where had the bastards got to now? He scanned the green down for hidden chasms and blind alleys. He cocked his head, imagining he could hear the dim clash of steel and the muffled thunder of hundreds of hooves over to his right. It could be their friends struggling up the hill to thicken the line, he thought furiously. Away on the slopes ahead of them he could see more troops appearing over the ridge, moving in echelon towards his left. Towards the deserted wilderness which was Roundway.

William Sparrow eased his hand under his crotch to pick the sticky breeches from his backside. The rough woollen mixture had chafed the skin from the inside of his thighs and he could have done without the unfamiliar charger's brisk pace. He stood in the stirrups, tried to match the bay's exasperatingly rapid rhythm. He'd spent half the night trying to match Mary's, he thought lewdly. Didn't the girl ever sleep? It had been light enough to see the webs hanging in the corner of the stall before he had finally managed to close his eyes. It was as if she had laid claim to his body, staked herself over his sweaty belly and heaving crotch. He'd kissed and cuddled the girl before, of course, but he had never imagined her bashful glance could conceal such elemental desire and lip-biting passion. He would have sworn she'd drawn blood from his ragged mouth. He had settled the horse cloth over her shoulders when she had eventually decided enough was enough and nestled into his chest with a satisfied murmur. He hadn't caught what she had said but he hadn't dare risk waking her up again. William had reminded himself he must be up at cock crow to get back in time for reveille – McNabb would have him flogged at the tumbler otherwise – and fallen fast asleep.

'You candle-wasting splinter! Didn't I tell you four thirty prompt?' he had bawled at the sleep-shocked stable lad when he had finally recovered from his erotic stupor.

'That you did, sir, but I imagined you'd be indoors, not sleeping out in the stable like a . . .'

'Never mind that now,' he rasped. 'Get my horse saddled and hurry up about it!' He stamped back into the cool and fragrant interior of the stable, buttoning his breeches and hauling on his buff coat as he went. Mary looked up from her straw bower, stretched like a cat under his warm cloak. William stared at her for a second, filled with a gut-cramping pang of fierce pride and anxiety. What was he going to do with her now? She had always been someone else's responsibility. Now he had responsibilities enough without worrying his head over a sweetheart. A wife.

'I have to be back, I'm late,' he said, dry mouthed. Mary straightened her bodice with belated modesty, sat up straight against the bales.

'I'll be back as soon as I can.' He fished his meagre purse from his tangled belt, fingered a shilling from the worn leather. 'This'll see you right for a room.' She frowned, took the coin in her warm hand.

'I shall have to follow her back, you know,' she said awkwardly, as if she was suddenly reluctant to name her wayward mistress. 'She'll be at her father's by now.' Mary's younger brother Jeremiah had driven the girl back to Chipping Marleward in the dog cart. Her blushing servant would have to risk the roads alone or wait for his return.

'I'll be back before the end of the week. I'll bring Gillingfeather or one of the other preacher men, he'll marry us under the sign there.' He nodded under the rafters at the creaking board. Mary Keziah climbed to her feet, brushed the worst of the crushed webs and straw husks from her dress.

'I have to go,' he said, as if he was convincing himself as much as the miserable girl.

Mary nodded, accepted his rather brusque kiss. He should have stayed with her, seen her settled before riding back to the army. There was nothing to do now Maurice's horse had fled except watch the empty downs and track down the deserters. William was seriously considering turning the horse and riding back for her when he saw the first tiny black stick figures on the hill ahead. A dozen men on foot, hurrying toward him. He reined in cautiously, watched them scramble over a stone wall and pelt off across the open field to his left. The fugitives wore tattered civilian clothes and didn't seem to be armed. Camp followers? Deserters? He shouted into the gusting wind after the fleeing men but they didn't even turn their heads. Sparrow felt uneasy, the familiar light-headed anxiety of the unknown. Gnawing at his resolve, a thousand times worse than sitting on a hill with your friends and watching the enemy move towards you. Up here, in these horrible expanses of red earth and bone white stones, the enemy could be anywhere and everywhere. He felt hopelessly alone, twisted the greasy reins through his fingers in agitation. Sparrow swallowed, urged McNabb's horse toward the quiet slopes, desperate for the reassuring company of his comrades and cronies.

He could hear the racket from the camp on the far side of Beacon Hill, the restless clink of pots and pans as the men cleaned up after their breakfasts. Sparrow sighed with relief, told himself off for his childish doubts. Better get the tired horse back to McNabb before he sent a search party out after him. There was a muffled crump as the batteries overlooking the town blasted more shot at the hopelessly trapped Royalists. Sparrow wondered for a moment why they didn't just give up. There was no point in dying for a heap of rubble two hundred miles from home, was there? He imagined himself down in the ruins, trapped with the Cornish barbarians. What would he do, trapped, hungry, isolated from all his friends? He could hear the idle cavalry cheering the fall of shot now, shouting and hallooing to wake the dead they were.

Sparrow urged McNabb's fine horse over the final leg of the steep lane which switchbacked up Beacon Hill and paused on the windy ridge to enjoy the view. It took him about thirty seconds to take in the horrifying panorama. They had begun the attack without him! Drawn the foot up on that hill away over the valley and thrown regiments of horse out over the lush green down to protect the flank. Protect the flank? What for? The enemy-held town was on the other side of the down! He shielded his eyes, peered over the wilderness towards the hazy eastern horizon. More cavalry had been flung out ahead of the main body, but General Waller had obviously called them back because they were coming towards the . . . Oh my God. It was the enemy. Paralysed by fear and uncertainty, Sparrow sat still on the ridge while the bold horse hoofed the turf. He squinted at the nearest cavalry units formed up quietly just along the slope, and picked out russet coats and orange sashes, green and white and black cornets fluttering gaily in the breeze. Waller's horse. He was sure of it. Sitting in their saddles like statues as they watched the almost supernaturally rapid enemy approach. He felt a surge of relief and then a childish urge to lose himself in the centre of the friendly crowd, surround himself by his comrades. Before he could think what to do he had clamped his thighs around McNabb's narrow saddle, touched the spurs to the Scot's fierce charger. Argyll leapt over the grass as if he was trying to catch up with the rest of the field at Newmarket races. Sparrow ducked down and held on as the wind buffeted his face, billowing white dust kicked up by the trotting ranks ahead. He closed in on the curiously staring cavalry, snatched his hand from the reins to give the suspicious troopers a reassuring wave. He didn't recognize any of them.

'McNabb's looking for you up ahead!' a cavalry major in glistening black armour shouted, waving his sword to the east. Sparrow slowed the charger to a ragged canter, overtook three ranks of unfamiliar cavalry. He stared at the flapping banners above each troop, looking for the black fist device he ought to be carrying. Where were they? He spurred past another three ranks of Roundhead horse and closed up behind the leading troop. Sixty men in two ranks riding boot to boot towards the long eastern ridge. He recognized Buchanan carrying the standard, that surly hound Hunt alongside. Speechless with relief, he urged the major's horse in behind Hunt's black charger. The captain looked over his shoulder, raised his stubbled chin.

'Where in the bowels of Christ have you been?' he bawled.

'Chasing deserters,' Sparrow gasped, his tongue suddenly too big for his dry mouth.

Hunt barged his own horse to the right, creating a gap for Sparrow's borrowed charger.

Buchanan handed the heavy cornet over with evident relief, shook his gauntlet to clear his stalled circulation.

'Yours, I think. And make sure ye hang on to it,' the dusty rider told him. Sparrow took the heavy pole, tucked the butt under the instep of his long leather boot. He tilted his head to the right to peer over the shoulder of the trooper in the front rank. All he could see was green grass and a windy ridge.

'Where are they then?' he managed to gasp, when he had regained his breath a little.

'Over yonder. Running us ragged, it looks like,' was Buchanan's laconic response.

Prince Maurice had kept his word, dismally delivered at the gloomy council of war held beside Hopton's sickbed. His tired cavalry had galloped out of Devizes on Monday night and covered an astonishing forty-four miles to clatter into Oxford, numb with fatigue, on Tuesday morning. Even so, some three hundred of his exhausted horsemen had insisted on turning round and joining the relief column which had hurriedly been patched together to rescue General Hopton and his brave Cornishmen. Lord Wilmot had drawn out his own brigade plus Lord Byron's. Two small galloper guns had been attached to the column, handy pieces which could be hauled by two horses and crewed by mounted gunners who could keep up with the flying force. They had no time to collect any further cavalry, and infantry would only slow the relief force down. Wilmot's scratch force had picked up the remains of Lord Crawford's cavalry which had been detailed to escort the ill-fated ammunition column. Pausing only to rest the horses at Marlborough, the column had set off down the

Bath road, firing signal guns to warn Hopton of their imminent arrival. The Cavaliers had trotted through the green breach in the Wansdyke and formed up in three great blocks in the shallow valley. The tireless cavalry were all for an immediate descent on the astonished enemy, but Wilmot angrily ordered them back into line. They must wait until Hopton had marched the Cornish foot out of Devizes to support their attack. The Royalists could see Waller's agitated army forming up on Bagdon Hill, at right angles to their furious approach. The Roundhead forces deployed from their pivotal position on the hill, wheeled north and then east to face up to the Royalist threat. Both sides ordered their troops, sited what guns they had wherever they could. It was early afternoon by the time the twitching, sweating armies were ready for battle.

BY
MORGAN'S HILL

JULY 13, 1643

Lord Wilmot had risked everything bringing his out-numbered relief force to a shuddering stand at the eastern end of the shallow valley. He had come within an ace of falling on Waller's unguarded camp, forcing a wedge of cavalry between the scattered Round-head infantry around Devizes and their supporting artil-lery, baggage and horse up on the hill. He had surrendered surprise and the opportunity of winning the day with one sudden swoop on the unprepared enemy in the hope that Hopton's foot would charge out from behind their barricades and assault Waller's wavering troops from the rear. Sitting on his sweating horse at the head of his brigade, the Cavalier nobleman wondered if he had gambled in vain. All his instincts, and perhaps more importantly, those of his arrogant and unbeaten troopers, had been for the lightning charge into the thick of the panicking mob of enemy troops dithering on the downs there. The King's cavalry had never been beaten in battle. They had come off the worst in the occasional skirmish, but it was the Cavalier horsemen which had swung the war in their sovereign's favour. It had been the King's cavalry which had ridden over the rebels at Powick Bridge, scattered them at Edgehill and half a dozen other fields across England. Lord Wilmot held them in check on

416

their prancing horses, while he patiently ran his glass over the town, fuming to itself at the foot of the colliding escarpments. What was Hopton doing? He must have heard the relief force's signal guns, they had heard Hopton's cannon roar in reply, so where were his blasted infantry?

Sir William Waller, astride his horse one and a half miles across the valley from his Royalist counterpart, had uttered silent prayers of thanks to the Lord for allowing him to assemble his army at all. The infantry companies had been prised out of their positions in Devizes and herded up the steep slopes to reform their ranks on Bagdon Hill. His cavalry scouts had trotted this way and that on the empty flank, isolated troops insolently impersonating whole regiments to buy time while the general assembled and deployed his scattered forces. The Roundhead commander had wondered why the enemy hadn't simply galloped into action, trusted to surprise and their superior horsemanship to carry the downs and win the day. Instead they had streamed into the eastern end of the valley and drawn up in three distinct bodies. Two astride the road and a third in reserve. Waiting. Why?

Waiting for Hopton to complete the pincer movement by marching his forces out of Devizes behind him, that was why. Waller aimed his spyglass to his right, down the quiet slopes towards the ruined town. He studied the ring of smoking rubble and trampled vegetable plots which surrounded the hovels and houses where Hopton had hidden himself with his three thousand Cornishmen. There was no sign of any movement yet, no frantic throb of drums or hasty display of bright colours to draw the

417

men out from their improvised fortress. Could Hopton have slipped away to the south, marched his men into the wilderness hills to outflank him or attack from the rear? Perhaps his scoundrel army had mutinied? Refused to follow the drums out of their hard-held defences? Whatever the reason, Sir William knew he must not allow the Cornishmen to join the battle. He knew if he granted the enemy time to assemble their army as they had allowed him to assemble his, he would be outnumbered. It was early afternoon, the men were still tired from their exertions climbing the steep slopes. They could not be allowed to rest any longer. He lowered his glass, turned to the formidably armoured form of Sir Arthur Haselrig, sitting stiffly in his heavily reinforced saddle at his right hand.

'They're waiting for a sortie from the town,' he snapped. 'We must shoo those horse out of the valley there, drive a wedge between them. Have the Devon horse drive in their forlorn hope, your cuirassiers to their support, sir.' The steel-suited MP nodded briefly, lowered his helmet visor. 'Bowl them aside, sir, let all the army see your triumph,' he encouraged earnestly.

The helmeted knight turned his heavy horse and spurred away from Waller's command post. He cantered down the hill towards his men. Six hundred fully armoured cuirassiers carrying carbines and swords and a pair of pistols. The segmented plates of steel over their arms and legs had given them their name: the Lobsters. The most talked about troops in England, one of the finest regiments in Parliament's service, according to the newssheets. Sir Arthur rode along the compact mass of men, six ranks deep, and took his place at their head. The lighter armed cavalry, formed up into three looser ranks ahead of them, moved off first. Devon and Somerset yeomen all. The Puritanically minded minor gentry of the south-west farming and clothing communities had been pushed north by the invading Cornishmen, driven out of their own counties by these Celtic savages who couldn't speak English, ate human flesh and celebrated the mass like the heathen papist butchers they were. The west country brigade picked up speed, clattered down the gentle slope towards the despised enemy forces.

A thousand points of light danced about them as they drew their swords to take their revenge at last.

'Well, I can't see a bleedin' thing,' Bill Butcher moaned, peering into the thin ropes of smoke sidling over the field. The batteries drawn up between the two massed foot formations and their cavalry supports on either side of Bagdon Hill hadn't even warmed up and yet his eyes were watering already.

'What are those bastards using for powder, that's what I'd like to know,' he moaned, taking off his black felt hat to wipe his forehead.

Colston Muffet tilted his head to blow on his match, radiating calm to the raw ranks of Roundhead musketeers. They copied him dutifully, glancing nervously over the empty down. The enemy troops seemed to be miles away, well out of range. What was all the fuss about, it was only a few cavalry?

'They're advancing in echelon,' Long Col had murmured.

The teenaged sniper had closed one eye, studied the veteran sceptically. 'Do what?'

'They're leapfrogging one troop in front of the other, from their left,' Muffet replied, pointing a dirty finger over the rolling grasslands. 'They pin us down in the valley, look, while the rest of them wheel off to get a good run in on the right.' His patient explanation was drowned out by a burst of delighted cheering from the nervous block of pikemen, sandwiched between the long ranks of musketeers. They had spotted the cavalry moving into the attack at last and given them a rousing send off, to relieve their own tension as much as encourage the gentlemen of the horse. Their own comrades and kin from the western brigade poured down the slopes toward the enemy forlorn hope. The silent infantry on the hill watched the two lines of horsemen come together like so many rutting stags. Just when the watching soldiers thought they must collide in complete and mutual ruin the charging horses pulled up, shied away or stopped dead in their tracks. Riders were hurled from their saddles or lost their balance and fired their pistols into their mounts, their comrades or themselves. There was a muffled clatter of steel on steel as the riders milled and mingled, hacked and jabbed at each other.

'I hate it when they do that. Why do they always hold back at the last minute?' Butcher wanted to know. Muffet rolled his eyes towards the eggshell heavens.

'Ever tried riding a horse into a brick wall at the gallop? No? Well, that's 'cus it won't. They're not as stupid as you,' Long Col growled. He was known throughout the hotch-potch brigade as a wily veteran of half a dozen actions, but the scowling apprentice was beginning to grate even on his nerves.

'Well, how come ... hello ... they've had enough.' The spectating infantrymen on the hill watched the confused scramble in the valley dissolve into a hundred desperate struggles, riderless horses running wild in all

420

directions, fugitives spurring back the way they had come. The lighter west-country cavalry streamed away, dividing around the solid black block of Haselrig's regiment or trying to force their way through the closely ordered ranks.

'Go round, go round, you dozy buggers,' Long Col murmured, watching the rout in helpless agitation.

'Hah, now they're for it! There go the Lobsters!'

Haselrig's discomfited cavalry closed ranks as the last of the west country horse spurred away down the valley. The disorganized enemy cavalry hurried out of their way, leaving the littered valley clear for Wilmot's Royalist brigade, three ranks deep at the full trot.

'Don't stand still, don't stand still!' Muffet called forlornly, Haselrig, bound into his steel skin half a mile down the slope, didn't hear him or much else besides. He could hardly breathe inside the steaming, clanging helmet, barely see through the thin steel slits. He drew his regiment to a halt and waited for the Royalists to do their worst. Wilmot's veterans did just that. They didn't slacken their pace at all, hardly flinched as the stationary enemy riders emptied their pistols and carbines at them. The Cavaliers endured the stinging fusillade and fell on with determined shouts and screams of abuse. A thousand blacksmiths beat furious tattoos on the unwilling anvils, the Royalists lapping around each flank of the tightly compressed mass of cuirassiers. Colston Muffet watched with his heart in his mouth as the brave Lobsters endured the frightful hammering for a few agonized moments before giving ground. The men on the windy ridge watched in helpless fascination as the mass of metal and men was ground backwards, inch by inch, foot by bloody foot. Wilmot's men redoubled their frenzied attack and broke them at last. The armoured regiment shattered into smaller and smaller fragments, like a sack of nails dropped on to a courtyard floor. They turned and cantered off the field as fast as they could go, parties of Royalist horsemen swooping in and out of their disintegrating ranks like so many cheetahs amongst a panicked crowd of wildebeest. They hacked and fired and jabbed and slashed, but the well-armoured cuirassiers bent over their horses' manes and held on for grim death. Sir Arthur's horse stampeded with the rest, the deafened, blinded and half-dazed MP reeling in the saddle as a gaggle of Cavaliers closed in for the kill. The bolting horse collapsed at last, the eager Royalists leaping out of their saddles to finish him off. A burly captain swung his sword straight at the prostrate knight, but the blade glanced off Sir Arthur's black carapace. The helpless MP tore his helmet visor from his stifled face, peered out of his sweaty steel prison at his exasperated captors.

'What good will it do you to kill a poor man?' he gasped as his would-be killers hauled the wretched prisoner to his feet. Sir Arthur picked at his sword knot in agitated alarm as his Royalist captors caught their breath and insulted his men.

'So much for that fine crew,' a flaxen-haired cornet boasted, wiping his bloody mouth on his greasy sleeve.

Waller had ordered his guns hauled from the wickerwork emplacements from which they had been energetically bombarding the town, and set up between his infantry on the hill and the cavalry support on either slope. The four-gun battery on the right-hand slopes had hardly fired a shot, the crews standing around watching the cavalry tussle degenerate into a series of manic steeplechases around the hill.

'Have they run out of powder or something?' Long Col wanted to know. Jamie Morrison nodded in agreement, hardly daring to trust his voice. He felt sure he would dirty his breeches at any moment, his bowels writhing like a sack of eels behind his tightened belt.

Muffet noticed the youngster's staring eyes and twitching lip, shook his head. 'You stay with the rest of 'em. I'm off to gee that idiot of a gunner up.' Jamie Morrison looked blankly at the lean veteran as he handed him his musket and bandolier, took the officer's sweaty halberd in their place.

'Well, they won't take any notice of a bleedin' sergeant, will they?' The stupefied captain watched as the sergeant and his cronies loped away from their breezy position toward the silent guns.

Long Col was infuriated to find the gunners lounging about their pieces as if they were on a Sunday picnic. They leaned on their linstocks and scouring swabs as the furious veteran stalked up on them, pointed the halberd at the shapeless mass of horsemen down the slopes.

'What are you bastards doing? That's your enemy there!' Muffet bawled. The artillery captain, a balding, watery eyed German in a red velvet suit, shrugged his shoulders and tapped his ear.

'He can't 'ear yer,' one of the powder boys called cheerily. 'He's been deaf since the siege of Breisach!'

Muffet grabbed the saucy youngster by his ragged shirt, lifted him from the ground and turned him toward the milling enemy cavalry as if he was some supernatural scarecrow who would frighten the gaudy Cavalier crows away.

'That's the King's men down there, you tosspots!' he shrieked. 'Fucking fire at 'em!'

'Those Lobsters were in the way,' one of the surly gunners objected. 'We'd have shot our own men!'

'We'll fucking shoot you if you don't give 'em a round right now!' The artillery crews closed in around their deaf captain, linstocks and scouring swabs held like fighting staves.

'Have a care, gentlemen,' Gillingfeather called from the carts drawn up behind the battery. They looked up to see the fanatic musketeer sitting on their powder barrels, unconcernedly blowing on his lighted match.

''Ere, Col, what happens if a spark gets into that powder there?' Butcher asked innocently. The gunners blanched.

'All right, all right, keep your hair on.' The artillerymen muttered and cursed, keeping one eye on the fanatical intruders as they wrestled their sakers around to face the slowly re-forming enemy cavalry. Gunners were often paid professionals, skilled technicians rather than keen followers of a particular cause. They weren't cowards, but they were careful. They had been happy enough pumping balls into Devizes from a well-prepared battery, but facing a mounted enemy on an open flank wasn't in their contract. The deaf German seemed quick enough to grasp Muffet's intentions though, and diligently laid his eye to the black barrel of each cannon. He stood back, lowered the glowing match curled about the steel linstock to the touch-hole of the first saker. There was a blast of hot air and the hill was covered in stinging smoke. The massive recoil felt like a sack of sodden laundry thumping into their chests. The ball cut a bloody swath through the milling Royalists four hundred yards away down the slope. The second, third and fourth guns followed suit, the reluctant gunners scrambling to swab the barrels and reload their smoking pieces.

'That's it, come on,' Long Col encouraged, peering through the hideous, sulphurous soup to study the damage they had inflicted.

'Give 'em another round, hurry up,' he yelled, throat parched by the rotten, smutty ropes of smoke. The battery opened fire again, a ferocious broadside which smashed legs, holed horses and took the head from one captain as he pointed his sword toward the hated heights. Long Col crouched down to peer beneath the drifting clouds, watched a dark mass of riders detach themselves from the battered main body and spur their tired mounts up the hill toward them. He straightened up, whacked the halberd over a sweating gunner's back.

'What are you waiting for? Reload, you poxy whore's abortions!'

The sooty artillerymen scoured their barrels, rammed home another pierced muslin bag of powder and rolled another ball into each hot barrel.

'Hurry up!'

'Col ... they're right on us,' Butcher fidgeted nervously, raising his flintlock into the sickening murk.

Muffet peered into the mist, saw the shadowy shapes of the enemy cavalry billow from the smoke.

'Fire!'

The bitter clouds were illuminated by enormous orange flashes as the guns blasted the oncoming cavalry. Horses disintegrated in the sudden cauldron of fire, their terrified riders crushed and slashed and hurled from their saddles. The dazed survivors spurred into the improvised gunpits, slashed at the gunners as they took to their heels. Gilling-feather rammed his musket into a Cavalier's coal-black face and fired. The rider toppled over the back of his crippled horse, nerveless fingers clawing the boiling air. Long Col swung the halberd like a scythe, taking one trooper's arm off at the elbow. A bellowing captain skewered him through his outstretched shoulder and he howled in agony, darted beneath one of the gun carriages to escape the slashing blades. Butcher had held his fire until he was sure of his target. He'd not have time to reload in this wretched confusion. He aimed calmly, shot the shouting officer through the right eye. Long Col scrambled out from beneath the carriage and waved them away from the undefended guns. A fresh gust of wind had lifted the grey curtain from the bloody, littered slopes and revealed fresh troops of Wilmot's re-formed brigade rushing up to second the squandered charge.

'Back to the pike, they'll have us in the open,' Muffet bawled, racing like a scorched hare for the safety of the patient infantry on the heights.

Sparrow felt himself carried away with the rest of them. The drumming of the hoofs, the fierce clatter of their equipment a soothing lullaby to help him drift off to sleep. He imagined for a moment he was lying in the unconcerned clouds above the downs, reclining like a Roman emperor while the armies played below. William blinked back to reality. The reality of being thumped up and down in a narrow saddle, grating his flayed flesh. Of grit and stones flying into his face. Of trying to breathe in a tightly bound buff coat while carrying an ash pole with a flapping flag which would act as a magnet for every ambitious young buck on the other side. He clenched the hated banner in his sweaty gauntlet, felt the borrowed horse surge forward into the sudden gap in the ranks as the racing troop broke up to impact against a wall of enemy riders. Byron's brigade had finally come into contact with the left wing of the Roundhead army. William cursed the impetuous beast as McNabb's horse carried him through the struggling front rank and slap bang into the middle of a press of astonished Royalist horse. A wrinkly veteran in a feathered hat was laughing like a maniac, pointing his sword at the terrified cornet. Another trooper brought his sword down against the flagpole. The blade was deflected down on to William's fist. He lost his grip, the flag fell away from him like a sapling he had chopped down in the woods back home. He hauled on the reins with his left hand, bringing McNabb's charger to a shuddering halt. The horse reared, knocking a stunted bay to the ground and spilling its rider into the stamping mass of hoofs and boots. The flagpole, jammed between William's boot and the sweating horse, dipped toward the massed enemy troopers. He reached out, noticed his gauntlet was drenched with blood. He held his hand up to his shocked face, realized the enemy's blow had removed the top of his index finger. He couldn't feel a thing. Another Cavalier came alongside, grabbed the wavering flag in his right hand and wrenched it away. Sparrow dropped the reins, ducked down and lifted the rider's pistol from its holster. The cursing trooper dropped the pole, clamped his right hand on Sparrow's left, still trying to tug the weapon from its leather boot. They wheeled and ground against each other, the horses and equipment locked and tangled.

'Let go, let go, you bastard!'

'Bastard yourself!' Delirious with terror, the frantic cornet worked his useless right arm behind the flagpole clenched against his thigh, pushed the pole down against his enemy with all his might. The Royalist, intent on holding on to his pistol, took the blow across his face, his nose splintering in a stream of bright blood. Sparrow wrenched the pistol out of the undefended holster and was about to fire when the furious press of men shifted again. The compressed mass of wrestling men and rearing horses broke apart, spilling the combatants away from each other. Sparrow's terrified horse leapt away with the wounded officer clinging to the saddle. A youngster in blue trotted into his path. Sparrow aimed the pistol with his left hand and fired. He missed. The youngster's equally astonished horse bolted off into the press. Another Royalist brought his sword down across Sparrow's back. His buff coat deflected the blade but the furious force of the blow knocked him into the borrowed horse's sweaty mane. His assailant brought his sword back, jabbed at the cornet as he was carried past, straight into another mob of Royalist horse. McNabb's charger skidded to a halt, spilling the terrified youth to the ground. Sparrow automatically curled himself into a ball, covered his head as the wild hoofs thundered and stamped. A horse trod on his leg and he howled in agony. Another caught him a glancing blow on his helmet, smashing his face into the springy turf. The ground was vibrating, the sinews of the earth singing and humming as the mad charge carried the Royalists up the hill and through Waller's hard-fighting regiments. Sparrow rolled over, stared at the sky as the mad stampede thundered by.

He sat up in the litter of broken men and slaughtered horses, looked about the bloody carnage like a steel-helmeted owl. Fifty or sixty other riders were sprawled over the trampled grass or had propped themselves up against heaped horses or slashed saddles. A Royalist trooper was crouched on all fours, vomiting into the grass. A bare-headed Roundhead trooper picked himself up, staggered off through the trampled chaos. Sparrow lifted his hand, tugged the bloody gauntlet off and yelped in pain. The enemy blade had cut through the glove and removed his index finger just above the knuckle. The glistening bone showed through the middle of the wet red flesh. And it hurt. Oh God did it hurt. He groaned, tore his sodden neckerchief from his throat and twisted the improvised bandage around his hand. His writing hand, he thought with a bitter flinch. Never mind writing now, get out of it, he thought, clambering to his feet amongst the dead and the wounded. He looked up in time to see the last of the brigade pursued over the ridge and off into the distance. The battling cavalry forces had laid a carpet of broken riders and crippled horses over the green slopes. To their left he could see the green, grey and red ranks of the unscathed Roundhead infantry, at bay on the top of the hill. Half a dozen other wounded riders were already making their way up the slope toward their friends. Sparrow knotted the neckerchief around the throbbing wound, remembered the flag. He cursed, looked around the scrap heap of men and lost weapons. The black fist banner was nowhere in sight. Sparrow turned and ran up towards the mass of men on the ridge.

BLOODY DITCH,
BEACON HILL

JULY 13, 1643

Not even McNabb's bawled curses and bloodied spurs could persuade the panting piebald to keep up with the rest of the beaten troop. The furious Scot was being overtaken on every side by bawling Cavaliers on better horses. They seemed content to overhaul his wheezing nag, leave the hopeless fool for their slower comrades. McNabb watched a trooper rein in alongside, squint at him as if he had grown an extra head. He realized the green youngster was trying to make up his mind whose side he was on. The furious major glanced over the youth's shoulder.

'Look out behind ye!' he called. The trooper jumped in his saddle, peered to his right. McNabb leaned over the piebald's heaving shoulders and slit the youngster's saddle girth with his razor-sharp dirk. Before the astonished youth knew what had happened he was rolling in the trampled grass, the breath knocked out of him. McNabb grinned, spurred the borrowed horse on again. He glanced to his left, the great immobile blocks of Waller's largely unscathed infantry at bay on the hilltop. He saw the white faces of the Roundhead musketeers blinking at the avalanche of horsemen, not daring to fire in case they hit their own men. He wondered for a moment about turning the wheezing beast into their ranks, taking cover with the foot. Isolated on that hill with two thousand knock-kneed cabbages? They were as good as doomed, he thought, spurring on past the dazed infantry.

The piebald lumbered over the ridge and cantered down the other side. The ragged remains of Waller's cavalry brigade were streaming across the slopes, hurrying towards the safety of the empty western downs. Small groups of Cavaliers were reining in, trying to regroup now the Roundhead army had been shorn of its cavalry support. McNabb wound up his pistol as he rode, gripping the horse with his legs as he poured more powder down the barrel. He dropped another ball into the sooty muzzle with his teeth. He drew up beside a Royalist cornet holding his sleeve to his forehead. He had stopped a spent ball and was seeing double. McNabb stuck the sooty muzzle in his back and fired. The cornet lurched forward, his horse carrying the body off towards Devizes. The red-eyed Scot peered over his shoulder in case any of the enemy riders had noticed his merciless revenge, held the hot barrel of the pistol to the heaving piebald's flank. The scalded cob took off again, cantered across the road after his fellow fugitives. McNabb peered into the distance, watched the leading Roundheads disappear into a hidden fold in the ground. More and more horses and riders dropped out of sight. A shallow valley perhaps, funnelling them to safety?

The Scot closed in on the milling cavalry, shouting and bawling and yanking their horses away from the edge. He cursed, hauled back on Jasper's reins to bring the piebald to a juddering halt twenty yards short of the desperately panicked mob of riders. They were teetering on the brink of a sudden precipice, a chalky chasm which had opened up under their hoofs. The first hundred or so riders hadn't been so lucky. They had spurred their exhausted chargers straight over the edge, crashing to their deaths at the foot of the hellish pit. A groaning, whinnying crush of broken-backed horses and snapped legs, a thicket of discarded swords and snapped banners. Some riders had hung on grimly while their mounts scrambled down the steep slope kicking up billowing clouds of white dust. Others had turned their frantic horses to the north, followed the trampled track down Beacon Hill. McNabb peered over the edge at the bloody chaos in the ditch, shook his head. If he had been riding Argyll, he would be down there with them. He uttered a brief Gaelic prayer, turned the drooping gelding to the right and trotted off after the last of Waller's brigade.

A mile to the south Sir Arthur Haselrig was riding off the field in good order, his dazed troopers crowding in about him like so many steel chicks. He had taken off his helmet to get some air, glanced nervously at his loyal troopers. They had rescued him from his cackling captors, just as he was about to ask one of the Cavaliers if they would cut his sword strap to speed his surrender. Well, it didn't do to go flailing about in the midst of a dozen well-armed cut-throats. The stray Roundhead troop had noticed their commander down, spurred to his rescue and then caught a horse for him. The blushing MP could hardly bear to look them in the eye. Instead, he twisted in the saddle, looked back up the green slopes to the besieged heights.

'God help the foot,' he called piously.

'God may, there's no other bugger left,' an unrecognizable trooper muttered at his armoured elbow. Sir Arthur faced about, led his battered regiment away from the stricken field.

William had pushed and shoved his way through file after file of nervous, sweaty pikemen, giggling musketeers and pale-faced officers. They opened their ranks to let the wounded cavalryman pass as if he was a leper, as if his pale face was blossoming with pustulent rosettes.

'Where's your fucking mates gone?'

'Don't put yourself out on our account, will you?'

'Bloody cavalry. One charge and they're off!'

Sparrow ignored their furious banter, shoved his way through the wild-eyed Gloucester men to the Bristol contingent, chattering and laughing like idiots on their bit of hill. Zachary Pitt recognized William's pasty features, drove his pike into the turf to lend him a hand.

'Should have stayed with us, Will, we've hardly had a scratch up here,' the simple-minded youth called cheerily, glancing down at the wounded rider's bloody bandage. Sparrow shook his dazed head, anaesthetized with fatigue. He could barely think straight in the humid confusion on the hill. Names and faces popped into his foggy mind like barely remembered fragments of a disturbing dream.

'Where's Jamie?' he asked hoarsely.

'Havin' a lie down. He came over a bit funny, the heat and all.'

Sparrow absorbed the information slowly, tilted his helmet to the back of his sweaty hair. The fresh breeze picking up over the downs blew some of the coiling cobwebs from his mind, brought their hideous prospects into sharper focus.

'They'd better order the retreat soon, we're buggered otherwise,' he said flatly.

Zachary frowned, pulled the pike from the earth as if it was the sword in the stone, shook it in his fist. 'Just 'cus you've had a pastin', Will, don't mean t' say we'll get one,' he called.

William accepted a water bottle from one of the Somerset levies, gratefully poured the cool liquid over his red face.

'Here they come!' The cry was taken up from one parched throat to another along the windy ridge. The musketeers blasted away at the foolhardy Cavaliers who had worked their way up the littered slopes to press in against the flanks. A hundred bullets hit three enemy riders from their horses, left them twitching on the trampled turf.

'Pick your targets, save your powder,' Colston Muffet groaned. Butcher and Gillingfeather reloaded beside him, trying to conceal their anxiety with a show of nonchalance.

'What we goin' ter do then, Col, leg it?'

'With half of the King's horsemen between us and Bristol? How the fuck are we goin' to leg it?'

'Well, I don't see as we're goin' t'old 'em.'

'Just shut your mouth and keep firing,' Long Col growled. 'As long as everyone keeps their 'eads, we'll be all right,' he called for the benefit of the rest.

Sir William Waller had watched the rout of his cavalry, the total collapse of his flanks. Now he had two thousand foot stuck on a hill, a horde of savage Cavaliers riding caracoles about his isolated position. The general had eased his fingers under the collar of his constricting breastplate, as if he was having difficulty swallowing his trampled pride. Hadn't he ordered the faultless dispositions of his well-disposed and well-equipped army? They had outnumbered the enemy cavalry by at least two to one. Waller hardly dared contemplate his own personal shame and dis-honour, let alone the damage his defeat might do to the tottering Parliamentary cause. He raised his glass for the hundredth time that Godforsaken afternoon, willing his muscles rigid, and squinted through the drifting smoke toward the town.

Half a dozen hedgehogs of pikemen were lumbering up the main road towards the downs, long files of musket-eers with their useless weapons over their shoulders hurry-ing alongside. Hopton had managed to get the reluctant Cornish on the move at last. Waller knew his army had little chance of surviving now. The best he could hope would be to hold the survivors together long enough to shake the pursuit away. The gleeful Royalists would have a camp and baggage and all his guns to play with, he might be able to save something. If they kept their heads. They must fall back by companies, each regiment covering the rear of the next. A checkerboard of troops, marching backwards, keeping the frenzied enemy horse at bay. Sir William had fought through some of the bitterest struggles of the German wars. He had seen the flower of the Swedish armies, the cream of the Spanish tercios in action. But he had never seen troops with the cold-blooded discipline to be able to carry out such a manoeuvre. He gave the orders anyway, urging the captains and majors that had remained to calm their raw troops.

The two massive bodies of foot began to give ground, marching deliberately down the bloody slope towards the west, towards their homes. The Cavaliers swarmed in, manhandled the abandoned guns Long Col had commanded. The apprentice gunners double charged the sakers, rolled Roundhead cannon balls down the cold barrels. The first four shots tore great holes in the cowering ranks of pikemen, flattened whole files of quaking musketeers. The dazed survivors, speckled with blood and brains and scraps of bowel, closed ranks over the heaped dead, ground on down the pitiless ridge. They looked over their shoulders at the sudden commotion, heard the mounted officers calling for the colours. In the sudden, eerie silence the raw regiments watched their banners furled, handed up to crying cornets and reluctant ensigns. The flags they had followed dozens of hard miles, followed over rivers and up hills. For those that cared – and a good many of Waller's composite army did – the colours represented their honour. Without them, there was none. Burdened as they were with the heavy poles, the mounted officers banded together, rode off across the lush slopes after their scattered cavalry. Waller, mortified by the unthinkable defeat, bowed his head at last and turned his horse. His staff officers and bodyguard closed in around him and whisked the general to safety in stunned silence. The abandoned foot stood in helpless rings on the reverse slopes of Bagdon Hill. The few officers who remained stamped about knocking them into line, trying to raise their non-existent spirits. The faint hearted or foolishly brave men on the edge of the battered formations made sudden dashes to imagined safety, scrambled down the ditches and tried to escape on foot. A lucky few evaded the loose cordon of Cavaliers, ran like hares to all points of the compass.

Sparrow swallowed, stared at his bloody hand for what seemed like hours, but he couldn't have told his best friend what he had been thinking about. A string of memories like autumn leaves running away down a brook, bobbing and turning and stopping against sudden stones. Each tiny brittle piece, every translucent fragment, another bit of him. He looked up at the sudden woody clatter, as if somebody had kicked over a heap of carefully stacked firewood. He saw instead white-faced pikemen hurling their weapons to the floor. Musketeers tearing off their bandoliers and hurling the leather belts out to join the sad flotsam and jetsam of a broken army.

'Pick up those pikes, you scum! You Welsh vermin!'

Sparrow didn't recognize the cursing fanatic striding through the wavering ranks, slapping the scared soldiers or thrusting their weapons back at them. Where did he find his courage, his determination in the face of such overwhelming odds? Sparrow shoved his way after the stranger, buoyed by his careless courage.

A few hundred determined men stuck together, formed a bristling hedgehog of pike and musket. Long Col had almost lost his voice, croaking reassurances to the resolute few. 'Stay together. Don't let them spook you. They'll be in after those cowards, they won't fight us!' he breathed.

Small groups of men divided from the main body, made their way toward the steep slopes which had claimed so many of Waller's impetuous cavalry. The enemy horsemen had spent half an hour re-forming their ranks. Now, troop after troop trotted closer, a noose of men and horses and guns tightening around the shuffling foot soldiers. The first Cornish infantry had arrived on the downs at last, and eagerly fell on the faint hearted and the fallen. Subjected to a week of constant shelling and sniping, they were only too pleased to have a chance to pay off a few scores.

Sparrow shoved through a bellowing herd of lost souls, shouldered his way into Muffet's defiant unit. He picked up a discarded pike, gripped the ash shaft in his left hand and steadied it awkwardly on his right wrist. Creeping away from the hellish chaos, one hundred, two hundred yards and they were still together. They were over the lane, imagining for a few precious minutes they had escaped, when three troops of Royalist horse materialized from the flanks and closed in around them, a pistol shot away. Sparrow watched the wary horsemen, wished these defiant bastards would surrender so he could surrender too. He thought about dropping his useless pike and running out on his new comrades, but it seemed easier to stick with the mob. So many somebodies stripped of their identities in the crush of nobodies. Together, they were a shoal of shimmering mackerel. On his own he was a stranded porpoise to be picked by the gulls and poked by scavenging beach boys. Somebody the sweaty, sooty cavalry could pick out, make an example of.

'You can do it the hard way or make it easy on yourselves,' a black-eyed captain called hoarsely. 'Take quarter or we'll cut you down all the way to Bristol!'

'You and who else, you pox-ridden coxcomb!' somebody shouted.

'We'll not take quarter from a bandit like you, we shan't!' Sparrow's ears rang as the ridiculous shout was taken up on all sides. We shan't! We shan't! His own throat was too tight to join in, and he wasn't sure he could have trusted it anyway.

'The cause! The cause!' the mad stranger bellowed at the constricting scales of Royalist horsemen, the flickering tongues of their bloody swords.

ACKNOWLEDGEMENTS

First and foremost my thanks must go to the Sealed Knot in general and my regiment in particular, for allowing me first-hand experience of standing in a depleted pike block on a lonely hillside while Royalist horsemen charge about waving swords at you. If you fancy the idea of dressing up at weekends in a good cause there are Royalist and Parliamentarian regiments all over the country just itching to get their hands on new recruits. Don't forget your wellies though!

For the most exhaustively detailed accounts of the Civil War in the west country I am particularly indebted to Stuart Peachey and Robert Morris, whose fine set of pamphlets from the Stuart Press are jam-packed with valuable information on who did what, where and to whom. Look out for their publications at Sealed Knot musters or contact the Stuart Press at 117 Farleigh Road, Backwell, Bristol BS19 3PG. For those wanting a slightly more general view of the Civil Wars and a good idea of uniform, tactics and weapons, look out for Philip Haythornthwaite's *English Civil War* (Blandford Press). For the military minded who want the details on the many skirmishes and battles of the three civil wars, then Brigadier Peter Young and Richard Holmes' *The English Civil War* is essential reading. Peter Young's *Civil War England* (Longman Travellers Series) provides a pungent guide to the best battlefields and castles to visit, as well as thumbnail sketches of some of the lesser-known combatants. C. V. Wedgwood's *The King's War* (Penguin) provides the full political and strategic overview of the conflict, and further details of the bloody struggles on the Continent can be found in her excellent *Thirty Years War* (University Press). The Osprey Elite series on infantry and cavalry of the Civil Wars provides good background on uniforms and organization, as well as including sets of excellent illustrations by Angus McBride.

While I have endeavoured to make 'The Shadow on the Crown' series as historically accurate as possible, there are inevitably occasions when a little journalistic licence is required. Please forgive any unintentional errors as to when and precisely where certain events took place. Also, a note on character names. As a general rule the more comical or unlikely the name means the person actually existed. One of the officers at the siege of Bristol was a certain Captain Shemmington Farewell. Strange, but true!

Nicholas Carter, pikeman and pamphleteer